ETERNITY

VIRUS WARS

MAGGIE LYNCH

Windtree
Press

This is a work of fiction. Names, characters, places, and incidents either are the product of the author's imagination or are used fictitiously, and any resemblance to actual persons living or dead, business establishments, events, or locales, is entirely coincidental.

Cover Art by Christy Keerins

http://coveredbyclkeerins.com

Windtree Press

http://windtreepress.com

Publishing History

First Print and Digital Edition: May 2011

2nd Print and Digital Edition: April 2018

Published in the United States of America

ISBN EBOOK: 978-1-944973-87-2

ISBN PRINT: 978-1-947983-51-9

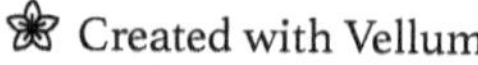 Created with Vellum

For Kim Campbell.
You were there in the beginning.

ACKNOWLEDGMENTS

As with any book, there are many people who are part of making a story come to life. Unlike some authors, who come to Science Fiction and Fantasy as a child or young adult, I came to the genre later—in my thirties. A special thanks goes to Rob Geiser for introducing me to Science Fiction, for sharing his knowledge of engineering, and for listening to my crazy ideas and stories. When I began this book, Rob was working on a part of the space shuttle program—a program that made the last shuttle flights in 2011.

Also, special thanks go to Mrs. Sleeper, wherever you are, my High School English teacher at Tustin High School in California. I always hated grammar and formal writing, but she made it wonderful and emphasized what was important—she made it something that could be a permanent part of me and has made a difference in every career I've pursued.

Finally, a very special thanks goes to my husband, Jim. He has supported my writing consistently. He has cried with me when I was frustrated and celebrated with me when I sold. He continues to be my greatest cheerleader in all my life pursuits.

A pilgrim of Eternity, whose fame
Over his living head like heaven is bent,
An early but enduring monument,
Came veiling all the lightnings of his song
In sorrow.
—Percy Bysshe Shelley

1

Rohin stood motionless, his eyes fixed on the platform and the funeral pyre directly behind it. Blowers fanned the flames to drive the stench away from the plaza. Resolute, he swallowed the bile rising in his throat. Until he accepted his part in these fiery protests, the demons from his past would continue to haunt him.

To one side a man and a woman removed their long robes and assistants lovingly poured oil onto their bodies. A plaintive, solo flute played a pastoral piece that merged the boundaries of joy and melancholy as the two nude protesters mounted the stairs on either side of the platform. They stepped slowly, but in unison, walking lightly, presenting a ghostly, slow-motion ballet. When both reached the top stair of the upper platform, they simultaneously turned toward the uncaring crowd and clasped hands.

"I ask death for us all!" the protesters proclaimed together. "For each of us a beginning and an end."

Rohin wiped his hand across his brow as nervous sweat beaded. He was no longer sure he could stand and watch. Was it true? Did they really prefer death? How could a discovery meant to lift up mankind be so detested? Mesmerized by their voices, the din of the crowd faded from his consciousness as every nerve in his body screamed "Stop!"

Two others wearing immaculate white robes moved somberly to each end of the platform, their hoods purposefully drawn close to obscure their identity. Acting as one in thought and motion they lit the pyre. The nude protesters neither flinched nor turned as the flames rose behind them. Rohin winced at the hiss and crackle of the flames.

"I beg each of you to join me." The protesters continued their exhortation in unison. "It is only through death that we can save our world! There is no change without death." They swayed in place, not yet moving any closer to the flame. A drum beat their words into a rhythm. "Die with me! Die with me! Together ... Together ...Together." Their feet stomped more brutally as their bodies writhed with frenzy. The drum beats thundered. The pulsating dance moved them in ever smaller concentric circles. A crowd of white-robed individuals gathered near the platform, shedding their cloaks to join the dancers. Now twelve of them writhed and chanted until they matched the volume of the drum. "Burn...Burn like the Phoenix. Burn...Burn."

Their words tore through Rohin's heart, imprinting his mind, drawing him closer. "Die with me," he whispered to himself as his feet stomped to the beat.

Yes, death would be preferable to this life. He hadn't found much meaning in the past two hundred years, and he wasn't sure the struggle was worth it anymore. His body swayed and his feet moved closer to the stage, keeping the cadence which called him forward. Hands reached for him and clawed at his shirt, ripping it from him. Other hands reached for his pants, shredding it into long strips. The chanting grew louder and closer, calling him forward.

Someone grabbed him from behind, "No! No more will go today." He turned to protest. White robes pulled him toward the light. Confused, Rohin shook his head and struggled to cast off everyone who clawed at him. He dropped to the ground and the hands moved away in search of another acolyte.

The drum's beat quickened and the protesters on stage wove their arms and bodies together until they seemed to be one. "Transform ... transform us ... transform," their chant continued. The newcomers shed their clothes as they joined the turbulence of the dance. Assistants rushed to pour oil on their now nude bodies. Sunlight danced off their skins, making it appear as if an aura of light surrounded all of them.

The cadence reached a frenzy and the sound of rolling thunder drowned their voices until only the thumps of the dance could be heard. Rohin closed his eyes, unable to watch their destruction.

All sound stopped. A deafening silence, broken only by the crackling flames, drew his eyes back to the entwined bodies. Unmoving, they stood facing the flames like statues in hell.

In one fluid movement, the twelve nude bodies surged forward like a wave crashing upon the shore, hurling themselves off the platform onto the flaming pyre. The drums picked up again, but not in time to cover the screams of agony as the fire engulfed them.

Rohin doubled-over in revulsion as the stench of burning flesh reached him. On his hands and knees he vomited until his stomach emptied all it held and spasmed over a string of dry retches. Once there was nothing left in his stomach, he forced himself to watch until the fiery end.

When the screams ended, the drums stopped and the flute returned with the same pastoral tune that had started the ceremony.

The hooded assistants stood on the platform and signed their final words in silence, the translation captioned above them on a screen. *Death is only change. We transform the world as we arise from the ashes of this life.* They bowed and retreated, disappearing as a crowd surged around them.

It had been much worse than he'd imagined. The stories he'd heard in the hives always belittled the protest, made it out to be more like a child's game. But it wasn't a game at all.

A gruff voice followed behind him, shouting "That's him. Get him!"

Without looking to see who shouted, Rohin instinctively ran in the opposite direction. He weaved between potted trees in the square, then ducked down an alley to catch his breath.

His pursuers converged on him, forcing him to spin into them as they closed. In a surge of terror, Rohin turned, kicking and punching at anything that moved. He left two of them on the ground and a third still on his feet, but staggering.

A blinding light engulfed him, followed by a broadening shadow, leaving him in conscious darkness. Rohin bit his lip to keep from crying out as he flailed his arms to defend from more attackers. Stinging numbness started at his toes and worked painfully through his limbs to his brain. The final convulsion struck him to the ground, where he struggled to maintain some semblance of consciousness.

"Don't move, or the next charge will break you," a woman's voice spoke harshly above him.

"Eternity," he groaned, noting the blurred insignia over the woman's breast pocket. No. Not again. He turned to his stomach and stretched his arms out, clawing at the earth in frustration, trying to get some purchase to push himself up.

A woman's voice babbled without meaning while he lay prone, his chin on his arm. The blindness had passed, but he could only see and hear through a veil of fog.

His eyes focused, then unfocused. The tall grass wavered in and out. In and out. A pair of thin trousered legs became clear, then fuzzy. He rolled onto his back and tried to lift the veil to look further.

"He's useless in this state," the woman said to some unseen assistant. "Put him out, then get him into the ambul."

The slight prick of the hypo pressed his bare arm, followed by soothing warmth. Finally, he surrendered to the darkness.

～

ROHIN AWOKE LYING on his back. A flat, hard, cold surface tremored beneath him. A second later he recognized the low, steady sound of a hover. His legs and arms ached. He tried to move them, but they were held—ankles, knees and wrists pressed tightly to the platform. He threw all his strength against whatever pinioned them but they remained immovable. The effort exhausted him and he slipped back into unconsciousness.

When he woke a second time he was still lying on his back; but the surface under him had become softer and motionless. He listened for a sound and recoiled when labored breathing came from somewhere in the darkness. Heavy footsteps trudged toward him, then a bright light glared into his eyes as a surgical mask bent toward him and nodded. He struggled against his restraints. Then he felt the pressure against his arm again.

"TDs?" Rohin whispered. The masked person nodded slightly and the pressure released. Rohin closed his eyes in resignation as the soothing warmth of the truth drugs diminished his fear. And any capacity to rebel.

2

Her eyes aching, Miki Yokoyama looked up from the terminal and sat up straight, stretching her tired back. A thunderstorm brewed to the southwest. Bruise-black clouds silhouetted a forest of giant pines outside her window, while distant lightning rippled along the horizon. The static in the air played on her nerves with a lingering tension. She was so close to finally figuring this out, but it always stayed just out of reach.

Miki bent again to the screen and scrutinized an enhancement of the gamma microscope output. Even after all this time, this virus left her in awe. In the world of viruses, the Eternity virus was a giant: about ten times the diameter and twenty-five times the mass of the virus that caused polio in the early twentieth century. The size and complexity of the Eternity virus defied traditional methods of examination, so scientists used computer enhancement to analyze the structure and simulate the features they couldn't detect.

She hit repeat and once more the simulation engaged. The virus attached itself to the cell and dissolved a hole through the cell wall—allowing its nucleic acid to seep in and steal the cell's energy—forcing it to make virus protein and nucleic acid for the production of progeny. For what seemed like the thousandth time, she noted which type of cells accepted this virus; particularly which small part of the cell membrane—a receptor patch—fit it exactly.

For the past seventy years, she'd been trying to create a counter-virus, with a null-protein, to stop it. Why was it so hard? She'd been successful with many other viruses in the past, but this one was different and she was running out of time.

The vidcomm buzzed, jarring her concentration. She slammed her hand on the bench in frustration. "Damn!" she muttered to herself. "Can't they leave me alone?"

She stomped to the terminal wall. Fingers poised above the keypad, she consciously calmed herself and schooled her features into bland professionalism before answering.

Thunder rumbled through the heavy air. The vidcomm buzzed again.

Miki hit the code converter simultaneously with the privacy augment switch. Only a few selected people knew her location; and even fewer knew the type of research she pursued.

Secured deep in the Mt. Hood wilderness, the Ager stronghold provided a safe refuge. It was one of the few places Eternity hadn't completely mapped or penetrated with their spies, but she could sense the lapping of the tide. Eternity was winning.

The decoded signal came through and a three-dimensional image of a beautiful blonde woman with shoulder length hair filled the screen. She immediately recognized her best friend, Anna. The locator indicated she was calling from Vivan Square.

"Miki?" Anna queried excitedly.

She secured the privacy lock before allowing the transmission of her image to be acknowledged back to Anna.

"Yes, there you are," Anna said. "You won't believe this . . . Rohin's showed up."

"What? Are you sure? I figured Eternity killed him long ago."

"I saw him with my own eyes. He hasn't changed much, a little thinner perhaps, but it was undoubtedly him. He was leaving the Anniversary protest when one of Eternity's goons beamed him and carried him into the I2 building."

"Did you follow him?" Miki asked. The Interrogation and Identification building was a nightmare. Miki wouldn't wish that on anyone, even her enemy.

"I couldn't get into the interrogation room, though I'm sure they used TDs on him." Anna shuddered as she spoke. "You know what happens to anyone going in there."

"I have a good number of questions for him myself," Miki replied derisively. "I wonder what Eternity wants with him after all these years?"

"Do you think they're prepping him for something special?" Anna asked. More than the usual strain marred her face.

"Anything's possible with Chawla. The question is *who* is he working for, and should we go after him?"

"Well, I hate to see anyone go through I2," Anna hedged. "But it's pretty risky for us to do a recovery project. I'm not sure he's worth it."

Miki was inclined to agree, but she wanted information more than anything else. "Damn it!" She shook her head, angry with her own conclusions. "We've got to get him. Maybe he knows something about the virus that can help us. He stayed on the Eternity project longer than either of us."

She clenched her teeth. Rohin Chawla was the last thing she needed right now. She turned back to Anna. "Crap – it would have been better for everyone if he was dead."

Anna smiled. "Maybe dead is what we should make him."

Miki frowned, thinking of the risk. "If he's somehow working for Eternity, I'll kill him myself. But right now, we don't really have a choice. Meet me at rendezvous H15 in one hour."

Miki signed off, quickly linked her terminal with the sat array and called her hover. She secured her terminal and rushed out of the building, voicing commands to the building's computer security.

In a matter of moments, her hover arrived outside the door and she climbed in, sitting stiffly upright as it rose straight up 100 meters then arced over the western flank of the mountain on its trajectory toward Vivan Square.

Rohin Chawla. A name out of the past come back to haunt her.

It was in 2050 that Miki, Anna, and Rohin had met in Antarctica on a research project. They were all young, promising biomed grad students serving a pre-employment internship with the leading biomed manufacturer in the world. In spite of the hardships of six months in Antarctica, it was the type of internship that could provide dream opportunities for their professional futures.

Their research project, funded by the World Health Organization, had been to determine if deep ice core samples could yield information on ancient diseases—viruses that had suddenly seemed to disappear. If any were found, WHO hoped to gain new insights into current disease processes that may have mutated from previous viruses. Little did the small research team know that their discovery would change the world, the economy, the balance of power, and every life on the planet.

When she, Anna, and Rohin were all one team it had seemed so wonderful—looking for cures to save the world. Then it quickly fell apart. Eternity Inc. took control and Rohin Chawla suddenly disappeared.

She had loved him fiercely, and his disappearance was a betrayal she would never forgive. She shook her head as if it would clear any lingering feelings for him. What was wrong with her? After all he'd done, how could she even consider there would be an ounce of regret? No. She would not let him under her skin again, even if he could help them. Even more important, she had to make sure he wasn't going to interfere with her project now.

The hover slowed, coming to a stop one hundred meters above the H15 coordinate. Miki queried the computer for close scan. Satisfied her approach hadn't set off any alarms with Eternity security, she parked at the public air lot, quickly stepped out the door onto the grav platform and descended to the ground.

It was only forty meters to the rendezvous point. She advanced from one cover position to the next, taking advantage of trees, bushes, and the sides of other buildings. She scanned the avenue in both directions, thankful for the dark, clouded sky obscuring the moon. The thunder and lightning of the storm seemed to stalk her. She looked up and shook her head. She hoped the churning clouds were not an omen of things to come.

Reaching the rendezvous point, she glanced toward a low-slung, elliptical-shaped one story building. It looked non-descript, not at all imposing. However, the bland facade of I2 did not reassure her. Miki was well aware of the types of interrogation practiced inside.

She surveyed the area for Anna. Where was she? Miki checked her timer. Four minutes until the agreed meet. Damn. Couldn't Anna be early just once? Miki stood across the street, a tall bush blocking any view of her from the building. Alert, she marked each second as it passed. When the time was up, she swore to herself angrily. She didn't like to be kept waiting, it was too dangerous. She and Anna had learned to be very precise whenever they met outside the Ager stronghold. Being caught loitering outside the I2 was not her idea of fun.

A red and white ambul appeared to the south, about fifty meters away. It came in close to the ground, then descended the last few meters to stop across the street, blocking her view of the entryway. She knew exactly what would happen. Ambuls were used to take seriously ill or wounded Eternity personnel to the hospital for treatment.

Because of the Eternity virus, in the past 200 years very few people actually died of illness. Most genetic diseases had been resolved in utero through gene splicing. Ambuls were usually a sign of a *planned death*.

She knew the drill. The attendants would enter the building and come out with an unconscious victim to surreptitiously take to the hospital. No one would be suspicious. Somewhere along the way the body would disappear and all record of the ambul's being at this location would be erased.

"Tarful," she swore in Frenger. "Where is Anna?" Miki rechecked her timer. Anna was now six minutes late.

True to form, one attendant immediately headed toward the building as the other opened the back end of the ambul and retrieved the gurney. Just then the sky opened up and a driving rain drenched everything in its path. Her soaked jumpsuit clung to every curve of her body and her dripping wet hair obscured her vision.

She quickly twisted her hair into a braid and capped it with a band. "Tarful! Can't I catch a break?" She looked down the street and saw no one approaching. Perhaps she could use the downpour as a good reason to run toward the building, pretending to take cover from the rain under the overhang.

She ran toward the overhang and the door to the building swung open. A security guard stepped out, leveling a dark cylindrical object straight at her.

"No loitering. Move along," he barked when she came within three meters of the door.

She came to a complete stop just outside the overhang. Only government security personnel were allowed to carry beamers; she had no defense against one.

Thunder boomed overhead and a streak of lightning illuminated the avenue. At the same time, someone leaped from a cluster of bushes at a ninety-degree angle to the guard. The shooter aimed at his torso and a white energy beam enveloped him. He slumped to the ground.

Anna pulled the guard around the side of the building, motioning for Miki to take cover in the bushes. Moments later Anna joined her, her breath ragged.

"Where the hell were you, and how did you get a beamer?" Miki whispered.

Before Anna could answer, the front doors of the building opened wide and the two attendants backed out, rolling a gurney toward the street. Miki recognized Rohin's pale face above the blankets.

"We have to move now. Once they get him inside the ambul, you take the driver and I'll take the other one," Miki instructed. "Then you get Chawla out of here."

Anna nodded.

Squatting behind the bush, Miki's leg shook with anticipation. She never took her eyes of the attendants as they loaded the body into the back. The door to the ambul slammed shut and she yelled as she sprung toward the attendant at the back door.

Miki delivered a powerful punch to the chest, shoving him back against the door, knocking the breath out of him and sending him sprawling to the side. She couldn't see how Anna fared. She heard the sound of scraping metal against the other side of the vehicle and turned to look. The attendant on her side rose, but she delivered a swift knife-hand chop to the left temple, followed by a well placed heel to his stomach. The man immediately lost consciousness. She didn't know if she had killed him or not, but he was definitely out cold. She carefully rounded the side to see if Anna needed assistance.

Anna bent over the unmoving body of the second attendant. Her beamer was no longer in sight.

"Well, what are you waiting for?" Miki asked. "Get Chawla out of here. Now! After you've secured him, strip the ambul memory and send it on a remote crash."

"But Miki, what are . . ."

"Just do it!" she commanded and backed away to the other side of the avenue.

Without looking back, Anna climbed into the ambul and closed the door. It rose straight up into the thundering sky and moved off.

Miki stood across the street from the building, huddled behind a tree, estimating her position. She shivered as the breeze played icy fingers across her damp skin. She nervously tapped her timer's commlink, sending a signal to her hover to leave the parking area and pick her up. Moments later, the hover braked with a whoosh of air in the street behind her.

She listened for running steps, then checked up and down the street for Eternity agents. Seeing no one she ran. She reached for the door and the distinct white light of an energy beam illuminated a broad circle on the handle, missing her only by centimeters and sending a teeth-clenching shock throughout her body. Lightning smashed into the street behind her, echoing the beamer's retort and the explosion of electricity deafened her.

For a moment, she thought she'd been struck. Then fire crackled.

She didn't dare turn to look. The lightning stroke terrified her even more than the beamers. She seemed caught between nature's fury and the unknown assailant.

A deep bass yell sent her running as the assailant rounded the hover. Her breath grating, she ran in a serpentine pattern toward the blaze. Feet pounded behind her, growing closer with each step.

Miki took cover near another tree and turned briefly to determine the distance between them. He was directly behind her and coming fast. Her heart pounded the terror of her mind.

Lightning struck again; the explosion knocked both of them to the ground and sent the beamer skating toward Miki. She reached for it, closing her fingers tight around the cylinder as she rolled to her feet. The assailant slammed into her, his callused hands grabbed her wrist and twisted it like a bottle cap. He trapped her against the tree trunk with his full body weight against her and the beamer fell from her hand. He kicked it out of her reach.

"No!" Miki shouted, and with all her strength she delivered a knee to his groin. He huffed an involuntary "Oof" as she connected.

He released her briefly and she grabbed for his neck, but he blocked her and grabbed her throat, pressing thumbs against her windpipe.

She let loose an X-block, dislodging his hands, then recoiled to smash her knuckle into his Adam's apple. His head jerked back. Miki followed with a powerful punch to his solar plexus, doubling him over in pain. Then she struck him on the back of the head with the heel of her hand, collapsing him flat on the ground. He put his hands to the ground and tried to lever himself up like a tripod, but she delivered a kick to his knee, then dropped to her haunches and swept his legs out from under him. He fell, smashing hard against the ground. His head hit with the sound of shattering bone.

She waited a breathless moment, expecting him to come back at her one more time. Smell. Sweat. Fear. Blood. Dirt. There was no movement. Gasping for air, she dropped next to him and felt for a pulse. Nothing. He was dead.

Sweat dripped down her back and under her arms. Blood spatters and the smell of salt on her skin washed away in the rain.

As the adrenaline drained from her, she noticed the man seemed very young—twenty-five, maybe thirty. Would his mother cry or even know of his death? For a moment disgust made her stomach clench. Though she had killed before, she still hated it.

A siren in the background warned her Eternity fire engines were responding to the lightning strikes. She had to hurry.

As her automatic survival instinct took over, her actions seemed more and more surreal. She dragged the body over to the blaze and rolled it into the fire. Then she returned to find any other bodies left from the battle. There should be four assailants—two drivers, one guard, and the person she had just killed. Anna had disposed of one. That meant there were two more corpses somewhere.

Finding one more body with the head snapped back and eyes rolled up, she dragged him quickly into the fire. Siren wails grew louder and her breath quickened in response. She did a brief reconnaissance of the area, looking for the fourth body, but couldn't find him. Time was growing too short. She gave up and staggered back to the hover.

Forcing herself to get in and close the door, she set the coordinates. Her breath sliced through her throat like a knife. The hover lifted directly overhead and followed the same trajectory as the ambul had earlier. She set it on autopilot and sank into the seat. Fear and questions assailed her.

Had it been too easy? She was certain the building was monitored. She'd expected more agents to come at them. Wasn't it convenient no one else was on the street to witness the fight or the fire? Was it possible Eternity was one step ahead of them or had they just gotten lucky? Mentally and physically exhausted, she shook uncontrollably. What if she was being set up? What if Anna was right and Rohin was still working with Eternity? Tears coursed down her cheeks at the possibility.

She was so tired. Tired of running. Tired of hiding. Tired of fighting Eternity and the damnable virus she'd helped to create. She wanted just to lie down on the street and let the rain wash over her, absolving her of responsibility. But. . . there was always a but . . . too many people were counting on her. To the Agers, the entire future of humanity depended on her and her counter-virus to return the world to sanity.

3

R ohin woke to a vague sense of heaviness. He moved his arms a bit and discovered that he was under a thick layer of blankets, but a cool breeze caressed his face. Painfully, he blinked until his vision cleared and he surveyed his surroundings. The dimly-lit room was furnished only with a desk, chair, and a bureau. Three doors led from the room. The breeze came from a window above his head. The only sounds he heard were the cool wind through the trees and a steady scratching of a branch against the side of the building.

Shivering, he wriggled deeper in the blankets. He wondered where he'd been moved. He barely remembered a cold slab, a surgeon's mask, questions...he couldn't bring up any of the questions. The tingling paralysis in his limbs was mostly gone now, but his arms and legs were slow to respond to his cautious attempts at movement. His head, however, remained foggy and pounded whenever he moved. When the room began to spin, he closed his eyes once again.

He poked through jumbled memories to see if he could recall anything. Rohin groaned, but cut the sound short as the agony in his head returned with the sound of his own voice. Where was he now?

Not too many years ago, he used to feel like this on a regular basis after partying all night; but he'd changed.

The click of an opening door and the sliver of light streaming in from the other room brought his eyes open again, followed by a shaft of pain.

"I see you're finally awake," a woman's voice spoke softly from the semi-darkness. The voice seemed familiar to Rohin, but it wasn't the voice he'd encountered before. Rohin had known so many people, been so many places in the last hundred years, that he couldn't place it.

He managed a weak grunt in response. His head pounded even with that little effort. He blinked harder, trying to make out the woman, damning himself for his weakness. Was she an enemy? Should he try to make a break for it? The pain he felt underscored the ludicrousness of any action.

Dimly, Rohin was aware that she was now beside him, sitting on the edge of the bed. Small, strong arms gently helped him sit up and steadied him while the room stopped spinning. More blinking brought her into focus—short, brown hair. No, it was tied back and secured with a clip. Dainty hands offered him a plastic cup. He drew back, but she smiled and said gently, "It's water."

Rohin paused, unsure. If she wanted to kill him or drug him, she'd had plenty of opportunity. Was she the one who had entered the room with the truth drugs? No...that was a blonde. Eternity? Something was different. Something was wrong.

With both hands he took the cup. The cool, refreshing water sluiced down his parched throat. He drank all of it. Damn the drug consequences.

The woman took the cup from him and eased him back onto the pillows. Her scent lingered for several minutes, cueing a familiar memory that sat just beyond his conscious. Chilled, Rohin pulled the blankets around himself as she retreated beyond his vision. A chair scraped along the floor near the desk.

"How do you feel?" she asked.

Rohin swallowed, testing his throat. "Unsteady." His own voice sounded strange and far away. Ignoring the lingering headache, he risked a question. "What happened? Uh ... do I know you?"

The woman hesitated, then said flatly, "You were stunned by the Eternity security forces in Vivan Square. Do you remember being in the square?"

Rohin shuddered as the memory of the anniversary protest came back to him full force. His vivid memory of those images, along with the frustration and pain he'd felt, washed over him. His stomach rolled as he shook his head, trying to clear the awful image from his mind. The stench. Rohin gulped.

The woman spoke again, distracting him from his misery. "I can only assume you were interrogated with TDs." She paused for a moment as though expecting him to speak, then continued a minute later. "I'm not sure what was planned for you next, or even if they've put a probe inside you. Our scanners didn't detect one, but we can't always keep up with their technology. In any case, you're here now. We need to determine which side you're on."

"What do you mean which side? I'm not on any side. What side are you on?" Rohin hardly recognized his own whispery voice. Eternity has many guises, he reminded himself. He could be the *guest* of any of a dozen factions of the organization. No matter who held him, he needed to recover soon and find a way out of here.

His eyes were adjusting to the darkness and the small bit of light in the room. He could see a petite form in the corner next to the desk. He squinted and tried to make out the woman's face, but it was too shadowed to see any features or even guess the color of her skin.

With each stretch of a leg or arm, he winced in pain. He felt like he'd been beaten senseless, then stretched on a rack.

"So you're supposed to be my savior, huh." He tried to goad a reaction from her. "Are you going to tell me where I am, and who you are? Or do I assume you're some heavenly spirit with no self-identity?"

A chair scraped back and he saw the shadow stand, outlined in the corner.

"It's Miki, Rohin—Miki Yokoyama." She stepped toward him so he could see her.

He froze, immobilized by a name that was tied to so many emotions—emotions he hadn't experienced for decades. Then the connections slammed into him as the store of drug-induced memories flooded him all at once and he groaned with recognition. She didn't look that different from his memory. With the Eternity virus in her system she would have aged only ten years in the past one hundred since he'd last seen her.

Her dark brown hair was shorter, even though it was held by a clip. When they'd been in Antarctica together, her hair had cascaded to her waist. Sharp angles of shorter hair were cut around her face as if she'd taken the shears to it herself. Her brown almond-shaped eyes still had no wrinkles around them, and her face was as smooth as he remembered. Her lips—that bow he had kissed so many times.

Then memory hit him again and he swallowed hard against the emotion. God, how she must hate him. He had taken over her prized research after she'd been forcibly reassigned. It made no difference that he'd wanted her to stay. He'd begged and pleaded with Eternity to keep her on. But she'd believed he arranged the transfer. That they were in love at the time only made things worse.

Just as the depth of their feelings for one another had made their relationship passionate, so had the reality of her transfer from the research unit made their parting cold. Even now, after decades of living a life without Miki, he still recalled the harsh words that had passed between them. If she still held that animosity for him, he was a dead man.

The silence hung, ominous, as though a vortex had suddenly created a void between them. After what seemed like a long time he found the courage to turn back toward her. He searched Miki's face for some warmth, but he found only the impersonal concern of a caretaker for a patient. No affection, no friendliness, no trust. Even her high-necked wraparound clothing purposely held her separate. He winced. Well, he deserved no less.

Miki finally broke the silence. "I can't tell you where you are; but I can guarantee your safety from Eternity . . . for now."

Rohin said nothing. His confusion mounted. What faction was Miki with? Was he still a prisoner? Her tone betrayed a mix of pity and anger.

"After I leave, the lights will come on more fully and you will be free to move around the house. There's food in the kitchen, and various sized clothing in the closet. I'm sure you can find something to fit." She paused a moment letting her instructions sink in. "Don't try to leave, Rohin. You were brought here over the objections of many in our organization and we can't afford to have this location compromised." Her voice hardened. "If you leave this house for any reason, I will personally kill you."

She let the threat hang in the air for a moment. He was inclined to believe her. When she continued, her voice was not as harsh. "I'll be back in about ten hours. I suggest you just relax and recover from the beamer and the drugs."

Before he could form a reply, her footsteps retreated. The door clicked shut leaving him alone once more.

～

ROHIN AWOKE a second time to an even colder wind coming through the cracked window. His head had cleared and his arms and legs responded normally at last. He slid slowly out of the bed and closed the window.

Trees and a darkening sky reminded him of Miki's admonishment not to go outside. Probably automatic defenses, he thought. With resignation he explored his newest prison.

One of the doors in the room led to a closet. He found a pair of corduroy pants and a sweater that fit. The bureau had some socks that he deemed acceptable. He found no shoes. "Why not," he muttered. "I'm not going out anyway." A hairbrush on the bureau prompted him to pause at the mirror on the wall. He'd changed his appearance so many times while running from Eternity that his image still startled him.

Streaks of gray in his black hair had seemed a good idea at one time; it made him look older, distinguished. The lines in his face were startling—some real, some not. But the empty, hollow stare of his own eyes stopped him. He couldn't remember the last time he faced a day with any hope. Knowing he'd found Miki again created a small seed of hope, but he wasn't sure whether to nurture it or hide it.

He explored his new surroundings with caution. The third door leading from his room revealed a bathroom, rustically fitted with a claw foot bathtub, commode and pedestal sink. The medicine cabinet held deodorant, toothpaste and other toiletries as well as first aid supplies.

The rest of the house, a sitting area, kitchen and dining room, were equally simple and unautomated. Quaint by current standards, it fit Miki well. She had always preferred things from a bygone era.

The main entrance gave him a glimpse of a dark and not too clean courtyard surrounded by trees on all sides. In fact, a casual passerby might think the place was abandoned or held only squatters. Carefully chosen and probably well hidden, it was unlikely anyone would find him here should he be sequestered for a long time.

A familiar feeling of fatalistic acceptance kept him calm. When he'd run from Eternity so long ago, he'd purposefully lost himself in one of the large hive cities, becoming one of the billions of faceless people who belonged nowhere, did nothing that mattered, and lived day to day without a plan beyond the next meal or finding a place to sleep. Menial jobs were posted each morning through main hive terminals. Workers were assigned on a first-come basis. Like most hive residents, Rohin had worked only enough to pay taxes and buy food. The rest of his meager existence was lost in drugged sleep or prurient entertainments.

Looking back, it was hard to believe he'd lived that way for so long. Living only day to day, one year was much like the next. Time was inconsequential without goals or meaning. Not only did he successfully hide from Eternity, but he hid from his fears—hid from himself. He'd lived in fear that someday a common man on the street would identify him as one of those who wanted the Lifer virus to remain only in the hands of the elite. And when they did, he would be tortured and made an example.

But it had never happened. Probably after the first fifty years or so, most people had forgotten how the virus became available—and especially forgotten any part he had in it. Somehow, in running from one hive to the next, he realized he was still willing to fight for his life —and for the life of others. That's what had led him to Vivan Square —led him to erase the ghosts of his past and take action again. Since witnessing that grisley protest, he would not shirk his responsibility ever again. He would seize this second opportunity to make a difference.

Rohin felt even better after he'd eaten. The well-stocked kitchen provided sealed foods of all kinds. He had just sat on the sofa with his second cup of kama when he heard voices outside. Miki stepped in, bringing a blonde-haired woman with her.

He felt the grip of fear, then steadied himself. The blonde hair triggered memories, but he couldn't summon the connections or who he saw, only the fear. He shook his head to release the unconnected image. He knew this woman...Anna Hollin... Hollinrake.

He suppressed a scowl. Though she'd been Miki's best friend on the Antarctic project, Anna had never been friends with Rohin. The feeling was mutual.

Anna pulled a chair in front of the sofa and fixed Rohin with a stern gaze. "Well, do you want to tell us about your little arrangement with Eternity, or do we have to coerce you?"

He glanced at Miki. She pulled up a rocking chair and sat on the edge of the seat, her feet planted squarely on the ground so the chair would not move. They both faced the sofa as if teamed against him. She stared back at him, her face as impassive as it had been earlier.

He turned back to Anna and smiled, being sure to show his teeth. "I see you haven't changed your sweet style and gentle personality. I'm sure your devious little mind has been busy thinking up tortures for me all these years. The rack perhaps? What about thumb screws? Or how about pulling out my fingernails? Now, there's a classic."

Miki stomped a foot on the ground. "Let's not waste valuable time with you two playing one up." She turned to Rohin and looked him straight in the eye, her voice confident and accusing. "What really did happen? How did you get chosen to lead the team after *I* found the virus? And how did you arrange to have Anna and me transferred?"

Unflinching, he held her gaze. Had she learned nothing in the past two hundred years about how Eternity worked? "I told you then and I'll tell you now: I told them...no I begged them to keep you on. I knew you'd done most of the definitive work on the project. I told them it would take me twice as long to do the same work, because I'd have to review everything first."

"Oh, come off it." Anna pushed her face within inches of his. "We know all about professional competition. Don't give us your it-was-a-surprise-to-me-too crap."

He ignored her, keeping Miki's gaze. "It *was* a surprise to me. Sure, I'll admit—once I realized they wouldn't bring you back—that I was happy for the opportunity. You were always so much better than me, Miki. I never dreamed I could replace you."

"I never dreamed I could replace you." Anna repeated Rohin's line in a squeaky mocking voice. "Ha! And I suppose you hated presenting the findings to Kant, too."

"How did you know I presented . . ."

"Get on with it," Miki interrupted again, her jaw hard as her eyes drilled into him. "You presented it to Kant and then what?"

Rohin ran a hand through his hair and sat back against the sofa cushions. How much did they already know? How much should he tell? How much did he even know about what had happened in the I2 building? What he had promised? His life may hang in the balance if they knew everything. He would tell as little as possible, yet what he did tell would be the truth.

Rohin paused for a moment, getting up to refill his cup of kama. His stomach knotted as he recalled the beginning of all his trouble.

Miki sat motionless at the edge of the rocker, waiting for him to return. Anna shifted in her chair as she watched his every move, her brow furrowed. He was sure if eyes could spew daggers, Anna's would do so right now. He took his time before settling back on the sofa, the cup of warm kama in his hand.

"You have to understand, there was no questioning Kant's plan. If I wanted to keep my job—and I did—I knew I would have to follow his instructions exactly. Even though I knew what was going on . . . "

Anna snorted and he turned to her, gritting his teeth. "Yes, I could figure out their motives. If they controlled the virus, they would live longer than any other world leaders. I'm not stupid!" He held his teeth together and took a deep breath through his nose, then turned back to Miki, pleading for her understanding. "You have to believe me . . . I'm not that low. I couldn't follow through with it."

"He's lying," Anna said in a tone that expected no argument. "That is exactly how Eternity got to where it is today. And it's mostly your damn fault!" Her voice rose quickly with her temper. She cursed at him and paced behind her chair, her hands balled into fists as if she were consciously trying to stop herself from punching him. "You could have stopped them," she said with quiet intensity—almost too quiet for Rohin's liking. "You were the only one of the three of us in a position to stop Kant. And you didn't." Anna's fist unclenched and she waved an angry finger in his face, raising her voice. "You're a damn coward! What did they offer you? Fame and fortune? All the fucking you could want?"

She looked down at him, her nostrils flared with each breath, daring him to move. "Don't let him sucker you, Miki. He's slime and I think we ought to get rid of him. The longer we keep him around, the more chance he'll have to play on your feelings." She laughed, a short, nasty sound and tilted her head toward him. "Look at him! The idiot thinks you still love him—after he betrayed you and all that has happened over the past century."

"That's enough, Anna." Miki's voice was edged with steel. "You're out of line."

"Am I? Need I point out how big a security risk he is? He knows how to play on your emotions." Anna stepped aside and pointed to him, still seated on the sofa, quietly facing Miki. " Look at him! He's giving you his best puppy dog, you-can't-help-but-love-me look right now. He'll do anything to get you to believe his lies—probably lies fed him under hypnosis. For all we know Eternity's recording everything we say here."

"I'm telling you the truth." He held Miki's eyes. He dared not look away. It was true. All he had to offer was the truth. He'd been a coward in the past, but he wasn't a killer and he wanted to make things right now. He wasn't anything like Kant.

"I don't know if they hypnotized me in I2. I don't know if I have a probe. I'm sure you already checked me."

"Yeah, we checked you all right," Anna said. "But unlike Eternity we don't have all that cash to keep up with their surveillance techniques. Each day we wake up and hope they haven't found us. Each day we wonder when they'll send in someone as a double agent. And wouldn't you know, here you are...all of a sudden. After over a hundred years of not hearing a word from you, you show up at Eternity and Miss Goody-two-shoes here decides to save your sorry butt."

Miki continued to stare at him wordlessly. She neither came to his defense or joined her anger with Anna's. He saw nothing in her eyes, neither caring or disgust. No emotion was worse than anger. He wished she'd feel something.

"Why didn't you contact me?" Miki's voice was flat, as if she already knew the answer. "I could have used your help to fight Eternity."

He looked away. "I know. I just couldn't." He matched her tone, tired of repeating the same lines he'd told himself for so long. His eyes focused, distracted, across the room. "I was on the run. Kant's people wasted no time contacting all my acquaintances." His voice grew softer. "Knowing me became a death sentence. I found that out too late—after they killed my parents and my brother." His eyes came back to hers, he felt them mist but willed them not to fill. He didn't want her pity. "I didn't want you hurt too."

"I...I didn't know," Miki said.

Anna snorted from across the room. "Oh, yeah. You weren't

running out, you were just trying to save us." She hit the table between them with her fist. "Bullshit!

"Well, guess what bozo. We didn't need your help. We're better than that. Eternity would have gotten us long ago if we weren't. And all that stuff that happened to your family? So what? We've all lost people we loved...and millions of people have lost even more...entire civilizations wiped off the face of the earth while you did nothing. So forget the pity party. Where have you been for the last, oh, one hundred years or so?"

Rohin ignored her, bent his head and reached for Miki's hand. But a quick shake of her head stopped him. "I didn't think you'd want to hear from me." His lip hitched on one side in a rueful smile. "I couldn't decide who hated me more, you or Kant."

Miki did not rise to his bait. "I did."

"Why were you at Vivan Square?" Anna challenged him.

Rohin winced as he looked up at Anna. He didn't want those memories to haunt him too.

"Six months ago, Kant's forces came after me. After eighty years of avoiding them in the hives, I thought they'd given up. . .figured I was dead. But they hadn't. When they found me, I ran. Instinct. I've been running for six months—running from one hive to another."

He stopped and turned again to focus on Miki. He needed her to believe him, to understand. He didn't expect forgiveness. He didn't deserve it. He already hated himself enough for both of them.

"While I was running, I began to see things as if for the first time. All these years I'd been in the hives I'd ignored everything. Stayed drugged up, told myself there was nothing I could do. But during the last six months I was forced to see...forced to understand what living there was really like. Without drugs I had no escape.

When I heard of the Anniversary Protest, I couldn't believe it. I had to see it for myself. How long have these protests been going on?" He shifted in his chair. "I couldn't believe anyone actually wanted to die."

"They've been going on about seventy years," Miki answered. "Believe it, there are many people who think death is preferable to living 800 years. And the protests are saying death is not only necessary, but natural and should be expected."

There was a sadness about her, a tiredness he hadn't noticed when she and Anna first walked through the door together. He wondered what had happened to her. If he didn't know better, he'd think she carried the weight of the world on her shoulders even more heavily than he.

"Yeah, yeah, yeah. Then you got beamed by that Eternity agent, and the rest is history," Anna hurriedly finished for him. "Or so you would have us believe. Well, I don't see that you've changed at all, Chawla. You're the same damn irresponsible coward you always were."

Anna strode to the door with an air of finality. "Miki, I've got better things to do than listen to this drivel. I've given you my recommendation. Get rid of him. He's no use to us."

She opened the door and stepped outside as if to leave, but then turned back flinging her blonde hair behind her dramatically. "But, if you want to keep him ... well, you know the risk. I won't be responsible. Keep him for a pet if you want—preferably in a cage. Come out here and fuck him every once in a while if it makes you happy. But be damn careful!   You've come too far to let your hormones override your brains." Then she stalked out, slamming the door behind her.

Rohin let out a breath. The room seemed larger now without Anna in it.

Was it possible that Miki still cared for him, after all he'd done? He searched her face, trying to read the emotions flitting across it in silence.

He rolled his shoulders back and twisted his head from side to side to relieve the tension. Miki had been the best thing to ever happen to him, and he'd screwed it up. She was obviously not with Eternity and he could certainly get onboard with that. Was it possible they could work together again? This time both of them against Eternity? Both of them helping to make sure the innoculation was also available to parts of the world that had been ignored.

Miki stood and went to the window. She shuddered and crossed her arms in front of her, her left hand rubbing her shoulder and neck. He knew she wasn't looking at the dark forest outside.

"Why should I trust you?" she asked softly. "Anna's right. You're a weak link in our security."

He felt his insides go cold. Security? What kind of organization was Miki involved with? What would she do if she didn't trust him?

He rose and approached her. Up close, he saw again how small she was. He remembered holding her. How good her body had felt in his arms. She'd been younger then, more trusting—naïve perhaps. A hundred years was a long time to feel betrayed.

A pine scent mixed with lavender triggered a memory. "Is that the same perfume you used to wear?"

She shook her head and took a step back. "It's a combination. The pine is new."

"It's nice." He stepped toward her again, coming even closer than before. He could feel the heat from her body, warming him and giving back a life he had forgotten. Cautiously, he reached for her, drawing her to him.

She stiffened immediately. "No!" She pushed against his chest and stepped out of his reach. "I have no feelings for you. . . and . . . I never will again." She strode toward the front door and opened it.

He turned toward the window, the pain constricting his chest and his breath shallow. "So, what are you going to do with me?"

"I don't know. I don't know what to believe anymore."

He looked back at her. Her entire body looked like it was ready to run.

"I'll be back tomorrow morning with a decision." She hurried outside, closing the door with a loud bang behind her. He heard the bar slide into place.

Rohin stood at the window and watched her leave. His life was in the hands of someone he'd loved, someone he'd wronged. He'd have to convince her they were on the same side again. If he died now, who else would make sure the Eternity virus was available equally to all?

4

Miki peeked in the bedroom. Rohin was stretching and making motions to get up. She quietly closed the door and sat in the kitchen at the dining table, listening. A squeal of pipes indicated the water had been turned on in the shower. She closed her eyes, willing herself not to think of him naked.

Last night had been rough. She couldn't sleep. She couldn't believe she still had feelings for him after all this time. It was like seeing a ghost. It had been so long since she'd even heard his name that she'd convinced herself he was dead. She had grieved heavily then. For two years she'd moved back and forth between anger and grief. Then she'd finally let him go. Or at least stuffed him so far back in the recesses of her mind that she didn't have to remember anymore.

She knew he was dead because she'd never wanted to believe he would purposefully leave her, or not try to find her. He had to have known what was going on. Her fight with Eternity's distribution of the virus had been in all the media for twenty years after she'd left.

She'd been made a criminal by the Eternity props—the propaganda machine—and the government. At one point she'd even been accused of treason. When she went underground, the props reported about her life as a prostitute in the hives with bogus sightings. Women who had some resemblance to her were probably forced to do sex acts while being filmed so they could provide evidence to the claim. She'd seen a couple of the bogus films with a man yelling out her name as he'd ejaculated and the woman putting her hand over his mouth and whispering, "Don't ever use my name again or I'll kill you."

What type of man could watch that and not seek her out? Surely, he hadn't believed the props. If he'd truly loved her, how could he have not at least looked for her? Even if it was just to tell her he was alive but he couldn't come to her without putting her in danger.

Her brain told her Rohin was holding back, but her heart wanted to believe him. She'd pushed herself into her work, guaranteeing she'd never have another relationship after Rohin. And now he was here. Here where in the deepest quiet of her sleep she'd always wanted him to be. Her heart wanted to believe they could work side-by-side together again and finally defeat Eternity.

The water stopped running. Shortly, she heard the sound of drawers opening and closing. He was probably dressing. She opened her viewer. She would not be caught thinking about him. Anna was right. He was a security risk and that was all she should focus on. She may never love another man, but one thing was for sure. Rohin Chawla was never going to be allowed into the Ager organization. She'd worked too long and too hard to take that risk.

On the small screen, Miki perused the Ager security reports for the immediate two hundred kilometer area. There had been a break-in at Zig Zag, not far from their current location, but nothing was missing. She would have to follow up on that later. Any break-in was cause for concern. She closed the viewer when Rohin entered the room.

He said nothing as he proceeded to the antique electric stove and set a pan of water to boil. He was wearing a pair of wool pants and an oversized sweater that somewhat emphasized his short height. Although he was a full fifteen centimeters taller than her, his one point seven meter frame was small compared to most men. She noticed he'd taken the time to use beard removal lotion, which gave his oval face a more youthful appearance. He hardly looked like the same man they'd abducted two nights ago.

He moved energetically about the kitchen, opening each cupboard to locate what he wanted: a cup and spoon, some kama flakes, and a little cinnamon spice. Evidently, the effects of the drugs had worn off completely. Except for the light gray circles under his eyes, he appeared to be in good health. Good. She thought to herself. Today we will return him to the hives and he can do whatever he was doing before Eternity found him.

She looked up to find his brown-green eyes staring at her. His hair was still wet, and a small curl fell forward onto his forehead. She licked her upper lip and her mouth opened slightly.

She shook herself and turned away. No. It was memory, not reality. There was no way she was seeing desire in his eyes.

He stood within inches behind her and touched her shoulder, then turned her toward him. "Miki?" He smiled in that way she remembered all too well. That way she thought she'd never see again.

Tarful! She pulled his face to hers without hesitation. She ravaged his mouth, digging her fingers into his full dark hair and he did the same right back. When she opened to invite him deeper, there was no hesitation. Their tongues darted, lips sucked, groans on both sides moved hands to clutch, knead. No softness. She deserved this before saying goodbye again.

When he reached his hands beneath her shirt she didn't fight him. Instead she reached for the zipper on his pants. God, she wanted him so much. She wanted to know if he still felt the same. She wanted him to make love to her. If only they could make love she would know if he were the same man she remembered or if he'd changed. He could never keep anything from her when they made love.

As the zipper slid in her fingers she came to her senses and pushed him away. She shuddered and backed up. Who was she kidding? How could she be so naïve? "No! This isn't what I want. It can't be what I want."

He didn't attempt to move forward. His breath ragged, she knew it was completely up to her.

She shook her head. Tarful! It wasn't fair that he could still move her like this. Who was she fooling? So much had changed in the past century. She wasn't sure *she* could even be honest anymore, so how could she expect it of him?

Sure, there had been men since Rohin. She wasn't the type to be without sex for a hundred years. She would take a lover for a few weeks once or twice a year. Then let him go. Once she'd had a hiatus from sex for six years before the next one. Then there was Robert. No, she wouldn't go there. That had been a disaster.

They all understood. She was the leader of the Agers. They understood she couldn't get attached. She couldn't show favorites. Only she knew that she'd been longing for him…for a dead man.

She pulled her blouse back together. "This isn't going to happen, Chawla." She moved to the kitchen and concentrated on slowing her breathing, keeping her hands steady as she made her own kama. "My fault. Completely. A mistake."

Rohin stepped behind her. He didn't touch her, but she could feel his breath on her neck. "Not a mistake, Miki. I've been dreaming of this…waiting…never able to believe it was possible."

"It's not," she said. "Never again. You're leaving today." She moved to the dining table and sat down.

"Why?" he asked. "Tell me what's going on. Tell me why I can't join you? Were a good team. We always have been."

"In bed, maybe," she said. "A century is too long. I can't trust you. I won't trust you."

He reached toward her cheek and she backed up. "We both want to stop Eternity. We both want the same thing. Tell me how I can help you. I want to be part of your fight…part of your life… again."

She felt a hollowness born of constant caution in sharing any information at all—even with a man who she used to trust with her life. She wrapped the mantle of leadership about her like a cloak. Her constant companion was that empty sense of isolation that kept her safe. Kept all of the Agers safe.

She hadn't discussed the details of her plan for Rohin with anyone, even Anna. She wasn't sure Anna would approve. But the decision had to be her own. She was the one with the past relationship. She was the only one who could decide whether to trust him. And if he was to be terminated, she wouldn't shirk that responsibility either. She'd brought him here, so she had to be the one to decide what would happen to him.

Each person in the Ager inner circle knew only pieces about the plan for the final Ager rebellion—the pieces that most pertained to each of their roles. Only Miki knew the arc of responsibility and consequence. A person in Miki's position learned to keep a lot of things inside. She'd been burned before by supposed loyal Agers who became agents for Eternity. She was determined that would never happen again.

◇

STILL RECOVERING from the shock of her pushing him away, Rohin sat next to her at the table and stirred his drink. He was not going to let go of her this time. When she'd pulled his lips to hers he'd felt young again, full of anticipation, full of the knowledge that together they could do anything. If she'd just let it continue he would have shown her how much he'd changed, how much he still loved her. How he would do anything to protect her and fight with her.

Maybe she just needed a little time to get used to him again. It was obvious by what just happened that she wanted him...maybe even still loved him.

He could slow down. He could lighten it up. Whatever it took to keep them talking, to keep them on the same side.

He raised his cup to her as if in a toast, then cleared his throat. "Hey, don't let what just happened throw you. We can slow down. We were both . . ."

"It's already forgotten," Miki interrupted sharply.

Rohin's lips barely parted in a half smile of understanding as he lowered his cup back to the table.

Miki closed her eyes as if she was trying to make up her mind about something. Then she rose from her chair and stood apart from the table, feet slightly apart, shoulders back. She narrowed her gaze to focus on him.

"You have no idea who I really am, do you."

What the hell? She was Miki Yokoyama. What game was she playing now?

"Right, angel." Rohin said. "Now you want to tell me you're a clone—and the real Miki is somewhere else."

"No," she said seriously, without even the beginnings of smile. "I want to tell you who I am now. I am not the same young, awestruck researcher you met in Antarctica."

"I didn't think you were," he responded quietly. "No one stays the same for a century."

He wasn't the same either, but their foundation was still the same. He knew it and if she'd give him half a chance, he'd prove it.

He took a slow sip of kama, then placed his drink on the table and pushed it away. He'd give her his full attention. Then he'd set her straight. He wasn't leaving this time, whether she wanted him to her not. He was no longer afraid she would kill him. He was more afraid he'd lose her again...this time forever.

She continued, her voice confident. "Last night you mentioned monitoring my efforts to bring the Eternity Virus to the general population. But you only know what was reported to the public by the props. Some of what you saw was true. Some of it was spin, convenient to both Eternity and myself—though they sure didn't know they were helping me in any way."

He reached for her hand, but she withdrew it from the table. Her eyes widened and her lips thinned.

"You were magnificent," he said. "Almost a martyr to the cause. Thousands of people were depending on you to help them. I understand, Miki. I admire you and everything you've done."

She stood and stomped away from the table. "You do not understand! How could you? You weren't there."

Her back to him, she took a deep breath and her shoulders slumped as she let it out. When she turned to him again, he could see the tiredness, the constant pace she must keep waking up each day and trying once more to go up against Eternity.

"I'm no longer that person either," she said. "I'm not famous. I'm not a hero. I'm not a martyr to the cause. In fact, for the past seventy years I've consciously tried to stay out of the public eye—and especially off the radar of Eternity."

Rohin shifted uneasily in his chair and turned away rubbing his neck. "You're right, I really have no idea what all you've been through. I was out of it." He turned back and lowered his hand to the table. "I never believed you were a prostitute, Miki. I never believed the props."

She stood stiffly and he had to look up to see her. Her eyes stared at him, but he couldn't read anything in them—not acknowledgement, not shock, sorrow, trust—nothing.

"I'm sorry I wasn't there for you. I'm sorry I didn't come looking for you. I have all kinds of excuses, but they don't matter anymore."

He tapped the table. "Will you please sit down? I'm getting a crick in my neck."

She moved around the table, chose the chair closest to him and turned it backward, straddling it as she faced him head on.

"I see you've changed," he acknowledged. "I've changed. We've all changed. That's life. But that doesn't mean we can't work together again. I'm not asking you to forgive me. That would be too much. I'm just asking you to give me a second chance. I know we are on the same side. We've always been on the same side."

She said nothing. Once again her face was devoid of emotion.

"I can take it slow. I'm willing to do whatever you need to prove I can be trusted again." He paused. He didn't have a new plan for going against Eternity. He knew only that he would—that he must. If Miki had been working a plan all these years, he could join her. All she had to do was give him a chance.

"Have you heard of the Agers, Rohin?" Her formal tone showed no attempt to be friendly.

"Ummm . . ." he murmured, searching his memory. "Only what I've seen on a slow 'cast day. Aren't they some fanatical group that wants everybody to be executed on their two hundredth birthday, or some such nonsense?" Vivan Square flashed again in his memory and he flinched. "They aren't part of that awful protest I saw, are they? Flinging themselves into fire and making it out like it's some spiritual calling?"

"The protesters are a fringe group," she said. "The Agers aren't fanatics. They're scientists, artists, educators. They seek to revitalize society by limiting the average lifespan to less than two hundred years," she continued. "They believe the stagnation of humanity is directly connected to the virtual elimination of death brought on by the introduction of the Eternity Virus."

He shook his head. She couldn't possibly believe that. "Now you're selling prop," he said. "That sounds like a memorized speech from some drug-crazed leader. Who have you been listening to? Those extremists are out of their minds if they think people will give up their long lives."

"We are not fanatics, extremists, or terrorists!" Miki's eyes flashed in anger.

Rohin struggled not to leave his mouth open. He waited a minute, hoping she would make a joke out of it. But she didn't. "Oh God, Mik . . . please tell me you're not one of them."

"Oh, I'm one of them all right," she laughed with noted sarcasm. "Not only one of them, Rohin, I'm their evil leader."

"Tarful . . ." he slowly placed his cup back on the table. How could she have fallen in with them? When they'd been at Eternity together, they'd agreed to work toward making sure the virus was given equally to everyone. They'd agreed that it was good to finally deliver the proverbial fountain-of-youth to the world. How could she have joined an extremist group like this?

"Slow down a minute," he said, taking a deep breath, trying to make sure he didn't get her emotions up again. "I agree we need to fight against Eternity. They've certainly gotten power hungry. The distribution of the virus hasn't been even-handed. But we aren't helping anyone by shortening people's lives. What happened to you? How could you have given up on our dream?"

She stood and marched into the kitchen. "Our dream?" She gripped the counter and her eyes widened. "You gave up on our dream when you stayed with those bastards. When you let them fire me. When you never came looking for me. Don't you dare even consider it *our* dream."

Rohin sucked in his cheeks. She had a point. But revisiting this same story wouldn't get them anywhere. He stood and joined her at the counter.

"You're right. I gave up. It was a mistake." He reached for her hand again. She tried to pull it away, but he grabbed it anyway. "I'm here now. We can change it. Together, Miki. We can change it. This small group of...what do you call yourselves?"

"Agers." She yanked her hand away. "Get it in your head, Chawla. Agers. And we are not small."

Okay. That was not the right move. Obviously, she was passionate about her direction. Misguided, but passionate.

"My mistake," he said again. "Tell me more. How did you decide to join this group?"

Her lips pursed.

He growled. "Lead... this group against Eternity?"

She took another breath and continued. "The majority of people have become completely dependent on Eternity for the virus, for work, for places to live. In return, Eternity has encouraged all of us to become docile, passive pets lulled into taking whatever they provide for us, never questioning and never wanting. They provide food, housing, drugs, sex, anything we want. They've created the only economics allowed in hives. That is labor or pleasure. We can choose to waste our lives in total self-indulgence and do nothing for others for the entire eight hundred years most of us will live. It's so easy to be lazy, to let them take over. That is what we have to stop. That is why the Agers have banded together."

"But you've turned it down," he insisted. "And Anna. There are others Miki. We can find them. They can help us teach others, show others. There's no reason to take away our long lives."

He stepped around the counter and lightly raised her chin to look into her eyes. She didn't resist. "Remember how happy we were when we first found the virus and knew what it could do? Remember how happy we were that it enhanced immune systems, that it stopped disease in its tracks? Remember how we believed that long lives would allow people to finally be more fulfilled—have even more chances to do all the things they longed to do? Write, paint, study music, make their mark in business. That's what we wanted, Miki. That's what we can help others to bring about."

She stepped away from him. "No. We have to go back," she insisted. "As long as we're unconcerned about health, jobs, income, we put up with the seemingly small inconveniences of dealing with Eternity. While everyone is feeling safe and secure, Eternity quietly exercises its power, taking a little more away each year and killing our spirit in the process.

Miki began pacing and gesturing emphatically, her dark eyes glowing as the fervor of her speech intensified. "Can't you see that the need for protest...the need for questioning power...the need for change... is what has ultimately kept us alive and moving forward?"

"There are those who still want change," he said.

"Not enough. Not enough feel an urgent need to strive for new goals. With nothing to strive for, what makes our lives worth living? What value do we place on our existence? Or, what matters about our death when we can't even perceive of death anymore?"

He couldn't believe it. She was passionate about this direction. How could she have changed so much? How could she have given up on humanity. More than that, how could she take the choice away?

"And you and the Agers have the answer? You believe that by cutting life short it will change everything?" His voice rose as he thought of how wrong she was, how little she must understand. "Do you really think that if you succeed in shortening our lives again that anyone will thank you?"

She shook her head. "No. I'm not that stupid."

"You're right, they won't thank you. They'll hate you. They'll seek out everyone of you and kill you. Can't you see that? Is that what you want? Then when they've hunted all of you down and put you in prison, or killed you, who will be around to help them with the change, Miki? Who will care?"

"It's not important what happens to me." She stood still, her voice quiet but confident. "I'm willing to take that chance to save the human race."

"By killing them?" Rohin asked incredulously.

"No! Not killing them, simply limiting their lives to a more natural length. Death is an important part of experiencing life. Some of the greatest wisdom came from people who could embrace death. Avoiding death is not the answer."

Rohin stared at Miki thoughtfully. "I know you took on the corporations of the United Americas before, but that was over a hundred years ago. Now, with Eternity in charge, there is a world order that is much more powerful. How can you and a small group of fanatical idealists do anything?"

"We are no longer a small group of two or three people," Miki said. Her hand scrubbed over her face and she massaged the space between her forhead and the bridge of her nose. "I don't know why I bothered to tell you. You have no clue what's happened while you were drugged and escaping reality."

He stepped behind her and kneaded her shoulders until she relaxed. "You told me because you know I care, because you know I want to be with you."

She shrugged and moved away from his hands, leaving cold air in her wake. She turned, her mouth turned down, her eyes dead. "I had this insane hope that you would understand. That somehow you really could join us...join me. I should have known. I should have known you wouldn't have the guts for it. Anna's right. You haven't changed much at all."

"Guts? What kind of guts does it take to remove choice? What kind of guts does it take to lead a band of fanatics that have no idea what the consequences will be. How many, Miki? How many do you lead? Fifty? One hundred? Even five hundred wouldn't be enough to go up against Eternity."

"I can't tell you that right now," she said.

"Ah, don't you trust me? Are you still afraid I'm an agent of Eternity?"

He pulled her face toward him, wanting to crush her lips to his—to prove he still loved her, still wanted her, they could still work to save humanity together. But he stopped short when he saw the panic in her eyes and let his hands drop.

She stood her ground, unmoving. "No, Rohin. I don't know how much I can trust you. I do believe you care...about me. I do believe you care about going up against Eternity. But that's all I know about you. You told me yourself that you were a coward. You don't understand anything I've told you. Why should I trust you? Why should I tell you any more?"

Rohin clenched his jaw together, but refused to look away. Yes, he'd been a coward but he wasn't going to be one now. And he definitely wasn't going to let her or her crazy organization of a few hundred fanatics take away the one gift he'd given humanity—longer life.

He worked to soften his voice, not to show the anger and fear that was rising in him. "You don't know what you're asking, Miki. You are riding into the maelstrom with half-baked ideas and disenfranchised fanatics at your side."

"So that's what you think of me? Half-baked? Stupid? A fanatic?"

"That's not what I said."

"Yes it is. That's exactly what you said." She pushed against his chest to move him back. Then she opened her viewer, pressed a button and pointed to a number. "Thousands, Rohin. Thousands."

Before he could read it, she closed it again. "The only thing I've done that is stupid was to hope you might join us. Or at least not stand in our way. But I can see Anna was right. It was my hormones talking...hormones and some long ago unresolved memory of you and me together. Well, I've seen you now, and its over. No matter what my body is saying, my brain knows better. There is no chance for us. I just have to decide what to do with you now."

He was losing her again. He would not allow that to happen. Not after his hopes were renewed. She had to still care. She'd rescued him from Eternity. She hadn't immediately ordered him killed. Maybe he could pretend to be part of the organization. Maybe he could change it from the inside, like he'd wanted to do with Eternity.

"I can't pretend to understand your organization or why you've chosen this direction," he finally said. "But you can trust me, Miki. I won't hurt you."

"You're already hurting me, just by being here. I've put Ager security at risk by saving you, by bringing you here." She turned away. "I wish you'd stayed dead," she whispered. She bowed her head. "I grieved for you when I lost you a century ago. I grieved for you again when I heard you were dead. I wish I could have continued my life without knowing you were still around."

He reached toward her, but she sidled away at his touch. He sighed deeply. "You don't mean that. I know you don't."

She turned back to him, her chin up, her nostrils flaring with each breath. "I'm putting my life on the line every day to do this. I expect the same from anyone in my organization. Even if you don't agree with my cause, I don't believe you feel any cause is worthy of that kind of commitment."

"I see," Rohin said. Maybe it was better this way. Maybe he could be more help to her if he was on the outside where he could keep tabs. He knew she'd try to send him off to some place where he couldn't track her down again. But he'd keep tabs. He would find a way to always know what was going on and when to step in to stop her—or save her.

"And what about Anna?" he asked. "Is she part of your Ager organization? Does she think I shouldn't be told anything?"

"Anna is my right hand, like she has always been since we were fired from the Antarctica project. As far as telling you anything, I'm sure she wouldn't approve of what I've already told you. Actually, Anna not only wants you dead. She's already volunteered to take care of it herself." Miki smiled slightly. "She always was one to just take care of any inconveniences and not analyze them. But, it is my decision."

There was a long silence as they stared at each other; neither one saying anything. Then Rohin moved to the table and fumbled with his cup, almost dropping it as he returned to place it in the kitchen sink.

"Well," he cleared his throat while running the water and rinsing the cup, "since it's obvious you won't tell me anything else, and I have nothing to offer, what do we do now?" He paused, turned off the water and turned to face Miki with a teasing leer. "How about taking up where we left off earlier? If I'm going to be killed, I want to go out having made love to you one more time."

Stiff-armed beside her chair, fingers curled into fists, Miki's sharp-eyed glare impaled him. Rohin chuckled.

"Just kidding, Mik . . . you've got to lighten up. Anna said you could keep me and come for a visit now and again. Maybe that's a start. If we're going to be spending any time together, you can't always come on like this overbearing military type."

She marched over to him and stood within inches of him, looking up to his face. Her hands fisted at her side. "I should slap that smirk from your face," she said. "In fact, if I were you, I'd have a bad case of castration anxiety right now."

He held up his hands. "Okay, okay. No need to get hostile here. I can take a hint." He knew she couldn't kill him. He knew from that kiss that neither one of them could purposely hurt the other. "Let's stop with the grandstanding."

Miki stiffened and her chin lifted slightly.

"If we just slow down a minute maybe we can work something out. We just need a little more time. Time to talk. Time to get to know each other again."

"We. Will not. Be spending. Any. More time together," she said. "Anna is taking you away today." She seemed pleased to note his surprise. "You're going back to the hives."

"Miki...please..."

"While you're there maybe you'll come to your senses. Maybe you won't. I don't care."

"And if I want to contact you?"

"There will be no contact."

"Never? Even if I decide to join the Agers?"

"We both know that won't happen, Rohin. Don't try to play me. Count your blessings that I'm letting you live. Many in my organization would vote otherwise."

She extended her hand to shake his. "This is the end of our acquaintance."

"Acquaintance?" he pulled her to him. "Miki, we are much more than acquainted."

She looked up and for a moment he saw a flicker of interest, then it faded to sadness. He bent and caressed her lips slowly, carefully. At first she didn't respond, as if it was a matter of honor. But he pressed forward, his hands in her hair, his lips massaging and encouraging. He would leave her with a promise. If she wouldn't listen to his words, she had to listen to his body.

Finally she responded. As if she knew it was the last time, she kissed him back with a combination of passion and sorrow. At first tentative, then giving and taking until it was hard to tell where she started and he ended. He felt a moistness on her cheek and hugged her closer.

"Oh, Miki...I can't let you go...I can't leave you again." His mouth endeavored to show the truth in his words once again.

As if on cue, Anna barreled in the front door, causing Rohin to jump back in agitation. She glanced briefly at Miki, then without any discussion or questions, she forcefully clasped Rohin's left arm behind him and led him toward the door. His fingers trailing along Miki's shoulder then arm.

"Come on, lover boy. The honeymoon's over," Anna said harshly, as she hustled him out the door and toward the hover.

Rohin didn't put up much of a struggle. He wanted to leave Miki with his promise of love...of caring for her...not his anger. She would come around. She had to.

"Think of what I said," he shouted to Miki as Anna propelled him into the back seat with a knee to his buttocks, her hand pressing his head down and through the door. She then secured him with a belt across his lap and chest.

"You can't play God with people's lives," he shouted out the hover door when Miki didn't respond or even move to wave goodbye. "Give me a chance to show you, Miki. Give me a..."

All sound was cut off as the security screen activated, closing and locking the hover door and effectively stopping him from reaching any pilot controls. He was trapped with no way out and no one to hear him.

～

"YOU TWO ARE REALLY A PAIR," Anna said, barely hiding her mirth as she joined Miki beside the hover. "The idealistic passions you shout at each other are almost sensual."

Miki turned and stomped toward the cabin. She hated it when Anna became so self-righteously controlled. She knew Anna was proud of having wrenched any seeds of idealism from herself. Anna felt it gave her a superiority over most people. Well, maybe it did sometimes, but not with the arrogance she usually displayed.

For Miki, it was her "so called" idealistic passion that provided the vision to guide the Agers and the endurance to keep going when she felt like giving up. Sometimes she wasn't sure why Anna continued to support the Agers. It certainly wasn't because she believed in the cause. The only explanation was that Anna appreciated friendship and loyalty. She may not be aligned with the Ager cause, but she was definitely against Kant and Eternity. Anna had a streak for vengeance, and Kant had definitely got on the wrong side of it. That was what Miki used in Anna, and so far it had served the Ager cause.

"Lover boy is secured," Anna said. "Where are we taking him?"

Miki raised her head to Anna's voice, removing the clip from her hair and fingering it in agitation. Thank God Anna had shown up when she did. Otherwise they would have...no, she couldn't go there. Not now. Not ever.

"Where do I take him?" Anna repeated, louder.

"Sorry," Miki apologized.

"You know he's just a . . ."

"I know," Miki quickly interrupted, before Anna began to lecture again. "I shouldn't let him get to me like this. It's just that sometimes I do have doubts about our work."

Anna grabbed Miki's shoulders and shook her forcefully. "Come off it, Mik. Don't let that ass get you to question anything. Can't you see he's trying to break you down? Get a hold on yourself."

Anna backed away, then said in a more sympathetic tone of voice, "Now, where do I take him? You know you can't leave it up to me. I'd dump him from the hover at four thousand meters."

Miki chuckled, grateful for a little humor. Actually Anna probably would do that. "Take him to Rho Hive 69219. At least it will be familiar to him. It's far enough away he won't know how to get back, but close enough we can keep an eye on him and see if he's working with Eternity. Be sure to blacken the windows."

"Gotchya." Anna responded, and started out the door. As she stepped over the threshold she stopped and turned back. "Are you all right?" she asked softly.

"Don't worry about me. I'll be fine in a few minutes. Thanks though," Miki answered absently.

Anna's moods sure seemed changeable today, she thought. Then she remembered what day of the week it was. "Are you still planning to report to Eternity headquarters this week?"

"Yeah. After I drop Rohin I'll head down to the city. I'm not expected until tomorrow morning."

"Kant doesn't suspect anything yet?"

"No. I don't think so."

"Good. Still...be careful."

"I will," Anna said, then she turned and walked out the door without a backward glance.

~

ROHIN WATCHED Anna's profile through the hover's security screen between them. He straightened in his seat and leaned forward to see if the mapping coordinates were still displayed on the console. As he'd suspected, they had already disappeared. He noticed Anna was wearing a helmet—probably getting all of her data directly to the visor. The windows had also darkened so he had no way of getting a visual on their direction or destination.

He leaned forward. "Can you hear me? Or am I talking to myself in this damn box?"

"I can hear you," Anna replied, her voice obviously being directed through a speaker in the back seat.

"Where are we going?"

"I'm dropping you at a hive. I'll just pick one at random so no one can find you." She chuckled as if it was a great joke. "I think Miki's crazy to give you another chance. Personally, my vote was to kill you. But the others went along with Miki."

"You don't seem like someone to take orders from anyone, even Miki," he said.

"You know nothing about loyalty. You never did and never will."

He swallowed, unable to answer her accusation.

"In spite of my strong feelings on the matter," Anna continued. "Mik still seems to care about your sorry butt—so your future won't end with me. Unless of course you want to give me an excuse to kill you. Then, I'd be more than happy to oblige."

"It sounds like you don't want me to join you."

"Your powers of observation are amazing," she sneered. "Personally, I suggest you go back to being a drugged out, pleasure seeker like the rest of them. It's much safer for you, and far less trouble for me."

Rohin refused to take the bait. They had never been friends in the past, and he wouldn't waste his energy trying to become friends now. He wondered what Anna really wanted? It certainly wasn't what Miki and the Agers wanted. Anna wasn't one to give herself to any cause except her own advancement. Was she looking to become the leader of the Agers? Was it possible that organization was big enough to draw Anna's desire for power? If so, Miki was really in danger.

He closed his eyes. He had to prepare for his return to the hives. It was never easy living there, but at least he knew how to survive. This time there would be no drugs and no pleasure. He knew what he needed to do now, and the hives were one of the best places for recruiting.

5

____

O*ne Year Later*

Maritza took a quick look from the hall into the main concourse of Rho Hive 69219, then pulled back instantly, flattening her body against an open heating duct which ran between the two hovels—vels. Deftly she pushed aside a piece of wire mesh and crawled into the duct. Folding her legs close to her torso she was able to replace the mesh screen to hide her entrance. EMOs—Eternity Medical Officers—were swarming all over, rounding up all children who had reached puberty, scanning ID bracelets and matching physical characteristics against data records.

She peered through the mesh, straining to see what the EMOs were setting up on their tables: two color-coded vials and the big compressed-air canisters that operated the hyposprays. She withdrew, having seen enough to recognize another inoculation effort.

The blue vials contained the Eternity virus, brought as an incentive for illegal children to be registered. Eternity knew illegal children were still being born. Their sterilization efforts had not been as effective in the hives, and it was difficult to keep track of the changing transient population. But Eternity had the right bait for attracting the children. They promised to inoculate even illegal children with the

Eternity virus if they were registered and a nominal fee was paid. Of course, that also meant they would use the red vial.

The red vial was for female children only. That was the one that ensured no unregistered pregnancies in the future. Females could not receive the blue vial until they first accepted the red one.

Both inoculations lasted a lifetime. However, the anti-pregnancy shot could be reversed for up to three months at a time once every five years. That was long enough for Eternity to harvest eggs for in-vitro fertilization for rich folks who were unable to get pregnant. They would lock up the hive girl until the eggs could be harvested. Once they got what was needed, the red vial was forced on her again. The hives were the homes of the unwanted, the unnamed, and the unnoticed—that is, unless the outside needed some entertainment or service only the hive people were willing, or forced, to provide.

Rapidly Maritza ran through her current list of mothers of illegal children whom she should inform—first, because they would pay her for warning them to hide the kids; second, because those who could afford it would pay her for stealing whatever Eternity virus she could. Over the past few years she had successfully lifted several hyposprays, and after a couple of experiments she became very adept at using them with the stolen blue vials.

First, she would have to change into a clean skinsuit and find a legitimate ID bracelet. Registered hive residents were issued one skinsuit a week—a form-fitting single unit that contained a wearable computer with message send and receive capability and some information retrieval—and their ID bracelet was updated at the same time. When they turned in the old suit it was destroyed and a new one issued. As she was unregistered, she had to wear whatever could be bartered from her customers; and hope an adult female ID bracelet could be found for the few hours needed to perform her hive duties.

Worried, she looked at her wrist bracelet. The ID she was wearing now was a month old and it would easily be noticed by the EMOs.

Grandma Leah was always good for fresh skinsuits and an occasional updated ID. She provided nice young boys and girls for the

Rho hive administrator's pleasure; and he, in turn, provided her with extras—or looked the other way when she rifled his files. Yes, Grandma Leah would cooperate, especially if Maritza went to her first with the news about the EMOs and cut her in on the profit. This could be a very good day.

Noting the EMOs had passed her level now, she crawled back out of the duct and headed for the center-shaft emergency stairs on her way down to Grandma Leah's vel.

Most of Maritza's ninety years had been spent in scrounging a totally unofficial living in the multi-ethnic Rho hive. She knew every passageway and vel in these old, unused buildings. Each hive contained thousands of hectares of concrete and steel buildings, connected together by remnants of plastic sheets to provide passage from one building to the next. The vels were established, on a first come basis, for the growing number of unemployed who could not afford housing.

She'd grown up in the hive culture. She understood the code. One where you minded your own business and didn't interfere with anything—no matter what was happening or who was getting hurt. She knew exactly how to engender loyalty for short periods of time, long enough to get what she needed. And, because she never missed a single trick, like today's unexpected EMO roundup, many people counted on her knowledge and paid her well. Maritza had learned how to escape the stringent controls, clever obstacles, and little traps ingeniously set up by the Rho Hive Administration Council and their Hive Security Agents supplied by a *benevolent* Eternity.

EMO's skirted on the other side and she ducked behind a plastic sheet, holding her breath. When she heard steps getting closer she sprinted the other direction and found an old elevator shaft. She shimmied down the cable and held there, out of view.

She listened carefully, holding her breath, until she heard no more boots above her. She pulled herself back up the cable, peeked over the rim and then scooted toward the security shaft where her vel was adjacent to Grandma Leah.

"Hey, Maritza," her friend, Theresa, called to her in a whisper. "Did you see the EMOs?"

Maritza grabbed Theresa's arm and pulled her toward Grandma Leah's door. "Yeah, I'm going after some vials for the illegals," she said. "I need you."

"I don't know." Theresa withdrew her arm. "I'm legal. I don't have to steal anything."

"Exactly why you're the perfect person to help."

"But, what if..."

"Don't what if me," Maritza shook her finger in Theresa's face. "What if I didn't tell you when Jolo was here? What if I didn't watch out for you when the Administrator is looking for threesomes, or worse foursomes—and smiles thinking of you with all those pervs?"

Theresa swallowed. "Okay. What do you want me to do?"

Pulling her into Grandma Leah's vel she explained the plan to both of them at once. Soon the three of them were part of a long line, slowly moving toward the EMO's table.

Trudging forward step by step, Maritza and Grandma Leah tugged on Theresa's hand. Theresa was the right age for the shots and, best of all, she was legal. As was the usual practice, the EMOs had divided the hive buildings among themselves, leaving only one representative on each level to administer the hyposprays.

When Theresa was only four people back, Grandma Leah pretended to become faint and staggered against the table. While the EMO was coping with that, Maritza swept two entire trays of the blue and red vials into her pack, hastily covering them with a smelly cloth. Then she ran to Grandma Leah's assistance.

"My stomach, my stomach!" Grandma Leah said in an appropriately plaintive tone, her gnarled hand flattened against her stomach. The pain in her voice was not entirely faked, considering the drugs she had indulged in the night before without eating that day.

"Move her out of the way! Now!" the EMO demanded.

"But she's hurt!" Maritza protested.

"Too bad. She's holding up the line. Now move along!"

Solicitous, Theresa and Maritza helped Grandma Leah to her feet and guided her slowly toward the nearest hall intersection. Once safely out of sight, Grandma Leah immediately reached for Maritza's pack and peered inside it.

"Ooooo," she exclaimed happily. "It looks like at least twenty! How many more floors do you think we can hit today?"

"At least three," Maritza answered, "but we'll have to hurry."

Over the next forty minutes, the three of them pulled the same stunt on other floors, netting at least one hundred vials. But the fourth attempt was one too many. The EMO officer began counting the remaining vials once some of them were retrieved from the floor. Realizing some had been lifted, she immediately yelled for security.

"I'll draw their attention," Maritza said quickly. "Give me a couple of vials to throw at them. Theresa, you get Grandma Leah out of here. Remember, she is supposed to be sick. Move slowly and deliberately."

"No, Theresa. I can take care of myself," Grandma Leah said. "You run ahead and get your vaccination on your regular floor. Then go and tell the others to come in small groups of four or five tonight, after the EMOs leave for the day."

The three of them split up. Maritza began her frenzied run, yelling at the top of her lungs. "You'll never catch me, you bastards!" She flung a useless red vial toward the oncoming EMO security officer. "You'll never sterilize me!" Then she took off running. As planned, the two officers chased after her, leaving Theresa and Grandma Leah alone.

The EMOs mounted an all out search when they discovered the missing vials on several floors. Maritza holed up in her vel, putting out the word she was unable to inoculate anyone that evening. After four hours of finding nothing, the security people finally disbanded. She knew they would leave some snoopers around for a couple of days, watching and listening for evidence of someone using the sprayers. But then they would give up. After all, what was a measly hundred vials to the billions Eternity produced. She smiled to herself. She could be patient.

Counting up the probable exchanges she would garner from her work today, she figured she would have enough food and supplies to last her three months. Maritza crawled under two blankets and slept soundly, dreaming of buying passage to another world for herself and all her friends in Rho Hive... another world and a new life.

~

"Jolo's here," Maritza shouted to Grandma Leah, pushing through the vel opening and squirming to give herself a little space in the crowded room. She wrinkled her nose at the palpable odor of unwashed bodies pressed close together. Restless customers awaited her arrival, since she was the only one who knew how to load the vials into the hyposprays. The past three days had been a nightmare – the constant waiting, hiding, changing locations, and waiting again.

She had been forced to change the locations of the illegal inoculation effort several times. As if concealing herself and the virus weren't enough, she also had to help move and hide many of the illegal children. Of course, she was paid in trade or credits for her assistance. It was her knowledge of Rho hive's duct system, balconies, and fire escapes that often kept children one step ahead of the authorities.

"Jolo?" Grandma Leah stretched to peer over the heads of the customers and wave Maritza forward. She gave a snort. "Jolo will roast in hell before I sell him another child." Her fingers tightened convulsively on the hyposprayer as she handed it to Maritza. "We need to get this finished today. We'll have to move quickly now. As for Jolo, you stay away from him. Though you're no longer a child, he would still like to take you just to spite me."

Maritza nodded soberly. As hard as her life had been with the men her mother found for her to entertain, it was nothing compared to a life with Jolo. It was thanks to Grandma Leah that Maritza's mother had not sold her to Jolo. But he had a long memory, and he was determined to exact his vengeance on Grandma Leah and still get Maritza too. In fact, she had narrowly escaped Jolo twice last year. She had no desire to go anywhere near him.

"But Jolo gives such a good price," Willa whined. She was Woman twenty-three in the local bedding stable. She had a girl child who had just reached her ninth birthday. The girl was prime selling material, and Willa didn't want to pass up any opportunities. Also, she desperately needed the underground fertility drug which was forbidden by Eternity. Her eggs were getting old, and it was becoming more difficult to conceive. The only way to ensure her ability to bear and sell a child every year was by an occasional sale to the likes of Jolo. "Maybe I should go get my girl," she fretted. "It's just one child."

"You will never sell to such as him!" Grandma Leah snapped in Engel—switching to her native language, black eyes flashing. "Price or not. Even selling to Kant's cruel security forces is better; and there the girls never leave until they die. But ten years with Jolo is worse than five hundred years with the security forces."

"Oh, I just don't know," Willa continued to whine.

"If you bring that child to him, I will cut you off," Grandma Leah threatened. "You may need that drug, but what will you do if we don't help to protect your illegal children until they are old enough to sell, huh?"

"You just don't understand. It's easy for you to say when you have smart Maritza to do all your work for you." Then the woman roughly shoved a plump thirteen year old toward Maritza. "Here, give her the shot now. We have to go."

Maritza smiled at the girl, but the girl wouldn't look up to meet her eyes.

Willa continued in an irritating tone, "I just hope it was worth keeping her for Eternity. If I can't sell my nine year old to Jolo, I better get a good price on this one."

The young girl kept her eyes to the floor as she offered her arm for the shot. She never spoke, and moved only when dragged or shoved by Willa.

Maritza bit her lip as she administered the hypo. She knew too well what the life of this young girl already entailed. She'd lived it until her mother died and she'd faked her own suicide to get off the roles of prostitutes.

She combed a finger through the blond curls on the girl and gave her head a pat, then signaled the next one in line to come forward for the spray. There were fairy tales about Harmony station, people who moved to the stars and could live a life without catering to men's base needs. Maritza used to believe those stories, and she still occasionally dreamed of what it might be like. But she knew now, deep inside, they were only tales to keep the girls from killing themselves. Even the tiniest hope of escape had kept her alive during the darkest times.

Next in line was a young man. Maritza looked him up and down and guessed he was about fifteen. She didn't see any facial hair but that wasn't the only sign of puberty. "Date of onset?" she asked the boy.

"Within the last six months," he answered head down, hands in his pockets. He already had a large patch of burned, exposed skin on his right arm.

"Okay. Number?"

"Child thirty-two dot seven, Rho west, level two." She nodded to Grandma Leah and watched her enter the data in her 'puter while Maritza loaded the hypospray again.

Hive boys sometimes had it even worse than the girls. The ones that weren't sold into prostitution ended up working in the bubbles— dangerous manufacturing zones that were previous dumping sites for manufacturing pollution, radioactive wastes or other chemicals. They were landfills lined with a concrete basin, covered by soil, then capped with a bubble to protect the environment. They were recalled for manufacturing as land grew ever more scarce and hive boys and men were the only ones willing to work there in exchange for food for their families.

Though their immune system was enhanced enough to ward off cancers, the pollution still attacked their skin often causing it to fall off in four to six inch pieces of raw epidermis. Many young men had the consistent visage of being recently burned. The hive economy felt it was better to risk sperm than ova; so, girls were not allowed these jobs.

The hypo administration became very orderly as Maritza and Grandma Leah worked in tandem. Grandma Leah rolled up sleeves, recorded names and arranged trades, while Maritza wielded the hyposprays and kept track of the vials. The line snaked around the small vel, out the front door, and down the hall. People, crammed shoulder to shoulder, spoke in whispers. Adolescent boys and girls with hopeless eyes continually shuffled forward as Maritza sprayed each person in turn.

Now that Eternity had given up their search, she was determined to complete the inoculations as quickly as possible. She especially wanted to hurry tonight, so she could warn the other illegal girls about Jolo's arrival. One of these days she would get enough credits to buy a black-market beamer, she thought. Then she would use it on Jolo at the first opportunity.

Three hours later, Maritza inserted the final vial. She finished and handed the hyposprayer to Grandma Leah for safekeeping, then backed toward the door.

"I'm not sure when I'll be back," she said. Grandma Leah nodded, understanding her need to warn the others. "If you need me, tap a vibe to my wearable." Then she was out the door and running through the maze of vels with her message.

Late that evening, Maritza slowly climbed the inside passage of stairs for the final seven stories to reach her vel. Few lights were burning in other vels on the corridor as she quietly edged the last few meters toward her door. In her wanderings Jolo had caught sight of her twice, but each time she managed to disappear down an adjacent hall or to duck through a vel to a connecting passage.

Checking the hall in both directions to ensure no one was watching, she pushed aside the blanket over her door opening next to the security grill. The minute she walked through the door, a hairy arm grabbed her around the middle and pulled her toward him, her face firmly implanted in his chest.

6

"Jolo!" she gasped, just before he placed his other hand around her throat as if ready to crush her carotid. He was twice her weight and easily held her tight against him. She didn't dare squirm out of his fetid embrace as he had the power to put her unconscious if he wanted.

"Oooo, you are a feisty one," Jolo smacked his lips before laying a sickening tongue on her neck. "I had to provide two years supply of free fertility drugs to Woman twenty-three to find out where you moved. I intend to get payment in full from you." He pushed her to the ground and yanked her head toward his crotch as he quickly unzipped his pants. His throaty laugh turned Maritza's stomach. Then he slowly gyrated his hips, "You know what I want," he said pushing himself toward her face. Maritza turned her face away, resulting in him rubbing against her neck. He pulled her hair then and pressed her back against the floor. Easily straddling her, he tore open the crotch panel in her skinsuit and laid his body on top of her, rubbing against her to build an erection. He licked her entire face like a thirsty dog who had finally found water after a week in the desert.

She squirmed, trying to avoid his tongue and his putrid breath smelling of rancid cigars, garlic, and at least a week's worth of unbrushed teeth.

"Stop fighting me," he whispered, "and I'll show you what pleasure is all about." He continued to gyrate over her, but was obviously having a problem getting it up. "I'm better than any man your mother ever put you with."

That immediately stilled her, remembering his promise of vengeance to Grandma Leah. She would endure him if she had to in order to protect Leah.

"That's better," he said. "Now, if I roll off you for a minute, we can get you out of that skinsuit and do this properly."

Maritza didn't move her head in acknowledgment or denial as she formulated a plan. She moved to stand, but he yanked her back down.

"Ow!" she rubbed at the arm he had pulled. "Let's go to the bedding stable, Jolo. I don't want to wake my neighbor, and I can get some sustain drugs for you there."

Jolo laughed long and hard. "Don't worry about the old woman, she's had an unfortunate...accident. She was bad for business, ya know. The fool was telling my customers not to sell their children to me."

Maritza choked back a sob for Grandma Leah. She knew there wasn't much hope for getting away from Jolo now. He was on a rampage and he would take what he wanted.

She put her mind in the same place she had as a child. This was not her. This was not her body. She'd survived before, she would survive again.

He looked down at her and unzipped the top of her skin suit to release her breasts. He bit down hard on a nipple and she screamed in pain.

"You're mine," he said, biting her again. "Repeat it."

"I'm yours. I'll do anything you want." She kneeled on the floor in front of him.

He grinned as he unzipped his pants and let them fall to the floor. Awkwardly, he kicked them aside.

She had a plan, if she could only force herself to execute it. She looked up and licked her lips.

He gathered a bunch of hair and yanked her head back. She screamed with the pain.

"Don't you dare," he said, holding her hair so tight her neck hyperextended. "I know what you're thinking."

She worked to get any words out. "No...I promise, I..." she choked and he released a little of the pressure. "I want to do it. With Grandma Leah dead I no longer have a protector. I want to please you, Jolo." She didn't have to struggle to let tears fall. The pain was enough. She bent her head as if in submission. "I need you, Jolo. I need a protector. My mother taught me many tricks that I can use to sustain you even without drugs."

She chanted in her mind: I will kill him. I will kill him. She kept that chant going to take her mind off what she might have to do in order to make any chance to get away.

Maritza took his greasy hand, took a deep breath and placed his middle finger in her mouth forcing herself to smile. She sucked on his finger demonstrating her technique.

"That's better," Jolo said. He withdrew his finger and grabbed her hair again to force herself to look up at his face. "Now put your mouth where I want it."

"Patience," she said swallowing hard as her stomach roiled.

He licked the saliva from his lips in anticipation and sneered.

She looked down at his pantsless legs. His erection had finally exerted itself. He was mindlessly stroking himself as he waited for her and panted.

"Ooooooo," she cooed as she stood slowly. "You are sooooo big."

He sneered. "That's right. All the women beg for me." He stroked himself faster. "Now, I want that mouth on me now. Then when I'm ready, I want to hear you beg when I skewer you." He reached for the zipper on her skinsuit, but she danced away.

"Let me do it," she said. "You are so big, I need to get ready for you."

She slaked her hands down the sides of her suit. She placed his hand between her legs and undulated against it. "It's been thirty years, Jolo. Let's go a little slower." She inched her zipper down. She panted faster as if she wanted him. She writhed in front of him.

"Fuck this."He reached for the zipper. "I said now."

He yanked the zipper down and reached to pull the skinsuit from her shoulders.

Maritza dropped to the floor and lunged to one side, kicked her right foot toward his ankle and tripped him.

He fell heavily onto the floor. Swearing loudly in Asi, he brandished a knife, slicing at her ankle as she rose.

She ignored the pain and rolled free. Her adrenaline pumping, she scrambled to her feet, picked up his pants and rushed out the door, pulling the blanket down in her wake. She dropped his pants down the elevator shaft and yanked her skinsuit zipper back up.

"Grab her!" he shouted at someone waiting a few doors down from her vel.

She turned the corner and darted into a small passage leading to stairs. Heavy footsteps clopped behind her.

She jerked open the fire escape door and stopped short, one foot hanging over a void below. The stairs had come loose from the building and were swinging free.

Trapped at the end of the hall she evaluated the drop. She looked behind her in time to see one of Jolo's guards closing quickly.

Taking a deep breath, she dropped over the side of the building, her hands grasping the threshold. She pushed out with her legs, then let loose to drop one story to the stairs below. On impact she screamed in pain. She had crushed the same ankle that Jolo had cut with his knife.

The henchman above her laughed cruelly and yelled to someone watching from a window. "That's her. Get her off those stairs. Strip her and bring her to Jolo."

Maritza tried to stand and move down the stairs, but she screamed once more when she attempted to put pressure on her foot and, unbalanced, she collapsed.

The man laughed as he looked down at her. "Feisty. All the

sweeter. After Jolo's done with you, he'll let each of us have you too." He rubbed his hands together.

She'd been so close. Tears streamed from the pain of her foot and the pain of knowing what was to come. For tricking Jolo she would pay. He'd probably kill her after using her and letting all his men use her. He would make sure he hurt her as much as possible.

She looked up at two men now on the ledge. The larger of the two, he looked to be about two-hundred and fifty pounds of pure muscle, was making his way down a different set of stairs and would soon be on top of her, stripping her, grabbing her, and dragging her back to Jolo.

She looked over the edge. There was no way she was going to let Jolo have her. She'd die first. A thirty to forty meter drop would definitely kill her. At least it would be quick. Determined, she put her hands on the deck and pushed up.

Suddenly, a pair of trousered legs dropped to the platform and straddled her position on the stairs, blocking her access in any direction.

"She's mine now," the man straddling her shouted to another running toward her.

She looked up at the face above the trousers. She had no idea who stood over her. Both of Jolo's men were now only a few meters from her position.

"Oh yeah?" Jolo's voice boomed as he stepped around one of his men.

She briefly wondered how hard it was for him to find another pair of pants and get dressed. He probably ordered one of his goons to give up his pants. She almost smiled. At least she'd bested him, if only for a moment. Unsure whether her savior would really be any better than Jolo, she waited and watched the standoff. She wanted to be ready to jump to her death if needed.

"Back off!" Jolo yelled from the floor above. "You're messing with my property! She's my woman, and I want her back."

"She doesn't seem to want to be your woman," the man standing over her answered. "And I have a long-standing contract with her mother that was passed to her. Back off."

Maritza squinted up at the man. She knew of no contract. Since her mother's death, she had voided all contracts. Most everyone thought Maritza was dead. What was he talking about?

"Hey, it's no big deal," Jolo changed his tone to a calmer one, almost friendly. "It's just a disagreement. You know how whores are." The man above her acknowledged nothing, remaining silent.

Jolo laughed. "I understand contracts. You don't want to be out any money." He reached for his wallet. "What's the contract price? I'll pay it off."

The man standing over her laughed. "She's that good that you are willing to pay?" The man looked down at her and winked. "Yes, I can see why you'd want her, but now I'm not willing to sell."

After several long seconds, Jolo's voice boomed again. This time not friendly. "You have no contract. Do you know who I am?"

The man took a deep breath and gritted his teeth. "Oh yes, I know you." If looks good kill, Maritza was sure Jolo would be dead already. She sucked in a breath. Maybe this man was her savior.

"I gave you a chance to live and make some money," Jolo said. "This is the last time I'll ask. Give me the whore."

The man stood his ground.

Jolo turned to the men behind him and gestured. "Kill him."

The two men brandished knives and moved toward Maritza. To her surprise, without even a blink, her temporary savior pulled out a beamer and paralyzed both of them. The two attackers fell, unconscious, to the floor as the man above her reset the load level. Immediately he aimed it at an astonished and terrified Jolo.

"This is for Lisi and all the other children you've hurt," he said savagely and again let loose the white energy beam.

Jolo fell on his side, writhing in pain and confusion but still conscious. The man quickly pulled himself up to the next level and dragged Jolo's writhing form from the doorway onto the stairs. Then he pushed him over the edge. The same edge from which Maritza had planned to jump.

She listened for the inevitable thud of Jolo's body. Although it was only seconds, it seemed like time stood still as he fell forty-four stories to the pavement below. Then finally she heard it. She shuddered. She knew that she and all the other girls at Rho hive would never have to worry about Jolo again.

She looked toward the man, watching him replace the beamer inside his pants as he approached her again. He bent to help her to her feet. She noticed his eyes stray to her torn skinsuit and bared breast. Immediately, he removed his sweater and placed it over her head, helping her thread her arms through the sleeves and pull it over her torso. The sweater was twice her size. It hung to her knees like a dress.

"Where do you live?" he asked in a whisper, easily lifting her into his arms like a child.

"You don't have to carry me," she said.

"You know that ankle won't support you." He walked toward the elevator as if he knew this section of the hive well.

"Look, I'm grateful for your help, but don't expect any favors from me."

"I don't want your body," the man replied stiffly. "Now, shut up and tell me how to get to your vel."

"Just remember, you'll have to beam me to get anything out of me."

The man nodded, and she directed him through the hive's maze of hallways and makeshift vels. He never stopped his pace as he carried her, easily following her directions through both inside and outside office spaces as if he'd lived there all his life.

When they arrived at her place, he gently placed her on the pallet of blankets she had in the corner, then looked toward the heater. Without speaking, he put a cup of water on the heater. "Ice?"

"Next door," she said. Then her eyes misted as she suddenly remembered that Grandma Leah would never be next door again. "If they didn't take it all," she added.

The man disappeared for a moment, then came back with ice wrapped in a towel. He applied it gently to her ankle until she reached to hold it herself. He watched her for a moment before returning to the now rolling boil of water.

He poured the water into a cup and took dried flakes from a small pack on his hip. Stirring the mixture, he offered her the warm drink. "Sorry I don't have any spice."

She inhaled the smooth aroma and her eyes brightened. "Kama?" He nodded. "I haven't had real kama in ages. Around here, we get the fake stuff...you know, similar vitamins but the taste is horrible."

He nodded again as she took her first sip, then another. He remained silent for what seemed like several minutes.

His silence scared her. What would he expect now? No matter her bravado she knew she couldn't hold off a man with a beamer. She would be forced to do whatever he wanted.

As if talking would save her, she filled the void with one babbled question after another. "Who are you? What do you want? Where are you from? And who the hell is Lisi?"

He frowned, then sat crossed-legged about a meter away.

Maritza self-consciously glanced at the floor, realizing she hadn't swept it for over a week. But she didn't offer any apologies.

He chuckled and stretched his legs in front of him as he sipped his Kama. "Do you always have a motor mouth?"

She went silent. Maybe he'd told the truth. Maybe he didn't want her body. For some reason she wanted to trust him. She wanted to know him better. She sipped her kama and watched his silent evaluation of her.

After a few moments he began to talk—stilting at first, then more freely as his story unwound. "I used to live in Rho hive, on the other side of the complex," he gestured behind him. She shot him a look of disbelief.

"I was a different...person...not a man...a shell...drugged." He looked over her head as if he was talking to someone beyond her, someone in his past.

"Lisi was a young girl. Her mother sold her to Jolo on her eleventh birthday." He shifted to lean against the wall, his knees drawn toward his chest. "I was there when it happened. She clung to me...as if I could change things." A tear welled in his eye, but hung on the edge of a lash as if knowing to fall would be to give in to the darkness in his soul.

Silence again. He closed his eyes. She wasn't sure for how long, but she knew she would wait. She knew the fate of girls in the hive. She had lived it. She had survived. Though Jolo was gone, there were others—many others who would keep the slave economy going.

His voice softened to barely a whisper as he continued. "A year later, I saw her again, with many other children brought in to an administrator's party. A party I would have never attended had I known the intent." His voice broke briefly. He swallowed before continuing. "After a year working in Jolo's stable she looked older than my own mother, though she had the body of a twelve year old." His voice quickened as if now he had to rush through the story before it consumed him again. "She recognized me. I knew it. Yet she had no animosity, no hatred for the man who failed to save her. She told me to run. She told me to hide and I did. God forgive me I ran away from her once more."

He paused and swallowed hard. Maritza reached toward him. It wasn't his fault...the economy of the hives was a given. She knew if he'd tried to save Lisi odds were he'd be dead now. With no one to stop Jolo, that meant Maritza would be dead now too. She covered his hand with hers and waited.

He squared his shoulders and looked her in the eye. "I promised myself I would find a way to come back and rescue Lisi. That was a hundred and twenty years ago. I tried to find her the next year, and the next. Finally, after five years I'd heard she suicided."

Maritza didn't flinch. She held tighter to his hand. She had been planning to suicide herself just moments before rather than face Jolo's plan for her.

"They all do within five or six years," she said. "It's for the best." She paused. "Some of the older women, like my mother, last decades because they find favor with only a few powerful men. But children don't have that choice...especially Jolo's children. It was for the best. Really, it was."

He shook his head and withdrew his hand from hers. "It's not right. It's not fair. No child should have their lives stolen like that."

For several minutes neither one spoke. She watched emotions flit across his face. So many hated Jolo and he was only one of the evils they had to fight. When his shoulders relaxed and he leaned against the pillows, she spoke again. "So, do you have a name? I don't know anyone who ever got away that wanted to come back to Rho hive."

"Chawla. My name is Rohin Chawla." His lips parted in the smallest hint of a smile for the first time that evening. " I want to somehow make up for letting Lisi down, for letting all the Lisi's of the hives down. I'm looking for others to join me. I want to offer hope and dreams to children again—not the despair they see every day." He looked away for a moment and swallowed hard.

Maritza nodded and closed her eyes. An idealist. She was safe. At least for now. She knew Rohin's dream would never come true. She'd seen many idealist flame, burn out, and die. But she'd go along with him for now. What choice did she have? Whoever was primed to take Jolo's place would want to prove themselves by capturing her. She took a deep breath and snuggled into the blankets. Sleep. She should get at least a few days of sleep out of this. Smiling, she let herself drift off.

7

———

Anna was anxious to get to Eternity. Her normal reporting time was at 0900 local, and she was calling it pretty close already. She set the hover for automatic pilot to coordinate E39. Then she tried to relax into the cushions, closing her eyes for the two hour trip.

The hover cruised by the headquarters building as the MC link transmitted the Eternity security landing code. The automatic pilot sounded an alarm when it received the parking coordinate from Eternity's MC. Anna opened her eyes and began reviewing the report she would make to Kant. She knew she would have no problem getting in to see him, and she was well prepared for this meeting. Her success depended on seeming fully cooperative with Kant, giving him no reason to question her loyalty.

She left the hover and strode with confidence toward the secure employee entrance of Eternity headquarters.

The building was the largest in the world. At its highest tower it rose over six hundred meters tall. And, with the exception of the internal parks, it totally enclosed almost nine square kilometers. By Kant's command no building could be larger. Over one hundred fifty thousand people were employed at this one site. To accommodate

their needs Eternity had spared no expense, including every convenience of a luxury resort. Restaurants, shopping malls, underground
transportation, overnight accommodations, and entertainment of
every imaginable type were available to all headquarters'
employees.

Eternity's board of directors knew that contented employees
would never leave, and never have reason to question their positions.
This policy had proven itself over many decades. Employee turnover
had been less than one percent for at least 40 years now.

Anna stepped up to the retinal scanner in front of the rear
entrance doors. Two young, fresh-faced security guards made no
move to stop or acknowledge her. If the scanner didn't recognize the
imprint, the guards would quietly beam her and ship her to the local
I2 building for interrogation. If an employee was ever suspected of
duplicity their record would be flagged and one day, without warning, the scanner would reject them. But Anna did not let that knowledge temper her confidence.

The scanner's seal held her head tightly until her eye pattern
matched the appropriate computer file. The match made, the
computer stated her appointment destination and automatic doors
slid open to admit her. She strode through the doors and stopped. A
glowing circular platform appeared and she stepped forward where it
affixed a directional chip to the bottom of each shoe. Then she
proceeded down the hall past the guards. A few steps farther she
stepped onto a moving conveyor system and grasped the railing to
keep her balance as it began a steep incline.

Each employee's destination was automatically keyed by their
retinal pattern. The chips implanted in their shoes allowed the
conveyor system to transport them to the correct office for either
work or a scheduled appointment. Any attempt to step off the
conveyor prior to reaching the programmed destination, or to leave a
designated work area, would result in an immediate disabling electric
shock followed by a staff pick up alarm. This allowed security
personnel to concentrate on entrances and exits instead of having to
patrol the entire building during working hours. Only the entertain-

ment areas and the main auditorium on the first floor were accessible without the conveyor system tracking you.

Anna relaxed as the system carried her toward Kant's office at the top of the building on the 205th floor. The conveyor quickly passed Anna through a large foyer with polished marble floors and smoked glass walls reflecting and recording each passing individual. Within two minutes she reached the northeast corner of the Foyer, where several p-tubes—private vertical transport tubes—would take a single occupant to levels above the eightieth floor. Anna stepped off the belt and carefully followed the blinking arrows pointing directly to the p-tube she was to enter.

The doors closed and the small circular tube darkened as a blue light bathed the area, causing her to feel slightly unbalanced for a few moments. This was the last security scan before the tube would allow for her ascent to Kant's inner offices. Without a sound, a small section of floor seemed to disengage from the cylinder and press her upward toward the top of the building. She felt the internal pressure in her ears increase. By the time she could swallow to equalize the pressure, the tube slowed. As it reached the top of the tower, the blue light disappeared and the natural light from the inner offices filtered through the now transparent glass. Finally, the tube opened and she stepped out into Kant's office, arriving only six meters from his desk.

Anna stood patiently just outside the tube, facing Kant's desk without comment. He was a tall, lanky man who could not seem to stop moving about his office. He went from his desk to a viewing screen, to the window, then back to his desk. Occasionally, he would give voice notes to his MC link, then continue his rounds again. From previous experience she knew not to interrupt his thoughts. He would indicate when she was to approach.

Although Kant's office occupied the entire 205th floor, this section was not overly large for someone of his stature. It was about the size of a medium-sized apartment, but filled with wall to wall windows to the outside. However, though employees could see out, anyone on the outside would see only a reflection of the sky or nearby buildings. One window wall was completely covered by large viewing screens, each one a video window on a remote Eternity manufacturing location. At the touch of a button any one screen could locate a particular individual within that facility and put them in contact with Kant, if he desired.

"Come," Kant finally said, sitting down at his desk and speaking a closing voice command to end his notes.

Anna walked forward and stood in front of him, a respectable distance away, while he tapped in a code to bring up a review copy of her latest report.

"Report, Hollinrake."

Anna hated being called only by her last name. But that was Kant's way of being impersonal. "I am continuing to monitor and interact with the Ager leader," she began. "I've been able to locate Chawla since Yokoyama let him go a year ago."

"Yes," Kant frowned. "How is it that after handling the abduction so well, you lost him Hollinrake?"

Anna said nothing. They'd been over this last year. The question had become Kant's normal greeting—his way of letting her know he always had the upper hand and he never forgot a mistake.

Kant waved a finger at her, indicating she could sit. "At least the tracking probe seems to be working."

Probe? Her throat went dry but she refused to swallow. Refused to let him know she was sweating. She and Miki had suspected, but when Kant said nothing over the past year they figured he hadn't put one in Chawla after all.

He laughed. "You didn't know, did you?"

Anna stiffened, wondering if his probe was able to also discern when Miki or Anna had been with Rohin. She said nothing.

Kant leaned back in his chair. Obviously enjoying his game. "Guess where he is now."

She looked over to one of the screens, debating what to reveal. She cleared her throat. "I'm sure you already know that I took him to Rho Hive."

"Hmmm?"

He was good. Not letting on whether he knew that or not. But She was better. She could play his game, and she was determined to win. "He refused to join the Agers and I assume he's already gone back to the drugged lifestyle he had before." She leaned a little more toward his desk, lowering her voice to a more intimate tone. "I've always believed he was worthless, Kant. Meeting him again a year ago has only reinforced my feelings."

"I'm well aware of your feelings about him, Hollinrake." Kant stood up forcing Anna to stand as well. "But we can't be too careful. Do you know exactly where he is at this moment?"

Anna swallowed. Of course she didn't. She hadn't bothered to check up on him at all. As far as she was concerned, the farther from Miki he was the better.

"Not exactly," she finally said. "If you have a probe in him, why don't you ask one of your technicans."

The left side of Kant's lip lifted in a smirk. "In the past year, he has remained at the hive. However, he has also had an interesting visitor three times."

Anna refused to ask the question of who. She didn't want to know. She didn't...

"Miki Yokoyama," he pronounced.

Anna stood perfectly still. Shit! He really did have a probe in Chawla. How dare Miki be seeing him and not tell her. How dare she mess up everything Anna had worked so hard to accomplish.

"Nothing to say, Hollinrake?" Kant leaned over his desk with a self-satisfied smile she'd love to slap off his face. "Chawla is a wild-card, but it seems he is still useful to us after all." He pointed his finger at her. "No one...and I mean no one will cross me without paying a price. If you are holding out anything, tell me now. Because I will find out."

Anna squared her shoulders and leaned on the desk toward him, coming within inches of his face. "Yokoyama is using him for sex. That's all. I didn't think it was something worthy of a report."

She'd make sure it stopped as soon as she could ring Miki's neck in person.

"They had a...thing...when we were all working in Antarctica.

She's using Chawla for her needs because he isn't part of the Ager organization. That keeps her from compromising herself with anyone on the inside. It's nothing more than sex. She just needs release. That's all."

"How sure are you of this?"

"One hundred percent," she answered, looking Kant straight in the eye as she lied.

"Wrong," he pronounced. "You know nothing. Don't pretend you do.

Fuck! Fuck! Fuck! What was Miki up to? She wasn't only going to get Anna killed. She was going to expose the entire Ager organization.

"Tell me what's at Qyzylqum," Kant said out of the blue.

"It's an R&R house," Anna lied. Where in the hell had he heard about Qyzylqum? Anna had never told him about it. "Think about it. Who would want a base in that godawful desert?"

Kant chuckled. "Really? Then you won't mind that I've programmed the probe to send Chawla there."

Shit! What was she going to do now. She had to find a way to get to Qyzylqum and to get Miki there for some kind of sexual encounter so that Kant wouldn't find out what it really is.

Anna took a deep breath and let it out slowly as she thought through he response. "Hmmm. You are clever, Kant. If I let on to Miki that Chawla is going to Qyzylqum, she might suddenly decide to plan a vacation. Nothing like having her own little sex slave for a couple weeks to take the edge off." She paced near the desk, as she thought through the plan. "This could really work. This could get me closer to the inner circle of the Agers, just like we want."

She paused as an idea came to her. She stopped and threw her shoulder's back with confidence. "Or...perhaps *you* are holding out on *me*. You didn't tell me about the probe. Perhaps you've programmed Chawla with some pheromone that makes it impossible for Yokoyama to stay away. Perhaps you programmed Chawla to take Yokoyama to Qyzylqum. Why would *you* do that without telling me?"

Kant stepped back and chuckled, a deep rolling sound from his chest. "You're good, Anna. Very good. I can see we both want the same thing." He sat again behind his desk and motioned for Anna to take the chair facing him. "I can assure you I did not program him with anything, though I wish you'd thought of that idea while we had him in I2. Then I would have done it."

Anna slowly relaxed and lowered herself to the chair in front of his desk.

"I will tell you, that in addition to the probe, we did load his memory chip with data—hoping he would correlate it and use it to find the Agers' headquarters, as you seem unable to get in deep enough."

Anna bit down on the side of her cheek, stopping herself from a retort. "I'm close," she said. "Yokoyama trusts me more and more each day."

"Not enough, Hollinrake. Evidently she doesn't trust you enough."

Anna nodded. She could feel her power slipping with the Agers and with Kant. She needed to reinforce her value on both sides before she got herself killed.

"Chawla wants something," Kant continued without acknowledging her. "He's gathering some supporters in the hives for something. I'm just not sure what." He finally looked her in the eyes, "That's what you must find out for me. I want you to find a reason to go to Qyzylqum and to learn what Yokoyama and Chawla are planning together."

"I will. I'll do it immediately." She stood, but he motioned for her to sit again.

Kant swiped a card across his terminal then placed a call. Anna sat, her hearing poised to pick up any nuances of his conversation.

"Jolo," Kant demanded to whoever answered the phone.

Anna listened closer. She didn't recognize the name.

"What? Dead? Dammit! Why wasn't I informed? Well who's in charge then? Get him to the vid now!"

Anna continued to sit at attention. Who was Jolo and why did Kant care if he was dead? She didn't like being left in the dark about any of Kant's underground contacts—especially now that she knew he could track Rohin Chawla.

"Zog?" Kant peered closer at the image on the vid. "When is your next visit to Rho 69219?"

The blurry figured answered, "Two weeks, sir."

Kant looked at Anna and raised his eyebrows, then asked in a whisper, "How long to get the information from Yokoyama about Chawla?"

"Give me seven or eight days. I don't want to raise suspicion with her," she replied equally quietly.

Kant faced the vid screen again. "Plan your visit in eight days. I'll make it worth your while. Chawla. Rohin Chawla is the name. When he shows up, let me know. No, I don't care what you do to him, just don't kill him and make sure he can talk. Don't leave Rho Hive until you have him. Got it?"

Anna flinched as she straightened her posture, watching Kant disconnect from the terminal. Obviously, Kant had already decided if he didn't get what he wanted from her, he would get it from Rohin himself. Would he then continue to use Anna or would she be superfluous at that point?

Dammit! Why did Miki stop her from killing Chawla in the first place? Now he stood between her and the Ager plans to infiltrate Eternity.

She stood cautiously. "Is that all you ..."

Kant interrupted. "You need to step up the pressure on locating the Ager central command."

"I expect to become part of the inner circle very soon." She took a step backward. "If I'm careful." She stared back at Kant in silence, debating whether to ask permission for her next plan. She took a deep breath and let it out. "If I can tell Yokoyama that you have a probe in Chawla it will make her trust me... and I would get accepted immediately in Ager command. I'm sure of it. She'd probably even invite me to go with her to Qyzylqum."

Kant stood and stepped toward her. "Interesting."

Anna swallowed. Had she gone too far?

"A risk...letting Yokoyama know anything about our tactics." He paused, his chin in one hand. "But one worth taking if it gets us their central command location." He stepped back to the other side of his desk and sat again, waving her away. "You tell Yokoyama about our probe, and how I personally know all about her sexual fetish with Chawla." He laughed for several seconds. "That should put her off center."

Anna took another step backward. "Is that all, sir?"

Kant looked up, as if he'd forgotten she was still there. "Ahhh. Right. You'll find your usual fee. Once you call me from Qyzylqum I'll send a nice bonus immediately. I'll expect your report in one week . . . unless, of course, you find out about the Ager headquarters location before then."

"Yes, sir."

Kant brought up the six vid screens on his wall. Her usual signal that she was dismissed.

Her back ramrod straight, Anna turned and walked back to the tube. She carefully withheld any emotions as the tube darkened and began its descent. Miki was going to get a piece of her mind. What the hell was she doing with Chawla now? This time Anna would get rid of him whether Miki liked it or not.

Miki rubbed her forehead as Anna paced back and forth. She hoped Anna's rage would settle soon.

"Dammit, Miki, why are you letting your hormones get in the way of knowing what we have to do? He's going to destroy us. Can't you see that?"

"I'm not killing him. Don't even try to go there."

"Why? If it were anyone else, you wouldn't hesitate. You'd do what had to be done."

"I don't kill innocent people."

Anna came to a halt in front of her and looked her in the eye and snorted. "Sure you do. Remember Tinaca?"

Miki blanched. "That's unfair and you know it."

"It's not unfair," Anna shook her finger. "It's an example of how you didn't follow up on everything. It's an example proving you can't trust anyone."

"There was no way I could know they'd been storing Influenza H and planned to use it and pretend it was the Eternity virus."

"And why couldn't you know, Miki?"

Miki closed her eyes. She had trusted him. She had trusted someone in her organization she'd known to be loyal for more than fifty years. "Because I trusted Robert. I needed..."

"That's right. Once again you trusted someone you were sleeping with. And what happened?"

Miki refused to answer.

"Sixty-eight thousand people died at Tinaca," Anna announced. "All because you let your hormones overrule your judgment. And now you're doing it again."

"This is not the same!" Now Miki began to pace. "My sleeping with Robert had nothing to do with my judgment. He was a loyal Ager for over fifty years. My sleeping with him didn't make him any more or less loyal."

"Are you so sure?" Anna asked. "Before him, all of your relationships were only a few weeks...but Robert was two years of, I think your quote was 'mind-blowing sex—the only thing that could relax you from the stress of command.' Two years was enough time for you to overlook his failings." Anna paused and her lip quirked up in a sneer. "Now that I think of it, Robert looked a lot like Chawla. Same height, same weight. With a tan it would be hard to tell them apart."

Miki sighed. "Cut the crap, Anna. You aren't going to manipulate me into changing my mind. Only my best friend could get away with reminding me of my worst failure. Thanks a lot."

Miki dropped into the chair behind her desk, opened her viewer, and called up Helios in Qyzylqum. She waited for the signal to decode and connect.

"I'm sorry." Anna sat on the edge of the desk. "I know I went over the top. Bringing up Tinaca wasn't fair. I'm just afraid for you, Mik. I don't want you to get hurt. I know how long it took you to get past Chawla before. I don't want to see it happen again. The Agers can't afford to lose you for two years again."

Miki was still back in Tinaca. Sixty-eight thousand people died because she trusted one man. Eternity had gotten to him—evidently before they'd started having a sexual relationship. She was sure the relationship was even part of Eternity's plan all along. She groaned. For all she knew, they'd recorded every time they'd done it, listening for any bits of information about her plans.

She shook her head. She'd worked through that mistake years ago. No one could have predicted Robert's betrayal. Even Anna thought it was a good thing for her to be with someone for a little longer.

She sighed. "If I can't trust someone who's been with me for fifty years, I can't trust anyone. Even you, Anna."

Anna laughed. "I wouldn't worry about me. You're never going to have sex with me."

"That wasn't the problem at Tinaca and you know it. And that's not the problem now," Miki insisted. "Rohin and I are not sleeping together. In fact, we haven't had time even if we wanted to. He has ideas. Ideas that are beginning to make sense to me. He's changed, Anna. I'm certain of it."

She put her fingers to her lips. She'd been trying to forget his last kiss. Trying to forget Rohin had walked back into her life, and now she was planning to see him again—planning to listen to him, to.... She shook her head. Was she planning to sleep with him or worse, join his cause?

Anna took her hand and leaned forward. "You're right, Rohin and Robert aren't even close." She paused and looked Miki straight in the eyes. "Chawla's a lot worse."

Miki shuddered and looked away. She stood and crossed her arms across her chest as she paced. "How can he be worse? You even said yourself that Eternity didn't get to him. They have a probe in him. That's definitely something to consider, but at least we know —and it's only been a year. We can use it to our advantage. We know he hasn't been working with them for seven years like Robert did."

Anna widened her eyes and stared straight at her. "Shit! You're still in love with him, aren't you? I knew you never loved Robert, which is why I thought the sex thing was great for you. But it was because you never forgot Chawla. Crap! He walks back into your life and you just pick up like nothing happened. You still love him. I can see it."

Miki shook her head. "I'm not..."

The connection pinged through and Helios' image appeared sleepy-eyed and only half-dressed. "Miki? God, what time is it?"

"Sorry, Helios. Muru is meeting someone at the airport and you need to get a secure room ready to receive him."

Helios rubbed at his eyes. "All right. Anyone I know? What are we supposed to do?"

Anna leaned over her shoulder. "It's Rohin Chawla."

Helios sucked in a breath. "The Rohin...the one who..."

"Yup, that one," Anna said, snapping her fingers together and nodding. "The one she never forgot. The one she still loves."

"I do not..." Miki said.

"Yes, you do."

"I just..."

"Don't fool yourself," Anna said. "At least be honest. If you're honest you're better prepared to deal with him."

Helios pulled on a shirt. "Love...so I guess that means..."

"I don't know what it means," Miki interrupted him. "It just means don't hurt him until I get there. Then we'll figure out if he's a threat."

"Why is he here?" Helios asked. "No one comes to Qyzylqum without a reason."

"He probably doesn't even know," Miki answered. "Eternity implanted a chip in him. Something to help him do correlations about Ager locations. He doesn't know it's there. He doesn't know why he wants to go, and I decided to officially invite him once I knew.

He probably just had a hunch and followed it. The problem is not Chawla. The problem is the chip."

"It's pretty hard to separate the two," Anna said. "The chip is in Chawla, so it seems to me the problem is Chawla."

Miki ignored her. She didn't want to get involved with Rohin again. But even more, she didn't trust Anna to be fair. At least not when it came to Rohin Chawla.

"I'll see you in twenty-two hours," she said to Helios. Then she signed off.

MIKI LEANED BACK in her seat, letting the pilot do his job. She'd been fortunate to catch this flight to Nyagra where they would pick up a replacement crew to take her on to Qyzylqum.

She reviewed everything Anna had said—that is between the yelling and the blaming. She knew Anna and Rohin had never liked each other. Even on the Antarctica project Anna had always seen Rohin as someone to step over on her way to the top. She had a feeling Anna was now holding something back about her report to Kant, but she wasn't sure what.

Was it possible Anna truly believed Rohin was that much of a threat to the Agers? Or did Kant want him killed to cover up the tracking probe and the chip Eternity had installed? Maybe he had made killing Rohin a test of Anna's loyalty to Eternity.

She sighed. Whatever the reason, Anna was too eager to get rid of Rohin and Miki wasn't going to let that happen. She might be willing to lock him up forever—or at least until she found and unleashed a counter virus—but she would not be a part of killing him.

She rubbed her eyes. They were so dry from lack of sleep that she didn't have enough film to close them comfortably. She fished in her carisack for drops, then tilted her head back to administer them. Blinking through the sting, she took a deep breath and leaned further into the seat until it reclined slightly. Maybe, in a few more minutes, the drops would do their work and her eyes could close even if she couldn't actually sleep.

She checked her timer. Muru should be meeting Rohin within the next half hour. She couldn't stop Chawla from arriving at Qyzylqum, but she could at least keep him contained. Maybe she could make some permanent arrangements for Rohin to stay in the desert—safely out of the way. She could trust Muru and Helios to keep tabs on him, make sure no one let him out.

She sighed. Her eyes were tearing. The drops must be working. She dragged a fist across her cheek to wipe the tears away and closed her eyes. Why did Rohin have to complicate things? Anyone else would have made the decisions easy. Why him? Why now?

Anna said Miki was still in love with him. She swallowed. It was true. Hard to believe after all that had happened. She'd never stopped loving him. She sighed. Hundreds of years was a long time to love someone—especially someone you could never live with again.

8

———————

Rohin woke when the alarm sounded at his landing in Qyzylqum. He exited the plane and a short, muscular black man with a pronounced mustache and wearing desert fatigues took his bag.

"I'm Muru," he introduced himself. "Miki Yokoyama asked me to meet you. She will be joining us soon."

"Miki?" Rohin was confused. How could Miki know he'd arrived? He didn't even know exactly why he was here. He just knew he had a hunch. He'd heard from someone in Rho Hive that there were rumors of a great library at Qyzylqum.

"Are you an Ager?"

Muru nodded. He pointed toward another, smaller plane. "This way please."

Rohin stopped. What if this really wasn't someone sent by Miki? What if Muru was working for Eternity? "I think I'd rather find a hotel here and wait for Miki."

Muru dropped Rohin's bag and in one swift move he had both of Rohin's arms clasped behind his back. "I'm sorry. There is no choice in this."

The man whistled a small warble, like a bird, and another man appeared at his side. The two of them somewhat forcibly shuffled Rohin into the private plane and locked him in a personal compartment. A minute later his bags were thrown in after him, and he heard the click of the security lock in the door.

As the plane's engines revved, Rohin sighed. It seemed even the Agers wanted to control his every move. Obviously, Micki still didn't trust him. He glanced around the room. A chair, a bed with tie down belts, a small toilet, and a small fridge. At least they hadn't tied him to the bed. He opened the fridge. Bottled water and the usual kama flakes.

The speaker in the room crackled. "I apologize for the difficulty in getting you onboard." Rohin recognized Muru's accented voice. "I suggest you take this opportunity to sleep. Whatever your choice you will want to buckle yourself in for take off. We will be in the air for about three more hours. Rohin looked at the bed and shook his head. He wasn't going there. Shortly he heard the engines roar so loud he had to put his hands over his ears. He fell backward into the chair as it ascended at a sharp angle. He quickly secured his buckle.

Once again, Miki seemed to have him imprisoned. How was it that the Agers knew where he was? He had surmised Eternity might have a tracker on him, but he didn't remember being poked or prodded in the cabin at the Ager camp. He was beginning to feel that this Ager organization was much larger than he'd first thought. The presence of personal jets, long distance flights, larger crews all pointed to a well-organized and financed group. Plus Miki, who had vowed never to see him again, was coming all this way to meet him. Certainly, there were a lot more secrets at stake here. Just what had Miki gotten herself into this time?

ROHIN WAS a little unsteady as he climbed down the stairs of the plane. They had landed just as the sun was reaching its zenith, and he felt the oppressive heat rising from the desert floor. The flat, arid land stretched clear to the horizon, dotted with an occasional red sand dune and rocks. No sign of housing or even animal life appeared as far as the eye could see. He looked around for any other people beside himself. Where was the two man crew of the plane? For a moment he wondered if maybe Anna had got her way. That somehow, when the Agers learned of his travels, Anna had finally convinced Miki to have him killed. Then he saw Muru coming down the steps with two small bags over his shoulder.

"Don't worry," Muru said in Uighur. Rohin had to struggle to remember this language. It was one he actually knew a little when he was young, but he hadn't spoken it for decades.

"I won't leave you here to wander and die of thirst," Muru continued, then noticed Rohin's forehead wrinkle as he rubbed it with his fingers. He switched to Engel, the language used by Eternity. "I won't leave you here," he repeated. "It's not as bad as it looks."

"Thanks," Rohin answered. Muru turned and headed toward one of the sand dunes.

Rohin hurried to follow a few paces behind, still looking from side to side, trying to gather any information that might help him know his location or devise an escape plan. Unfortunately, given the amount of time they spent in the air, this could be any one of several deserts in this part of the world. He didn't even know which direction they'd flown from the airfield at Qyzylqum.

Most deserts were only lightly inhabited, if at all. Once Eternity started providing housing, food, and occasional jobs even the desert dwellers moved toward the city and its suburbs. No one chose to eek out an existence in these horrible places.

Rohin's forehead dripped sweat into his eyes and his parched mouth begged for water by the time they reached the closest sand dune and Muru walked around the back side of it. Astonished, Rohin noticed a door with a small window in it. Muru shouted something he didn't recognize and soon a face appeared in the window.

"Muru!" the man shouted. Then the door swung open and the man ran to Muru, lifting him from the ground, bags and all, in a bear hug. Rohin stared at the large, beefy individual who stood before him. He stood a full head taller than Rohin, and at least twenty-five percent heavier.

"You must be Chawla," the man said gruffly, extending a huge hand. "I'm Helio."

Rohin extended his hand for a brief shake, but instead the man's hand engulfed his and squeezed, pumping his arm up and down vigorously. Finally, Rohin pulled lose and folded his arms in front of him, surprised at the friendly greeting. Maybe he wasn't slated to die after all.

"Come in, come in," Helio encouraged in a friendly tone. "I am so happy Muru has returned." He placed the bags on what appeared to be a sandstone table, then again caught Muru in an embrace. Without letting go, he looked into Muru's eyes. "It was too long this time. I was worried. But not now that you are home." He stroked his back affectionately. "Yes, finally you are home."

As if suddenly noticing Rohin again, he let Muru go. "As you can see, our home is rather small but it serves its purpose."

Rohin nodded in agreement. Just inside the door he could see one large room with stairs leading down. He assumed sleeping and eating quarters were below. It made sense to have the majority of the housing underground to keep it cooler.

"Can I offer you anything to drink, Rohin?"

"No," he responded, his voice cracking with the dryness.

"You must be tired. Or did you sleep? You want to talk a while, or see your room, or what?" Helio moved nervously from side to side as he spoke, as if he wanted time alone with Muru but also knew his duty for taking care of Rohin.

Rohin smiled. "Actually, I'd like to stretch my legs a little more. It was a long flight." He gestured toward the outside door. "Any chance of me walking around out there and living?"

"Not too much," Muru responded. "There are a few other homes among the dunes within about four kilometers, but I doubt anyone would let you in. People around here don't take too well to strangers. That's one of the reasons this is such a safe place to hide people. Everyone minds their own business."

"I am free to move about the house though? Free to leave?"

Helios smiled. "We have a little surgery to do first. Eternity has a tracking probe in you."

Rohin slapped his thigh. Pulled his pants down to look at his torso. "Where? How do you know?"

"Miki told us." Muru said. "We must remove it."

Rohin immediately stripped. "Miki? How did... Never mind. Take it out. Take it out now."

"As you wish." Helios pointed to a chair that had already been covered with a sterile sheet. "Please straddle the chair, your back to me."

Rohin open his eyes wide? "On the back? They put it on my back? Tarful!" He immediately did as asked.

Muru swabbed an area just above his coccyx. Rohin felt a slight pin prick then nothing. Within less than a minute, Muru had bandaged him and handed Rohin the probe.

"You may think you should smash it, but I would not suggest it. We do not want Eternity to know it is removed."

"What? You expect me to carry it around then?" Rohin asked.

Helios chuckled. "No. We will keep it here while you and Miki visit, then we will send it with someone else who will do some traveling."

"When is she expected to arrive?"

"Soon" Muru said. "I do not think the true love of Miki Yokoyama would want to leave before her arrival."

"The true love?"

Helios elbowed Muru in his side. "Miki will be here in the early morning hours. Then we will all know what to do." His eyes strayed to Muru again who smiled.

Muru brushed a hand along Helio's jaw. "I'm going to get resettled. I've been away a long time and I have some messages to send before I can rest. Helio will show you around our home." Then Muru left to descend the stairs in the far corner of the room as Helio watched after him and sighed.

"Work is always first." Helio crossed in front of Rohin and opened a door at the back of the room. "You don't feel it now, because of the anesthetic; but your back will start to hurt in about two hours. You will want to be resting by then." He gestured into the room beyond the door. "This is the only other room on this level," he said, turning slightly to speak over his massive shoulders. "This is as good a place as any to think and rest." Rohin followed him into the room, wondering if it was less spartan than the main room.

As he walked through the archway he stopped mid-stride. Everywhere he looked were printed books. Floor to ceiling bookshelves lined every wall. There were books in piles scattered around the base of most shelves, and even more books piled on top of books on the floor in every corner. Rohin had never seen so many books outside of a museum. Most everyone got books on electronic devices now. Only the very wealthy could afford the space or the cost of printed books.

"Geez," Rohin breathed, as he slowly wound his way to one of the shelves and gingerly ran his fingers along the bindings. Was this the library he had sought? How would anyone in Rho Hive know about this? "What are you, some type of curator or something?"

"In a way," Helio replied, almost shyly. "I'm a historian. I know I can get most of this information through MC nets and Eternity research services, but I like having my own copies. I like to personally trace history from the original historical records themselves. You never know what another researcher may have mistranslated, overlooked, or deemed unnecessary to report. Or worse, change the reported history.

"When Eternity started burning all the books, with Miki's help I began saving them. I had friends in each of the hives who would sneak out and find me books and get them to me. We did this for ten years. We have many libraries around the world, guarded by Agers who know their worth."

Helio wandered to another wall and pulled out an especially large book. It looked to be about thirty centimeters tall and twenty-five centimeters wide. But more than that, it was at least ten centimeters thick. Rohin had never seen such a large, thick book. He opened it eagerly when Helio offered it to him.

"The Holy Bible." Rohin fumbled with sounding out the words. It was written in an antique version of Engel, before the language was combined with parts of German and several African dialects. Opening the cover, he haltingly continued reading the inscription on the first page. "With love to Sheena and Kavan, on the occasion of their wedding, 1908, Dunoon, Scotland."

"This is actually a family Bible," Helio said with pride, guiding Rohin toward a desk and chair with better lighting. "Before the Eternity virus, and the massive increase in information storage capabilities, my maternal great-grandfather passed this to me. I was only nine years old. The Kavan named here was his great, great, great grandfather, and he made me vow never to give it up.

"My great-grandfather belonged to a little known religious sect known as Christians, and he was very proud of it. As far as I know there have been no followers of that cult for at least two hundred years now. With the advances in technology and our ability to explain most natural phenomenon the need for religion really is obsolete—though there seems to be a rise in churches of humanism lately. Hmmm..." he absently ran his hand through thick black hair and stopped talking, as if he was lost deep in thought.

Rohin smiled to himself, then raised his voice. "Your great-grandfather was a religious?"

"Oh, yes. Sorry, I was debating why the humanist churches are so important today.... Anyway, back to my grandfather. He really wanted me to follow him. But even at the age of nine I never felt the need to join anything like that. It's funny though, now that I'm older and I've studied the history of world religions, I somehow feel we've all missed the ability to get caught up in that optimism—in spite of the fact that ..."

Helio paused for a moment as he shifted his bulk behind Rohin, watching him carefully turn the pages in admiration. He spoke over Rohin's shoulder. "As you can see, I still kept my vow to my great-grandfather. This book has been in a place of honor in my library. In fact, it probably had a great deal to do with my love of history. One day I hope to truly understand the faith of my great-grandfather and many of the people of his time."

Helio pointed to a shelf at just about eye level with Rohin. "I have other religious books as well." He pointed to each one as he named them. "The Qur'an, the Tripitaka, the Shri Guru Granth, Daodejing ... and many smaller texts from other practices. Because these beliefs were so widely practiced, I have often dreamed that one day one of these books will provide an insight to an important historical truth. Sounds crazy doesn't it?"

Rohin didn't answer. He ran his fingers across the page of the Bible he held, then reverently closed the book and carefully handed it back to Helio. "While I'm here I would like to read some of this book and some of the others. Perhaps you can give me some background, point out some stories that are most meaningful to you in each book."

"Sure," Helio responded eagerly.

"That is assuming I live long enough to read anything after Miki arrives."

Helio chuckled and shook his head. "Miki is not the killing type. Some might say she is too soft or too trusting. But I know better. She is wise. She knows that trust is the foundation for loyalty."

Rohin nodded. "Nice to know there isn't a death notice already made out for me. Well, if I'm to be stuck here for awhile, then I need something to do besides contemplate my navel."

Helio laughed heartily. "Navels can be interesting too. Muru has the most amazing navel..." He returned the book to the shelf and stepped back toward the door. "Religious history is my area of expertise, and I rarely get to talk to anyone about it these days. It certainly doesn't interest Eternity. And, at least so far, the Agers have no use for it either."

"Religion and the Agers?" Rohin contemplated aloud. "Hmmm... I'm beginning to see a connection. Both movements require a group of fanatics." He paused a moment then continued thoughtfully. "But, until now, I would have never pegged Miki for a fanatic. Never."

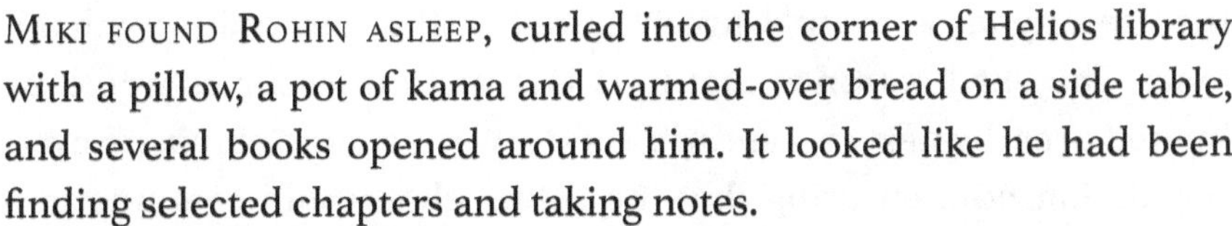

MIKI FOUND ROHIN ASLEEP, curled into the corner of Helios library with a pillow, a pot of kama and warmed-over bread on a side table, and several books opened around him. It looked like he had been finding selected chapters and taking notes.

Gingerly, trying not to wake him, she picked up a piece of paper closest to her. Scribbled at the top was a quote attributed to Sir Walter Raleigh.

> *Even such is time, that takes in trust*
> *Our youth, our joys, our all we have,*
> *And pays us but with age and dust;*
> *Who in the dark and silent grave,*
> *When we have wandered all our ways,*
> *Shuts up the story of our days.*

BELOW THE QUOTE Rohin had written words at all angles on the page: Jerusalem, Isralarabia, death stench. Piles of corpses, mass graves, desert. Starved, sick, dying people, aimless. Then a full sentence at the bottom of the page: *Whenever I stopped for a moment, the expressionless refugees gathered about me, staring, as if waiting for me to join the dead.*

Miki let the paper flutter back to the ground. She remembered learning of the state of Isralarabia herself about fifty years after Eternity began the virus distribution effort. The ruling elite had distributed the Eternity virus as directed, but only to the chosen groups—select sects of Jews, Muslims, and Christians who agreed with the politics of the moment. Then, to ensure the quick demise of the unchosen, a subtle biological warfare was waged on the unprotected. Over a period of ten years, entire cultures were wiped out. The Kurds were one of the first groups to die, closely followed by Orthodox Jews and Fundamentalist Christians.

This same scene was repeated wherever she'd traveled. In New

Austral-land, the last remnants of an aboriginal tribe faced the same kind of death. And in Uzbek, the ruling elite had chosen to distribute the Eternity virus to only five hundred of the four million inhabitants. They had reasoned that food and natural resources would be limited over the next six centuries; and it was better to eliminate over-population now, ensuring that the ruling elite would continue in a comfortable lifestyle.

Is it possible that what Rohin had told her was true? That he had traveled and seen what the unequal distribution of the Eternity virus had wrought?

She picked up another quote and read another story of his travels. After four or five more, tears streamed from her face as it became apparent that he was racked with guilt over his role in finding the virus. In one note he'd written that suicide was all he could offer but, being the coward he was, he was unable to go through with it.

A sob escaped her as the words blurred in front of her eyes. He did still care. He had tried to change things and she'd pushed him out of her life.

A hand reached out and gently tugged her toward him. She followed without thinking, sinking onto his lap. Rohin's arms enclosed her. "Shhh..." he comforted. "It was a journey I had to take alone. It's behind me now. Purged."

She looked up into his dark eyes and all the feelings of the past came back to her. All the times they'd laughed together, made love together, believed in their ability to make the world right.

His head lowered. When their lips met it was like a refreshing rain after a long drought. Her hands fisted in his thick, dark hair as she pulled him closer. She opened her mouth, her tongue slicking his lips, inviting him to deepen the kiss.

He groaned and plundered. Pulling her so tight against him she believed they would never come apart again. As the heat burned between them, she clawed at his shirt, yearning to be skin to skin.

"Miki," he jerked his shirt over his head and pulled her shirt out of her pants.

Craving his touch, she tugged at her top, lifting it over her head.

His hands slaked along her sides and he dragged her back to him. She shuddered with the feel of her naked breasts finally against the smooth expanse of his chest.

He lifted her and shifted to the floor. Lowering her with care to the soft rug below, he loomed above her. Her heart slammed against her chest as if her ribs could contain it no longer. She looked into his eyes as he stared down at her. "Please...please, I need you."

He kissed her hard and deep until she could barely get a breath out. When she thought she could take no more he let her mouth go and moved down her throat, trailing kisses along her shoulders until he stopped at a breast. He took her nipple into his mouth and suckled, then opened wider and took in more of her breast. His tongue teasing. His mouth molding. His breath driving her up so fast she thought she might scream. His other hand played her other breast like a consummate musician, knowing when to finger a counterpoint to his mouth or to work his hands and mouth together driving the fortissimo to a frenzied pace.

Sobbing with need, she pushed him away and rolled him beneath her. She shucked off her shorts and pulled at his pants, begging for release. "Rohin, I can't wait. Please, help me now."

He rolled her again onto her back. "I will, Miki. I will." He stepped away and the loss of his warmth had her yanking his pants down, hurrying him back to her. He laughed and pushed her back to the rug.

She stared at his full erection and gasped. He was still as strong, and dark, and virile as she'd remembered. Though she knew in her mind that his body would have only aged ten years over the past one hundred, she hadn't allowed herself to imagine what it might look like. She hadn't allowed herself to believe they would ever be together like this again.

She ran her fingers across his belly, then trailed them down until she held him full in her hand. She moved her head to envelop him with her mouth, but he stopped her, raising her chin and looking her in the eye.

"You are as beautiful and wild as ever," he said. "Please, let me take you."

He kissed her softly and lowered her back to the rug. She dug her nails into his back and lifted toward him. "Now. I don't want to wait any longer."

He knelt between her legs and took each one to drape over his shoulders. "Do you have any idea how often I dreamed of seeing you again? Loving you again?"

She tilted her hips toward his erection, dying to have him inside her as fast as possible.

Instead, he put his hands beneath her hips and raised her womanhood to his mouth. Burying himself, his tongue drove her over the edge so fast she screamed out his name and clawed at the floor beneath her. Then, he took her up once again, and when she thought she would die the little death, he entered her. He stroked quickly and deeply. Her legs still draped over his shoulders as he leaned forward on the floor taking full advantage of all she had to offer. Her hands clutched his back, holding on, guiding him deeper.

They found a quickening rhythm and her senses were bombarded with every part of him. The slickness of their bodies together, the musky aroma of pheromones, and the blessed slick friction building and pulsing inside her until that was all she knew. Pumping and building. Breaking down every wall they had so carefully put between them. The sensation of nerve endings being massaged and pressed pushed her higher.

Pressure intensified as he grew even larger and yet she wanted more. She urged him onward until there were no thoughts, no conscious knowledge of each individual—only the rhythm of them together as one. The breathing, the pulsing, the pumping. Faster and faster. Clutching to each other. Faster and faster. Sensations colliding. Faster and faster. Tension mounting. Arms straining. Hands clutching. Lips plundering. Faster and faster. Tears falling. Faster. Screams. Faster. Her world tilted as he pressed down on her, her knees to her shoulders and captured her mouth as she called on the gods. Release...blessed release.

9

———

Awake again, Miki looked at Rohin's long lashes as he lay asleep at her side. She listened to his steady breathing and wondered what was next. She'd just done exactly what Anna had warned her not to do. She'd let her emotions lead her body into territory that would only complicate things. Worse, she'd reinforced in her own mind how much she still loved him.

She slowly rolled onto her shoulder to escape his embrace, but he woke and his hand pulled her back, spooning her into his side.

"I'm not nearly done," he said.

She swallowed. Her memories of making love last night were enough to sustain her for years to come. She didn't think she could take more in the light of day and what she had to do. "I...I can't." She half-heartedly tried to pull his hand from her stomach.

Instead he rolled her onto her back, and trapped her between his legs. When she put her hands on his chest to push him away, he grasped them and held them out to her sides, his fingers entwined as he plundered her mouth.

He raised his head and smiled. "Now, was that so hard to take?"

"No...but..."

He covered her mouth again and this time she just surrendered. She could wait a little longer to tell him.

Knock. Knock. Knock.

"Miki?" Helios called through the library door. "Rohin? Breakfast is in the kitchen." Then steps retreated along with a chuckle and whispers she couldn't make out.

Rohin groaned and pulled himself up, bringing her with him to a seated position. "How long until it's really obvious to everyone what's going on here?"

"It's already obvious," Miki chuckled.

His fingers moved to chafe at a nipple. "Well then, it won't matter that we keep them waiting a little longer."

She covered his hand and removed it, looking him in the eye. "It will matter."

"Miki, we need to talk."

She stood and pulled on her pants and shirt. "Yes, but not now."

"When?"

"Later. Maybe this evening. I have to think." She moved to the door, her hand on the button to open it. "Right now, I'm taking one step at a time. I'm taking a shower. Having breakfast. That's all I can handle right now."

She pressed the button and the door snicked open. She looked at him, wondering if there was even the slightest chance it could work. Then she shook her head and turned, closing the door behind her.

EACH NIGHT they went to sleep making love. Each morning she woke in Rohin's arms and they made love again. She knew she had to talk to him, say something, make a decision, but she couldn't bring herself to do it. She couldn't bring herself to say goodbye again.

On the fourth day, as she made breakfast while Rohin showered, Helio and Muru hugged her goodbye as they went to visit friends.

"You must tell him today," Helio said. "You can't leave him hanging. It's too cruel. Either you will allow him to join us or you must let him go."

She took in a deep breath and let it out. "It's not as simple as that," she said. "He doesn't believe in the Ager cause. He can't join us."

"He can't? Or he won't?" Helio asked.

"Give him a chance," Muru said, clasping Helio's hand. "Do you remember when I joined? I wasn't sure of your cause. But I was sure of Helio." He looked to Helio's eyes and smiled. "Because I loved him...because I trusted him...I listened and waited. I listened and eventually understood. Maybe Rohin can do this too."

The sound of running water stopped. Helio tugged Muru toward the front door. "We will leave you alone," he said. "You will know what to do."

"But..."

Muru kissed her forehead. "You will do what's right. You always do. Trust your heart."

Then the two of them stepped outside. The door closing with a resounding clunk, as if emphasizing the finality of what she must do.

"Good morning, angel." Rohin entered the living room sans shirt, remnants of water still glistening on his golden-brown chest. "Was that Helio and Muru leaving for the day?"

Miki tore her eyes from him. The last thing she needed was to think about making love again.

"Only a few hours," she said. "They're visiting a friend about ten klicks away."

Rohin encircled her with his arms. "I can make a few hours feel like a lifetime of pleasure if you give me the chance."

She turned in his arms and extracted herself. She reached to the stove for his hot plate of scrambled eglos and tofu strips and set it in front of him. "You need food." She set a fork on the plate.

He chuckled and took a bite. "Afraid I'll run out of energy before they return?"

She stood on the other side of the counter and played with her own plate of eglos. "No, I'm afraid I'll lose my nerve."

Rohin's brow furrowed. He covered her hand with his. "What is it? Did I do something wrong?"

She shook her head and opened her mouth, but her throat closed and her eyes misted. It was so hard to say goodbye again.

He immediately rounded the counter and drew her to him. "Oh God, what is it? What's happened? Is it Anna? Is it one of your Ager compounds? Let me help. I'll do whatever you need."

"You can't help," she whispered, pushing herself away again and wiping the tears from her eyes with shaky fingertips. "You can't join us."

"Ah..." He lifted her chin and kissed the tears from her cheeks.

She closed her eyes and he kissed her eyelids too.

He grazed her cheek with his thumb. "So, the honeymoon's over."

She opened her eyes and looked at him. "Is it even possible you could come to understand why the Agers must develop a counter virus."

He held her close and she turned her cheek to his chest. He put his head on top of hers. "I understand why you believe this is the right path. But it can't be my path."

"I know," she said on a shuddered breath. He hugged her even tighter.

"I want to be with you, Miki. More than I've ever wanted anything in my life. But I can't join your cause."

"Then we can't be together," she said. The finality of her statement shutting a steel door on her emotions.

He held her far enough away that he could look at her. "Why? Just because we disagree doesn't mean we don't love each other."

"I know, but..."

He put a finger to her lips and she stopped. He brushed the lightest of kisses across her lips, and she gasped at the trail of cool air as he stood back again.

"Just because we disagree doesn't mean we can't be together."

She squared her shoulders. "I can't, Rohin. Thousands of people are counting on me."

"Thousands?"

What would it hurt for him to know? She knew now that he couldn't hurt her. He also couldn't stop her. The Ager's were too far ahead for him or Eternity to catch up.

"There are over one hundred thousand of us," she said.

"That many want..." He shook his head.

"Yes. That many and more every day."

"I don't understand."

He stepped toward her again but she backed away and put her hand up. "I can't do my job as the leader of the Agers and worry about what you will do to stop me."

"I'd never hurt..."

"You wouldn't mean to," she interrupted. "But when the counter virus is ready to be released and you truly believe that I'm wrong, I know you'll do everything in your power to stop me."

"You really believe you can create a counter virus?"

She backed toward the door. "I don't want to hurt you, Rohin. I know you're a good man. I'll give you one more week here if you want it. Then Muru will take you back to Rho Hive. If by some miracle you change your mind, let Helios and Muru know. They know where to find me."

"Miki?"

She pushed the button to open the door. When it opened she stood in the entry. "I love you, Rohin. I always have, and I probably will until the day I die."

She fled into the desert, calling her hover to pick her up two klicks away. She needed to run in the heat. She needed to let the emotions evaporate in the desert. She needed to be exhausted when she shot into the sky and left him...again. The quicker she could leave, the quicker she could get back to work—back to a life without Rohin Chawla.

~

THE FIRST TWO DAYS, Rohin barely remembered eating or sleeping. It seemed that time stood still as he tried to accept that he had lost Miki again. He spent hours in the library, pouring over Helios' books. When he finally roused himself to talk he engaged Helios in detailed discussions about the historical relevance of religion to today's world.

Helio's knowledge was immense, examining the spread of religion as humanity expanded and diversified its cultures, progressing from the early days of Mesopotamia to the exodus and the origin of Israel. He was also able to temper Rohin's belief that religion was only used for self-aggrandizement. Helio pointed to many instances where those who believed in a higher power used it as a way to give life meaning and to help others.

Rohin was careful to make mental notes on each key point of discussion along the way. Over the next few days he spent several more hours in Helio's library, reading pertinent passages Helio had referenced, and cross-checking their historical significance with other books. Occasionally, after long stretches of discussion, Rohin would walk into the desert, as many teachers had done before, in his own form of silent meditation and searching. On the sixth evening, as the full moon illuminated the dunes dotting the landscape, Rohin was finally ready to leave.

In the morning, Helio and Muru had prepared a special meal of fruits and vegetables to add to the nutrition of kama for their breakfast. Though six cups of kama provided all the necessary nutritional requirements for a day, Rohin still valued the rare opportunity to taste real food.

"I had hoped you would join us," Muru said quietly. "But in my discussions with Helio and the quest you have taken, we understand your decision."

There was no talk for a number of minutes, just the clinking of forks, and the sound of cups raised and then lowered as they drank in companionship.

"Do you know what you will do next then?" Helio asked.

"Not exactly. All I know is that I must begin my own search for a type of universal power—not for myself but for the masses. I want the power to make changes in individuals rather than creating a political struggle to rule over others. I'm not a religious leader, but I am going to lead like them. I must find a way to help people once again build dreams for the future—a way for people to have hope."

~

MURU TOOK Rohin from the desert the next day. Following Mike's security protocols as before. Muru returned Rohin to Rho hive as requested. Rohin was eager to be home where he knew the rules, the economies and the needs of the people. For it was the people in the hives—not Eternity and not the Agers—who would be the ones to change the world if his plan worked.

Rohin did have a plan, but he didn't trust to share it with anyone yet. If Eternity or the Agers knew his way would eventually stop both of them, his life and those of his followers might be in danger. But if his plan worked, no one would feel threatened if he went quietly about offering hope to individuals—making no move to take control of the political or economic balance of the world.

First, he wanted to find a core group of people he could trust. People who saw the same vision for humanity. He would first seek out recruits in the hives. They had nothing to lose and everything to gain. The hives were built on loyalty and protection because it was the only way to survive. It was the perfect group to get started.

Rohin laughed at himself for even thinking it. Utopia. That ideal life that every great individual throughout history sought, but no one could really make work. I can't create Utopia. No one can, he thought to himself. But the dream of Utopia may be just the leverage I need.

~

ROHIN LOOKED up at the concrete edifice of Rho Hive as rain spilled from the elevator header, slicking his hair to his scalp. The doors opened on the fifth floor and plastic sheeting flapped around him in the wind, leaving little warmth to the resident vels. He thought he would start with Maritza. That was the only person he actually knew here who might help him. With her street smarts and contacts, she could be the best recruiter he'd ever find.

He turned left and headed toward the fifth group of vels.

"Chawla," a low deep voice yelled out, followed by two sets of heavy, booted shoes running in his direction.

"Eternity!" someone whispered as he passed. Rohin ran, randomly choosing when to turn left or right.

As the men closed on him, he jumped into an elevator and pushed the button for the basement. The last thing he wanted was to endanger anyone here.

The elevator didn't move.

He swore. These must be some special agents. Only Kant's men carried electronic interruptors.

He braced himself for the blast as the doors opened.

He fell as the beam hit him. He closed his eyes and let the darkness come.

ROHIN SHOOK HIMSELF AWAKE. A mask hovered near his face. It was like he was caught in a repeating nightmare.

"We're done here," a woman's face said behind the mask. She held up a probe.

"Give it to me," a harsh male voice demanded from the darkness.

A click and a slight whirr caught Rohin's attention.

The male chuckled. "I knew there was something at Qyzylqum."

"What should I do with him now?" the woman asked.

"But him under and drop him back at the hive. Let's see what else he can find for us."

ROHIN FELT a cool compress on his forehead. He reached up to move it.

A hand stayed his fingers. "Good, you're coming around."

He recognized the voice. "Maritza?"

"Yes, Rohin. Eternity agents left you in front of the building and a couple of my customers brought you to me. They remembered that you saved me."

He tried to sit up but the headache was far too painful.

"Shhh," she trailed a finger along his chin. "I'm sure they drugged you. It may be days before you can walk."

He sighed. There was something he needed to do. Someone he needed to see.

"Who's Miki?" Maritza asked. "You've been asking for her."

Memories flooded back. He flailed his arms trying to get up again, but to no avail. "I must talk to her."

Maritza whispered to someone else in the room. He heard the light padding of feet as the person left. In only a few minutes, feet padded back in.

"What's her vid code?"

Rohin groaned. "God, I don't know. I don't know."

His leg kicked out as if he could walk. Maritza smoothed her hand over it.

"Deep breaths," she instructed. "Don't try so hard to remember. It will make it worse." She paused. "How about someone else who knows how to get in touch with her?"

Rohin took conscious breaths. In and out. In and out. He tried to clear his mind. "Helios," he finally said. "13-248-521-9."

"Good." Maritza dialed a portable vid. When it connected she held it in front of Rohin's face.

"Rohin? What's wrong? God you look awful. What happened?" Helios gestured wildly and Muru came to stand in the picture as well.

Rohin concentrated on his words. He kept breathing deeply. He couldn't afford to be agitated. "Run." He said. "Eternity knows..." He took another breath. "Qyzylqum. Eternity knows..." He struggled again. This time taking three breaths before he could speak again. "Ager library...stronghold."

"God no," Helio said. "Thanks, Rohin. We owe you."

The screen went blank and Rohin closed his eyes. He hoped they could get out in time. He hoped all of the Agers could get out in time. He didn't know how many their were, but he knew those books didn't get there just by Helios carrying them.

Maritza worked her fingers along his temples. "Relax," she said. "You've done what you could. Go to sleep."

Finally, he let go.

10

———————

Anna walked in as Miki hunched over a viewer, frowning in concentration. It had been a long night and she still wasn't seeing what she wanted.

"Getting any closer?" Anna asked, as she pulled up a chair and set down a tray with two cups, a pot of kama, cinnamon packets, and a small bowl of fruit.

Miki looked up and snatched a piece of apple. "No. This is the fifty-second vaccine we've tried." She turned the viewer toward Anna. "Look at the serum protein fractions. I can't get them to elevate any higher. That damn Eternity virus really has control."

Anna looked into the viewer. "What do the lymphocyte transformation studies look like?"

"Not much better. The same three antigens still work. I can't seem to find anything to increase the suppression of the T8," Miki answered. She sat back from the table and rubbed her temples. The pain there indicated that she was unconsciously letting the stress level get to her.

Anna clicked the viewer through the slides. "I see what you mean. Perhaps it's impossible to create a vaccine against the Eternity virus."

"I hate to think that," Miki said. "After seventy years of effort and sacrifice . . ." She couldn't finish the sentence, as her eyes began to mist over. She was putting in too many all night stints lately. Her emotions lingered too close to the surface.

"Maybe we're taking the wrong approach," Anna said softly.

"What other approach is there? It's not like there is some miracle counter-agent out there." She stood and stretched her arms to the ceiling, listening to her vertebrae realign.

"Why not, Mik? Two hundred years ago, we never would have dreamed there was a virus like this. Why couldn't there be some naturally occurring agent to counteract it?"

She sat back on the stool at the counter. "If there was, it would have shown up by now."

Miki and Anna reached for the pot of kama at the same time. They exchanged silent glances.

"I'm sorry." Miki sighed and withdrew her hand to massage the tenseness from the back of her neck. "I shouldn't be taking this out on you. You have enough on your mind—with having to make up tall tales for Kant every week."

"I think you just need some rest." Anna replied. "Maybe there's something we're missing. Why don't you get Helios doing some research? He's itching to be useful. He doesn't know much about biochemistry; but he's a wizard at tracking down data files. Maybe having someone with a fresh perspective—someone to bounce ideas off—will help you think straighter."

"That's not a bad idea," Miki replied, opening a packet and stirring cinnamon into her cup. "I've pretty much let Helios wander since he and Muru arrived here. Thank God Rohin got in touch with him."

Anna didn't say anything.

Miki looked at her. "He may not agree with us, but you have to admit his warning saved the Agers of Qyzylqum."

"If we'd never let him get to Qyzylqum he wouldn't have had anything to tell Eternity," Anna said.

Miki shook her head. Why did she bother? Anna would never change her mind about Rohin and his intentions.

She changed the subject. "With Muru shuttling people out of

Snohomish, Helios has been feeling pretty lost. I guess I've been too busy to pay much attention to him."

"Well, he sure looks like he's staying here awhile." Anna spread her arms wide. "Did you see all those books he unloaded with his personal cargo? You might as well set up a museum and invite the public."

Miki smiled at the memory of Helios unloading his belongings and Muru complaining about how the hover practically crashed with the weight of it as he flew between the port and the compound. She never realized how much more he had collected while he lived in the desert.

"Why don't you take a shower and a nap?" Anna suggested. "You look beat. I'll see if I can get Helio to come up in a couple hours or so. With his research background, he might kick start your search."

Miki stood. "Good idea. Only a good friend like you could put up with me looking this way."

Three hours later Miki entered the dining lounge. She noticed that Helios was seated at the table closest to the west window. She watched him for a moment, wondering if he was feeling homesick as he stared at the sunset above the trees. The Mt. Hood wilderness was quite different from the sandy desert where he had spent the past 95 years.

"Are you adapting okay, Helios?" she asked before taking the chair directly across from him.

"Oh, sure," he said, turning away from the window. "Actually, I like it here. So green . . . so much more water. Was it hard to get this place?"

"No, not really," Miki responded. "It's too remote for Eternity to want anything to do with it. There's not enough people in the area for them to justify the trouble and expense to modernize it. Besides, with all the entertainment requirements of the masses, there's little concern for the few last remaining wilderness areas. That's why it's perfect for the Agers."

"But doesn't Eternity know about our people in this area?" Helios asked.

"Well . . . yes and no. They know that an old fashioned group of environmentalists is doing forest research in the region; but they have yet to correlate a relationship between them and Ager command. They do have records of one or two known Ager members who are also environmentalists. However, they calculate that as of little statistical significance to the overall organization."

"You said yet. Does that mean you expect them to figure it out eventually?" Helios asked, a little wary.

"We have to plan for that eventuality," Miki responded. "But don't worry. If necessary, we can evacuate up to four thousand Agers to underground caverns which we've made accessible from several locations in the central complex. There is an entire series of caves near here that haven't been used in three centuries. They don't appear on any of the satellite mapping networks and we've camouflaged all entrances and exits. I'm hoping any maps of the area were lost in the virus wars one hundred fifty years ago. With a few other precautions, we should be safe."

"I wasn't worried," he said. "I just want to be prepared in case anything happens. Since we fled the desert I don't feel safe anymore." Helios turned from the window. "How do you keep track of Eternity's intelligence on the Agers?"

"Pretty much the same way they keep track of us—only I hope we have the upper hand. We have a controlled program of leaks to Eternity. I believe Kant is feeling very comfortable with the spy I've provided him. Our contact has surreptitiously passed him selected information on our research, as well as secret locations of some of our people. As long as Eternity continues to believe we're just another small group of harmless radicals, and that they know everything about us, we'll be left alone."

"That's small consolation." Helios sampled a small piece of bread before taking a sip of his kama. "Eventually Eternity will make the correlation between the Agers and the environmentalists. I just hope it doesn't lead them to find all the other groups joining the Agers."

"I agree." They both were quiet for awhile thinking of the awful possibilities. Then Miki continued, "That's why I've been working so hard on this vaccine."

Helios reached for her hand and held it for a moment. His eyebrow raised. "Chawla returning really hurt you, didn't it?"

Miki stiffened. "I'll get over it. I shouldn't have stayed those few days. I shouldn't have let my passions get the better of me. I know better. I've done without him over a hundred years, it's not like I can't do it again."

She returned to looking at the viewer, her jaw clenched.

"Were we wrong to let you and Chawla enjoy yourselves?" he asked. "You both seemed so happy, so light those first few days. Muru and I wanted you to find someone—someone to love, a lasting relationship like ours."

She opened her mouth but then closed it without a word. Better not to say anything. Better not to start down that path.

Helios shook his head and let go of her hand. "I'm sorry. It's none of my business. I just wanted you to know I care...we care."

Miki curled her lower lip under teeth. The small pain she experienced as she put pressure on it with her teeth took away the sting of memories.

"I don't have time for a relationship," she said. "I have a counter virus to create."

"You aren't doing all the work yourself, are you?" he asked. "You can't stay up for weeks on end doing all the work yourself."

"No, of course not." Miki answered, somewhat defensive. "It's just that the other three research groups don't have as much experience as we do here. Though they're excellent, my experience with the Eternity Virus sometimes allows me to see things they don't.

"Unfortunately, we've hit a huge wall. We've just completed testing of the latest vaccine, and it's a dismal failure. Nothing seems to work. We've isolated several Eternity effected cells, and tried to mutate them using null protein counterparts, followed by the re-introduction of disease strains. We keep hoping to get a dominant mutation that would supplant the existing one. But each time the Eternity virus works with the body's immune system to counter the new strain, like it does with all the other disease-type viruses it destroys.

"It's beginning to look like we've run out of options. I was really hoping a null protein replacement would work. But now it looks like only a more complex combination of the existing infected cells will produce the mutation we need. At this rate it could take hundreds of years for us to research all the possible combinations. I don't think we can continue to fool Eternity for that long."

The weariness Miki had tried to wash away with her shower began to show again as she described her dilemma to Helios. She had let this last failure really get her down.

"Is there any way I can help?" Helios asked.

Miki smiled slightly and shook her head. "I don't think so. You don't know much about biomed."

"No...With the exception of a couple of historical articles I wrote . . . way back when you discovered the Eternity Virus," he responded. "But, I can listen. I'd really like to have a better understanding of what we're trying to do."

Miki smiled at Helios empathy. What would it hurt. Going back to basics may help her focus too. She outlined how basic immunity worked and how several types of immunodeficiencies had similar problems with a particular type of T cell, and the difficulty found when enhancing the T8 marker. Helios asked questions about antigens and specificity showing he had at least a little more than basic knowledge.

When she finally wound down, for several moments neither one said anything. Miki watched silently as Helios seemed to digest the information. He was looking down at the table in earnest, as if the answer to some burning question written there. Miki had done this herself several times, so she waited patiently for the question he was bound to ask.

"Very interesting," Helios said, finally breaking the silence. "Especially from a historical perspective."

"What?" Miki questioned, confused. "Do you know something about biological history?"

"Well, as long ago as the fifth century BC., Greek physicians noted that people who had recovered from the plague would never get it again." Helios paused for a moment, collecting his thoughts, then continued. "They didn't have the concept of immunity then, yet they noted a pattern."

His face visibly lit up with a thought. "Maybe I'm over simplifying things, but it seems the answer would have to be another virus. Have you ever thought there might be another virus in Antarctica, one which developed in the same way, or near the same geologic time as the Eternity Virus?"

"Anna asked me somewhat the same thing earlier today. It seems unlikely though. We know, for instance, that Eternity has been researching this aspect to ensure they could counteract that type of introduction. Probably any external agent having an effect on the Eternity Virus would have been found by now."

She wrinkled her forehead in thought, trying to weed through the thousands of reports she had read in the intervening years since finding the Eternity virus. "What makes you ask me that question? Have you read a report somewhere?"

"Well not exactly," Helios was hesitant. "It's a number of religious references. A variety of early religious documents describe people who had lifespans of seven to eight hundred years, though this was the exception rather than the norm. But these historical documents are from a combination of written and oral records, some over four thousand years old, long before the types of advances in medicine we take for granted."

Miki stood, her arms across her chest. It seemed he was talking any circles. "Religion? Myths? What are you getting at, Helios? Where's the science in this?"

"The science is iffy—or none existent," he said. "There has never been a good archaeological explanation for the myths. No one has ever found any skeletons that would concur with those long lives. The only logical explanation has been that people in those stories measured the passage of time differently than we do. Perhaps, what the translators read as a year was really more like one of our months.

Language is such a cultural phenomenon that it is very difficult to document certain concepts—like time and distance."

Miki paced. Impatient. She waved her finger in a circle, asking him to get on with it.

"The point is that, whether myth or not, there is some question that people may have lived that long—maybe more people than is mentioned in these passing references found in Ebla and Qumran." He paused. "When you did the core samples, in what era was the Eternity virus found?"

"Somewhere between 2100 and 1700 B.C."

"That does fit the period described. Isn't it possible that a strain of the Eternity Virus was responsible for the longevity of those people mentioned in these religious records?" Helios stood and practically danced in place. "Around the time of Moses, 1500 B.C. there is no longer any mention of long-lived people. It's as if it stopped. So something must have happened, some disease or virus that could not be stopped by the previous one.

Catching his meaning, Miki began to smile. "It is grasping at straws," she said cautiously. She looked up to the ceiling, as if the answer could be found there. Then she closed her eyes, concentrating, talking the logic out. "A second natural agent, easily passed from one person to the next. It would have been strong. Almost twin viruses, but mirror opposites."

She paced again, zig zagging back in forth, thinking of everything that would need to be done now. If this were true, one of the best places to begin the search was back where the Eternity Virus was originally found. She should send one of her teams back to Antarctica. To prevent Eternity from stepping in and trying to stop them, she had to move quickly and carefully. She stopped pacing and looked directly at Helios.

"Can you research the Qumran and Ebla findings for me? Can you get a better fix, within say two hundred years or so, as to when the Eternity Virus died out? If we can get that, we can go back to Antarctica and dig at the appropriate level in the ice to look for the counter agent. It's a long shot, but it's the only one we have right now.

And we have to be fast and secretive to make sure no one else finds out. Don't share this with anyone, Helios—not even Muru."

"But I trust Muru with my life."

She grasped his hand in hers. "I know you do, but I don't want anything to slip accidentally. I don't want anyone to know until we are ready to launch a major project."

"Of course," he answered. "But I hope it's not long. I can not keep things from Muru for too long. Especially happy things."

"I'll have to get the council together to plan a project. But I can't let on the reason yet." Miki said, already planning the next step.

Lost in thought, she listed what would need to be done in order to pull off this meeting in the near future. Anna will have to contact the eastern sector, while I coordinate the western groups. We'll need to put together a team quickly, and then start coalescing our organization. If this agent is found, we have to be in a position to move with it.

She stopped for a moment and took a deep breath. She looked up and gasped, startled that Helios was still there.

"Thank you Helios. Thank you. I have to get work." She immediately opened her viewscreen again.

Smiling, Helios quietly left the room.

11

"Yes, have you found something?" Kant looked at the vid and saw the secretive smile and twinkle in Anna's eye—that special twinkle she always had when her news was particularly important, news that gave her the power to make or break him and his plans. He could feel his pulse racing with anticipation. When she was like this—playing her game of chess—he wanted her in so many ways. But he waited. He would never beg, and he knew she was dying to tell.

She licked her lips slowly, then smiled. "The Agers are going to Antarctica." She stopped, stringing it out as long as possible. "Yokoyama and a couple of her top people will be traveling the next couple of weeks putting together a team of scientists. I can probably come up with the schedule if she plans it at all."

"Good work," Kant reached toward the screen, wanting to touch her, then slowly dropped his hand to the desk. "If you bring me the schedule personally, I'll pay more than triple your bonus, plus something even more pleasant."

"I'm counting on it," she said. Then the vid screen blanked.

KANT WAS GRANDSTANDING AS USUAL, Anna thought with contempt as she watched him greet the line of guests. His charm was at full strength and every person in the room, no matter whether they were a head of state or a lowly staffer, would think of him as being as protective as their father and as companionable as their brother. Mix in a strong dash of sex appeal for the single daughters of the rich and famous and he was almost unassailable.

But Anna knew who he really was, and she hated having to go to these types of gatherings. Oh, she knew how to finesse and charm as well as Kant, but if it wasn't going to get her anything there was no reason to waste the energy. She wanted to be back with Miki and be on top of what was going on with the Antarctica plans. She knew she'd be traveling soon and she just didn't feel that being here was going to help anyone.

Anna glanced again at the woman in front of her and turned her lips up in a half smile. She realized she was still going on about nothing. Anna was adept at nodding every once in awhile as if she was interested in banal conversation, when in reality she had no idea what the woman had been talking about the past ten minutes.

She spotted Kant moving toward the prince of Isralarabia and she excused herself quickly. She wanted to be closer to hear what was going on. She caught a drink from a passing waiter and moved herself a little closer, being careful to wave at people just to the right of Kant so she didn't look like she was following him.

She saw Kant was greeted warmly by the prince and then the King joined them shortly. A couple of women—model types—stepped up briefly and flirted with all three men. She wondered briefly if they were hoping for a great date or just making the rounds. They seemed to really coo over Kant.

It was only that invisible aura of power that surrounded him that made Kant seem like a hero to everyone. Yes, he played the "I'm so kind and compassionate" card whenever it suited him—doling out the Eternity virus as the aid organizations used to dole out food, trading on it with poor countries for slaves and upping the ante for rich countries by making the leaders beholden to him for centuries to come.

"He seems indomitable, doesn't he?"

She felt his hand first, casually placed on her shoulder as if it belonged there. He turned her easily so that her back was to Kant and then slowly inched her toward a potted palm. He looked over her head, staring admiringly at Kant.

"You'd think with all the threats from the Agers these days that he'd cancel this kind of soiree." Hurley lifted his cocktail in a half salute, then looked down at her.

He was a good eight inches taller than Anna, but rather slender and not nearly as good looking as Kant.

"Well, better him than me," he smiled. "Nice to run into you, Anna."

"Not much danger here on his turf with all this security." Anna pasted a smile on her face. "But maybe you're right. Discretion is the better part of valor."

"I didn't say he was making a mistake," Hurley said quickly. "We can't let those terrorists scare us."

"You'd never do that," Anna said. "Everyone knows what you stand for, Rushton. We all rely on you. Kant most of all."

She executed a little pirouette to get out from behind the palm and started to leave, but he grabbed her hand.

Kant was motioning the King and Prince toward the open doors leading out to the terrace. A moment later the three strolled out and closed the doors. Immediately, two armed guards took up positions on the terrace facing outward and another two were inside near the closed doors.

"I wonder what he's up to with King Ghabra," Hurley murmured in her ear, but didn't turn her away this time. "They usually don't have much to say to each other."

"No telling." Anna shrugged and moved a few inches away. She didn't want to feel his breath on her neck. "Remember that little slip when the Prince's wife was found dead in Upsilon Hive and was immediately on all the 'casts?"

"Oh, yes." Hurley almost bubbled with excitement. "King Ghabra almost nailed the Prince for that one. But Kant squelched the 'casts and put a completely different report on the nets—making it look like it was all a big mistake from a jilted mistress."

"Maybe Kant's trying to show everybody he and Ghabra are still a united front." Anna inclined her head toward the terrace doors.

"Hmmm..." Hurley murmured while taking another swallow of wine, and then turned her back toward him. "Who knows? He can be a bit secretive."

"And you're so open." Anna didn't hide her sarcasm.

Hurley laughed. "I'm just a simple guy trying to do my job."

Tarful. Anna thought to herself. There was nothing simple about Rushton Hurley. He was scheming and tap-dancing his heart out while positioning himself to replace Kant at the next possible moment. In fact, Anna wouldn't put it past him to be behind some of the so called terrorist threats.

She knew the Agers weren't making those threats. On the contrary, they were going out of their way to stay off Kant's radar. She shrugged a shoulder. She might as well make small talk. It didn't look like Hurley was going to let her go, and they both wanted to know what was going on behind those terrace doors.

"I have a favor to ask." Kant said. Neither he or Ghabra looked at each other. They both gazed out over the garden and the terraces with pooled water and small streams running from one end to the other.

"One that means a lot to me," Kant continued. "—for which I am willing to compensate you and your country very well."

"You know I'll do whatever I can," Ghabra smiled. "Especially since you helped with that little incident with my son's wife."

The Prince lowered his head and visibly took a step back from the railing. "I thank you again for your discretion. Of course, I'm honored to help the great Kant... if I can."

"I've received news that the head of the Agers, Miki Yokoyama, will be making a move back to Antarctica soon," Kant said. "We believe she has information that may lead her to find a counter-virus to ours. I'm sure you understand that we can't let her find anything. I spent billions looking for any counter agent in Antarctica after we began distributing the Eternity virus, but we found nothing. I was convinced there wasn't one, and since no one has pursued anything for more than two hundred years, I really thought she had given up by now."

Ghabra said nothing; he only continued to stare toward the horizon. The breeze ruffled his scarf behind him like a flag of power.

"I've been informed that she will be personally contacting several researchers around the world," Kant continued. "She always was a hands-on leader. I'm sure she wants to personally approve each one. We know where most of her Ager sites are now, just not all of them. Unfortunately, we've had a very difficult time finding out which researchers are associated with her—at least finding out if anyone really important has signed on to the Ager cause."

Kant stepped away from the rail and looked at Ghabra. He noticed the Prince was now on the far side of the terrace, probably not even able to hear the conversation. Kant waited for what seemed like several minutes.

Slowly Ghabra also turned from the terrace and grinned. "And you want me to find a way to stop her," Ghabra finally spoke.

"Yes. I'll feed you information as I get it, but I may not have anything exact." Ghabra's eyes looked beyond Kant toward the closed doors, as if checking to see who else was listening.

Kant smiled. "I have the privacy screen here. Even the guards at the end of the terrace can't hear us."

Ghabra nodded. "It's not going to be easy. We don't have many Agers in our area and I don't have anyone placed within their organization. Why me? I'm sure you have other contacts who can do this."

"I have the people in the right places to get the information. But you have the means to make people disappear. We both know your people are the best in the business." Kant paused and waited.

Ghabra nodded. "Any special treatment?"

"I don't care what you do." Kant's voice roughened with suppressed violence. "Just make her stop. Permanently."

"Not a problem," Ghabra said.

"I don't want her death tied to Eternity in any way, and I don't want her to become a martyr to the Ager cause. Just make her disappear. No body for anyone to identify."

Both were silent, then Kant laughed. "Maybe I could work up a little scandal to go with her disappearance. Pictures with the Prince perhaps?"

Ghabra looked to the corner where the Prince was standing. "I'm sure he will oblige you."

The Prince nodded his assent.

"And my payment for taking on this risk?" Ghabra asked.

"I can help you stop the bombings."

The Prince stepped forward with his fists clenched. "You know who did this and you didn't tell us?" His father's eyes flew to him with disdain and a silent order passed between them. The Prince turned and stomped through the doors, exiting the terrace.

"What do you know?" Ghabra asked with dead calm. "Three hives gone and even my best people have been unable to find more than a few leads. It's not like the usual small hits by dissatisfied religious extremists. Whoever is doing this is very clever and they must have a hell of a lot of money and contacts. It's ruined my manufacturing. They've killed most of the workers now. And my bedding stables are ruined. "

"I've recently discovered a lead that no one has shared with you before," Kant said. "No one has dared tell you of this because it appears that someone in your inner circle is helping these terrorists.

"I see. And you did not see fit to share this with me until now?"

"As I said, *recently* discovered."

Kant waited, watching the play of emotion on Ghabra's face. It wasn't easy to read. Ghabra was practiced at hiding his feelings; but Kant could tell he was definitely interested.

When Ghabra stared back to the garden, Kant spoke again. "As a show of good faith, I'll tell you something now. Begin with Hassan."

Ghabra's teeth clenched and his face turned red. Kant knew he had hit home. Hassan was the number three man in Ghabra's organization.

"Then, it would be my honor to help you in this assignment," Ghabra said, his jaw tight. "We must pull together in times like these."

Yes, they did, Kant thought wearily as he signaled the guards at the door. They pushed the buzzer to unlock them.

He offered his hand and Ghabra shook.

"United we stand," Kant said, then turned on his heel and exited the terrace.

He would stand with Ghabra for now—for as long as he proved useful.

Kant paused and glanced around the room for Anna. There was no way of slipping in or out of any function, but everyone seemed to be pretending they hadn't noticed he'd been gone.

Finding Anna with Hurley. Kant coolly nodded his head toward her in acknowledgment. He noticed that Hurley was attempting to hold her attention and Anna didn't seem particularly pleased to be talking to him. Yes, Anna was bold as brass and full of personal magnetism when she wanted something, he thought. He doubted Hurley could even begin to hold his own with her. He walked toward them.

"Everything okay?" he asked Anna.

"Fine." She smiled brightly at Hurley. "Rushton was telling me about his latest tennis match, but I'm sure he's much more interested in what you and King Ghabra were discussing." She sipped her wine, her eyelashes batting like a virginal debutante. "Aren't you, Rushton?"

Hurley blinked. "Not at all. I had no-"

"No? Then I must have been mistaken." She slipped her arm through Kant's, easily disengaging herself from Hurley. "I think it's time to say my good night then." She looked up at Kant and ran her tongue along her lips. "Will you walk me to the door, please? It seems I've had one too many, and things are getting a bit mixed up." Over her shoulder, she gave Hurley a smile, "You'll excuse us?" She didn't wait for an answer as she gently nudged Kant forward.

Kant chuckled and walked with her toward the foyer. "What the hell are you up to?"

"You have everyone in the room wondering what you said to Ghabra. I'm just helping you move away from the questions, and you're helping me escape from Hurley's roaming hands."

"Hurley doesn't stand a chance against you, and I'm sure no man has ever touched you without your permission."

"Except you," she said. Her voice had a sweet edge to it.

Kant smiled as he acknowledged a couple waving at him across the room.

"It's more likely you're the one wondering what was said, not him."

"Sure I am," Anna confirmed. "But I'm sure you'll tell me if you think I need to know." She searched his expression and then shook her head. "Nope. I don't think I need to know. At least not right now."

She smiled when they reached the front of the room. "Thanks for the escort." She bowed just before mounting the three steps to the foyer, and then turned and walked toward the front door alone.

Kant stood for a moment, then smiled to himself. He should have expected both the curiosity and the perceptiveness. They knew each other so well. In many ways there were alike—both wanted power and both knew how to get it. Not for the first time, he wondered why Miki was the one leading the Agers and not Anna. He knew Anna's heart certainly wasn't involved with the Ager cause, but then when did that stop her from seeking power?

He chuckled again. She was a challenge...and he loved a challenge.

❧

MURU AND MIKI arrived at Coromandel, New Austra-land shortly before noon local time. The use of the ramjet for the long distances made the trip from New York to Coromandel only three hours. A solar car was waiting for them at the airstrip. Before heading to Whitianga, they stopped at a convenience store on the corner for take-out sandwiches and toiletries. Another wonder of travel in this part of New Austra-land was that most of the people had not converted to Kama as their primary source of nutrition. Miki was really looking forward to eating something more substantial.

"Why don't you get a little sleep while I drive," Muru suggested when they had settled into the car.

"I can't sleep now," Miki responded. "I was tired during the flight, but I want to enjoy the drive and the scenery before we meet Dr. Finn. It's only an hour and we can both catch up on sleep once we make the wharf and get our rooms for the night."

Formerly a gold mining and timber town in the early 20th century, Coromandel held no interest for Eternity—in fact outside of Auckland, the entire North Island was still too rugged and remote for them to find it useful. Populated primarily by fishing villages and beaches, the mines had long ago run out. Most of Eternity's elite just didn't find it profitable to pursue business interests there.

They left the native Maori to their customs, and felt that the rest of the population was probably safer here in their eccentric enclaves than trying to incorporate them into Eternity's larger plan. As long as they didn't try to influence anything, Eternity was happy to ignore them.

For the past hundred years this island had been a quiet haven for artists, crafts people, and conservationists—also a refuge for many Agers. Coromandel, Whitianga, and Whakatane were the primary Ager strongholds on the North Island.

Tomorrow, however, Miki and Muru would be visiting a top oceanographer living at Lonely Bay. She was well known and first published at the young age of sixteen when the Eternity virus swept the world. Because of her politics, she purposely left the spotlight after only thirty years at the university, pursuing her work in private until she joined the Agers. Miki was hoping she could offer some help with the Antarctica work.

As they drove along the coast, Miki reveled in the scenery. The island at the mouth of the gulf had acres of long, white sandy beaches on its eastern shore, deep-water sheltered inlets on its western shore, and a rugged spine of steep ridges running down the centre. From a previous trip, she remembered that natural hot springs, towering kauri forests and a serene aura made this island a perfect escape and the reason that many Agers chose to live there permanently. A succession of picturesque bays led them to their final stop. Muru pulled into the parking lot and climbed out of the car to check in.

He walked out of the office with two room keys. "The rooms are adjoining," Muru said as he handed her the key. "Lock your front door and put a chair in front of it. Our host said that yesterday someone was asking around about you—someone no one here has met before." Miki's eyes narrowed slightly, but she didn't say anything. "We'll enter and exit through my room," Muru continued. "I need a shower, then I'll be ready to eat. Your room or mine to enjoy those sandwiches?"

"I'll come to yours," she said, suddenly weary. "While you're in the shower I'll see if I can raise Anna on a secure link. I need to verify our contact is still in Lonely Bay and that no one has been asking around about her."

She didn't like the sound of what Muru had said, but she couldn't deal with it right now. She went into her room, shut the door, and locked it. She didn't move for a minute. After what seemed like several minutes, she pushed herself toward the small round mirror over the sink and worked on the knots in her hair. She felt as drained and lackluster as her appearance.

She sank down in the chair by a small desk and opened her 'puter. She tapped a two-digit code that immediately rang Anna, but it pinged back an "offline" response. She left a voice message with a code key, asking Anna to call her when she was available.

The week was finally catching up with her, she thought. And this was not an auspicious beginning for her travels as she tried to put the

Antarctica trip together. She laid her head on the desk and closed her eyes. She'd just take a little time to rest. Not long..."

"Are you all right?"

Her lids flew open and she saw Muru standing in the doorway of the adjoining room. She took a quick glance at her screen and noticed she'd been out only twenty-five minutes. "I'm fine. A little tired."

She gingerly moved her head from side to side. It had stiffened when she fell asleep on the desk. "I couldn't get in touch with Anna. Here, I'll try again."

"No." He crossed the room, flipped her screen down and handed her a sandwich. "Eat first. I don't know when you last ate, but I'm starved. We'll talk a little, make plans, and then you'll call Anna and I'll call Helios, and we can both catch up on sleep. You need to rest, Miki. You can't keep going like this."

"I'm not hungry." She picked up the tuna sandwich and unwrapped it with the plan to hand it to Muru. Then she smelled it— fresh tuna. "Or maybe I am. It looks pretty good." She bit into it and smiled. "Mmmmmm....I'd forgotten how good real food could be." For a few moments she could only hear her own chewing as she savored each bite. In what seemed like less than a minute, she found she had eaten the entire thing. She let out a surprising burp, then giggled.

"Must be really good." Muru smiled as he finished off his own sandwich. "You ate a little fast for someone who wasn't hungry."

Miki sat back in the chair and grinned from ear to ear, satisfied. For a few moments they just looked at each other. Finally, Miki looked away.

"You're right, Muru. I've been pushing both of us too hard. This is our fifth stop and I haven't let either of us sleep much. I'm getting punchy. We can get up at the break of dawn and hit the computer just before we head out to Lonely Bay."

Muru took her sandwich wrapper along with his and placed it in the recycler. He looked at his timer. "That should give us a good ten hours of sleep if we take advantage of it."

"No staying up at the 'puter, Miki."

She stretched and moved to the bed. "No worries. I'm dead."

Muru nodded and disappeared through the adjoining door.

MIKI STARTLED AWAKE. She struggled against the hand covering her mouth, and the body on top of her.

"Stop it," a voice whispered. "It's me. Rohin."

She stilled.

He switched on the small light next to the bed and she blinked him into focus. "What the hell? Get off me. How did you find me? How did.."

His hand covered her mouth again and he put a finger to his lips. "We don't want to wake Muru."

She nodded, her eyes wide as a hundred emotions went through her mind in a matter of seconds.

Slowly he moved off her, watching her as if she would suddenly spring at him and scream for help.

"How did you know where I was?" she asked again. This time her voice barely above a whisper. "What are you doing here?"

"Kant is planning to kill you. Here on the island." He reached for her, but she backed off the bed and stood.

"That's not possible. He doesn't know where I am."

He looked up at her, saying nothing.

"Right. You found me, that means Kant can find me."

Rohin nodded. "I'm not sure when or how, but they have your entire schedule here."

"And so, evidently, do you."

Miki finally put it all together. Somehow Rohin knew what Kant knew. Or did Rohin find out and tell Kant? She looked at him. No, he wouldn't hurt her. He promised and she believed him. She had a spy in her ranks. Again.

"Miki, come here," Rohin held out his hand.

She shook her head. "Look, I appreciate the warning, but you are not staying."

"Yes, I am," he said.

"No, you're not."

"It's not safe for me to leave," he said.

She swallowed. Of course it wouldn't be. He probably risked his life coming here.

Then she blanched. "The tracker."

She rushed to her bag and threw her toiletries into it. "I've got to get out. I've got to get Muru."

She started toward the adjoining door, but he stood between her and Muru. "The probe is gone," he said. "After the Qyzylqum incident, I found someone who could find it and remove it."

"But Anna reported that..." She stopped.

Rohin smiled. "I should have known. You have Anna spying for you." He chuckled. "I bet she's very good. That's exactly the kind of game she'd find challenging."

Miki sank to the bed. It seemed she couldn't keep anything from him. She was always letting down on her guard. It had been two months since they'd last been together, yet it felt like years...and only weeks at the same time.

She sighed and Rohin joined her on the bed. "So, where is the tracker? Kant still thinks it's inside you."

"Mostly in Rho Hive, being passed around from one person to another every few days. Every once in a while, Maritza passes it off to the Administrator in a small pocket of his luggage where he'd never find it. Then he carries it around for a few business trips just to make Kant think I can travel whenever I want."

"Maritza?"

He leaned toward her, a finger traced a single curl of her hair. "Jealous?"

She slapped his hand away. "Why would I be? We are not together. We can't be. You can be with whoever you want. I don't care." She turned her head away.

He turned it back and brushed his lips against hers. "Anyone I want?" He hovered within a centimeter of her lips.

She swallowed and gritted her teeth. She forced herself to look him in the eye. "Yes, anyone."

But she didn't mean it. She couldn't stand the thought of him with anyone else. She knew it wasn't fair to hold him. She knew she couldn't expect him to be celibate when she kept turning him away. Just because she often chose to go years without sex didn't mean he would.

He brushed her lips again. "Good, because the only one I want is you."

12

Miki had just closed her eyes when the flashing light got her attention. She checked her timer. 0300. Only one hour until Muru and she had planned to leave. She groaned and rolled over.

Rohin was gone.

She'd done it again. Despite all her promises to herself, she'd just spent the night tangled with Rohin in every which way. After they made love for the second time, she'd fallen asleep. She vaguely remembered him waking her to say goodbye before sneaking out of her room.

She grabbed the skinsuit and pulled it to the bed. She looked at the flashing light on her breast pocket and swore briefly. "This had better be good."

She swung her legs over the bed and wrapped herself in the sheet, then walked to her 'puter across the room. She entered the ten digit code to connect the caller. Almost immediately Helios appeared on her screen.

"Sorry to wake you," he said.

She nodded. "What you got?"

"I finally found it—the Ebla findings."

"Just a minute. I need to get Muru."

Miki turned away from the screen and shook her head from side to side, then patted her cheeks making sure she was alert. She knocked on the adjoining door and Muru, already dressed opened it. He raised an eyebrow in question.

"Don't ask," she said.

Then she turned back to the 'puter and pointed. "Helios has found something." She sat.

Muru joined her at the small table as she voiced the command "Record."

Helios began his briefing. He presented Miki with a more defined timeframe. He estimated the counter agent to have historically become available between 2100 BC. and 1900 BC. Armed with this information, Miki set in motion a search for the old research station on Antarctica.

The coordination of all the logistics was mind boggling, but the three of them had put everything in place when Helio started on this research. She had wanted to be ready, just in case it turned out as she'd hoped.

She, Muru, and Helios divided up the tasks now.

After packing and changing back into her clothes, Miki made calls to three geologists to begin research on the ice flows since the initial Eternity Virus study. Before global warming became so uncontrollable, it would have been easy to go back and find the exact site. But now the poles melted at an extremely fast rate, and that melting created a weather pattern that caused immense blizzards to cover or destroy any buildings at the site, thereby obscuring any landmark pointing to the location. In addition, the polar ice tended to shift as glaciers melted and broke away. Sometimes the debris would be carried hundreds of klicks away from the original coordinates. Since all the countries abandoned their research stations within sixty years of the Eternity virus being implemented, she was sure there would be no sign of buildings or equipment now.

Muru put in motion his contacts with the Ager security team, coordinating plans with transportation and supply and a safe way for getting people to Antarctica, setting up facilities, and establishing communications. It would be Winter there now, so getting in and out was next to impossible. But they had to be ready when the summer season opened two months from now, and without the notice of Eternity until the last possible moment.

For once, she was grateful Eternity had diverted the further development of reconnaissance satellites in favor of entertainment and other space-based communications. Miki was counting on Eternity's general belief in their economic and political invincibility.

The final hurdle was putting together the actual research team going to Antarctica. She had already selected twenty-three people with a combination of biomed and geology education. Helios agreed to follow up with all of them now that they had an actual timeline in place.

"Let's go." Miki stuffed a map into her jacket as she closed the door to her room.

The last piece of the puzzle was to meet with the New Austra-land oceanographer, Dr. Finn. Finn had no loyalties to either the Agers or Eternity, but Miki knew that getting her cooperation was paramount to their success. Dr. Finn was very careful about sending directions. She wanted to wait until the last possible moment. They probably arrived some time in the morning, when she and Rohin were...

Miki sighed. She hadn't heard her 'puter beep with a message. But then with Rohin demanding all of her attention, she probably wouldn't have heard it if fireworks had exploded from the thing.

Muru followed Miki with the bags as they left the motel and walked toward the wharf. Miki reviewed Dr. Finn's credentials as they walked.

It was the paper she wrote for *Atmospheric and Oceanic Sciences* that had caught Helios' attention. She'd submitted a proposal to the Global Entertainment Foundation for Natural Science, GEFNS, suggesting that the cruise ships that visited Antarctica were not negatively impacting the environment as long as landing parties were kept to one hundred or less. Then she asked the World Council for eighty-five million gurons to establish a new research station and to seed a new crusing industry to the continent. Her proposal had already received favorable approval by the Enviro24—twenty-four countries that provided research funding on the global environment and entertainment impacts.

When they reached the end of the wharf, Miki pointed to a small speed boat tied at the wharf. Then easily stepped into it and sat at the wheel. "This must be it."

Muru eyed the craft warily.

"I haven't driven one of these for at least half a century," she said.

"You sure we can get to that island and back in this little thing," Muru asked.

Miki laughed as he finally lowered himself to the bench still holding onto the pier as the boat rocked slightly. He settled into the seat and immediately found the life jacket and tied it securely.

"I've heard Dr Finn is rather eccentric," Miki said as she turned the key and revved the engines.

"Or she's just crazy," Muru offered, bracing his hands on the gunwales.

"Maybe. But for us she's brilliant crazy."

"How so?"

"If we can somehow buy cruise ships already licensed to take tourists to Antarctica, it will give us a way to drop off a couple hundred people to do research through the summers. With Dr. Finn's credentials, she would also be allowed aboard as teaching staff and that would give us a way to do our research as well. Because of her climate studies, she would naturally be taking ice core samples."

"Do you really know how to drive this thing?" Muru asked.

"I won't make any promises," she said. "But I do know how to swim. So, if the boat sinks there is at least a fifty-fifty chance I'll not let you drown." With that she cast off the lines, started the engine like she did this everyday, and began moving the boat across the water toward a small point that could bearely be seen from the dock.

It was a good hour and a half later that she noticed the warning buoy. A huge mesh web that looked like net, but upon closer inspection was solid rods of some type. The cross-hatch pattern stretched from shore to shore across the entire opening of the small bay and it stood a good six feet above the surface of the water. On top of the rods were foot long, spear-like structures or spikes that looked like they could really hurt you if you tried to climb over the top.

"So what do we do now?" Muru murmured. "Nothing will cut those rods."

"We wait." She cut the motor of the speedboat. "I left a message on her 'puter that we were coming. It's her move. We may be out here awhile."

Her gaze fastened on the small elliptical structure hugging the shore. It looked like a giant piece of river-washed stone jutting out of the landscape. The only thing that suggested it might be something else was a faint trail of smoke snaking over the top from behind the structure.

"Geez, this is a beautiful place," Miki whispered as if talking would jar that illusion. Jewel-blue water, green mountains, and tropical breezes swaying the trees. It was like something from a travel brochure. She closed her eyes for just a moment and let her sense of smell and touch take in all the sensations.

"Hey, I see a woman heading for the pier." Muru's observation woke her from her reverie.

Miki placed a hand at her forward to shield the sun's glare. Yes, the woman wore khaki shorts and a tank top. Her feet were bare. She was tall and sturdily built, with shining black flowing hair loosely tied with what appeared to be only a piece of string. She jumped into the motorboat at the pier and took off. She breathed competence, forcefulness, and vitality as she gunned the boat toward them.

The woman stopped fifteen meters on the other side of the net and studied them. Miki knew from her research the woman was at least two hundred forty years old, but her biological age looked to be about fifty-five. Her huge, dark eyes exuded definite boldness in the cool glance she was giving Miki.

"Miki Yokoyama?" she shouted across the barrier.

Miki nodded.

"You don't look like the picture I've seen of you on the 'casts."

"God, I hope not," Miki said. "It's been a few years."

The boat came closer to the barrier, so they wouldn't have to shout quite as loud.

"So, you want to piggy-back on my research." Elsie said. "I know a little about the Agers, and I'm not so sure I want to put myself in the limelight like that. Some people may think I'm keeping bad company."

"Depends on who you listen to," Miki grinned. "We might be trouble, but we can also make your proposal a reality. I have the staff and the financial resources to begin this cruising business within a few months. If you wait for someone else, it could take years or even decades before you get your chance."

It seemed like several minutes before Elsie finally nodded assent. "Alright, I'll give you a couple hours to convince me of your plan. Then you leave and I'll let you know in a week."

"You can trust us," Miki stared at her openly. "We don't want to get caught any more than you do."

"I don't trust you're not with Eternity." Elsie was silent a moment and then shrugged. "But I don't have a lot of other choices right now."

She started the boat and skimmed along the bars until she reached a spot a few meters from where Miki and Muru waited. She bent over the side of the boat, and a moment later a three meter section of bar slowly retreated below the surface.

"Start your motor and then cut it when you reach the entrance," Elsie instructed. "Then coast over the bars with the engine out of the water." She paused. "If you don't coast, the retractable spikes will put holes in your boat. They're set to engage anything with a motor in the water or traveling faster than the current. Believe me, you'll sink quickly."

Miki obeyed. The moment they were on the other side of the entrance Elsie reached back into the water and the bars returned to their former height with spikes intact at the top. Then, without another word, she turned her boat around and sped back toward the shore.

"I guess that means we follow." Miki dropped the engine in the water again and started it up. Even at top speed she didn't catch Dr. Finn before she tied up.

By the time Miki and Muru reached the pier, Elsie was striding toward the stone structure on the other side. She glanced over her shoulder. "Come on. I can't be dallying all day. I have things to do."

"Sorry." Muru helped Miki tie up the boat as he was the first one off. "I won't be hurt if we don't get inside too fast," he said.

Miki chuckled as she double checked Muru's knots. "She's not offering us tea, but it seems we have a chance to convince her. Let's just see if we can state our cause in under two hours."

When they arrived at the rock-like structure, Miki could finally see a small entrance at the back. They gingerly entered the door and stopped for a moment to let their eyes adjust to the darkness of the interior. She could see only one window that looked out toward the bay. Other than that, all the light for the building was provided only by sun streaming through multiple overhead skylights. A spot of sunlight highlighted a desk piled with data disks and a larger than average 'puter. Another lighted area was over what appeared to be a dining table—though it looked more like a large tree trunk with four large branches that had been cut level just enough to put down a plate or a cup of kama. One other lighted area was in the middle of a hallway that led to some other part of the building.

Elsie was tapping her foot in the hall as if she'd been waiting hours for their arrival. "Start talking," she said. "Just summarize and that will be sufficient."

"Well, we would like..." Miki started.

"Forget the niceties, just blurt it out," Elsie interrupted. "I don't have a lot of time."

Miki stared her in complete silence, as if daring her to push further. Finally, after counting to thirty she spoke. "Let's stop with the games, Dr. Finn. We are not going to be intimidated by rudeness or bad temper. We came for a reason, and we both already know you want to work with us at some level or you wouldn't have let us come. Now, can we all sit down and have a civil conversation?"

Elsie blinked. Then she threw her head back with raucous laughter that shook her entire slender frame.

"Maybe I do trust you ... a little. At least you don't bullshit. Call me Els." She crossed the room and threw the front door closed. "Come in and have a lemonade. It's fresh."

"We'd rather have conversation," Muru said as they followed her and sat at the unusual dining table. "And your full cooperation."

"Then you'll be disappointed. I never fully cooperate with anyone." She went toward the kitchen and opened the fridge. "So take the lemonade and let's see what happens."

"Thank you," Miki said and she pitched a pointed gaze at Muru, silently telling him to shut up and listen.

"We need your help," Miki began. She outlined her plan and the mutual benefits of them working together, filling in as many details as she thought might be helpful. After a little more than an hour, Elsie held up a hand.

"You don't need to say anymore." Her lips tightened. "Thanks to Eternity most of my countrymen are without work or livelihoods, but they will not bow to the pressure of drugs and entertainment to keep them satisfied. Most of them have also chosen not to take the Eternity virus or to have their children take it. I can't trust Eternity, and I probably can't really trust my own government as it is practically owned by Eternity already. If we weren't such a small island and it wasn't so difficult to move great numbers of people, we would probably be their next industrial site."

Elsie stood and poured another round of drinks. "The question is, can I trust you? I can see from the 'casts that you are not on Eternity's top ten favorites list. So I figure you can't be all bad. You're going to be moving fast and trying your best to take Kant down. Right?"

"Yes."

Elsie rolled her shoulders back and took in a deep breath. "All right. I'll tell you then that my proposal was accepted just yesterday. I'm preparing to travel next month. You begin your cruise preps and I'll get all the research equipment we both need. I'll submit the names of the five people you gave me as half of my research team.

Those five must come on the first ship. I think it's best that we do not contact each other again until we are both in Antarctica."

"Right." Miki agreed.

Elsie led the way back to the pier outside her home. "I'll take you back and lower the barrier."

"Are you totally alone on this island?" Muru asked. "I'm surprised no one's investigated you."

"Oh, I've been investigated—so to speak. Once two boatloads of assholes came to teach me a lesson after I wrote a particularly telling research article about the effects of growing population on the climate and these industrial zones that Eternity runs. I think they just wanted to teach me a lesson or make me an example on their next 'cast of some illegal researcher. Fortunately, I have a few good hiding places in Lonely Bay, so they didn't catch me. But they did destroy my last house and most all of my equipment. That's when I built this one to look like one huge stone. It's pretty hard to get into if I don't want you in. At the same time I built the barrier. Not only is it difficult to get through with the rods and the spikes, but it's also electrified. If you're lucky enough to get past that, I also have a couple of laser towers in front of the house that can pop up and disable a boat in less than ten seconds when it's within one hundred yards of the dock."

"Laser towers?" Muru gulped.

Elsie laughed. "I haven't killed anyone. The lasers just disable, not kill—unless of course the idiots are standing in the boat and fall overboard after being hit." She smiled so big all of her teeth seemed to show.

Her boat peeled out over the water, rushing toward the mesh barrier.

Miki and Muru followed. When Elsie let down the barrier, they repeated the process of raising the engine and coasting over the barrier. Before they could even start their engine again it was back in place. Miki glanced back at Elsie to thank her, but she was already skimming toward her rock house.

Twilight burnished the waves and bathed the woman and her light-colored boat in a golden haze. "Beautiful." Miki said. "I wonder what it must be like to live on an island and be able to close everyone out."

"It didn't sound like the choice was really hers," Muru said. "The island concept is nice, but it seldom works. Civilization always interferes, emotion interferes."

Miki thought of how she'd been wrapped in Rohin's arms this morning. How wonderful it would be for the two of them to escape to an island like this. Safe. Secure behind the mesh screen and the laser towers.

She sighed. "I'd still like to try it sometime."

Muru shook his head. "You couldn't stand it, Miki. You're too involved with living life, and making it worth living for the rest of us. You couldn't ever stay away for more than a couple of weeks."

Miki started the engine and slowly headed back toward the mainland. Her thoughts on Rohin, his hands all over her and wondering when she would see him again.

After about twenty minutes on the water, she noticed two rigid hull inflatables heading toward them at a fast speed. She squinted her eyes to make out what looked like four people in each one. Momentarily, she wondered if they were just kids racing in the water. Then she saw the mounted gun turrets.

"Tarful! Muru get down!" She yelled, then gunned the engine and made a ninety degree turn out of their intersecting path. The boat skipped across the water as she pushed the engine to its limit, but she could see they were gaining. Her only choice was to somehow return to Lonely Bay and get behind the rods that Elsie had protecting herself. She made another ninety degree turn and headed back at full speed.

Muru immediately picked up on the plan and put in a call to Elsie. Miki couldn't hear what he was saying, but he was nodding his head. She was trusting this was somehow going to work out without being killed by Elsie's mesh, or hauled to an I2 building by Eternity agents.

Muru completed the call then carefully made his way toward Miki and yelled animatedly. She blanched at the suggestions but figuring they had only moments to execute a plan, it was her only choice. A stream of warning fire strafed across the bow. They were ordering her to stop and be boarded. She did not slow down.

Miki could see the steel net now. She headed straight toward it at full speed as the inflatables closed on her position.

When she was within twenty feet, she and Muru jumped off the boat and dove straight down. She could feel the explosion above their heads as the boat crashed into the electrified rods. Her ears weren't clearing fast enough as they continued to dive lower. She pinched her nose closed with two fingers and blew. Finally she felt the pop, but the effort used the last of her lung capacity.

Her lungs began to hurt, she figured she could probably last only twenty more seconds without air. She wasn't one to panic, but she couldn't stay down any longer. She kicked toward the surface to get air—drowning was not an option. She only hoped the inflatables weren't going to be on top of her when she popped to the surface.

Muru grabbed her ankle and pulled her back. She kicked at him angrily and mimed no air. He pointed to his lips then hers. Miki's eyes widened as she realized what he would try to do. She'd heard of the maneuver in an old dive book but she'd never had to use it. He pulled her head toward her, sealed his lips to hers and blew the rest of his air into her. Then he grabbed her hand and pointed to a circular break in the rods that seemed to be connected to a 4 foot diameter pipe. He motioned that they would swim into the pipe.

She let him lead her in, hoping that Elsie's plan wasn't a trap because there would be no turning back now. The minute they were both inside, a door closed behind them. She looked in both directions alarmed there was now no way out and no way to surface. Her eyes widened in panic as she looked directly at Muru.

Whoosh.

She felt herself pulled to the bottom of the pipe like gravity had suddenly increased three fold, then the water suddenly drained away. On their hands and knees, trying to keep balance, they both coughed and gasped for air. Within moments the door at the other end opened and Elsie was standing, hunched over.

"Good thing you trusted me," she smiled. "Your friends have donned diving equipment and are searching the area looking for your bodies."

Muru and Miki stood hunched over in the four foot tall space.

"Follow me," Elsie turned and walked back along the length of the pipe. "It's a bit of a walk, but it's all pretty dry. After a hundred yards or so the pipe widens and you can stand up." She looked back over her shoulder. "You okay?"

"Yeah... thanks." Miki said, still gulping air as if it might suddenly disappear again. She saw the pipe door close behind them, then heard the sound of water rushing in behind the door. It squeaked with the burden.

She shrugged and continued to follow Elsie. "I guess you weren't kidding about a few hiding places."

"This is one of the older ones, not quite so nice as some of the others. But it has its interesting features. The noise you heard was my next surprise for your visitors. As the divers come to investigate, it will dump out foul smelling sludge. Nothing bad for the environment, but they'll think I'm dumping sewage and won't spend anytime trying to investigate. I hope some of it gets on their wetsuits. It has a way of sticking to polypropelene." She grinned.

Elsie straightened to her full height ahead of them. She turned and smiled. "I told you could stand up soon."

Miki rushed forward, anxious to stretch again.

"I'll put you up until your Eternity friends have given up," Elsie said. "It may be a couple of days though. They looked like pros."

"Thank you," Muru said. "I need a rest. Besides, Miki was just saying how she wanted to try the island thing for awhile."

13

———

Maritza and Rohin sat in a circle on the floor with fifteen other members. Crossed legs, knee to knee, and hands joined, Maritza led the opening meditation.

"Bring us together to abolish evil."

"We dedicate our lives to the light."

"Give us strength to support each other as we lead others out of the darkness."

"We dedicate our lives to the light."

"Now each one's supplications...Destroy those who bring horror to children," she offered the first one.

"We dedicate our lives to the light."

"Bring peace to women of the hives," Rohin offered.

"We dedicate our lives to the light."

"Strengthen the men to retreat from the demands of industry," the next voice whispered while choking back tears.

"We dedicate our lives to the light."

A stranger entered and waited as each of the fifteen offered their entreaty. When they were finished, they opened their eyes, and he stepped into the room.

"I am Johari. May I join?" he asked, his eyes downcast. "I come from the side of darkness and evil, but I wish to seek the light."

Maritza stood and nodded holding out her hand. The rest of the circle then stood and the one nearest him, led him into the center. She hugged him and said "Welcome to the light," then put his hand in that of the person next to her. The next person did the same, and he was passed from one person to the next in the same manner until all had greeted him.

ANNA CHECKED her timer before exiting the hover. 2030. She looked up at the imposing mansion that was Kant's home. She knew it was important to talk to him immediately or the plan could easily be waylaid.

Kant's home was even more secure than Eternity headquarters. Anna figured he felt less at ease alone in his house than he did surrounded by the large Eternity structure and thousands of workers. But Anna had wanted to meet him here, where she had more of an advantage.

Kant's home security required her to pass three levels of security staff personnel, as well as the identigraph. After twenty-five minutes she was finally escorted to his study.

"What's the rush to see me, Hollinrake?" Kant asked irritated. "Has something come up about Chawla?"

"Rohin?" Anna questioned, surprised that he would be brought up.

"Yes," Kant said brusquely. "Since we learned he disabled the tracking probe, you had accepted the assignment to keep tabs on him. Remember?"

She waved her fingers in the air as if the request was useless. "Oh yes, I remember. I think last I heard he'd started some religious commune in New Mexico." Anna snickered with disdain. "I think he's trying to help people realize their own potential, or some such rubbish. In any case, he's useless and not a threat to us. But that's not the reason for my request to report at this time."

"If you're not reporting on Chawla then why couldn't you wait to see me Tuesday at my office as planned?" Kant questioned.

"I may not be able to leave the Ager group for several days without arousing their suspicions," Anna said, with growing impatience at having to observe protocol with Kant. She stood tall and raised her chin. "In case it still matters, I'm now officially part of the inner circle."

"Remarkable," Kant looked at her with admiration. "You've proven to be most resourceful. Another bonus will be put into your account. So, what important news do you have?"

"I believe the Agers are about to make an important move," she began cautiously, selecting and analyzing each word before uttering it. "I'm not certain what is being planned, but I think it's big. And I intend to be a part of it."

"Yes . . . yes," Kant motioned for her to continue but to hurry it up. He had moved from behind his desk and stood very close to her now, so he could carefully read her expressions as she spoke.

"They intend to set up some sort of tourist attraction in Antarctica," she continued.

"Antarctica?" Kant's voice sounded higher. His nostrils flared and he took a step backward. "Can they find something there? Why else would they want to go to that frozen place?"

"At the moment they're planning a tourist museum touting the Eternity Virus discovery," Anna answered calmly.

She loved catching him off guard. It gave her a sense of power. She loved feeding into his paranoia about losing control of his vast empire. He was so much easier to manipulate this way.

"Miki found out about Finn's research approval and some new company named Circle Lines is going to be running the cruises. They plan to take advantage of the tourist trade by setting up a museum describing how the virus was found and how it works to assist the natural human immune system."

"Ridiculous!" Kant shouted at her, as if she could change the plan.

"I won't allow this. Their only aim is to discredit us. Is Miki Yokoyama behind this?"

"I'm sure it's not her idea," Anna lied. Then she lightly touched Kant's arm, and lowered her voice to a conspiratorial whisper. "I think you might want to go along with this," she said. "If we can have one of your own people directly involved with the museum, like greeting the visitors and checking the ships and the compound . . ." she let her voice trail off suggestively.

"Yes, if I put someone there who knows the Agers by sight, and is accepted by them," Kant continued her thought. "That person can provide me with information about every step of the Ager plan." His eyes gleamed with satisfaction.

"Great idea," Anna approved. "May I suggest, sir, that you select one of your best and most trusted agents. We don't want to accidentally tip our hand."

Kant looked at Anna and smiled knowingly. "Why not you?"

"Me?" Anna responded, pretending surprise. "I'm flattered. But I'm not sure if I can arrange it." She paused and turned away. "I only recently made it to the inner circle. I don't want to jeopardize my status."

"Hmmm...I see your point," Kant replied.

Anna turned back toward him slowly, then saw the twinkle in his eye that indicated he already had a plan.

"I know you, Hollinrake. If it will meet your needs, as well as mine, you'll find some way to make it work." He snickered. "Yes, I see through you too. We are two of a kind, you and I. I wouldn't turn my back on you; but as long as I pay you well, I think you'll serve me. Let me know your decision within the week."

"Of course, sir," she returned more formally. "Good night." She turned and quickly exited, not giving him a chance to respond or to give her permission to leave. She wanted to be last to score.

Kant was an excellent game player, she thought to herself. *When I finally replace him I'll almost miss him. Almost . . . but the power will make up for it.* She tossed her head, and with a broad smile she cruised past the guards and out the front door.

14

---

ix months later

Waiting for the next Vernal Service to begin, Rohin watched Johari smooth the white cassock down his torso and hips, his hand lingering at the folds of the hood which draped down his back. A useful costume, Rohin thought. Though it seemed silly to resort to such timeworn symbolism to captivate attention, it was an integral part of the theatrics that brought him into contact with the people he needed for his mission. Johari was well-suited for this role, and Rohin was glad for it. Though he agreed with the need, he doubted he could carry off the role without feeling dishonest.

His eyes strayed to the window in the suite at the pinnacle of the Church of Dreams. He looked up at the ever-present brown sky above. He could barely remember blue skies, clouds. Even sunsets were dull now. The dull red sun often dipped behind the horizon often without any colors.

Air pollution had long ago broken past the troposphere into the stratosphere. He doubted it could ever be eliminated again. He wasn't even sure it was possible to improve the skies anymore.

What would Miki think of the Church of Dreams? He was certain she knew about it. He hadn't tried to hide the Church from anyone—

Eternity or the Agers. He expected both groups had their spies among the dreamers, just as he already had his own spies in their organizations. It was all a nightmare game of politics. The difference was that Eternity still had the upper hand.

Rohin imagined Miki would understand the underlying context —the need to bring hope to humanity again, the need to build a better future without Eternity at the helm. But she probably wouldn't approve of the tactics. Her world never had allowed for many greys. For Miki decisions were black and white, right or wrong. For him, it had always been grey. He thought he could work within the greys to improve the world. Sometimes he won. A lot of times he lost.

His decision to take over her job at Eternity was a prime example. He knew she would be hurt, but he believed she would understand that at least one of them remaining embedded with Eternity was the only way they could stop the genocide. But she didn't buy it. She ran away and started the Agers. He stayed and failed miserably at stopping it. Had either of them succeeded? Not yet it seemed.

Miki believed Eternity was evil and that staying within their walls allowed that evil to overtake you. She thought they should leave together and fight outside of Eternity. Black and white. But Rohin saw the grey. The hope that he could still make a difference. The belief that there were still many leaders who could be turned toward the light. He'd been wrong then. Was he wrong now to embrace the greys and use The Church of Dreams to accomplish his mission?

"Earth to Rohin," Johari interrupted his meditations. "Anything out there I should be worried about?" He joined him at the window.

Rohin looked down from the seventh story suite to the long line of people snaking around the building. He estimated there were probably five hundred waiting to attend this Dreamer service. The Vernal service was used specifically for new recruits, so he was always interested in the people waiting in line.

Rohin heard the buzz of the intercom in his room. "Open," he said to the MC.

"Rohin?" He immediately recognized Maritza's voice. "Is Johari there?"

"Yes, he's beside me waiting for your signal to enter the service."

"Zoom in on the first third of the line," she said.

Rohin pressed a button near the viewing window and the glass zoomed to twenty times magnification. He stopped and focused his gaze on a small group just outside the entrance door. There were two men and one woman arguing with each other—at least it looked like they were arguing, although he couldn't be sure from this height.

"I have it," he spoke again. "What am I looking for?"

"I see him," Johari said as he pointed to the taller man in the group. "That's Dr. Leonard Yeske. Remember? You asked me to make sure he had a special incentive to come to a service."

Rohin now focused his gaze on the man. Dr. Yeske, he recalled, had been one of the top ocean habitat researchers before the discovery of the Eternity Virus. He was one of the few successful developers of deep sea living and research stations. Unfortunately the last station, which contained living modules and research facilities for over one hundred people, had been decommissioned by Eternity over seventy-five years ago. Consequently, thousands of scientists were no longer employed in their fields of expertise.

Only a few of the top scientists had been offered other research positions in Eternity's labs. The others had been left to fend for themselves—which usually meant they could find no suitable employment and were relegated to the general entertainment industry. If they were lucky, their well-honed skills would find some meager use in public marine-life museums and zoos. Similarly, astronomers had been relegated to offering star-gazing tours to remote hikers. Space engineers were completely unemployable, except the one or two still tracking ancient satellites. And other scientists considered themselves fortunate to find positions as technical advisors to vid productions like Star Trek 2800.

"This is very good," he said, finally breaking his silent reverie. "Do you recognize the other two with him."

"No," Johari said. "Maritza?"

"They may be Yeske's previous colleagues," Maritza offered. "He's been known to only associate with those who had done research with him before."

Over the past two months Rohin had noticed that scientists who attended the Vernal services often came as part of a group of colleagues. Rohin wondered if they believed the support of their fellow scientists would ensure they were not deceived by pseudo-magical occurrences.

Scanning further down the line, Rohin looked for other scientists he might recognize; but the remaining attendees seemed to be the usual entertainment seekers. It would be nice, he thought, if there were several more scientists in the line. Previous experience had shown they were the best candidates for permanent conversion.

Contrary to Miki's admonition, Rohin had found large numbers of people who were willing, if not eager, to venture beyond the confines of Eternity's dictates. He only hoped he could reach enough of them and prepare them in time. He wasn't sure what the time-frame was; but he could feel its limitation as though it had physical walls closing around him.

Within moments the sweet welcoming melody sounded throughout the building and the doors opened automatically to admit the line of people. As Rohin watched them enter the downstairs auditorium the sun dipped below the horizon—another dull red sky turned grey, and the Church of Dreams pyramid lit up with the colors of sunsets past—oranges, reds, purples swirled across the glass. The people below looked up in awe.

This building was the headquarters for his mission. Standing as a sentinel against the sky, its singular location dominated the high desert landscape—reminiscent of the ancient pyramids of Egypt.

Rohin had carefully selected this geometry because of its symbolism throughout religious history. Although originally a tomb design for ancient Egyptian royalty, the pyramid shape still evoked a mystical quality—one with memories of unexplained powers and great wisdom. Even those who professed no belief in religion or superstition could not deny the ancient urgings of the collective unconscious. Early in his planning, Rohin realized he could use the symbolism of the pyramid to lure thousands of people to the Church of Dreams.

The Church of Dreams had the reputation of being a new entertainment, and something much more. The rumor was that whoever entered the pyramid departed a changed person—not physical but spiritual. There were also many reports that some individuals entered and never returned. It turned out that the myriad of rumors was a better recruiter for the Dreamers than any advertisement could be.

In only four months Dreamer membership had grown from one hundred to over six thousand. While one cadre of scientists worked on projects to move people off planet, another worked on projects to make earth a more hospital place to live. It was the second group that produced the money products—money that was sorely needed to the Dreamers to continue their work and to take care of thousands of people in the hives. In fact, membership was growing so quickly that Rohin had recently commissioned the building of three more churches in strategic regions around the world.

Rohin watched the end of the line go out of his sight. He turned from the window and embraced Johari. "Ten minutes. Are you ready?"

"I'm always ready," Johari said. "With Dr. Yeske in this audience everything must be perfect."

"I think we need to change some of the subliminals," Rohin said. "Maritza? Can you get the media changed in the next ten minutes?"

Maritza yelled to someone in media.

"I want the subliminals changed to include the words: 'Oceans of space' and 'Ocean space habitats'," Rohin said. "Also, be sure the dream sequence draws a parallel between the ocean habitats and the planetary biospheres."

"Do you want all the subliminals changed to this?" Maritza asked doubtfully. "I wish you had talked about this when we began recruiting Yeske."

Rohin could tell she was somewhat hostile to the quick work required by his request, but it was important to use everything at his disposal to get Yeske and others like him.

"I didn't think he'd come so quickly," Rohin said, adding a little apology to his voice. "But with Johari's great help, he's here now."

Maritza sighed. "Yes, Johari is the best recruiter we have."

Rohin smiled. Maritza and Johari had hit it off immediately, and it was only a few short weeks and they'd already chosen to become a bonded couple. Rohin knew he was very fortunate. They worked tirelessly and both had become invaluable to the work of the Dreamers.

"Just a few subliminals," Rohin said. "Maybe twenty percent or so. We don't want to overdo it." He paused, waiting to see if she had other questions. "Today we will add some very important dreamers to our fold—dreamers who will change our world."

Johari moved toward the transit tube. He silently signaled the special effects manager. He exchanged a smile with Rohin. "Don't worry," he said. "It'll be perfect. We have this down. Yeske will join us tonight."

Rohin nodded his head.

"Are you ready?" Maritza's voice softened.

Rohin swallowed, wishing Miki were here with him, guiding him like Maritza did with Johari. Meeting him at night, sharing the same goals. Making love, reveling in their triumphs. He shook his head. Miki was stubbornly set on her own path. His life with Miki could only be the occasional surprise. She would never turn him away from her bed, but he knew she would also never join his cause.

"Live the dream!" Maritza said with confidence as Johari entered the tube.

"Dream on," Johari answered with the customary response.

"Yes, dream on." Then she closed the connection.

Johari turned as the door closed in front of him. He stretched his arms toward the heavens, his palms facing in, and the tube began to move downward. Rohin went to his desk and turned on the viewing screen. He settled back for the show to begin. Johari would be mesmerizing. He always was.

In the large auditorium, specially constructed with an elevated three hundred sixty degree stage, the ceiling lights dimmed to black and the conversations ceased. Only the diffused light of the stage floor remained, focusing all eyes to the center as the music swelled. A fog curled over the edge of the stage as a spotlight directed all eyes upward. Johari descended from darkness near the roof, without apparent support. He appeared as a white cloaked figure with arms outstretched. The lights changed and bathed him in the palest rose color and the music slowly quieted, leaving the congregation with the subliminal messages of *love, trust, hope.*

Invisible to the audience, the tube allowed Johari to slowly reach the raised stage in the center of the room as if he had control of gravity. He turned leisurely, greeting each side of the room, and then the tube invisibly opened to allow his exit. Once he stepped forward the tube retracted silently through the ceiling.

The audience's eyes were riveted to his cloaked figure as he moved slowly about the outer rim of the stage. The lights illuminated his outstretched arms. As he pointed toward someone, a ray of light appeared to connect from his hand to illuminate the member's face. Doing this made it seem as though he were cherishing each new member individually. On occasion, he would reach out both hands and select a specific person, then a holographic halo of light would descend upon the individual as he reached toward them. It would disappear when he turned away to reach toward the next chosen member. He could hear a gasp each time this happened, creating the illusion that he had actually touched someone though he was several meters away. Completing the circle, he lowered his arms to his side and bowed his head. Then he fell to his knees, and finally lay prostrate on the floor.

His body shook and his voice cried out in agony, imbuing the audience with his mourning. "I cry for our world," he began. "I cry for our people. I cry for the hope you have lost."

The music swelled and hidden subliminals whispered *pain, hopelessness, tears.* Johari continued to shake and cry until he could hear sniffles around him. He allowed the feelings of sadness to encompass the audience for a full three minutes before moving again.

Then he slowly rose to his knees, his features seemingly etched with the pain of the ages as he reached toward his audience, turning to face each quarter of the auditorium and silently begging them to listen to his next words.

"I beg for your forgiveness. I beg for your help. I beg for your hope." Again he fell prostrate to the floor as if he could no longer stand the agony; and the music swelled once more.

Now the subliminals suggested a chant: *help the child, help the man, help the world*. Soon Rohin heard an occasional muffled whisper from members of the audience, "Help him... help him." A woman stood and cried out. A spotlight immediately caught her with tears streaming down her face.

"I can't reach you," she cried. "I can't move. Help him! Help him!" Then she fell to the ground, silent.

"I'll help."

"I want to help."

"Yes, please let me help."

Other people stood and reached out to him, then attempted to move toward the stage, but ushers quickly moved in to restrain them, soothing their desires with promises of hope as they led participants back to their seats.

As if being pulled by the audience's urgency, Johari struggled back to his knees and painfully rose to a standing position. He walked shakily around the rim of the stage, slowly gaining new strength as the number of voices grew and shouted, "I'll help. I'll help. Tell me what to do. I'll help."

With each infusion of good will he strengthened a little more. He smiled a silent thanks to carefully selected audience members. As he began a second circle around the stage, Johari's new found strength became self-evident. The lighting cast a pale blue aura about him, showing him mystically transforming from a physical being to a ghostly spiritual entity. The audience gasped as it appeared they could see through him. Now the frenzy began, as several members were swaying back and forth, crying and screaming, "Take me. I'll help. Take me."

As he basked in the glow of the audience's desire, his body became whole again—all ghostly images removed. Then he smiled as broad as possible, which sent a surreptitious signal to the ushers to begin the selection process. Quickly, Dreamer assistants moved to help a few participants to the center stage.

The Church of Dreams' MC link had been processing the participants' sounds and movements via directional microphones and vid units that ringed the hall. Maritza directed the ushers, by audiocom, to those seats where the offers to help originated. She specifically tracked Dr. Yeske and made sure he was included. As these chosen ones were led to the stage, Johari embraced each one enthusiastically which resulted in a halo of light surrounding the chosen one. As he moved to the next person, an assistant placed a red cassock over the previous person's clothing then led him or her to a circle illuminated on the floor. Each chosen one was greeted by a new assistant who shepherded the participants to form a circle around the outer edge, facing toward Johari in the middle.

When all the chosen were assembled, they formed a circle around the outer edge of the stage.

In the middle, his arms outstretched, Johari addressed the circle. "Welcome dreamers. You are the chosen! You have the vision! You have the dreams!"

Now the subliminals were urging the audience to focus on the circle of celebrants, saying *Dream with them. Dream their hope. Dream their fear. Dream their rise to saviors.*

"Help us to dream," Johari continued addressing the circle. "Dream us a world of hope. Save us, Dreamers!"

All the lights darkened at once and a large, holographic spinning prism appeared in the center of the circle above Johari's head. The audience, and particularly the circle members, were drawn to watch the spinning prism as it released bolts of blue, green, and red lightning across the room.

"Look into the dream," Johari directed both the audience and the circle members. "Look into the dream spinner and see what the chosen ones will tell us. Join with the World Dreamers."

As everyone focused their eyes at the spinning prism, Johari provided the hypnotic cadence required to lead them into a group trance.

Rohin shifted in his seat and bit his lower lip. This part of the performance was where Rohin always felt the most uncomfortable.

When they'd started the church together, Rohin didn't know of Johari's talents as a hypnotist. Johari and Maritza convinced him that using a group trance would speed the process of recruiting. Of course, they'd been right, but Rohin wondered if the hypnosis encumbered free will. He wanted people to choose to be part of his mission. He didn't want them to be deceived. Yes, he manipulated their feelings with ancient symbolism, but so did novels and movies. Most people knew the difference between the fantasy of a book and the reality of decision. But with hypnosis Rohin wasn't as sure that everyone made a true choice.

Johari promised that the hypnosis was only temporary. It was no more unethical than the use of subliminals, which were used in all types of entertainments—not just at the Church of Dreams. In the past four months, they'd not lost a single member who'd come to them through hypnosis. Rohin had tested them, tried to talk them out of their decision, done everything he could to make sure they were each choosing the Church of Dreams with their own free will. He'd grown to accept the necessity of the hypnosis as part of the show, but he still felt uncomfortable with the need.

Johari now signaled the holographic projectors and pointed into the audience where the three-dimensional pictures floated above them.

"Look upon a new world," he shouted. "A world of growth. A world of happiness. A world of adventure. A world of limitless...opportunities."

The congregation saw familiar works of art seem to come to life. They saw underwater habitats reformed as biodomes on other planets. It was as if they were living in a science fiction vid, their hypnotic state supplementing the images to make it seem as though they were participating in the action. They saw worlds where children were abundant—playing and growing without fear, and where humanity transited between the stars in large, comfortable space ships.

After half an hour of these repeated images Johari directed their eyes closed once more and the projections melted away. He then quietly approached each dreamer in the circle and whispered in each person's ear.

"When I direct the audience to let go of the dream, you will not respond. You will not open your eyes until I speak the words 'Live the Dream'. You will not be frightened by anything that happens to you. When you awake you will be filled with trust, and hope, and happiness."

When he completed his message to each individual in the circle he continued with his directions to the audience. "Soon you will return to your everyday life. But do not forget what you've seen. Do not forget what you can make possible. It is up to you to save us. Now, awake and thank the dreamers before you." As the audience opened their eyes, they saw the scene set just as it was before—a circle of red-robed participants about a white cloaked figure. But, unlike before, the audience was now filled with hope and an amazing sense of wonder.

"Thank you, circle of dreamers," Johari continued, turning slowly to glance at each individual in the circle, making sure their eyes were still closed and each one remained in a trance. "You have given us hope. You have shown us your saving grace. For your dream you have been elevated to golden dreamer."

At that command the entire circle of participants began rising toward the ceiling seemingly without support, just as Johari had previously descended. The audience gasped as they watched them disappear. Johari smiled as a double halo descended within inches of his head, his arms outstretched as if he were the one performing the levitation. Once the circle finally disappeared into the darkness he turned for the last time to address the audience.

"Your love has brought a new springtime to the world! Remember this spiritual journey. Keep it in your hearts and your minds, watering the seeds of change with your good will. Help us bring forth a garden filled with hope. Already we have seen the elevation of a few chosen dreamers. You can earn this honor as well. You can make a difference and set us on the way to a new world—a world given to us by your own people who have shared their dream. If you wish to join us, please follow the Dreamers in blue robes as they leave the auditorium. They are waiting to answer your questions, waiting for your help in melting the ice of our wintry world."

Once more the lights dimmed, the fog rolled in, the rose colored light bathed Johari in its glow and he raised his arms toward the heavens slowly backing toward the center of the stage where he could enter the invisible tube.

The music swelled, and the subliminals whispered once more *love, trust, hope, love the dream, believe in the dream, live the dream.* Johari rose silently above the stage and disappeared into the darkness, leaving the audience with an overwhelming sense of well-being.

After Johari's departure, the lights came up slowly and the ushers directed the audience out the side doors where they were met by deacons of the Church of Dreams. Here the participants were encouraged to ask questions and take information on additional services.

Rohin shut off his viewscreen and headed for the auditorium to greet the new circle members. When the auditorium was finally cleared, and the doors were secured, Rohin directed the still hypnotized circle members to be lowered back to the stage. The lights dimmed once more and he joined them in the fogged floor and rose colored light.

"Go, and live the dream!" Johari commanded.

The circle members opened their eyes and looked at him. Not one spoke as the continuous music softened and the subliminals of love, trust and hope filled them.

"Thank you for your dream," Johari said as he clasped each hand individually. "You have done a wondrous thing today. You have offered your dream—your hope—to save our world." He paused and gestured toward a large arched doorway. "You stand now at the portals to the Dreamer's world. Step forward and join with us. Your desire to help, and your natural ability to dream will help you to move quickly through Dreamer education."

He walked to the stairs and the group followed him without hesitation. "Follow your dream partner to the door." He pointed to a line of people clothed in sky blue cassocks standing at the base of the stage stairs. "They will answer your questions and structure your education as your needs merit."

Then once more he stepped into the invisible tube and raised his arms heavenward. "Go in love. Live the Dream!"

"Dream on!" the circle answered, unaware of why they said the words.

Rohin smiled as the lights dimmed for the final time and Johari lifted toward the ceiling, disappearing as mysteriously as he had come.

Rohin stepped forward and took the hand of Dr. Yeske. Awestruck, the remaining circle members slowly separated into twos, each holding hands with a dream partner, following along a fog-filled trail toward the door.

Rohin nodded and smiled as each new couple passed him. Then he turned to his new partner and gestured for him to proceed. If Yeske was the only one to join his cause today, all of the services—all of the grey—would be worth it.

ROHIN REACHED his office and slumped into his chair. It had gone well. Yeske was onboard for now. It was as if the researcher had just been waiting for an opportunity to use his talents for hope. Eternity had killed hope in so many scientists that they were ripe for the picking.

He'd turned Yeske over to Lilah for indoctrination. Most recruits took two to four months before they were ready to make a decision. Lilah was one of his best teachers. He knew he could count on her. All he needed now was to have the private lab set up and Yeske would get started. Things were moving even more quickly than he'd hoped.

Buzz. Buzz.

Rohin tapped his desk to check the caller, then he brought up the comm viewscreen. "Yes?"

"We have it."

Rohin tensed with excitement. "Is it what we think?"

"I think so. I'm transferring it to the lab now."

"How long will it take to know?"

"Twenty-four, maybe forty-eight hours."

"You've destroyed the notes?"

"Yes. There's enough there to make it look like the notes are intact. But the most important parts are destroyed."

"Good. Keep me posted."

"Live the Dream."

Rohin nodded. "Dream on," he replied and shut down the screen.

He closed his eyes and took in a deep breath, then let it out slowly. They got it. Thank whatever dreamers, gods, heavens there were. He'd been scared that the Agers were close, but before they even realized how close, he'd shut it down.

He swallowed and bowed his head at his loss. His shoulders shook as he bore the burden of his decision. He'd sealed his fate now. When Miki found out, she would hate him for the rest of his life.

15

The headlights of Morgan's ice rover threw everything into sharp relief—the rippled ice, the moonlit shadow of another rover parked just beyond, and two sullen tour guides huddled against the cold, their breath clearly visible.

Morgan signaled Antarctic security of his arrival, then prepared himself for the task. He placed a wound, knotted nylon winch rope over one shoulder, several evidence bags in his jacket pocket, and a small spade in the other pocket. He doubted these two would be eager to help him. Finally, he got out of the rover and moved slowly toward the couple. Neither one seemed eager to report what had happened.

"Well, where is it?" Morgan finally asked.

"Right up there," the woman barely whispered, pointing behind her with a shaky, gloved hand, then turned into the chest of the man next to her.

"Do you know who it is?" Morgan addressed the man.

"Probably Randy, but it's hard to tell. Most of the face is gone. But I'm pretty sure it's him."

"How'd you discover it?"

"We were running one of the large tour groups out here for our usual Antarctic lunch experience—you know, cooking in the ice, how to build a quick shelter, that sort of stuff. Showing them how difficult it was for the first crew to get started here. While we were cleaning up, a couple of the kids took off, toward that ice shelf. Next thing we knew they were screaming bloody murder. We thought maybe one of them had fallen into a fissure or something. But, when we got there we found the body."

"How many people were in the tour group?" Morgan interjected.

"About 20 to 25 I'd guess. When we found the body, the other tour guides took them back immediately. We stayed, waiting for you."

"Did you get the kids' names, home locations, all that stuff?"

"Yup. I can beam it to you."

Morgan held out a small card and pointed it toward the one held by the tour guide. A light blinked once, then he placed the card back in his breast pocket.

"OK, let's go see it," Morgan followed the tracks up the ice shelf. Cresting the top, he shined the bright beam down the other side. Just ahead was a black mass that looked like a small stump with something draped over it. Morgan turned his beam on it and the stump suddenly became the head and shoulders of a young man, his damp brown hair plastered against his head. One hand lay palm upward, its fingers clutching desperately at a recorder, held open to the night air.

"Looks like the killer didn't even try to bury him," Morgan commented as he moved closer to the body. He noticed the other two had stopped at the crest, obviously not willing to venture down here again.

He slowly paced around the body. The corpse's head lay to one side and Morgan could see that a good portion of the frontal part of the skull had been smashed beyond recognition. The entire face looked like it had collapsed. He shifted the light slightly so the rear of the head was in the beam. The entry wound, though small, was well defined.

Morgan hunkered down on the ice for a closer look. "Damn," he swore under his breath. A sharp needle-like arrow protruded from the occipital region behind the left ear. No doubt this was a professional execution. He was sure the needle would be found to carry a poison that causes instant paralysis and death. Worse, to achieve this accuracy it had to have been fired at point blank range. Morgan shook his head. Kant must have an internal spy stationed with the Agers. He would have to report this to Anna Hollinrake and get a security lock down for all labs. He only hoped it wasn't already too late.

Morgan pulled the needle from the wound with his gloved hand and placed it in an evidence bag. Then he wrested the recorder from the frozen fingers and zipped it into his jacket pocket. Now he had to get the body back to the rover. He looked up the hill to the couple still standing there, thinking to call for help—but thought better of it. He doubted he could convince them to come down any further.

He bent low and spaded the ice away from the body. Taking the knotted winch rope from his shoulder, he placed it under the body's shoulders, let out some rope, then tied it around himself. Moving up the hill, the rope tightened around the body as he dragged it behind him. Cresting the ice shelf once again he noticed the couple had carefully kept their distance, always staying several meters ahead of him. Sweating, he finally made it back to the rover.

The woman had already hidden in the other rover. The man was waiting next to it, conscientiously trying not to look at the body. Morgan waited to catch his breath before speaking.

"I guess I can handle it from here. You two can go on back to your quarters. I'd appreciate it, though, if you didn't talk about this with anyone else until we clear it up."

The man nodded and gratefully rushed into his rover and sped away.

It was colder now that Morgan had stopped working. He shivered inside his jacket. He removed the ropes from both himself and the body, then rummaged in the rover for a tarp. He laid the tarp on the ice, rolled the body into it and wrapped it like a cocoon. With one final heave he hoisted the body into the back.

Morgan took one last look toward the ice shelf before climbing into the rover himself. Anna's really going to be pissed, he thought. And the war hasn't even begun.

THE CHILL MORNING air blew across the Visitor's Center entry. When anyone entered or exited the airlock, the warm air inside mixed with the cool air outside and created a momentary fog in ragged streamers. Anna huddled deeper in her coat as she left the entry and trudged up the walk to the maintenance building. Though it was only a few meters away, in this cold it could seem like half a kilometer.

The location of the maintenance building had been a compromise between practicality and security. It needed to look natural and uninviting to visitors and satellite imaging, yet be close enough for personnel to easily move between the two buildings. Hidden below the maintenance building was the extensive laboratory of the Ager counter-virus expedition.

At the gate, sensitive monitors scanned each person nearing the maintenance building. Anna approached and faced the scanner impatiently, waiting for it to match her facial characteristics with the appropriate file and admit her. Though the security was nothing like that of Eternity, it seemed to be sufficient for this far away outpost.

Finally the gate opened and Anna gratefully entered the compound. Only a few more feet and she was in warmth once more. It had been a lousy night and the morning hadn't been much better. Morgan had called late last night to report the murder of Randy Barrows. From his description, he believed that Eternity was behind it. Only Eternity used that execution style. Evidently there was also a recorder with a message. The unidentified voice said, "I know what you're doing and I will stop you. You will not succeed."

Anna hadn't called it in to Miki yet. She wasn't sure it was that important, and the last thing she wanted was to delay the work here. If the workers who found Randy could keep their mouth shut, she might be able to allay the panic that would work its way through all the Agers if they found out. Bad news spread like wildfire. There was no choice. She'd find a way to handle it all here and now. She may even speed up the work, get people to work longer hours. The Agers needed a win—something to celebrate. And Anna needed to move things along or the entire plan would fall apart.

Reaching the animal lab, Anna knocked. When nobody answered she pushed tentatively at the door. "Shandra?" There was no answer and she walked quietly into the small room. A light illuminated Shandra's desk and half a dozen printouts strewn across the top. A small tick of worry started in the back of Anna's mind. "Shandra, are you here?"

No answer. She edged closer to the experimental examining room. Peering carefully through the translucent glass she could make out a vague thin form hunched over a small black Labrador puppy. Quietly she entered the examining room and recognized Shandra's voice.

"All right, Einstein, if you don't like that you'll just have to go hungry." Shandra had been kneeling down, coaxing the thin puppy to nibble at a bowl of dog food.

"Shandra?" Anna spoke louder this time.

Shandra's head jerked back and she glanced up at her angrily. "You shouldn't startle me like that, Anna." She bent back toward the dog. "Honestly, I don't know why Randy was ever allowed to bring a puppy here. He just hasn't adapted well. If it wasn't for me forcing him to eat, he would have starved long ago." She reached out a slender hand to scratch the dog behind its ears. It turned away from the bowl of food and laid down at her feet. "Well, I guess somebody has to take care of you now that Randy's ..." Unable to finish the sentence, the words choked in her throat.

"Shandra, have any of your latest samples provided something unusual? Did Randy have more information than he let on to me?"

She looked flustered. "What do you mean? Are you accusing us? We reported everything to you."

Anna tried a gentler approach. "No, I'm not accusing. It's just that evidence suggests Kant's operatives were behind the murder. If they were, that means they suspect we have something. Where did Randy keep most of his records?"

"In the 'puter of course," she answered. "We both kept the records together."

"And the password?" Anna was already at the computer, trying to access the data files.

Shandra hesitated.

"Let's not play games, Shandra. We need to know how close he was."

"Freud," Shandra finally answered. "A joke really. Having to do with the anal retentive behavior of certain politicians." She smiled for a moment, then saddened.

Anna began skimming the research findings in file after file, trying to draw some basic conclusions. The data was spotty, but there seemed to be some trend toward killing the Eternity Virus. She searched further, looking for any conclusions Randy may have drawn.

She skimmed the final file in the directory. "Damn! It's like there are bits and pieces of missing information and no conclusions at all. Do you remember anything about this sample he keeps referring to? Sample Epsilon IV?"

Again Shandra hesitated.

"This is no time for confidences," Anna said angrily. "Randy's dead and you may be next if Kant's people suspect you know something. Now where is this sample?"

Shandra looked dubious. "All right. But I don't think it's anything special. Randy was excited for awhile that it might be the counter-agent, but the tests were inconclusive."

Anna followed her to the back of the animal lab and a locked refrigeration unit. Shandra deftly entered the combination and drew out a sample tray from the fifth shelf. Then her dark tanned skin suddenly turned white and she gasped.

"What? What is it?" Anna practically shook her to get her to respond.

Shandra set the tray on the counter and pointed, her finger trembling. In the second row, four samples from the left was a spot marked Epsilon IV. But there was no sample.

Whatever the results Randy was achieving, they could not duplicate them now. Somehow, between Shandra's memory and the small bits of information still left in Randy's files they would have to reconstruct the sampling site and depth and draw this again. Anna was sure Randy had found something important. What she didn't understand was how Kant had found it before Randy reported it—and why Kant was checking up on her.

"All right, Shandra," Anna soothed. "Put the tray back. We have work to do." Shakily, Shandra returned the tray and closed the refrigerator unit. "I want you to compile every note, file, even napkin that Randy may have written on in the past few days. We will find where this sample was drawn and begin testing again. I'm assigning four more researchers to you and the lab, and increasing security. We must be close now. I am not going to allow Kant or anyone else to stop us. Now get back to work."

Back in her own office, Anna took a deep breath before securing the comm line to Kant's office. If he was behind the theft of the sample that meant he didn't trust her. And, if he didn't trust her, she might be the next murder victim. She swore under her breath as she worked her way through the various security people before getting connected to Kant. Finally, she heard the familiar scramble tones of Kant's receiver. Well, it can't be all bad, she thought; at least he's still taking my calls.

Kant's visage filled her screen. "Anna. Have they found something? Is there a counter virus?"

Anna hesitated before answering, trying to read his face, pick up on any body language that would indicate what he already knew. He betrayed nothing—but then he was an expert at hiding his true intentions.

"First things first," Anna began. "We've had an . . . accident here. No, not an accident. A murder." She stared directly into the screen, watching his face carefully. "And evidence seems to indicate you were behind it."

He shifted in his chair and smiled. "Why would I want to sabotage your efforts? You are still working for me, aren't you, Hollinrake?"

Anna squinted. That was a typical Kant response, but she wasn't convinced he knew nothing about it.

"That just makes it all the more interesting," she said. "It seems that Randy, the murder victim, was getting very close to the discovery of a counter agent. Unfortunately, not only is he dead but his files are corrupted and the one sample that could be the breakthrough is missing."

Kant's nostrils flared and his jaw tightened. "Then I suggest you have a leak, Hollinrake, and you better get it plugged quickly."

"I think Randy was the leak, and his murder was a gift to you."

Kant slammed his fist on his desk. "I don't need gifts like that. I need results, results that I can use. Are you telling me he had a counter-agent and you've lost it?"

"It wasn't developed, it was a sample," Anna said. "Did you find out about Randy's work and then make arrangements to get his research for yourself?"

"What was there to find out?" he countered. "That's what I have you for. What are you holding out on me, Hollinrake? What did you conveniently forget to tell me and now it's blown up in your face?"

Anna faced him square on and opened her eyes wider. She wasn't going to tell him anything and she wasn't going to let him see her squirm.

"Someone is on to you, Hollinrake, and you better handle the problem or I will. And right now I consider you to be the problem. I want results." Kant cut the communication and the screen went blank.

Anna swallowed. If it wasn't Kant, then who else knew?

She sat back and a prickling sensation worked its way down her spine. Was it possible? Did someone see her kill Randy?

Last week she learned that Randy had been feeding information to Dreamers. When questioned, he defiantly admitted it and dared her to stop him. He had the look of a fanatic, completely unafraid for his own life. She had no choice but to eliminate him.

She next suspected Shandra was in collusion with him, but her reaction to the missing sample was too genuine to implicate her. No, Anna believed Shandra lacked any knowledge of Randy's involvement with the Dreamers. She had only recently joined the team in Antarctica. It wasn't her fault she was assigned to work with Randy.

Was it possible Randy had already smuggled the sample out before she killed him? She shook herself angrily, questioning her actions. "Dammit! Why didn't I check this out first?" She already knew the answer. She had no idea he was close to discovery of the counter virus. She only knew he was keeping in contact with the Dreamers.

Next time she would be more careful. They would somehow reconstruct Randy's work and find the agent again. Then no one would stop the plans. She would push this crew until they could be pushed no more. She was in charge, and she was going to make it work. She would trust no one but herself from now on.

She got up and stretched before placing the next call. Miki would need to be handled very differently from Kant. She wanted to look relaxed and be able to reassure Miki that there were no leaks in the organization. And maybe Miki could have some influence over the Dreamers—that is, if she still had any influence with Rohin Chawla.

After several minutes of working out her tension, Anna sat before the terminal and secured the comm line for the next call. Soon Miki's face filled the screen.

"Anna. I've already heard about the murder from Morgan. Can you fill me in? Do you know who did it or why?"

Anna smiled, exuding confidence. "Yes. I did it." She noticed Miki's eyes widen. But, to her credit, she didn't speak, waiting for Anna to continue. "He was a spy for the Dreamers. He was transferring research information back to the Church of Dreams offices."

Miki frowned and she closed her eyes for a moment. "I should have suspected Rohin wouldn't run a benign operation," she said. I didn't think he could get a group together so quickly. I didn't think..."

"It was your body that did the thinking," Anna reminded her.

"It was more than that," Miki said. "We connected again, like before, and I knew he wasn't bad. I knew he wouldn't hurt me. I believed he could join us and we'd be together, like before."

"Chawla used you, Mik, and now we are paying with his spies at our compound."

Miki sighed. "According to Helios, when Rohin left Qyzylqum, he was filled with a determination to change the world into some utopian dream."

"Sounds like a young researcher I once knew," Anna said.

Miki frowned. "Yeah, but I soon learned there is no such thing as utopia. I guess Rohin has yet to learn that."

"We can't afford time while he does his lessons," Anna said, careful to keep the anger from her voice. "The problem goes beyond a leak that I was able to plug. Evidently an important research sample is missing. From what I can piece together of the data, it may have been the counter virus. I believe Randy somehow got it out of the compound and to another Dreamer."

Miki leaned forward, her eyes wide. "Counter virus? You mean they actually found it? Are you sure? Why didn't anyone tell me? How could Rohin know before me?"

Miki paced back and forth in front of the viewscreen. Anna watched her go out of the view and then back in it as she spoke. "Where is it? How much is there? Is the sample site as large as the Eternity virus? How does it work? Is it passed quickly? We must get more staff on it right away."

"Slow down," Anna cautioned. "Did you hear me? The sample is missing. M-I-S-S-I-N-G."

Miki dropped back to her chair in front of the screen and Anna could see her entire face again. But she still didn't seem as worried as she should be.

Anna leaned forward as if Miki were in the room with her. "It had just been identified. The sample is probably in the hands of Rohin Chawla right now."

"But there's more, right?" Miki asked.

"I don't know."

"What do you mean you don't know. What about the notes? What about other people in the lab? What the hell is going on there, Anna?"

"Calm down a minute." Anna leaned back in her chair and steepled her fingers. "I'm trying to piece together the data to find where that core was drilled. Randy did something to the files. They are in the computer, but not intact. Critical information is missing. I'm confident we'll find it again, but it will take time. Then we have to redo the testing to make sure we have the right one."

"I can't believe this," Miki said. "We barely get set up and we actually find the damn counter virus and Rohin steps in and takes it. It's impossible. How could he get there so fast? His damn church has only been going for what? Four months? Six?" She paused. "Are you sure, Anna? Are you sure Randy was a Dreamer spy? Are you sure he wasn't working for Eternity?"

"Of course I'm sure. I talk to Kant all the time, remember? I'd know if he was sending a spy here. I'm supposed to be the spy."

"Right." Micki looked down. "You're right." She drummed her fingers on the desk. "Dammit to hell. How could he do this?"

"You have to get in touch with him," Anna said. "He still loves you and he'll talk to you. You have to go to the Dreamer headquarters and do something."

"If he has the sample, the last thing he'll want to do is talk to me," Miki said.

"You damn well better find a way to convince him you've had a change of heart and want to join that stupid Church of Dreams then. Because if he has the counter virus, he could be working on a way to negate it right now."

"I just don't know..." Miki trailed off.

"He used you, now you use him," Anna demanded. "Put those hormones to use and do whatever you have to and convince him you're with him. Then make sure that sample and anything related to it are destroyed."

Miki visibly shook herself. "All right. I'll find a way to get to him. You just keep looking for the location of the sample, Anna. You hold up your end in Antarctica and I'll take care of Rohin Damn Chawla and the Dreamers."

16

———

Rohin rounded the corner of the hall, approaching the dormitory section of the compound. He seldom visited this section, normally interacting with new recruits only in formal church settings. However, Lilah had informed him of Dr. Yeske's amazing progress and his desire to fully cooperate with the mission of the Church. Rohin felt that Leonard Yeske's cooperation warranted the personal touch. He slowed perceptibly as Yeske's room number came into view.

Len Yeske fit the profile perfectly. Rohin already had plans for his specific talents. The acceptance of a utopian dream was not as difficult as some believed. In fact, in a world seemingly without desire, it was natural to want to grasp at anything that held the promise of a meaningful future. This was one of the many lessons Rohin gleaned during his religious discussions with Helios Melucci. He smiled to himself, wondering if Miki realized what a gift she had given him when she led him to the desert.

Rohin counted nine doors before finally stopping. He stood outside the door with his head bowed in thought. It would take a moment for him to prepare for the meeting. He wanted to be open to all of Yeske's questions, yet able to imbue the same trust and hope in himself that Lilah had successfully nurtured toward herself and the Church as a whole.

He had not seen Yeske since the Vernal service two nights ago. Although he fully trusted Lilah's judgment, and admired her excellent ability to appropriately indoctrinate new recruits, it was always difficult to meet a new member before the full eight week indoc period was over. But, in the case of important scientists—scientists who could be assigned to lead new research teams—Rohin always made an exception. He wanted to be one hundred percent sure that the new member understood the gravity of the Church's mission. Having been a scientist himself, he felt he was best prepared to answer any difficult questions, in spite of the personal pain it may cost him.

Finally, feeling ready to begin the tour, Rohin knocked confidently on the door. When Len opened it and smiled warmly any vestiges of Rohin's misgivings disappeared.

"Good to see you, Master Dreamer," Len greeted him warmly, as if they were long time friends. "We will Live the Dream."

"Dream on," Rohin responded as expected.

"Please come in." He gestured toward his small dormitory room. Rohin smiled as he entered the room, letting the door close lightly behind him. "Lilah said you would be coming by this morning. I must tell you, Lilah is a wondrous woman."

"I'm glad you found her instruction so beneficial to you," Rohin replied with a knowing smile. As he recalled, Lilah and Len had become almost inseparable during the indoctrination period. Even the cool-headed Lilah was making noises about a permanent living arrangement with Leonard Yeske.

"If you're ready, Len, I would like to take you on a tour of our facilities," he continued in a friendly tone. "I want you to completely understand our mission, so that you can make an educated decision about your commitment to the Church of Dreams."

"I'm already committed, Master Dreamer."

"I appreciate your enthusiasm, but I don't want you to make any commitment until you fully understand our mission, and what part in it we would like you to take. And, please call me Rohin. Dreamers are a family and should be treated as such. Although there is a hierarchical structure for learning purposes, we do not believe in positional recognition through titles. My friends call me Rohin, and I would like to count you among my friends."

"Sure, Master . . . I mean Rohin. Thank you for honoring me as your friend."

"Shall we begin?" Rohin held the door open and gestured for Len to precede him into the hall. Before exiting Len dashed back into his room to retrieve his 'puter; then he hurried through the open door. As they started down the hall toward the research facilities Rohin asked a few key questions, primarily aimed at confirming the report of Len's personal ambitions and how much he had changed since embracing the philosophy of the Church of Dreams.

SHORTLY, they stopped in front of the first of what appeared to be several large rooms, each with heavy double doors and no windows facing into the hall. After Rohin spoke a voice command, the first set of double doors opened. He gestured for Yeske to enter.

Len looked about the lab facilities in awe for several minutes. To his left were three or four banks of freezers with multiple compartments, each covered with glass doors and a label. Directly in front of them were two L-shaped lab benches with several cases of petri dishes, a variety of test tube racks, small and large microscopes, a MC interface to the chemical analyzer, and a number of other lab tools he didn't even recognize. A lone woman, looking somewhat overweight and grandmotherly, was hunched over a MC terminal. She did not look up or greet them as they came in the door.

"I didn't know labs like this existed outside of Eternity," Len said with respect.

"Oh they do," Rohin said smiling. "But, like ours, they are secret. There are many wealthy people in the world who underwrite labs in many places. It's a way for them to make sure they are always on the winning team. I suspect the Agers have something similar as well, probably funded by the same benefactors even."

"The Agers?" Len questioned. "That fanatical group that spouts some sort of doctrine about needing death to bring life?"

"Yes," Rohin replied thoughtfully. "They are much larger, much better organized and well financed than anyone knows. One of our goals is to stop them. We must ensure they don't bring early death to anyone without that person's knowledge and consent." As he spoke Rohin led Len toward the heavy set, older woman. "I would like you to meet Dr. LaVerne Bohn. We often refer to her as Grandma Bohn, because in many ways she will be grandmother to a new generation of children. She is in charge of the species regeneration lab."

"Species regeneration?" Len turned his question toward Dr. Bohn, as he shook her hand. "Human or animal?"

"Children," she replied with a challenging glint in her eye.

"Children?" Len asked again, unbelieving. "You know we can't have children without a permit."

"Ah, yes Len," Dr. Bohn answered in Frenger.

Len was slightly taken aback. He hadn't heard Frenger in a long time, since Eternal was spoken in most places where Eternity had large compounds. Most people rarely spoke the other five primary languages except in families. Then he smiled to himself—Dreamers were a family. Perhaps each person was encouraged to return to their own language.

"Tell me more about your regeneration project," Len then asked in Frenger as well—honoring Dr. Bohn's heritage.

"I am responsible for ensuring that we can still have the children we want. It is our children that will colonize the planets."

Len could see why she was referred to as grandma; she must have been at least in her 60's when the Eternity virus was distributed. She had a plumpness that reminded him of illustrations in children's books from ancient fairy tales or rhymes—illustrations like the Old Woman in the Shoe or Mother Goose. He could picture her making cookies for a passel of children, or baking pies to set in a windowsill.

"I don't understand," Len continued, forcing his attention back to the discussion. "Are you suggesting in-vitro?"

"Yes, that and much more. Many of our fetuses are implanted in Church members who are willing to stay within the confines of the Dreamers compounds and consequently raise the child here. As long as the children are never seen, Eternity will never know they exist. Once they reach adulthood they can move freely outside the Church, as long as we are capable of providing their economic needs. However, our hope is that most of them will choose to work with us and become an important part of the colonization effort."

"But what about the Eternity virus? How do they get their shot? How do you account for Eternity's records?"

"We have developed a method to culture enough Eternity virus from our own members to maintain the shots for these children," Rohin interrupted. "As for the records, unless they need to work for Eternity there is no reason for records. There are millions of people in this world without a corresponding record. My years of hive living taught me a great lesson in avoiding Eternity's recordkeeping. Though they institute periodic raids, Eternity simply can't keep up with the numbers of unregistered adults anymore."

"I noticed the freezers," Len gestured past Dr. Bohn. "I assume these hold frozen eggs and sperm." Dr. Bohn nodded her head, almost imperceptibly. "Or, are they already fertilized eggs, frozen and waiting for implantation?" He asked as he realized the unbelievable enormity of this project. "Are all of those ready to be implanted? You can't possibly have that many women available right now."

"Oh, no, of course not," she giggled, almost girlishly. "We grow the child in the lab to viability—about a six-week fetus—then implant it into the woman, for those women available for implantation now. However, most of these samples are separate sperm or ova samples. Many of these will then be fertilized and implanted years from now, when we are ready to send members off this planet—ready for colonization of the stars. Some of the rest will be carried on the ships themselves for later implantation."

"But it's never been proven that sperm or egg cells can be frozen and remain viable for that long. You must be hundreds of years away yet," Len responded, incredulous. "What if it doesn't work?"

"We will take that chance," LaVerne continued. "To date, Eternity has been able to rejuvenate sperm and fertilize eggs over one hundred fifty years old. I believe that the length of freezing time will leave these results unchanged. You see, we must begin now in order to maintain a large gene pool. We cannot depend on the procreation of only those within the first colonies to create enough children without defects."

"And LaVerne is the best in her field," Rohin interrupted again. "She is one of the few people Eternity actually hired to do what she was trained to do. However, lucky for us, she attended one of our Vernal services and saw how much more she could do for humanity as a whole.

"Then, after recruiting two of her lab assistants to maintain a continuing spy network within the Eternity labs, the Church arranged an *accident* and Dr. Bohn disappeared without a trace. Eternity finally gave up searching for her when evidence was presented that she was on the ill-fated Larkin pleasure cruise that capsized in the Atlantic four months ago.

"Yes," Dr. Bohn laughed heartily. "See what drowning does for you?" She ran her fingers over her plump figure. "It's true that you become bloated." Len laughed with her. He liked this woman, and there was so much he wanted to ask about her research.

"There is much more to see, Len," Rohin said, indicating they should proceed down the hall.

Reluctantly, Len said goodbye, promising Grandma Bohn to return soon. Then once more he followed Rohin down the hall toward the next room. He noticed they passed several doors before arriving at their destination. At one point they went through two glass doors in a row, similar to an isolation barrier. The temperature change from one portion of the hall to the next was very noticeable. Whereas the hall had been a comfortable air-conditioned coolness, Len now found he was beginning to perspire. He wondered momentarily if the environmental conditioning unit was malfunctioning.

Before he could ask the question Rohin stopped and spoke a voice command for entry again. This entrance appeared much the same as the previous one—heavy double doors, no windows, and a similar looking security system. Len assumed it was another lab.

However, when the doors opened and Rohin ushered him in, it hardly seemed to be a lab at all. Unlike the other lab, which provided a very sterile environment, this one was like a tropical jungle. Plants of varying sizes were densely placed throughout the room, including many that Len could not identify. To one side of the room Len recognized the usual equipment used for hydroponics. He had worked with similar systems himself. But what held his attention was the large square box in the center of the room. At first glance it appeared to be a large sandbox. As he drew closer he realized that it was more like a cultivated garden plot.

"We're experimenting with a variety of root plants," Rohin said, noticing Len's examination of the box. "For example, manroot, or ginseng, has proven to be very effective for a number of common complaints. During space travel and initial colonization we can't carry an endless amount of medication or food. For those who do not choose to take the Eternity virus, we will need to care for them in traditional ways. Here we experiment with other ways to achieve similar medicinal results." Rohin gestured toward a tree which Len had never seen before. "For example, this Halta tree bears a very tasty fruit." He plucked off the silver, oblong shaped fruit and handed it to Len. "Try it, it won't hurt you."

Len cautiously took a bite, then smiled. "Mmm, a combination of coconut, orange, and apple taste. What is it?"

"It's something we've made up through a combination of genetic manipulation and interspecies grafting. Not only is the fruit tasty, but the skin provides your full daily requirement of calcium. And, the seed inside," he waited a moment for Len to notice the large seed, similar to that of an avocado, "can be crushed and encapsulated in pill form as a protein. One seed can make up to 22 pills. Each pill is the equivalent protein of about 113 grams of meat."

"Amazing!" Len said as he took another bite from the Halta fruit.

"In my previous undersea biosphere work we had just begun studying alternate food sources. Do you realize what a boon this would be even today?"

"Oh yes," Rohin smiled. "We knew long ago that Kama didn't provide enough nutrients on its own. It will keep you alive, but not provide much energy. Our development of alternate food sources is one of the ways we make the money needed to keep all these facilities going. Every lab produces one or more products that can be sold today. Many of them are bought by Eternity and then repackaged. Of course, each lab is under a different corporate name. We wouldn't want Eternity becoming suspicious of the competition, now would we?"

"No," Len agreed. "That wouldn't do at all." Out of the corner of his eye Len noticed a young man half hidden behind one of the bushes, moving quietly between several plants along the wall to the left. Len estimated he couldn't have been more than fifteen or sixteen years old. "Hello?" he called somewhat hesitantly.

Rohin glanced over his shoulder to see who Len was addressing. "Oh, Donal, come on over and meet Dr. Yeske." The young man delightedly stepped forward and offered his hand.

"*The* Dr. Yeske? The oceanographer in charge of underwater biospheres?" The young man was appraising him with respect, simultaneously pumping his hand enthusiastically. "I've read everything you've ever written. That was why I got interested in this project. Wow! I can't believe it. Are you with us too? Wow, Rohin, now I know why you are the Master Dreamer. You sure are good at finding the right people."

Donal was talking a kilometer a minute and still pumping Len's hand in excitement. Rohin had to speak up to get him to stop. "Enough Donal," he raised his voice sternly, then quickly chuckled as he patted him on the back. Embarrassed and apologetic, Donal quickly withdrew his hand.

"The answer to all your questions is Yes," Rohin continued, unable to hide the grin for Donal's boyish excitement. "As a matter of fact, I expect you and Len will be doing quite a bit of work together."

"Really?" Donal asked, obviously ready to start right away.

"You mean . . . he . . ." Len Yeske began, "this young man heads this project?"

"That's right," Rohin said. "Donal was one of Grandma Bohn's first secret successes. Long before she joined us, of course. Because Donal was an illegally born child, he had to be kept out of sight and out of the public schools. So Grandma Bohn and Donal's parents took it on themselves to educate him. Consequently, he probably has a better education than anyone who has gone through the regular academic training. He began his work here immediately after Dr. Bohn joined us."

"I'm impressed," Len responded.

"Thank you," Donal said vivaciously. "I can't believe I'll get to work with you. Wow!" The boy was practically jumping up and down. "Let me introduce you to the rest of the team. Is that okay?"

"That would be fine," Rohin replied, smiling at Donal's enthusiasm. "In fact, I'll let you complete the tour and I'll just trail along and listen."

Over the next two hours, Yeske met many more prominent scientists. Dr. Antonio Gomez headed a research team on terraforming. Dr. Evelyn Sullivan was studying interplanetary transportation systems, while conversely Dr. John Moser was in charge of planetary transportation. Along with Donal's work, Julia Pierce was already modeling biosphere food development; and Xa Hoang was designing a variety of oxygen suits to help people adapt to the varying planet atmospheric conditions. The Church of Dreams currently supported over thirty different research projects and approximately five thousand workers in direct pursuit of the colonization dream.

Every new member had research assignments in addition to certain recruiting duties. And every member kept important contacts in the outside world as well.

After Donal delivered all of them back to Rohin's office and left, Rohin gestured Yeske and the boy toward a counter. He poured everyone a drink of pure cool water.

"Speaking of work, Rohin," Len began after draining his glass in long gulp, "what exactly is it I can do for the Church of Dreams? It seems to me you have quite a few projects already and so many good people working on them."

Rohin put his arm around Len's shoulder protectively, while drawing Donal into the circle with his other arm. "You know biospheres, right?"

"Yes."

"What better way to use your knowledge than for space habitats on new planets."

Len's mouth dropped open and Rohin smiled. "You have the best background, the best experience. With you and Donal together there will be no stopping our colonization efforts.

Yeske cleared his throat. "Well, I would be honored, of course. But … it's been so long since I did anything…more than fifty years since my last project died. And at least 50 years before that since I was really involved in any design efforts. I would hate to let you down— especially since it is so important to the Church's mission."

"Trust me, Len." Rohin responded, giving his arm a fatherly squeeze. "You won't let us down. I know you can do it. We will give you the best facilities and the best assistants. And you'll have Donal here, who can probably quote all of your research papers by memory."

"Maybe not all," Donal piped in, "but what I don't remember I can find in two seconds flat.""Well …" Len continued to hesitate, but Rohin saw the excitement rise in his eyes.

"Live the Dream, Dr. Yeske," Donal whispered encouragingly.

"Yes," Len responded, a slight shake to his voice. "You're right, young man." He clapped Donal on the shoulder, then looked to Rohin and smiled. "Dream on!"

"Dream on." Donal and Rohin echoed, hugging Yeske between them.

～

ROHIN'S VIDCOMM buzzed two times then stopped and buzzed two more. That was the code for an intelligence briefing. He quickly dismissed Yeske and Donal and secured his office. Keying in the codes for his top intelligence officers, Langtree and Kim, he worried the bottom of his lip as he split their vid images on the screen.

"I have bad news," Kim said the minute they were locked in to the briefing.

"I can assure you that Miki Yokoyama is the head of what used to be a rather loosely knit organization. The Agers have successfully recruited and organized thousands of small protest groups under their wing."

"What has Kant done with the information on these people?" Rohin asked. "Has he ordered arrests, or is he simply following them?"

"So far he is only watching them—but very closely," Langtree responded. "He is also keeping a close eye on the Antarctica research of Dr. Elsie Finn. There are some suspicions that Finn is somehow working with the Agers, though no one has been able to prove any connection to any known Ager participants."

"I can confirm that Finn is in deep with Miki Yokoyama," Kim said. "I can also confirm that the Agers have the capability to mobilize their protestors worldwide for distribution of the counter agent when it becomes available."

"I've been receiving reports that Miki Yokoyama is already beginning this mobilization," Rohin said. "Do your sources seem certain that the Agers will actually find this counter agent?"

"Unfortunately, they have found it. I just received confirmation of it when I checked with my Antarctica contact." Kim replied. "Evidently it was originally destroyed after Randy was murdered. But all it did was put their research back a few months. They increased security and relocated the sample site. They haven't been able to mass produce it yet, but it's under such tight security now that my contact was unable to destroy it a second time."

Langtree groaned, closing his eyes as if shutting out the light could change this reality. Rohin simply shook his head in resignation.

"Do we actually have a Dreamer on the Antarctica research team?" Rohin asked, his tone subdued. He knew the Dreamer contacts were growing faster than his ability to keep up, but he could barely believe his good fortune in this one.

"Yes, we do. Actually, the team has been back from Antarctica for a little over a month now. Rumor has it they are already testing the agent on a few human volunteers. My contact is a biomed assistant assigned to the project."

"How did you find this person?" Langtree asked.

"Well, Shandra was my first circle member recruit. I had met her in the two days before the Ager meeting, and we struck up sort of a . . . well . . . a relationship. Within the first week of Dreamer education I contacted her and implored her to attend just one service. She came mostly to humor me, but I made it my personal *sacrifice* to bring her into the fold." She finished with obvious tenderness in her voice.

"The Ager plan was to locate the counter agent," Kim continued, "hopefully within a six month timeframe, then bring it back to Ager command and immediately begin experimentation. They missed their deadline by only one month. They found what they believed to be a counter virus, and they are testing it in earnest.

"According to Shandra, recent tests confirmed the virus does work, at least to some extent, to negate the immune system enhancement of the Eternity Virus. This week they are beginning two year clinical trials on 200 volunteers, injecting them with this new Ager virus. Simultaneously they will continue animal testing over the next three months in conjunction with carefully controlled disease injections. Then, if all goes well, Miki Yokoyama's organization will begin stealth distribution throughout the world. Because of Randy's murder and the subsequent missing sample, the Agers have been forced to move the timetable up."

Langtree stood, unable to sit any longer. "So, Kant guessed right. It wasn't just his paranoia. His worst nightmare is about to come true."

"Not if we can help it," Rohin's voice was filled with determination. "Langtree, from your contacts in Eternity, where does Anna Hollinrake fit in?"

Langtree paced nervously as he answered. "As far as we can tell, she is playing both sides of the fence. Kant has set her up as a double agent. He has her baiting Miki with information while actually reporting to him on Ager secrets."

"Are you sure it's not the other way around?" Rohin asked. Though he had never been real friends with Anna, he didn't want to believe she could stoop so low as to betray her best friend. "Perhaps Miki has set her up as a double agent for the Agers—baiting Kant with misinformation while reporting back to Miki."

"Or worse," Kim interjected, "she could be working only for herself, leading both of them in some unknown direction." Langtree stopped pacing and he and Rohin looked at each other.

"Now the pieces are falling into place," Rohin said reluctantly. "I should have guessed Anna would be the final link. I just couldn't believe . . . Yes, she is the one piece of the puzzle that could be disguised to fit anywhere." He rubbed his jaw thoughtfully as he reflected on what he could remember of the selfishness and lust for power Anna had displayed in the past.

During the initial virus research they had come to verbal blows many times. He had only put up with her because of Miki. Eventually, however, they came to a kind of understanding—working in respectful silence, each contributing professionally.

Though the facts suggested her personal mark of involvement, in this instance it was still hard to grasp that Anna was probably the master manipulator. He knew Miki would be devastated with the news. She considered Anna to be not only her political ally, but her closest friend. Was it really possible Anna had manipulated even Kant?

"Anna probably fed just enough information to Kant to get him thinking about the Ager organization," Rohin said aloud. "But it's obvious she hasn't told him about the counter agent."

"That seems likely," Langtree agreed. "He probably suspects that possibility, but I don't believe he has any reports or hard facts."

"But what is she after?" Kim asked. "I know that she is second only to Miki in the Ager organization. By what you've indicated, she is also very close to Kant. What more could she want?"

"She wants it all," Rohin said distastefully, rising to stand behind his chair. He leaned on the chair back heavily, transferring his anger through his firm grasp to the immobile structure. "You have to know evil to understand how someone like Anna operates. I've seen that type of lust for power in only one other person—Kant." He released his grip on the chair. Then, standing more erect, he shook his head. "Dammit! I should have known. I should have recognized it when I first saw Miki again. I was too caught up in old memories—too caught up in finding myself."

Neither Kim or Langtree spoke. Their silence was the only bond they could offer him.

Finally Rohin spoke, his voice tinged with sadness. "Our path is clear."

"Yes," Langtree responded. "I will find a way to get additional Dreamers into Eternity. We will concentrate on getting more information on Anna Hollinrake."

"And I will keep in close contact with Shandra," Kim continued on the heels of Langtree's response. "Perhaps she can once more find a way to either destroy or steal the counter agent before it can be released."

"The sooner we can stop Miki and the Ager organization, the better," Rohin added. "And Kim, let's concentrate on stealing the agent, not destroying it. The Agers now know how to find it again. The Dreamers must thoroughly research this agent, and find a permanent method of stopping it. Kim, you coordinate with Shandra to steal it for us. Once she's successful, pull her out of Ager command and bring her here to head up a research team at the Church of Dreams. Destroying the counter virus now will only buy us a little time. But, once we have the antidote we will be able to destroy it forever—even in the future. The Dreamers will prevail."

"We will live the dream!" the other two said confidently.

"Dream on!" Rohin responded.

17

———

Miki bent her head back and looked straight into the sky. Tarful. A pyramid. How literal. Did Rohin have no imagination? Was it possible that humanity had become so filled with entertainment, that this symbolism actually called to them? She sighed. Of course they had. Wasn't that one of her own tenants of belief? Wasn't that one of the reasons she fought so hard for the Ager virus? She and Rohin weren't all that different. They both fought against Eternity. They both wanted the best for everyone.

She shook herself. No. She couldn't afford to sympathize with him in any way. He may want the best, but he was working against her. He'd sent spies into the Ager camp. He'd stolen the Ager sample. He was not the kind-hearted, good man the Dreamers believed him to be. How could he be when he sold unrealistic dreams? When he brainwashed his believers with symbolism and entertainment? Colonization of the stars. Who was he kidding? Eternity had stopped all starship research and manufacturing efforts.

She squared her shoulders and watched the play of light and shadow on the side of the pyramid. The background of other buildings and the brown sky reflected off the sleek glass-like sides. She stared toward the pinnacle. She'd bet Rohin sat at the top in some luxurious office. Did he come out like the ancient god, Ra, and make demands of his supplicants?

She laughed at the thought. Even she couldn't imagine him doing that. Rohin had never been good at playacting. If anyone was representing Ra, it was someone who could pull it off. Someone who had no problem pretending. She'd heard about the services—something about a god descending from the heavens without any assistance, and the feelings of happiness and warmth that filled the audience. She had no doubt they'd achieved that, just as many entertainments did. The only difference between the Dreamers and others was their focus. Okay she'd give him points for having a positive future as the focus. But no way did some god actually appear and pull off a miracle.

Miki took a deep breath. One foot in front of the other, she told herself, looking straight ahead at the door into the pyramid. I can do this. I can do whatever it takes to find out where they are keeping the sample and get it back. She lifted her chin and strode through the door without a second thought.

A freckle-faced young woman in a light blue cassock stood just inside the door. She smiled broadly at Miki and touched her on the shoulder. "Live the dream!"

Miki furrowed her brow and stepped away from the touch. What the hell did she mean by that?

Undeterred, the woman bowed. "I'm sorry if my touching was a violation of intimacy. How may I help you? Have you come to change your life? Have you come to find true meaning and happiness?"

Miki laughed. "You really have it down don't you? Is everyone inside the pyramid an actor?"

The woman's eyes widened. "I'm not acting, Miss. I'm a dreamer. I'm a believer."

"Sure you are." Miki snorted through her nose with a barely concealed smile. "Look, I'm here to see Chawla. Rohin Chawla."

The woman smiled again, even more teeth showing—beautiful, white, straight teeth. "Oh, the master dreamer." It almost seemed as if she genuflected at his name. "You must really want to change your life. He will show you the true way. He will offer you true happiness."

Yeah, he would change her life all right. He would change everyone's life as soon as he gave her back the Ager virus.

The woman gestured toward the back of the lobby. "Follow me. I will contact him and I'm sure he will see you immediately. That is if he isn't with another dreamer at this moment." She practically ran to the back of the lobby, gesturing at Miki to follow—as if she was afraid of losing such an important convert, someone who had asked for the master dreamer. Master Dreamer, what kind of conceit was that?

At the back of the lobby was a small vestibule to an elevator. It was brightly lit, but very calming. Soft music played and a cushioned bench was along one wall. Very zen.

The woman gestured for Miki to have a seat, then she pushed a button and spoke. "Live the dream, Rohin."

Ah, so he didn't demand everyone call him Master Dreamer. Miki listened carefully.

"Dream on," she heard his voice respond from the wall.

"I have someone who has asked specifically for your guidance," the woman continued, her voice quick and her body moving up and down as if the excitement would escape at any moment and wreak havoc if she didn't get Miki to the master dreamer as quickly as possible.

"Is she one of the ones on the list?" Rohin asked.

"Oh!" The woman's eyes widened and she frowned. "Oh, I forgot to ask. I'm so sorry. I'm..."

"Not a problem, young one. Just ask her now."

"Yes, Master Dre..."

"Rohin," he said. "Remember, we are all family."

"Yes, Rohin..Yes. Just a moment."

"Miss, please what is your name."

Miki smiled. She wished there was a vid connection instead of just voice. She wanted to see his reaction. She stood next to the young woman and spoke to the speaker. "My name is Miki Yokoyama."

She smiled at the audible intake of breath. At least no spy had forewarned him.

"Of course," Rohin said quietly. "Ms. Yokoyama is always welcome in our home. Please send her up right away."

~

ROHIN CLICKED off the intercom and stood. So, she already knew they had a sample of the Ager virus. How was she going to play this? Surely she knew he wouldn't give it up. He sighed. Why did they have to be on opposite sides?

It had been what? –three months...four...since he'd been with her in New Austra-land. It seemed that whenever they were together they'd put aside the differences for a short time. He chuckled. No, they didn't put aside their differences. Instead, they allowed their sexual attraction to take over—to take them away from the realities of the world.

Rohin sighed and swallowed back a sorrow that had been sitting heavy in his heart since Miki had saved him from Eternity. Maybe that was all they would ever have. Stolen moments of passion over the years, when they could use each other to forget their burdens, to forget that they could never truly be together, and to hope they might get one more chance before one of them was caught. One of them was killed.

He shook himself. He wouldn't...he couldn't let Miki die, no matter how much she disagreed with him. He would do everything in his power to make sure Eternity didn't get to her—including keeping her among the Dreamers.

The elevator doors whooshed open and he walked forward, consciously shuttering his thoughts. For this moment he wanted to protect her, but not at the cost of the dreams for all humanity.

He smiled as she approached. "Hello, Angel."

Miki clenched her teeth and faced him squarely. "I'm not your angel, and you know it."

"Oh, but you are." He reached to bring her into an embrace, but she stepped backward.

"We are not going there, Rohin. I am not letting you confuse me with sex. I told you last time, it wasn't going to happen again."

He chuckled. "No, Angel, you told me you would never see me again." He paused and the side of his lip quirked up. "In fact, I think that was the second time you told me that. And here you are...again."

She swallowed, but her spine stiffened. It appeared as if she grew another inch or two before his eyes. "You have forced my hand. I would not have chosen to see you again."

He could see they were going to get nowhere until he settled the true reason for her visit. But if he capitulated and admitted that now, would she immediately walk back out the door? He didn't want that. He needed her. He needed her to stay. He needed to touch her, to love her, to shut the world out and pretend once again that it was just the two of them. That all the insanity was just a bad dream.

He offered her his hand. She still stood like a stone.

He sighed. "Yes, we have it. Is that what you want to hear?"

She shook slightly. Was that relief? Or fear he saw pass over her face.

Enough playing. Enough procrastinating. He put his arms around her and held her close. She resisted, unmoving—playing the stone maiden. But he held on. He kissed the top of her head. He inhaled the left over lavender scent of shampoo in her hair.

There were no secrets between them. They'd both been honest with each other about their passions, why they each pursued a different path. Eventually, she softened. He felt moisture upon his shirt. "Oh, Angel. Don't cry. It's not hopeless. We'll work it out. We always do."

"I'm so tired," she said. "It's too much. It's too much to fight Eternity and to fight you too."

He hugged her tighter. "But we aren't fighting, Miki. We aren't fighting. We're accepting."

She looked up. Her tear stained face tore his heart. How long could they go on? How long could they continue to be on opposite sides and still come together. It hurt more each time. Would there come a time when the pain of seeing each other was even worse than the relief?

"Miki, come with me."

Rohin's voice rang out again, and she started in surprise. He was standing right next to her. He turned to one side and his hand pressed at her back, leading her toward a door at the side of the room. No, she thought. No, I am not going to bed with him again. I am not!

"What is it? Don't clam up on me now. Let me help you forget. Let's help each other."

Her breath came quickly, and she struggled to slow down her racing heart. She dug in her foot and strained against him, suddenly desperate to get away—away from his quiet voice, the siren call to forgetfulness—but he had a tight grip at her waist.

"The only way you can help me is to return what you stole. Return the Ager virus."

"You know I can't do that. You knew that before you entered the building."

She shook her head in denial.

"Come on, Miki. No matter what has happened in these past months, at least we've been honest with each other. Don't try to fool me now. Don't try to fool yourself. All we have is our honesty."

"I thought...I hoped you..." She paused. No, he was right. When Anna had told her to seek out Rohin and get the sample back, she'd known it would be futile. She'd known there was no way she could go against him, threaten him. "Okay. You win. I came here because I had no choice. Because I had to try, even though I knew your answer. Are you satisfied?"

"I don't think so." He tilted his head to one side, his gaze thoughtful.

She stared at him for a long moment. There was a spark in his eyes that told her she was asking a loaded question, a question she already knew the answer to. She wanted to say nothing. She wanted to turn around and walk out the door and forget she'd ever thought, even for one moment, this would work. But she knew Rohin wouldn't let her go until he'd gotten everything out of her.

Her breasts tingled as she remembered the heat of his touch. She cleared her throat, trying to get a grip on her emotions. "I want to leave...now."

"Liar."

"Just leave it alone, Rohin. For once. Please." She didn't dare look at him. She knew if she looked at him, he would have her within two seconds and she would capitulate. She couldn't go there again. She couldn't go there...and leave...again.

"You know I never leave anything alone," he said, his voice sensuous, quiet, confident.

She swallowed hard at the look in his eyes. "Rohin, it's not fair," she said, not sure what else she wanted to say. Should she tell him to stop, to let go, or to pull her closer, to kiss her like he'd done in New Austra-land? Like he'd done in Qyzylqum? Oh, God. She counted the days of happiness in her life purely by the times they were together—by the times she could forget.

Rohin didn't give her a chance to decide "Life is never fair," he whispered as his mouth descended on hers with passion and purpose. Each time was so much better than the last. Each time she was sure that it would be the last—that she would give up her dream for the Agers and stay with him. She opened her mouth to his, their tongues tangling in a dance of heat and desire. The spark that had been smoldering since she walked in the door burst into a full blaze as she melted into his arms. She slipped her hands under his shirt. She wanted to touch him, to taste him, to strip off his clothes. There was nothing else in her mind but him, and she relished the pure focus of her thoughts as everything else slipped away.

She banished the rolling edges of reason trying to make their way back into her brain, the tiny voice saying this wasn't the right place or the right time. This wasn't why she came here. She was letting down millions of people.

No! Go away! She tried to chase her responsibilities out of her head. It felt right, dammit. It felt like what she'd been waiting for since meeting with Dr. Finn, since the last time they were together. She wanted him. She needed him.

She tore her lips from his, and it felt like tearing her skin and leaving a blazing open wound. This wasn't how it was supposed to go.

"Rohin, I can't." Tears filled her eyes and she swallowed hard for them not to fall. She forced him from her, her chest heaving with rough, ragged breaths.

He stared back at her in shock. She knew he wouldn't force himself on her. God, she'd counted on that. She could read the questioning in his eyes. She was questioning too, but now that they were no longer touching, her reason came back.

She re-zipped the front of her suit. "We can't do this now. *I* can't do this now."

Her own words made her stronger. Embarrassment at her weakness came with the realization that she'd completely lost her mind a moment earlier. Forgetfulness was not what she needed. She needed promises. Promises that the world was going to be a better place. She could no longer play the pretend game—pretending that she and Rohin would somehow magically end up together in utopia even though they were fighting against each other.

Rohin looked at her long and hard. She wondered what he saw— now that they weren't caught in the clutches of passion.

"You're right. I'm sorry," he said. "I wanted you. I wanted you to be part of my dream. Perhaps I've been too caught up in my own symbolism, too caught up in the future when I should be focusing on the present. I got lost in the dream."

She lifted a hand toward his cheek. She wanted to feel the firmness of his jaw, trace his lips once more. She thought better of it and dropped her hand back to her side.

"I wanted it too," she said. "I want the dream as much as you do.

But it's not real. It can't be real until something happens, until Eternity is no longer in control."

"Can we start from there?" he asked, reaching to her again. "We do have some points of agreement."

She took a step back. She needed space, air. She couldn't listen... shouldn't. He'd trick her with his talk, with his dreams, with his body. He was too much for her. She'd get lost in him, and she'd never find her way out. She tucked a stray hair behind her ears and shifted her feet. "I need to go."

He looked straight at her, as if he could read every thought, every feeling, every dream. She shuddered at his power.

"If you walk away now, there truly is no hope," he said. "No hope for us. No hope for our world."

Her brow furrowed. Her breath shortened. "I...I don't know." She shouldn't trust him. She shouldn't listen. But he had her and he knew it. What was he offering. They couldn't work together. They didn't see the same path.

He took her hand and guided her to a long sofa in front of the windows that looked out on the New Mexico mesa. She sat, unable to leave, but stole herself to question every thing he said.

"We both hate Eternity."

She nodded, unwilling to give words to any agreement.

He squeezed her hand. "We both love each other."

Her eyes teared again. That was so unfair. That's exactly why she was in this dilemma. She couldn't seem to leave him. But she couldn't stay.

"I'd protect you with my life."

Her eyes widened. What was he saying? What did he know that she didn't? She couldn't imagine a situation where he'd be asked to do that.

"It doesn't matter that I have a sample of your counter virus," he said.

"It does matter. You'll work to stop my work. If you find a way to negate it, you've chosen to stop my dream in favor of yours."

He shook his head. "No, I haven't changed anything. The only difference is we are both racing to see who wins. Why not just accept that only one of us can win? What does that have to do with us? With what we have between us?"

She sputtered in disbelief. "Do you believe that if the Agers don't prevail and it's because of you, that I can stay with you?" She paced, her arms flailing as her anger grew. "You treat my dream as if it was nothing, as if it was a passing fancy."

"That's completely untrue," he said, his voice even quieter than before, forcing her to stop her pacing and listen.

She worked to regulate her breathing, to stop her heart from pounding so hard.

"I know that only one can win," he said. "But it doesn't stand in the way of my feelings for you."

"You're just saying that because you don't believe I can win. You've already forgiven me for trying because you don't believe I have a chance in hell. Well, I can't forgive you, Rohin. If you stop me and you get your way, I can't forgive you."

Rohin smiled and pulled her to him. She struggled in his arms, but he only held her tighter. Finally, she stood still.

He braised her temple with his lips. "But you do, angel." He sighed into her hair. "Every time we make love you forgive me. Every time I touch you, you forgive me."

"No," she said. "That's my body betraying me. That's not my heart. That's not my soul. It's only my body."

"Really?" He bent to her mouth and plundered.

She couldn't help herself. She tried not to kiss him back. She tried to fill her mind with steel and stone, but he kept pushing and pushing. The warmth worked from her lips to her breasts. They tingled and peaked. Then it moved down her torso to her stomach. Her heart hammered. He delved deeper, opening her mouth, pulling her tongue in with his. She couldn't help it. Heat pooled between her legs and she rubbed against him and responded to him with desperation.

It's just sex. It's just sex, she chanted to herself as her eyes closed and the sensations took over any logic, any fight, as if bound to prove her wrong.

He eased off her lips and she sagged against him. He lifted her chin and looked into her eyes. "Miki, at least be honest about this. Whatever else is between us—our organizations, our path to save the world, you can't deny that we love each other."

She shook her head, "No, it's just sex, it's just…"

He captured her mouth again. This time he barely allowed her to get a breath. He moved his hands firmly along her back. He pressed her buttocks to bring her closer. His erection made it clear exactly what she did to him.

He tore his mouth from hers and she cried out. Her hands clawed at his shirt, at his pants. She needed him. She needed to be one with him. Now.

"Tell me this is only sex," he held her to him almost violently, as if letting her go would throw him into the depths of hell. "Tell me you've felt this with any other man."

She groaned.

"Tell me!" he demanded. "Tell me and I'll let you go, right now."

"I can't," she whispered in desperation. "I can't lose you again. God help me. I love you. I've tried not to, but I do. Oh god, I do."

He bent and took her lips. First softly, as if questioning his right. Then deeply, a promise hanging between them. As she stretched to accept that promise, he tore himself away.

"Eternity is going to come after you, Miki. They are going to come after you and kill you. I can't let that happen. You must stay with me. Stay here and let me protect you."

She leaned back from him, her eyes wide. "What do you know? Why do you say that?"

"I know they have spies in your camps."

"They've always had spies. You have spies. I have spies. Everyone has spies."

The fear in his eyes seeped into her. Why was he so scared? What had changed? "Tell me, Rohin. Tell me what you know."

He put his hand on her shoulders and squeezed. "You won't believe me. You won't want to believe me."

She looked up at him. Could she trust him? Could she trust him to tell her the truth? "I'll try."

He swallowed. "My information says that Anna is an Eternity spy."

Her shoulders sagged in relief. She laughed. The laughter felt so good, it almost turned to hysteria.

"This isn't the response I expected," he said. "Anger or denial, maybe. Not laughter."

She smiled and brushed his lips. "Anna is a spy for me in Eternity, and our plan has been for her to lead Kant to believe she is also a spy for him. We plan what information she will leak about the Ager operation. It keeps us in control of the information." She brushed his lips again. "Thank you for caring." She kissed him more deeply, passionately."

She reached for his shirt, and pulled it open. She shucked her own top and pressed herself against him, her fingers rolling through his hair. To hell with her plans not to make love this time. He was the only one in her life who truly cared about her. Whatever their differences, they would always have this. They would always be honest with each other.

He pushed her away. "As much as I'd love to have you now, you have to listen to me first."

"More?" She crossed her arms over her breasts, suddenly feeling exposed. "Someone else?"

He scrubbed a hand through his hair. His jaw tightened as if he had to force himself to speak. "It is Anna."

"No, I just told you..."

"Miki, think." He shook her shoulders. "Forget how you've planned things with her. Forget that she's been a part of the Agers for a long time."

"More than one hundred years," Miki reinforced.

"Think about those one hundred years. You know Anna better than anyone. Do you really believe she has taken up your cause?"

"Yes, she has proven her loyalty. She has..."

He shook his head. "No. Think. Put aside what logic tells you and look deep in your heart. You know Anna better than anyone."

She couldn't believe it. She would not admit Anna could be double-crossing her. It wasn't possible. "You've never liked her, Rohin. You don't know her. I do."

"I know she has always wanted to get ahead."

"So, what's bad about that?"

"At any cost?" He paused. "Remember how she pushed you aside when we were first in Antarctica? How she wanted to be the head of the research team?"

Miki thought back to that time. Yes, Anna had told some lies to her then. But they were all struggling to shine. They were new researchers at the beginning of their career. It wasn't a big deal. It didn't really matter who was the head as long as they worked together.

Rohin interrupted her reminiscence. "Then, when you were fired."

"You mean when you got me fired," Miki said, her voice obstinate. They'd been over this ground before and there was no way she would believe that Rohin had nothing to do with that.

"When you were fired," he continued. "How loyal was Anna then?"

It was true Anna hadn't been fired with her. But later she'd quit, and when she joined Miki's movement she'd told her how she'd tried to stop them from firing Miki but couldn't.

"She didn't find you for more than thirty years," Rohin persisted. "Isn't that right?"

"Yes, but then she..."

"That's because she took over the project from me, Miki. That's because she was working her way up in Eternity. I don't know for sure when she left Eternity...or if she ever really left...but I know that she told lots of lies about you. You were being blamed for everything that went wrong."

"No!" Miki refused to believe him. "She wouldn't. She told me that..."

He shook her again. "Think. I know this hard for you, but think."

Miki shook her head again. What proof did he have? He wasn't there. She wasn't there. How could he know?

"Think about everything that's gone wrong with the Agers," since Anna joined you.

He wouldn't let go of it. Why? Why was he so desperate to implicate Anna? What would it get him?

"You can't blame everything on her?"

"Think about what's happened lately? Do you think my spies could have found your virus without Anna's help?"

She inhaled a breath and held it. "You mean she told…"

"I mean she told one of my spies who is inside Eternity."

She shook her head violently from side to side. No. It couldn't be true. He was trying to trick her. He just wanted her to come over to his side. No.

He took her face in his hands. Stopping her shaking. He gently turned it up to him and looked her in the eye. "I love you." He grazed his thumb along her chin. "I love you so much I will die to protect you. Please, Miki. Please stay with me."

Tears threatened her again. Die for her? How could he? How could he say that and be so sure, so vulnerable to her?

"I have never…never…lied to you," he said.

She crumbled against him, her entire body shaking as she accepted everything he'd said. Once she let the truth of it in, she could see all the signs. She started to put together all the incidents that had been occurring over the years. She questioned every report Anna had given her on Kant, on Eternity, on anyone else within her organization. Was it possible that the damage was so much, the Agers could never win now? Anna knew everything. Everything of importance.

Her sobs racked her very being. She crawled completely into Rohin's lap and he rocked her. "I'll help you," he promised. "I'll protect you." His promises made her cry all the more.

She turned her lips to his bare chest. She kissed him and her desperation grew. She worked her way up to his mouth. Her lips pleaded with his begging for release, begging for a promise of light, for a promise of a future together.

"Miki." He breathed her name on a note of husky desire.

"Take me somewhere," she said. "Take me to your utopia."

"I'm not sure this is the right time. We need to talk. I need you to tell me you'll stay."

"I can't stay," she said. "You know I can't." She looked up, begging him with every part of her body. "Please, Rohin." She could no longer hold back the tears. "Please, take me away. It's too much. Please."

He gently lowered her to the sofa, his lips never leaving hers.

With reckless abandon, she exploded into his mouth, a mix of desperation and wonder tangling their tongues together in an impatient dance of need and desire. Miki didn't want to think anymore. She didn't want to consider the past or the future, just the present—in Rohin's arms. She wanted to feel him on top of her, beneath her, inside of her. She wanted to take his strength, his confidence, his power, and make them her own. She was being selfish, but she didn't care. She needed to take, and he seemed more than willing to give.

Rohin tugged her shirt off of her and tossed it to the floor. His mouth immediately sought the curve of her neck. He sucked her skin between his lips, and she gasped at the sharp tingle that spiraled through her. His mouth moved lower, his tongue tracing the edge of her breasts. His strong, golden-brown hand palmed her breast, his thumb grazing her nipple.

She let out a small cry, then wantonly pushed her breast into his hand. His mouth moved lower, his tongue sliding down the valley between her breasts. She felt a line of fire race through her veins. And when his mouth closed over her breast, she pulled his head closer, twisting her fingers in the strands of his thick, black hair. She sank further into the cushion as he tugged on her nipple with the edge of his teeth. Then his mouth moved lower, laving a sweet trail down to her belly. He unsnapped her pants and pulled them off along with her silky white thong.

As Rohin's eyes met hers, he whispered, "I love you, Miki. I can't live without you."

For the first time, she really believed him. She knew that what had happened in the past was exactly as he said. She knew that he would truly do everything in his power to protect her—even to die for her. She knew that even though they'd chosen different paths, that he would find a way for them to be together—forever. He knew everything about her—what she was thinking, what she wanted, what she needed. She didn't know how, or why it would work. But she believed. She believed in him.

She sat up, grabbed the edge of his pants, and helped him out of them. She pulled him back to her until he covered her body with his. She wriggled against his erection, wanting him inside her as quickly as possible. Wanting the joining that would keep the promises they'd made to each other.

He put his hand under her head and kissed her with deliberation. She didn't want to go slow. She wanted it hard, fast, wild.

Impatient, she pulled him into the cradle of her hips. He touched her intimately with his fingers, driving her crazy with desire. But she wanted all of him.

Her fingers dug into his hips as he finally thrust into her. He took his time at first, drawing out every movement.

"Please, Rohin. Hurry! Hurry!"

He chuckled at her desperation and his pace quickened. "Whatever you want, Miki. I'm here for you."

She urged him on, wanting nothing but the mindless pleasure that was washing over her in huge, caressing waves. Her thoughts blurred, her emotions collided with his. She'd never felt such an intense connection to him, as if they were one mind, body, and spirit.

The unity they shared suddenly worried her. How could they possibly continue as before? How could they possibly continue on their separate paths but stay together. She stiffened, holding back, questioning, unsure.

"Let it go, Miki," Rohin urged, each thrust taking her higher, deeper. "Trust me. I put my life in your hands from the beginning. Now give me yours. Give me everything."

He didn't know what he was asking. He didn't know the risk she

was taking. And what was she asking of him? What was she promising. Would she die for him too? But it was too late to stop. They came
together, her cries mixing with his. She gave him everything she had.

Yes. The answer was yes. She would die for him. Anything to keep
their love together. For surely she would die without him.

18

Miki paced anxiously in the small room off the main cafeteria. This would be the first time all the factional leaders would be in one place. She only hoped the precautions taken in getting everyone here had been successful in confusing Eternity's agents. She knew Kant's organization couldn't keep track of every small protest group. Eternity had neither the personnel nor the inclination to follow them all at the same time—they lived by the philosophy that small groups were tolerated rather than squelched. If they attempted to stop every group it would only make the protests stronger. Miki just hoped that no one knew how many of the leaders were going to be represented here today.

The cafeteria normally served the Eco-Awareness Research facility's two hundred and fifty three employees. Unknown to Eternity, Eco-Awareness Inc. was one of the many arms of the Ager organization. Eternity perceived Eco-Awareness as a small group of fanatics concerned about the environment, usually found at protests near industrial sites, and often found in communal living areas with the "back to nature" crowd. Unconcerned about wilderness acreage on the steep slopes of Mt. Hood, Eternity had granted them a fifty kilometer wilderness area for their research facility and commune—

mostly to keep them out of the news and out of Eternity's offices. The group lived completely off grid, using passive solar buildings, hydro and wind power from the river running through the property, and kept everything very rustic.

There was a knock at the door a few minutes later and a member of her security team entered. "They're almost all here," she said. "We only have two more people to go—Shaban, from Syria, and Lareina, from Wales."

Miki nodded. She was familiar with both of them. Shaban was the regional coordinator in the middle east. He spoke for three different protest groups represented in fourteen countries. Lareina was the leader of the Anniversary Protest. She had been the most difficult to convince to join the Agers. However, her dwindling membership forced her to realize that eventually there would be no one left to burn publicly—not to mention the deaf ear that society had turned to her group's pleas.

For the past month Miki and Anna had been contacting leaders of a variety of subsidiary protest organizations. Arrangements for bringing leaders from around the world had been a logistics challenge, many of them switching routes and back-tracking several times, while also doing their normal protests. Over the past two weeks people had been arriving and filtering into the facility, learning to blend in with the daily routines of the full time residents.

Helios and Muru had handled the logistics and the cover stories, with Muru making the final shuttles for each of the leaders. Each leader had made arrangements for meetings or conferences to attend, and no more than three leaders had attended any one named conference. For each of the spurious meetings, typical conference materials and souvenirs had been created. Thus, all returning members would have viable stories of what they learned at these meetings. Carefully selected Ager Command security personnel were responsible for ferrying attendees to this facility without being noticed. At the same time arrangements were made for many regular employees to be absent from the facility. This allowed the total numbers of personnel in the area to appear consistent. Temporary lodging had to be found for the most watched leaders along with disguises, keeping them safe from prying eyes. Miki didn't dare trust even the employees at Eco Awareness headquarters—one never knew when Kant may have turned one into a spy.

By the time another ten minutes had gone by Miki was growing even more restless. Anna knew almost everything about this meeting. It was because of that knowledge that Miki had been able to convince Anna not to attend. She'd told her she wanted Anna to tell Kant about it, to give her something big to share with Kant. Together they'd decided what he would be told. Then together they'd decided what would happen at the meeting. Miki made sure to slip in information that was untrue. Then she'd know exactly what lies Anna was telling on both sides.

"What time is it?" she asked the guard.

"1830."

"I can't wait any longer." Miki moved toward the door. "If the other two aren't here yet they will have to see me later. We have to start moving people out again."

She sent a silent signal to guards at the two entrances, then she entered the cafeteria. The guards secured the doors and activated a transparent privacy field around the perimeter with pre-recorded background noise, ensuring that none of the discussion could be heard outside the building but the din of talking and plates moving and being washed would sound normal.

Miki went through the cafeteria line, selected a regular meal, then wandered into the main seating area. Once she selected a table, she set her tray down and made the rounds of introductions to the highest level leaders. She would sit at the table for awhile and have a discussion, then move to another table. Although she had been in contact with all the major leaders via Vid and MC link she had rarely met any of them in person. Furthermore, it had been a relatively short time since many of these factions had been convinced to come under the Ager umbrella. Miki's reputation of successfully fighting world governments was the primary unifying force. When each of these groups had to make their final commitment to follow the Ager plan she realized that her physical and emotional presence could be the determining factor.

Each faction was represented by at least one individual. Japan had two representatives: one for the Historical Preservation Society, and one for United Martyrs. The Mediterranean had one representative for all the Anniversary protesters in Italy, Greece, and Spain; then a separate representative for each of the European republics. The regional representation remained uneven, due to the continued difficulty in recruiting dedicated members.

Exactly one hundred seventy-eight separate factions were represented in this room. These leaders together commanded the resources and loyalties of over twenty million individuals. Although a small number in comparison to a world population of 30 billion, their dispersion throughout almost every populated area was the key to instituting great change when the time came.

After completing the usual introductions of key members, Miki returned to her own table and began to eat her dinner. She wanted everything to appear normal to any possible outside spies.

A casual onlooker would see into the cafeteria and notice people eating meals, workers removing trays, and what appeared to be normal dinner conversation for the commune. However, if they tried to enter the cafeteria, they would be stopped by a worker explaining this seating was full, and that they could return for the 2100 seating.

Miki was dressed casually, like the other members seated at the various tables. She had selected a central table where they sat together with three other Ager command representatives. As Miki moved her food around her plate she began talking in a normal speaking voice; and the wireless mike on her lapel broadcasted her message to ear pieces worn by each leader in the cafeteria. She spoke in Frenger, the common language used by Ager command.

"This is Miki Yokoyama," she began. "Thank you for your patience and cooperation in coming here. Please remember, as I speak do not look up. Do not look around any more than you would during a regular meal. Continue eating, occasionally moving your lips silently as if in conversation with your tablemates. If anyone is observing us from the outside we do not want to draw undue attention to ourselves." She paused for a moment and slowly surveyed the room to ensure everyone was doing as she asked. It was a strange sight to see people moving their mouths all around the room but not hear a sound. Assured that it looked fairly normal, Miki continued.

"I'm sorry this has to be so short," Miki said to them, turning her head only to those at her table. "But any longer meeting would call attention to your absence from your group or, worse, your presence here. I especially appreciate the . . . shall we say . . . diversions provided by those of you who are regularly followed by Eternity's spies. After this meeting we will be contacting you individually to carry out the details of the plan I am proposing this evening. As I give my remarks the cafeteria personnel will distribute individual mikes to each table. They are attached to the dessert trays. As questions arise please pick up the tray and it will be activated immediately. There is only one mike per table, so be sure to pass the tray to give an opportunity for everyone to ask questions."

She paused a moment, allowing the workers to move through the room picking up some trays and delivering the mikes. When approximately one-third of the mikes had been delivered she began again.

"I have asked you to be here so that you could meet one another and begin to work toward our common goal—the elimination of the Eternity Virus. Though each of your organizations have a slightly different focus and philosophy the time has come to pull together our resources and to put aside our differences. We must prepare for the final phase prior to implementation of the aging process back into society." She heard an audible gasp as the members realized that the past seventy years of research may be coming to fruition.

"We have information that there may be a counter agent, in the form of another virus, that can stop or mutate the Eternity Virus enough to make it ineffective. We currently have a research team working on obtaining this agent. I believe it is only a matter of months before we will find it and have it available for limited testing.

"We plan the first testing to be on a population of two hundred volunteers. To ensure the counter virus is equally effective in all races

I will need volunteers from every region of the world. These volunteers will have to be confined at the Ager compound Z25, living in quarantine in the cave quarters we have built for emergency evacuation. They also will be restricted to a ten kilometer wilderness area which will be marked by security screens. Certain research facilities, libraries, recreation facilities and physicians will be transported to the caves as a part of the quarantined area.

"It is absolutely imperative that the volunteers do not leave the compound, under any circumstances, until we are ready to introduce the counter agent into the general population. If the counter agent transmission proves to be unpredictable or the physical aging process begins to show, and we are not prepared for the popular response, the chaos that would ensue could be devastating to our cause."

Miki paused again, giving her words time to register in each leader's mind. Thus far there were no questions; however this first step simply outlined the plan in a form they would have expected.

"What personal risk will there be to us?" a male voice asked shakily. "Is there any possibility of immediate death after coming in contact with this agent?"

"From our preliminary research we believe this agent, by itself, does not cause premature death." Miki responded. "It will simply return your immune system to a state that allows for the natural aging process to occur. Of course, you will be more receptive to disease again; and there are a number of diseases that can be fatal. However, our medical advances should keep you safe from the worst of them. Actually, if you are caught transmitting the virus, it's more likely you will die at the hands of an Eternity spy than by the virus itself."

"What time frame are we talking about here?" a feminine voice spoke up.

"Again, I'm not sure," Miki responded. "I anticipate a minimum of a one year trial with the limited introduction to the volunteers. If the limited testing proves viable, then we would make it immediately available at that time."

"A year seems a long time to wait and plan," the same feminine voice said.

"We also need the next year to increase the education process in your areas. If this agent is only transmitted by forceful means, like injection, then you will have an uprising to work against, unless you have subtly prepared them previously. It is up to all of us to begin making people aware of their need to change. We already know preaching and protesting doesn't work. We have to implement specific methods to counter Eternity's brainwashing. Buy commercial time in their vid movies. Come up with subtle campaigns for aging. Develop positive images of older people. Make entertainments, games, art, theater—all that show aging as a normal part of life. If the general population begins to see enough of this, it won't come as such a shock later. All these things need to be a part of your alternative planning."

The sound of a mike being passed to someone else alerted Miki to wait. Then a nasal-sounding masculine voice began speaking. "The Earth Day Coalition questions your plan. True, we support the end of the Eternity Virus. The increase of population, and dominance of man with no predator, has created a frightening unbalance in the ecology. However, the introduction of another unknown agent may only swing the earth to the other extreme. What assurances do we have that this won't get out of hand?"

A murmur of agreement passed through most of the room.

"There is not a one hundred percent assurance," Miki answered. "Our research suggests that this virus, which existed thousands of years ago, became a natural selector in humankind. In fact, it was an important part of creating that balance you seek. In the very unlikely event of a violent reaction, we will have that two year period to assess the proper method for use of the counter agent. But I strongly believe we will be returning humanity to a natural path of development, not another uncertain trail. If you don't agree with this assessment, please offer an alternative."

There was no further response from table one. Miki then indicated activation of the next mike. Several tables passed before another question was presented.

"Birth Rights Worldwide doesn't see how this plan can help our cause," a soft, almost shy feminine voice responded. "We agree with the introduction of a counter agent, but how will that stop Eternity from limiting our ability to have children? We need Eternity stopped permanently, not eventually. If you can't do this, we will go our own way."

At the end of that speech the tension in the room rose noticeably. Several people threw heated words toward the speaker. In return supporters of her philosophy fought back with their words.

A skirmish appeared at table five where the mike had been activated. Miki glanced over and noticed that one of the male council members was standing threateningly over the speaker. In addition to using a tirade of swear words, his fists were pumping open and closed as his arms flailed in impassioned gestures. Miki recognized him immediately as James Cosgrave, the leader of Stars First, an organization which wanted to pursue colonization of other planets. Since they were one of the most oppressed by Eternity, they had become one of the most violent and fearful factions under the Ager umbrella.

"You're all fanatics," he yelled. "You want to bring Eternity down on us so quickly we'll all disappear? I'll kill you first before I let that happen!" Then he lunged at the previous speaker, missing her throat by a few inches as several other members held him back.

Miki rushed over to the table and personally took control of the situation. She placed herself between the man, now being held by three people, and the female who was cowering beneath the table.

"What are you doing?" Miki demanded. "Everyone is allowed to voice their opinions here. If you decide to kill everyone in opposition to you, you might as well join Eternity and become one of Kant's people. You are no better than them!"

The man glared at Miki but stopped struggling with his captors.

"The rest of you," she spoke authoritatively to the people in the room who were now all staring at table five, "go back to eating and pretending to talk. We don't know who might be watching." All eyes turned back to their tables, and they began moving their mouths again in pretended conversation. However, all ears were perked, waiting for the next outburst.

"If you disagree so strongly with our activity here that you must resort to a physical attack, then choose me for your attack," Miki addressed the man. "I represent the majority opinion here. I'm as much to blame as anyone. But beware, I guarantee it will not be as easy to take me down. Let him go," she ordered the three men holding him back.

The man stood in front of her, his body coiled, ready to spring. But he made no move toward her. After less than a sixty second standoff, the man backed away slowly, still locking eyes with her. As he approached his table, he felt for the edge and stopped. Seeming to suddenly lose all energy, he stared ahead vacantly.

"Please, sit down," she pointed to the man's original chair.

Miki watched cautiously as the man slowly took his seat, his normal coloring beginning to return. When she was assured the situation had been completely diffused, she signaled to a member of the security detail to stand nearby and watch him until the end of the meeting. She would deal with his lack of discipline later.

"Now, are there any more questions or opinions?" Miki asked, returning to her own table. "I trust we can proceed in an orderly manner."

Although all the mikes were activated no further questions were asked. The previous scene had evidently acted both as an emotional catharsis for several members, as well as a reminder of Miki's ability to maintain control.

"If there are no further questions then let me leave you with some final thoughts," she continued. "Remember, we are taking on Eternity, the most powerful organization in the world. And we are forcing humanity to make a most difficult change, to give up the prospect of very long lives. We must persuade people that the reality of the dream of living for eight hundred years is, in fact, a nightmare. We must show humanity the societal nightmare that those of us in this room have witnessed."

Miki paused to catch her breath and then rose to begin moving around the room, taking an opportunity to stop at each table briefly and address them personally. For the next hour she answered individual questions, provided assurances, and listened to complaints and suggestions. Finally, it was time to leave. She moved toward the front of the room and placed her tray on the washing conveyor before making her final comments.

"I can't do it alone," she continued. "I need your help. All humanity needs your help." Then she turned away and slipped through the door with Muru on her heels.

"20:07. Not bad," Muru said with admiration. "For a minute I thought we were going to have a riot. But, as usual, you handled it well."

"Thanks," Miki responded, as she hurriedly walked out the back door and down the stairs. She was glad it was over, and she felt a need to put distance between herself and the crowd of people inside. It was the first major step in a long fight. She was emotionally exhausted.

Reaching the bottom of the stairs she stopped and leaned wearily against the wall. She raised a shaky hand to push her bangs away from her perspiring forehead. "Thank God I don't have to do this again! I know they're scared, but so am I. I just hope when they return home they will truly evaluate the situation. I'm sure those who search their hearts will stand with us. But I'm afraid many of them will find it much easier to give up without really trying."

"Don't worry," Muru consoled her. "They won't give up. They're just testing you."

"Right," Miki said, resigned. Then she pushed herself away from the wall, prepared to tackle the next step. "Is the hover ready?"

"Yes. You can leave right away," Muru responded. "It's parked behind the lab."

"Thanks." She touched him on the shoulder. "You've been a true friend."

"I'm sorry you've had such a shock," he said.

She turned her head away and swallowed. Beyond Rohin, only

Muru and Helios knew about Anna. She had to let someone know, someone who could watch with her.

Muru cleared his throat. "I think I'll stick around here and listen to how they react. I might be able to steer a couple of conversations in the right direction before everyone leaves. I can also make sure everyone departs as scheduled and that we haven't picked up a few unwanted Eternity guests."

"Thank you," she said. "Thank you...for everything. I'll see you tomorrow before you leave for Antarctica with Anna?" Miki asked.

"As planned," he responded.

Miki left, moving slowly up the hill toward the lab and her waiting hover.

KANT's private vidcomm buzzed insistently in his bedroom. Grumbling, he rolled over in bed and gave the MC a voice command to transfer the call to his wall screen. Within a microsecond a young male, dressed in a silver skinsuit bearing the Eco-Awareness Inc. logo was displayed on his bedroom wall. Kant vaguely recognized the logo, but not the man.

"Yes, what is it you want?" Kant asked impatiently, blinking as he adjusted his eyes to the light.

"Observer 133 with a priority report, sir," the agent answered.

"Go ahead," Kant said, pulling himself upright in bed, trying to focus his concentration.

Standing at attention the young man began his report. "I have been monitoring the air and foot traffic into and out of Eco-Awareness Inc., as usual. In the past two days I noted a thirty-eight percent increase in vehicular traffic into the research facility, sir."

"Did you check to see if they were conducting some sort of conference?" Kant asked, growing more interested as he became instantly alert.

"Yes, sir. There was no conference scheduled. On your standing order number four I infiltrated the compound under the guise of an employee."

"Excellent. Go ahead," Kant encouraged him.

"I counted the total number of personnel and only noticed an increase of five. Unfortunately, this could be easily accounted for as temporary visitors." The young agent began to perspire slightly and had some difficulty maintaining his composure.

Kant noted his nervousness and refrained from smiling. He enjoyed having this kind of power over people. A little fear never hurt, he thought to himself.

"Still I was determined to ascertain reasons for the unusual increase in vehicular traffic," the observer continued. "I followed a large group of employees to the first dinner seating at the company cafeteria."

"Good," Kant interjected. "Do you have access to the cafeteria yourself? Were you able to ask some carefully placed questions of other employees?"

"No, sir. All employees are coded and monitored for meal taking."

"Of course," Kant remarked, while at the same time instructing his MC to pull up the summary file on Eco-Awareness Inc. "Ah . . . yes," he said to himself.

"Sir?" the young man inquired, hesitantly.

"For the most part I have ignored Eco-Awarness for the past fifty years or so," Kant continued, as he read through the computer summary. "It seems, however, that restricting meals to coded employees is not unusual. When the company first incorporated it was running on a tight budget. It probably couldn't afford to feed anyone not registered."

"Sir?" Observer 133 interrupted again, unsure if he was to wait or proceed with his report.

"Yes," Kant answered distractedly. "Please, go ahead. Did you resolve this problem?" Kant knew there must be more. He was impatient to get to the meat of the problem. An observer would not have been patched through to his private vidcomm until he was interrogated by at least three levels of security personnel.

"Sir," the young man straightened once more before proceeding. "Although I was unable to obtain access to the cafeteria I did position myself so I could see and hear everything."

"Go ahead," Kant said.

"Well, sir, that was when I knew something unusual was happening. First, I counted one hundred seventy-eight people entering the cafeteria for the first seating. In a facility which only employs two hundred fifty I found it unusual that so many would be dining at the same time."

"Perhaps," Kant sighed. He could think of nothing particularly valuable about that information. "What else?"

"As I watched the cafeteria I heard the usual sounds of clanging dishes and the hum of voices inside. However, once the seating was closed and the doors locked, the noises ceased for a full second and then started up again."

Kant stared at the young man, his eyes growing wider as he tried to assimilate this report and analyze all the possibilities. However, he said nothing, indicating the report should continue.

"The problem was I could see inside the cafeteria and everything appeared normal. But that one second with no sound at all bothered me." The young agent was beginning to show signs of agitation. His hands trembled slightly at his side as he struggled to stay at attention. Kant wasn't sure if he had been frightened by these occurrences or he was simply frightened at reporting directly to Kant.

"Obviously they have a privacy screen and some pre-recorded noise," Kant commented. "Did you monitor any type of screening device?"

"Well, sir," the young man gulped. "I was in such a hurry that I forgot to bring my screen recorder with me. I thought this would be a minor reconnaissance exercise, easily completed." His forehead perspired profusely as his speech became halted and difficult to hear. "There have been so many times I've suspected something unusual, which later turned out to be easily explained, that I just didn't think to uh . . . bring it . . . uh . . . sir," he winced.

The young man visibly shook from head to toe. Though miles

from Kant he knew discipline could be swift. Kant made a point of all his observers knowing that a mistake would result in discipline that would be painful, but worse was not reporting an important incident. That would result in life in the hives, and Eternity withholding the Lifer Virus from any children the observer was allowed.

"I understand," Kant replied, patronizingly. "You did a good job except for that small error. Return to your post and tomorrow morning file a full report through the normal MC channels."

"Thank you sir," the young man replied, relieved. "Sorry to disturb you sir."

"Good night," Kant closed the connection then immediately sent a signal to Level Two security. This time the image of a slightly older man filled his wall screen.

"Yes sir!" the man said as he popped to attention.

"I immediately want observer 133 picked up for disciplinary action. Take him to retraining tonight, and after sixty days reassign him to sector six," Kant commanded.

"Yes sir. Is that all sir?" the man asked, as he recorded the instructions with his local MC link.

"At the same time I want fourteen Level Two security observers at Eco-Awareness Inc. by 0400. I want an ID on any person leaving Eco-Awareness within a twenty-four hour period."

"But sir, I'm not sure that we can get . . ." the man hesitated.

"I have no time for your excuses!" Kant said angrily. "The entire security of Eternity depends on this. I want to know exactly who is involved and what their plans are!" Kant's voice rose in frustration as the full impact of the observer's report assailed his consciousness. "If you fail me in this it will be more than disciplinary re-education for you," he let the unveiled threat hang ominously.

"Yes sir!" the man responded. "Your orders will be carried out immediately sir!"

Kant cut him off without further comment. Between losing his top spy, Anna Hollinrake, to remote Antarctica for several months, and now this report, it was getting more and more difficult for him to sleep at night. He climbed out of bed and changed into comfortable clothing. He would spend the night personally cross-referencing all subversive protest groups and their known leaders and philosophies. If his conclusions were correct he was determined to put a stop to it long before these divergent groups could effectively organize as one unit.

19

R ohin switched on his wall screen and distractedly accessed the blueprint files for three new church buildings. He knew he should be more interested, but he really didn't care about buildings or colors. Others could take care of that. As the buildings were being fashioned in the same pyramid style of the Dreamer headquarters there weren't a lot of decisions to be made.

He turned and stared out the window, looking past the glass, yet seeing nothing. It had been three long months since he'd seen Miki, and each day brought them closer and closer to disaster. Now with Anna so embedded in Eternity, he wasn't sure even the Agers and Dreamers together could stop her anymore. Each day he grew more afraid that he would not be able to protect her. That he wouldn't be there when she needed him the most.

Though they spoke at least weekly and renewed their vows to each other, they'd both been flooded with an ever-expanding membership. Every time they tried to make a trip coincide, something would happen to delay them. Even his dreams of her were being interrupted these days.

It was obvious she would never join the Dreamers, just as he would never join the Agers. He'd worked hard to replace her image in his dreams with the looming shadow of a woman standing in the way of humanity's destiny. In the beginning his picture of Miki was clear, and her shadow was small. Perhaps when he'd made his promises he felt he would eventually convince her that her approach couldn't possibly work. Sometimes he convinced himself that though her organization was large, it wasn't well organized—they didn't have a single vision like the Dreamers did. But it was all a convenient lie to himself.

Lately, when he dreamed of Miki, she was consumed by the shadow; and the shadow grew monstrous as further reports came in about her continued pursuit of an Ager virus. That brought her closer to danger every day—closer to the time when Anna would turn against her, maybe even be ordered to kill her. He shuddered at the thought.

How could he protect her from all of that without convincing her to give it up? If she never found the virus again, Kant would give up on her. Anna would do whatever Anna wanted in terms of her power within Eternity. But it didn't have to touch them. It didn't have to put her in danger.

The door to his suite buzzed. He brought up the viewscreen. He sighed. Another intelligence report from Langtree. He closed his eyes as he unlinked the door lock and braced for the worst.

Langtree greeted him then sat immediately in front of the desk, consulting his 'puter as he spoke. "One month ago there was an Eternity special priority observer report to Kant regarding a meeting at Eco-Awareness Inc. From our new source in data processing, we discovered that Kant had ordered a correlation analysis of all identified attendees. Unfortunately, we just received the analysis last week. Kant has had it for nearly three weeks."

"Farna!" Rohin swore in Uighur. "Why does it take so long to get good information?" He took a deep breath to calm down. "How many did they ID?"

"There was a ninety-nine percent probability of over one hundred and thirty outside participants at that meeting," Langtree continued. "Most of the attendees disappeared before the ID team could arrive.

However, twenty-two were identified as small protest group leaders, including two specifically from the Agers. Although no direct correlation to the Agers was found, Kant is suspicious that Miki Yokoyama was behind the gathering. Personally, I'm not sure if she was, or if he is just paranoid regarding her. He has carried a grudging fear of her ever since she forced his company to bring the Eternity Virus to the general population."

Rohin sighed and closed his eyes. "She was there. I'd bet on it."

SHANDRA'S long stride carried her quickly across the tree lined quad toward the Ager lab on the other side of the compound. The setting sun softened the angular features of her sharp square chin and high cheek bones, while enhancing the smooth coffee color of her skin. Her long slender fingers reached up to momentarily shade her eyes from the sun's reflection off the bright white building ahead. She squinted her dark brown eyes, recalling the coded message she had just received from Kim.

The Church of Dreams needed more specific information on the counter agent. What could she tell them? They hardly knew its full effects themselves. Somehow, she thought, she must personally accelerate and expand her own experiments. She knew that her work could well be the key link in the Church's plan to stop the Ager virus from being used.

I'll just have to take it one day at a time, she thought. If I pay special attention to my routine, note where additional tests could be run, then perhaps the Church can provide the expertise to help me. She knew she must not, she could not, fail the Church now. Hopefully, once this crisis was over, then she and Kim could be together again.

Shandra reached the small one-story building just prior to her normal work shift. This building contained the key lab in the quest to confirm the Ager virus' potency. She stepped up to the ID board and raised her palm to the scanner, waiting while the door slid quietly to one side. She stepped inside, allowing the exterior door to seal, then waited patiently for the inner door to open. The familiar chatter of animals greeted her. Despite the cacophony of sounds, she could pick out Darla's insistent screams. She heard her banging on the cage and screeching at the top of her lungs.

"Just a minute, you nut head," Shandra answered with amusement. She wound her way around several cages of rats, cats, dogs, and pigs, before finally reaching the monkeys. Her favorite was a coal black Rhesus which was always full of playfulness.

"Here you are, Darla," she said, reaching into her pocket and pulling out a half-eaten banana. "Don't you dare tell anyone where you got this." She stroked the monkey's head and was rewarded with shrieks and whistles.

She knew she wasn't supposed to become attached to the test animals or supplement their strictly controlled diet; but she couldn't help herself in this one case. Besides, half a banana was insignificant to Darla's diet.

"How are you feeling today?" she asked.

Darla downed the remaining banana in one gulp, then stuck her hand out for more.

"No. Sorry. No more."

As if she really understood, Darla slumped in her cage dejectedly.

Shandra unlatched the door, beckoning to her. "Now, now. Is that any way to act? Come here. Let me take a look at you."

Uncharacteristically, Darla refused to move. "What's wrong with you today? You're acting like an old woman—one minute you're full of complaints and demands, and the next you're sulking."

She reached in and offered her hand to Darla. Still the monkey wouldn't move. Finally, Shandra reached in with both hands and lifted her out. She placed her on the counter near the cage and tried to coax her back to friendliness; but Darla continued in her despondency. Eventually, Darla tiredly put her arms around Shandra, wanting to be held and hugged. Shandra responded by rocking her back and forth like a baby.

"Oh, you poor thing," Shandra cooed. "You just aren't feeling well, are you?" Then she heard the clunk of heavy soled shoes behind her. Turning quickly, Shandra almost dropped the monkey at the unexpected sight.

"Shandra, I didn't know you were here," Anna interrupted.

"Anna . . . I . . . I didn't think you worked this shift."

She grasped Darla even tighter, as if the action would keep her in control. Kim had warned her about the possibility of Anna's duplicity with both the Agers and Eternity. She hadn't realized, until now, how much that warning might effect her.

"This is my normal shift," Shandra continued. "Is there a problem?"

"Oh, no, not at all," Anna responded a little too blithely. "I just wanted to check on a few of the records here. Is everything all right with the monkey?" Anna seemed to be struggling to make friendly conversation.

"Well, I'm not sure. She seems to be more tired than usual. I think she's running a fever. It just doesn't make sense. We've only introduced the Ager virus in combination with Cold Virus B. The cold virus shouldn't have hit her this hard."

"Well, I'm sure there's a simple explanation," Anna responded somewhat absently.

Shandra noticed Anna's reflexive placement of a hand in her pocket and then a bulge, as if she was checking for something. But Shandra said nothing.

"It could even be as simple as her diet," Anna remarked.

"I guess I'll have to double check the virus samples she's receiving," Shandra purposefully looked in another direction. She hoped Anna wasn't suggesting an extra banana would effect the test results.

"That's a good idea," Anna responded, moving impatiently toward the front of the room. "Let me know what you find out." Then she hurried away.

Shandra waited to hear the door slide open and closed before she breathed a sigh of relief.

"Come on, Darla," Shandra addressed the monkey, putting her on the floor and taking her hand like a child's. "Let's go look at your records. I think it's time for another shot."

The two of them walked awkwardly together, winding past the cages to a section of lab which contained a single bench, an MC link with all the current records, and a small refrigerated unit containing the Ager counter-virus and disease serum samples. There were over six hundred different virulent diseases cataloged within the unit; most of them hadn't been seen in humans since the introduction of the Eternity virus.

With a firm reminder to behave, Shandra lifted Darla to one of the two stools near the bench. Seating herself on the other stool, she opened the appropriate 'puter file and quickly recalled Darla's record.

"Hmmm. That's interesting," Shandra said aloud. "The shot records seem to have changed. Instead of giving you Cold serum 12B, they've changed you to Virus 22A." She called up the serum index files to discover what was contained in virus 22A. "Ebola! Oh no! No wonder you're sick." Frantically pushing herself away from the bench she turned toward the refrigeration unit. "Let's see how virulent this sample is."

She opened the refrigerator door and scanned the labeled shelves for the specified serum. Finding a tray labeled 20A through 26A, she removed it from the unit; and quickly withdrew the small bottle labeled 22A.

"Now," she said, continuing to talk to Darla as if she were a human patient. "Let's see how bad this is." She knew that if by some grand mistake it was still an active culture it could be potentially fatal now that Darla's immune system was compromised by the Ager virus. Shandra straightened, attempting to temporarily close her mind from that possibility.

Caressing Darla reassuringly, she placed her into a holding pen near the desk. The last thing she needed was the monkey jumping on her while she was handling any of these virus samples. Though her Eternity enhanced immune system should easily counteract any viral attack, she wasn't one to take chances. After all, she was one of three researchers in constant contact with the new Ager virus. Since the tests were still incomplete, no one was sure of the variety of ways it could be transmitted.

She carefully donned a pair of latex gloves, and sealed them to her long sleeved shirt. Placing the bottle upside down beneath a protective glass shield she popped the seal from the injection bottle, inserted a syringe and withdrew a small amount for the slide sample. Moments later she placed the sample in the MC enhanced gamma ray microscope and waited for the automated analysis. The report, when finally displayed on the terminal, was totally unexpected.

"What? That's impossible." She requested a double check on the results. After another minute the results were again presented to her vid screen. "Someone has been tampering with these. There's nothing in this except a glucose and saline solution."

With shaking hands she removed a different disease sample, checked its reference in the computer, and identified it as Influenza A. She carefully noted its number on a piece of paper. Again she prepared a slide and waited for the MC's analysis. Again the answer was the same. She initiated an internal calibration of the machine, and when satisfied with the results she returned to the refrigerator. At random, she chose several more samples: smallpox, cholera, bacterial pneumonia F, until she had twelve possibilities to analyze. Every sample showed the same inert ingredients.

What happened to all of the test samples? And why were they changed? Whatever the reason, now she was certain this tampering went far beyond effecting only Darla. Immediately she accessed her vidcomm and initiated a call to Ager security.

"This is Shandra in Lab three," she told them quickly. "Someone has tampered with all the virus serums and placed the experiments in jeopardy." It was difficult for her to keep the rising hysteria from her voice. Anna's bulging pocket and her sudden appearance kept niggling her unconscious. "They've replaced the samples with sugar water. I haven't tested all of them, but I've tested enough to believe they are all the same."

"One moment," the security woman said. Shandra immediately noticed the flashing yellow light in the lower left corner of her vid, indicating a conference call. Abruptly the screen was filled with Miki's face.

"What happened, Shandra?" Miki asked.

She listened carefully as Shandra repeated her story about the testing, and her suspicions about Darla's condition. "The only person you saw in the lab today was Anna?"

"Yes," Shandra answered carefully. "Although I wouldn't dare to question her right to be here, her behavior seemed somewhat strange. I'm almost positive she had something in her pocket. But she couldn't possibly have carried out all the samples."

"No," Miki agreed. "And we shouldn't jump to any conclusions without more information. At least three other people have access to that lab. For all we know, these switches may have been occurring for several days. Have you checked the safe for the Ager reference sample?"

"No, I didn't think of that," Shandra responded, her voice shaking with the possibilities that thought brought to mind. "Just a minute, let me check."

Switching to the portable vidcomm, she ran to the large refrigeration unit and pressed a button near the floor. A keypad appeared and she entered her security code. "My code is in," she spoke without looking at the vidcomm. "I need a corresponding senior identification."

"Mine's in," Miki answered after a short pause.

A piece of the floor slid to one side and Shandra peered into the hole. "My God! It's gone. It's completely gone!"

"Security," Miki addressed the third party to the conversation. Shandra's screen image split in two to reveal both Miki's and Tran's faces. "I want an imaging team at the lab immediately. I want a forty-eight hour image report on any and all traces of human hair, scent, skin follicles, absolutely anything on or near the serum refrigeration unit or that key pad. I want a complete lockdown of the entire camp. No one leaves and no one enters. Immediately, pick up anyone who has been in or near that lab within the last forty-eight hours, including Anna. As you find suspects, confine them separately in building D. Tell them nothing about this investigation. I will personally do the interrogation. I expect a report within two hours. Sooner, if you can do it."

Security signed off and Miki's image encompassed the entire screen once more. "Shandra, I don't want you to mention this to anyone. Understand?"

"Yes, but . . ."

"No buts, Shandra. And don't leave the lab or you will be under suspicion as well. I'm sending security to make sure you are undisturbed. Until we find out who's involved, we can't afford to let anyone know that we've discovered the switch."

All Shandra could think about was her new knowledge of Anna's well-guarded contacts within Eternity. She shuddered at the thought of the counter virus getting into Kant's hands.

"We have to handle this cautiously," Miki continued. "Now, more than ever, we need the element of surprise on our side."

"I understand," Shandra responded, her voice trembling slightly. "Let me know what I can do."

"Right now you could be the most helpful by accurately diagnosing Darla's condition. Do a full bioscan and rerun all her bloodwork. I want to know what she's been given, and what the effect has been."

"I'll get right on it."

"Thank you, Shandra. Thank you for your loyalty." Miki's image disappeared from the screen as she signed off.

Shandra continued to stare as if the image was still there. She could almost taste the guilt of her divided loyalties. The bitterness consumed all of her immediate thoughts. Consciously shaking herself she managed to gather together her bioscan tools and walked slowly back to the pen where she left Darla.

There was nothing to feel guilty about, she chided herself. This was exactly the reason she had joined the Church of Dreams. They were quite right in wanting to stop the Ager counter-virus. Otherwise, there would always be the possibility that it could fall into the wrong hands. If the Church's suspicions were justified, Anna's plans for the counter-virus could prove even worse than Eternity's.

Drawing blood from a protesting Darla, she wondered how she would ever be able to contact the Church now that security would be watching everyone much more closely. She knew of at least two other Dreamers within the Ager compound. Somehow she must contact one of them, and quickly. She believed that the Church leadership may be the only ones capable of quickly intercepting Anna.

"We will live the dream!" She chanted the slogan like a mantra. "We will live the dream!"

20

Anna's hover signaled ahead to Eternity security. She had placed an immediate priority call to Kant, and expected direct routing to his office. Within moments, security signaled for her to park at coordinate T19. She acknowledged the signal with a self-satisfied smugness. They were indeed routing her to the rooftop parking area, usually reserved only for Kant and his security chief. Anna smiled at the knowledge of how much this obviously meant to them. She had the counter-virus, and now she would make them pay dearly for it.

As the hover touched down, the security chief approached immediately, alone. Anna retracted the dome and allowed him to help her out of the seat. As they walked toward the private entrance to Kant's office she confidently closed her fingers around a small syringe in her lab coat pocket.

A concealed door opened and they stepped into the familiar surroundings of Kant's inner office. As usual, he was sitting behind his desk. However, she did notice that all the wall screens were blanked. She had never before spoken with Kant and had his complete undivided attention. This spoke well of her importance, she thought.

"Anna," Kant said, standing and offering his hand.

Anna paused a moment before clasping it firmly. He'd never greeted her by her first name before; their meetings had always been more formal. She wondered if this was also indicative of her new stature with Kant, or some ploy to catch her off guard.

"So, you have the counter-agent." Kant stated.

Anna simply smiled and inclined her head toward the security chief.

Kant returned her smile but didn't dismiss him. "John is involved in every aspect of this operation. He knows everything I know."

"I don't want him to know everything *I* know," Anna replied between tightly clenched teeth. "This is between us, Wojin." She drew out her use of his first name. She could play this game too. Kant nodded to the security chief and he immediately withdrew from the room. Anna waited several seconds before continuing. "Yes, I have it," she said. "Not here of course. In a safe place. You might also like to know that it is not a manufactured agent. It is another virus."

"A virus?" Kant asked. "How can that be? Why didn't we find it before?"

"Probably because you pulled out so quickly before. Once we discovered the effects of the Eternity virus, all you could see was the money and the power it would mean. Your greed denied us any opportunity to fully explore the area."

"We've been through this before," Kant responded impatiently. "Tell me how it works. Can it negate the Eternity virus? Can we re-inoculate if it effects someone?"

"Patience, Wojin," she chided him. "I'll tell you what *I* think you need to know."

She watched his eyes flare in anger, but he didn't say anything. She took her time, wandered his room, then found a chair and sat leisurely before continuing.

"So far, testing has shown that it completely negates the Eternity virus. Once the Ager virus has consumed the immune system they have been unable to successfully reintroduce the Eternity virus. Of course, they don't know if the Ager virus' effectiveness reduces with time because these are only preliminary tests."

"Naturally you destroyed everything the Agers had and we now have the only serum left."

"*I* have the only Ager serum left," Anna corrected him. "There is no we. Yet." She looked directly at him, challenging him to disagree. Kant remained still, not a single movement conveying his feelings.

"You did destroy everything left with the Agers?"

"Of course. Do you take me for a fool?" Anna responded.

"No, never a fool. Careless on occasion, but never a fool. My greed is only surpassed by yours, Anna. That's why we understand each other. I just want to be clear on where we stand—before we begin our negotiations." Kant paused for a long time, until she shifted anxiously in her seat. "So, what do you have in mind? A promotion? More money? More power?"

Anna noted the glint in his eyes, but she answered without hesitation, hoping to throw him off guard. "I want your job."

"Ha!" Kant laughed boisterously. Anna continued to lock her eyes with his, but her gaze lapsed as her tension built. Her fingers curled more tightly around the syringe in her pocket.

"I've been the one doing all the dirty work here," she said. "Without me Eternity would be lost. Either you meet my terms or I negotiate with the Agers." Kant's laugh died down, and he raised an eyebrow in disbelief.

"Just think, I could become a hero," Anna stood and looked down on him. "I could be the one who recovers the stolen Ager virus and returns it to them. Then, because of my loyalty to their cause, I would help them release this virus as they originally planned, and watch your precious financial and political empire crumble into dust."

She paused, looking for a reaction from Kant. He continued to sit unmoved, but he was no longer smiling.

"So you see, Wojin," she again strung out his name. "I alone determine Eternity's future."

"Don't you think you're a little presumptive, Anna?" Kant asked, returning the same name emphasis she used with him.

She glared back at him with determination. But he continued boldly. "Certainly you have all the serum at the moment. But there is nothing to stop the Agers from returning to Antarctica for more samples and then manufacturing all they need. Furthermore, can you promise me that they can't simply manufacture the virus from test animals already infected with this virus?"

"I really doubt that's a possibility," Anna replied. Her voice was somewhat quieter than before. She hadn't thought about the already resident virus in test subjects.

"And what about human subjects," Kant continued, as if he could read her fears. "Have they begun testing on human volunteers?"

Shit! She thought to herself. I was so damn careful about destroying all the lab samples, so excited when the accelerated testing showed positive results, I didn't stop to consider the volunteers.

Masking her uneasiness, Anna sat slowly. Crossing her legs, making sure she showed a great deal of skin, she smiled maliciously, as if she refused to answer his question.

"Well?" Kant questioned.

"Yes," she replied confidently. "It has been introduced to approximately two hundred Ager volunteers. But all preliminary testing shows that once the virus is resident in the animal or human immune system it cannot effectively be removed and used for other serum."

Kant raised an eyebrow as if he doubted what she was saying.

"This isn't like the Eternity virus," she said. "Eternity must always be on guard against the black market. Eternity serums are often derived from animals, then sold in the hives. But the Ager virus is only effective if it is derived from the reference sample." She knew there was no research to back up these statements; but she was counting on Kant's lack of immunology background to keep him from questioning further.

"Of course," Anna continued, gaining confidence with her mixture of lies and truth. "The human volunteers show no signs of aging yet; but they were only subjected to the virus a month ago. Naturally, the Agers aren't infecting the human volunteers with disease like they are the animals. It might be years before a significant change in the human subjects is evident."

Now it was Kant's turn to be silent for awhile. Anna allowed herself to relax, just a little, while she studied his features. She tried to gauge whether he bought her lie or not.

Just then his desk vidcomm buzzed. Kant pressed the receive button angrily. "I told you I wasn't to be disturbed." Then his expression changed and he immediately engaged the privacy shield, barring the other end of the conversation from Anna's hearing. "Oh? Interesting. Yes. Yes, I do understand. Obviously we will have to take care of it. Thank you. I'll let you know my decision in a few minutes." He terminated reception and stood with a smirk.

Anna schooled her features to appear uninterested in anything he might have to say. She knew that Kant was a ruthless negotiator, and she wasn't going to let any phone games make her uneasy.

"So," Kant smiled condescendingly. "You haven't covered all your bases yet, have you Anna dear?" Then he leaned forward and took her hand in his. She stiffened at his unnatural warmth and immediately yanked her hand from his grasp.

" There is no serum left at Ager command," she reiterated.

"Oh, that," Kant gestured nonchalantly. "That is the least of your worries now."

Anna stared at him, determined not to give him any inclination that he was getting to her.

"It seems that you have been implicated in the theft, Anna dear. Such a shame. Just when I had the best mole ever to get close to Miki Yokoyama."

Anna couldn't believe her ears. How could they have found out so soon? She had counted on at least two to three weeks before they would even suspect her. She'd planned it to implicate Shandra.

That was it—she hadn't expected Shandra to find her in the lab. Dammit! She had let the little Dreamer spy get the best of her. Damn! Damn! Damn!

"That's all right, Anna," Kant said, again curiously warm toward her.

She knew he was enjoying her discomfort. She also knew this meant she couldn't press her demands now. At the moment he was back in control of the game.

"You have done everything I've asked of you and more," Kant continued. "I like your spirit. I even like the fact you want my job." He chuckled, reminding her of a grandfather encouraging a small child. "Maybe one day, when I'm long gone from this earth, you will have it. But not today, Anna dear. Not today."

"I still have the Ager virus," Anna said, continuing to push that advantage. "We haven't completed our deal for that very important item."

Kant nodded. "Point taken. By the way, where did you say it was?"

"I didn't."

Kant smiled.

She held herself firmly, her lips pressed tight together with determination. She was going to walk away a winner this time. It was time to show him he wasn't always in control.

"How about making it safe here?" Kant offered.

"How much and why should I?" she said, upping the ante in her mind.

"Money has no meaning if you become part of The Ten." Kant said casually, waiting for her to jump at the bait. When Anna didn't immediately respond, he continued. "How about number six? I will, of course, provide you security and protection as needed."

Anna thought for a moment. It wasn't the deal she had come to negotiate. Number six in Kant's inner circle meant she would still have to surpass five others to become next in line for his position. However, under the circumstances, it was probably as much as she could demand. She also knew it meant she had to watch her back. Previous inner circle members had been known to disappear when their usefulness waned. She certainly wasn't going to let that happen to her.

"Accepted," she finally answered. "I'll transfer the virus reference sample to bio-security tomorrow." Kant nodded. "But," she paused for effect. "I will keep a small amount of the reference sample in a safe place for myself. Not that I don't trust you, Kant." An impish, slightly malignant grin crossed her face. "But our deal does not include my releasing full control of the serum to you. Let's face it, there are a number of unsavory people in your organization who wouldn't hesitate to use that power for their own ends."

"Not to mention yourself," Kant interjected with a smile.

"And, should I accidentally become infected, you just remember who still has a reference sample safely hidden with loyal friends. I can always get to you, Kant. Even from the grave."

"Such trust, Anna." Kant chuckled, his eyes twinkling with the knowledge he had won this round.

"Let's call it my personal security," Anna said. "I may be number six in succession, but this way you and I both know this makes me your equal." Kant laughed heartily as he pressed the button to summon her escort.

The security chief entered immediately. Anna turned confidently, and without a word she exited the office, leaving the security chief to hurry after her as she walked toward her hover. She felt she had more than recovered from her oversight, and already she had a second plan in mind. She would still replace Kant, she thought. And she wasn't going to quietly wait the five hundred years left for his enhanced natural life to run out.

Half-way across the rooftop Anna feigned a fall as though she had tripped, causing the security chief to reach out and grab her as she twisted in his direction. He tried to steady her, but she slyly pulled him toward her keeping him unbalanced while at the same time removing the syringe from her pocket. With an affected exclamation of panic she fell backwards, pulling him down on top of her. Then, apologizing for her awkwardness, she quickly switched their positions, rolling him over and simultaneously inserting the syringe at the base of his neck just before his head hit the rooftop.

John swore at the pinprick sensation and she rolled away from him, continuing to apologize. Levering herself up behind him, she slipped the protective cap back on the syringe and repocketed it while brushing off pebbles from her lab jacket.

"Damn! What stabbed me?" He asked, as he rubbed as his neck and looked closely at the ground before getting up.

"Oh, were you hurt in the fall?" she asked solicitously. "I'm so sorry I grabbed onto you like that. I must have tripped." Anna stooped to the ground to join him in the search for the culprit pebble. "There are so many little rocks here." She offered several small sharp stones as possibilities.

Finally, John gave up and helped her back to her feet.

"Thanks for breaking my fall," she said, offering him her most seductive smile. "I'm usually not so clumsy. I must have been thinking about our next move on the Agers."

John didn't bother to reply. He angrily pushed her toward the hover, loaded her into the seat, punched in the destination and autopilot. The airdome lowered and the jets engaged as he backed away quickly. As the hover rose from the rooftop, Anna waved happily, watching him turn and run back into the building.

Time for him to start planning for retirement, she thought. Now we will see if a little Ager-Ebola mix works as effectively on a human subject as it did on the monkey. She smiled at her ingenuity.

"Wojin, dear," she said aloud. "You're next.

~

THE SECURITY GUARD carefully watched Shandra as she analyzed another set of blood samples. She had been entering the data into her terminal for over two hours now. She glanced at him furtively, once more switching files and entering another line of her coded message for the Church of Dreams. Completing the message, she moved it to her comm file, readied for encrypted transmission.

The problem now was how to transmit the message both to Miki's command monitor and Rohin Chawla without the guard noting the transfer. Then the germ of an idea formed in her mind. Cautiously, she engaged the vidcomm connection and voiced the numbers for the command center.

"Who are you calling?" The guard immediately asked, rising from his chair and standing menacingly near.

"I thought Miki would want these results right away," she answered. "The quickest way to send them is vidcomm transfer. Unless, of course, you would rather take them by hand." She held up a data disk, daring him to take it. Uncertainty crossed his face. She knew he wasn't allowed to leave her alone.

"Go ahead." He finally said, moving closer to get a good view of the screen. When Miki's image filled the screen he visibly relaxed and made his way back to the chair across from her.

"I have the results," Shandra spoke to Miki's image. "I thought you'd want them immediately."

"Good work. Shunt them to me now."

Shandra keyed in a code which would simultaneously send the Darla data file to Miki's comm code and the coded message file piggy-backed on it, but diverted to Langtree's terminal.

She spoke as soon as she hit send to distract any attention that might be called to her transmission. "As I suspected, Darla did receive the Ebola virus. It is active and her Ager-weakened immune system has allowed it to completely consume her. I expect she has at most a month more to live."

"Thank you. I have the data now," Miki responded somewhat distractedly. "I'll review it and call you if I have any further questions." Then her image disappeared from Shandra's screen.

Shandra sat back on the stool abruptly, nearly toppling herself in her nervousness. She hoped Langtree would delete the message immediately after receiving it, and delete its backtrail. She didn't want any time for Miki's system to generate an alert. If the system alerted, she knew Miki would immediately engage a cipher agent to trace it and read it.

The incessant beeping of the guard's timer set Shandra back on edge. His eyes opened wide and he stepped briefly into the next room, holding his wrist near his ear. She could hear his hushed questions, but could make no sense of their meaning. Then he reappeared and marched confidently toward her.

"You are to be removed from this facility at once." He grabbed her arm roughly, putting an insistent grasp at her elbow as he steered her out of the building.

"What's the problem?" She asked, her voice squeaking slightly. "Was there a problem with the data?" The guard said nothing as they now moved across the quad toward the command center.

Finally she stopped struggling. In response he loosened his grip slightly; but there was no doubt he would grab her again if she made any attempt to escape. They found out, she thought to herself. They intercepted the transmission and had probably begun decoding it. As they drew near the command center she forced her chin up and marched with the determination of a martyr to meet the interrogation. We will live the dream, she chanted silently to herself. We will live the dream!

In the office attached to her private lab, Miki was pacing back and forth in front of a small desk. When Shandra entered with the guard, Miki stopped mid stride and gestured toward him. "Thank you. You may go."

Shandra stood facing her, eyes looking straight ahead. She held her hands stiffly at her sides, her body in rigid attention as she waited to be addressed. She was determined not to say anything until forced.

Miki locked eyes with her for what seemed like several minutes, then she finally looked away in disgust. "Sit down!" she ordered impatiently. "We don't execute spies here. Besides, I wouldn't give you that satisfaction."

Shandra stiffly took the chair nearest her.

"I noted your additional transmission," Miki began, her voice heavy with fatigue. "Who was it to? What did it contain?"

Shandra blanched, but she stubbornly held her pose, giving no indication that she even heard the questions.

"I see. You think that your silence will help further the cause of your church." Shandra's eyes opened wide at her reference to the Church. "Oh yes, we are quite aware of your membership in the Church of Dreams," Miki continued pragmatically. "We also know that you have been passing information to Rohin Chawla about our progress with the counter virus. And that you have other Dreamer contacts within the Ager organization. How am I doing so far?"

Shandra's eyes opened still wider, but she remained stiffly seated in the chair. "I don't know what you're talking about," she insisted.

"Shall I call Langtree in here and have him corroborate these facts?"

Shandra's face fell as she realized Langtree had been captured on the receiving end of her transmission.

"I see that you are quite capable of spying on your own people!" Shandra accused. Then she lowered her gaze, as she shifted in the chair, drawing her arms across her chest. "But I won't reveal anything about the Church. You have me and you can do what you will. But we will live the dream!"

"There will be no dream for you to live if that virus gets in the hands of Kant," Miki replied forcefully. "If your suspicions are right and Anna's working for Eternity, then all your romantic ideals and Dreamer slogans will do nothing in the face of his evil. Don't you see that?"

Shandra twisted her hair anxiously, unsure what to say. She felt confused and scared. Somehow she had let everyone down.

"There's nothing I can do," Shandra said, her voice barely above a whisper. Then she started to cry. "I don't want Eternity to get the Ager serum, but I have no power to affect the outcome. You've taken it out of my hands. But you can do something, Miki. You can make a difference."

"Don't you blame this situation on me."

"Did you let the message get through? Will you let the Church know? They'll know what to do, how to stop it." She clasped her hands tightly in front of her.

Miki sighed. "Yes, I let it go through." Miki said softly, adding a hint of understanding to her voice. "I've let all of your messages go through. Rohin knows everything."

Shandra shook her head in disbelief, not responding.

Miki continued soothingly. "I don't want to hurt you. I want to help you, and to help the Church."

"This is a trick, right?"

"No, it's not. Anna has beaten both of us. Rohin and I have been working together. As much as possible without letting on."

Miki pulled a chair up and sat facing Shandra. "Don't you see? Our chances to recover the virus are slim, unless we work together. The Church of Dreams and the Agers have always had a common enemy in Eternity. Now that they have the virus neither of us can afford to try and fight Kant alone. The only way to prevail is to join forces."

Shandra looked at Miki questioningly. "But what can I do?" Her voice caught as tears threatened again.

"I'm going to contact Rohin Chawla," Miki said softly.

"The Master Dreamer?" she asked, with a new uncertainty as to Miki's motives.

"Yes." Miki brushed away the reference. "And you will tell both of us everything you know. Including things you've left out of your transmissions."

"I don't know . . ."

Miki turned on her vidcomm, and dialed his direct address. Shandra's mouth opened wide. "How do..."

"I told you. We've been working together."

Shandra stood suddenly, her face going white as she crossed her arms around herself. She watched Miki bypass each successive security check. Finally, Rohin's visage filled the screen.

"Miki." His voice was soft, inviting. Miki smiled at the memory of their last time together, at the promises they'd made with their bodies.

"I have someone with me," she said quickly. She didn't want any intimacies shared with Shandra. She turned the screen toward Shandra.

"Live the dream!" She said. "I didn't want to..."

"It's okay, Shandra," he replied. "Miki and I have agreed to work together. I'm sorry I couldn't tell you earlier."

The color returned to her face. "I trust you, Master Dreamer."

"Rohin," he reminded her. "Langtree forwarded your message.

This is what Miki and I have been waiting for...to catch Anna out and know what she was doing. I'm sorry you were caught up in this, Shandra."

"I am willing to do anything you ask of me."

"Thank you," Rohin said. "You may leave now. But you are to tell no one that you know the Agers and Dreamers are working together. All of humanity is dependent on your silence."

Shandra bowed. "Live the Dream."

Rohin smiled. "Dream on."

Miki released the lock to her office and Shandra strode through the door without looking back.

Then she returned to the viewer. "Can she be trusted?"

"I believe so," Rohin said. "Though no one is sure anymore outside of you and I."

"So, it's come to the final battle," she said. "What now?"

"I still have all my Eternity contacts," he offered. "My spies are on the inside and waiting. What do you have?"

She'd put too much trust in Anna, she thought again. She hadn't wanted to trust anyone else to infiltrate Eternity, but now she needed Rohin's contacts. "I don't have a connection into Kant's organization anymore," she said. "But I know the security system; I know the lab layouts inside and out; and most of all I know Anna better than anyone. I know where she'll be. With your current contacts and my inside knowledge, we have a chance of getting to her."

Rohin didn't respond for several seconds. His image on the screen looked serene as he bowed his head and closed his eyes in thought.

"What are we going to do, once we find her and the virus?" he asked, almost in a whisper. "You know I need to destroy it and all your files once and for all."

She nodded. She'd never allowed herself to imagine this part of the plan. When they finally had to choose whose dream would be trampled, hers or Rohins. She still couldn't find a way for both of them to win. Could they still love each other afterward? She refused to think about that now.

"Let's just worry about getting in there for now," Miki finally said. "At least we both agree that the virus should not be in Kant's hands."

"I love you," he said. "Don't do anything without me, Miki. I can't protect you if you go it alone."

"I won't," she said. "Just help me get it out of Eternity. Then will decide what happens."

21

Coordinate L259 was a seedy entertainment palace known as Plato's Pleasure Dome. Miki had agreed with Rohin's suggestion to meet there because it was unlikely they would be noticed among the revelers. Visitors usually participated by donning costumes and masks to add to the anonymous feeling of the festivities. In addition to the regular full-wall vid shows, one could drink, dance, gamble, work drug trades, or pursue countless carnal pleasures. It was usually so rowdy that most of the public enforcement personnel even avoided it. The Laws figured anyone crazy enough to go in there deserved anything that happened to them.

Miki, along with two well-trained security types, entered Plato's Pleasure Dome at 2100 hours local. Not comfortable with costumes, Miki had only changed her hair color to a flame red, and wore a skin-suit that had the look of black leather. Her two cohorts were similarly clad, the only difference was the dog collar around each of their necks with a length of chain that Miki held in her hand. She threaded her way among tiny tables until she saw Rohin with two others in a booth. He was wearing a gray cassock, looking close to what he wore in his dreamer ceremonies. He hadn't bothered to change any other part of his appearance. Sitting with him was an incredibly tall, lean woman, with closely cropped hair and pearl-like, gray-blue skin. Miki squinted as she looked at her, wondering if the color was a combination of lighting and body makeup, or her natural skin color. The other person looked like a forgotten figure from some ancient myth, a looming bronze statue that somehow had acquired life.

As she approached, the three of them looked up from the booth and rose in unison. No one moved or spoke as Miki and Rohin silently locked eyes. After a few tense moments Miki extended her hand and Rohin shook it perfunctorily.

The two groups took their seats, facing each other across the table, no one speaking. Rohin finally eased the tension by entering his account code into the tabletop menu, and asking Miki and her entourage for their drink preferences. Miki ordered for the three of them, depressing the keys on her side of the table and then confirming the order when the screen acknowledged the selection.

"Privacy?" Miki asked once the bot served their drinks.

Rohin nodded and pushed a button at the side of the table. A shimmering field surrounded them. "It's even Eternity proof," he said.

Drinking deeply from a tall, slender glass, Rohin put it down and gestured toward the two people with him. "Jasmine and Scully are two of my contacts within Eternity. They will provide our team with the necessary access."

"Volney and Penn," Miki indicated the two men with her, "will be our cover. Their specialty is security systems and, if need be, they can probably hold off a squad of Kant's men."

Rohin whistled appreciatively.

"Our main problem will be getting through security," Miki continued. "If you have that covered, then the next question is where we'll be routed. In Anna's previous visits she explained that all people passing through security are placed on a conveyor system which ensures their direct transportation to their destination."

"That's right," Jasmine spoke up, "unless you're on visitor status. The conveyor system is for permanent employees and visitors or temps staying longer than three days. Also, the short timer temps don't come in under the identigraph. They're ushered through security screening by a departmental approval card that is read at the main desk. That's our plan for getting everyone in except you and Rohin."

The drink bot signaled for access, interrupting the discussion. Robin disabled the privacy screen and the bot attached itself to the table. Three new orders were served. Scully punched in an acknowledgment and the bot departed which automatically reactivated the screen.

Miki took a long, grateful sip on her bourbon, put the glass down and said, "I can appreciate that Rohin and I can't suddenly appear as temps. I'm sure that my identity is firmly implanted in every Eternity MC and in every guard's chip. Since Rohin has been a guest of Eternity's I2 twice, the guards probably have a memory implant for him as well. So, how do we get in?"

"You'll have to come in during the noon break. Several employees meet family members or dates and share a meal with them at one of the restaurants inside the compound. There's no problem getting into the quad just inside the main gate. Two other dreamers on the inside will arrange visitor passes for you. Rohin, you will be an employee's visiting Uncle. Miki, you will be another person's out of town cousin. Naturally, you will have to be disguised."

"Right," Jasmine continued the description. "We'll send you a picture of the person you need to look like. So make sure someone who's good with makeup sets you up. We'll give you exact hair color the day before we go. During the noon break you'll exchange clothing with the person you're meeting and effectively take their place within Eternity."

"Do you mean employees don't have to go back through the identigraph again?" Penn asked.

"Most do," Scully responded. "But not those going to a general assembly, which both these people are scheduled to attend. However, once the general assembly is over they have to go through identigraph to get back to their offices."

Jasmine picked up again. "We've planned a significant diversion that should create enough panic that the entire assembly will run scared. That way, hundreds of people will be rushing past the identigraphs. Assuming the guards won't just begin beaming people randomly, you can run through with the crowd and confusion.

"What kind of diversion are we talking about?" Miki asked warily. "Explosives? Fire? What?"

"Several small explosions and a little gas," Jasmine answered, her smile wide. "Nothing really harmful—just scary. The gas will smell but have no real effect."

Volney shifted uneasily, pushing himself slightly away from his caged position near the wall. "I'm not sure I like Miki being in such a precarious position. Why don't one of us take the lead in the assembly?"

"You're missing the point," Rohin stated. "The rest of you will already be reconnoitering the lab. As you will be inside Eternity several hours before us, you will pave our way to Anna. Believe me, Miki can take of herself."

"Thanks. I think." Miki allowed herself to smile for the first time since they'd entered Plato's. She wasn't sure if he'd said that last part with admiration or he really believed it. Since he'd promised to guard her with his life, she'd worried about what that meant. The last thing she wanted was for him to make some stupid hero move and die on her.

Miki raised her chin. "The question is you, Rohin. Can you take care of yourself? I don't want to play babysitter."

Rohin winked at her. "You don't, Angel? And here I thought you liked these daring rescues."

Miki looked away with a slight flush to her cheeks. His use of the nickname Angel reminded her of all that had gone before. God she loved him. If anything went wrong on this operation and Rohin was lost, she wasn't sure what she'd do. Please...please don't let anyone get hurt. She didn't know to who she prayed, or if she even believed anyone could answer. But right now, she'd accept any help—supernatural or otherwise. They were sure to need it.

"It's a go then," she finally spoke, agreeing to the plan.

~

Anna surveyed her private lab at Eternity with great pleasure. Five uniformed technicians worked feverishly at their stations, ready to jump at her command. She watched them a few minutes before returning to the screen in front of her.

It had been two weeks since the sudden death of Kant's chief of security and the subsequent minor illnesses of nine other highly placed Eternity personnel. Well done, Anna thought, as she smiled at her ingenuity. Except for John, she had chosen non-fatal illnesses for creating the panic she wanted. She had to admit, she was surprised at how quickly the Ager virus had changed John's immune system. As no one had tried it on humans yet, no one knew how long it would take, so she had quadrupled the dose they'd used in the monkey tests. It was only a week after injecting John that he became visibly ill, then a matter of days after that before he died.

She'd greatly enjoyed the rumors about John's demise. Evidently, when John passed out in Kant's office he was immediately removed and taken to Kant's personal physician. Anna had several bouts of near hysterical laughter, imagining Kant bathing himself several times a day to ensure he didn't catch whatever John had, and then having his blood rechecked daily to make sure the Eternity virus was still working well.

The virus had moved so quickly in John that the physician was unable to diagnose it until the autopsy. The diagnosis was Ebola, a fatal virus usually passed from monkeys to humans. The disease had not been seen for several hundred years—and worse the physician had never seen a compromised immune system. Soon, a rumor began that perhaps the Eternity virus had a time limit, or that some of the serum had been contaminated due to poor security. Eternity's PR people had to work quickly to quell the stories.

Terrified, Kant had ordered all lab monkeys destroyed and immediately summoned Anna. At first he suggested that the Ager virus may have escaped the confines of the biolabs. Then he accused Anna of purposely doing this.

Anna laughed again at the memory. She loved the challenge of proving to Kant that she was as loyal as ever. It wasn't all that hard. He was eager to have her loyalty. After all she was leading the research team and had the most information about the Ager virus.

Cleverly, she'd suggested that her team of researchers would work twenty-four hour shifts, perfecting a test to verify who might have contracted the Ager virus and how. Of course, he immediately authorized additional funds and expanded her lab resources.

Anna halted the report's automatic scrolling and backtracked a few screens. With her wandering thoughts she'd missed the results of the last four series of tests. Again she concentrated on the graphs of Ager injected animals versus those of the control group. Something was wrong but she couldn't zero in on it.

"Janos," she called to the assistant in charge of the control group, "are you still using the same control animals?"

He looked up from the desk. His ruddy skin seemed to be stretched tightly across his face. "Yes, except for the monkeys of course."

"What about the pigs?" she asked. "Are you sure some of the pigs haven't become mixed with the Ager infected ones?"

"Of course I'm sure," he answered impatiently, his thin frame springing from his stool and storming to her desk. "What are you accusing me of this time?"

"I'm not accusing," she answered. "And, I don't like your attitude. There is something wrong with the damn pigs! Look at this data."

Anna backtracked to the beginning of the tests with the Ager injections in the pigs, pointing out the differences between the control group and the experimental group. "Do you see the first two weeks of graphs?"

"Yeah, I see 'em. They look exactly like we want them to look. No matter what disease we give the control group their immune system destroys it."

"Right, while the experimental group becomes sick."

"So? What're you so upset about?" Janos's bony fingers restlessly tapped on the edge of her desk.

"Now look at this." Anna forwarded the screens to this week's data.

"Whoa!" Janos exclaimed. "What in the hell happened?"

"Exactly." Anna said. "Why did the control group stop showing 100% immunity? Haven't you been watching them?"

"I've been swamped. I haven't had time to review this latest data. You have me on too many things at once. I'm only human, ya know."

"Well, you better become a superman then," she said. "Or you may be the next one to get sick."

Janos stared stubbornly back at her, as if daring her to carry out her threat.

Anna ignored his look and continued. "You better check those pigs personally. Double the rate on the bioscan timings, and find out how and why they are getting sick. Also, try the new test on the control group and see if we get any Ager positive results." Janos turned away, but she stopped him with one last comment. "For your sake, I hope there hasn't been a screw up. If you didn't keep the pig identities straight in the database, you are . . ."

"I've got it straight." Janos interrupted, gritting his teeth. "I'm sure there is a simple explanation."

"There better be. Now get out of here and get me those test results. Quickly."

Janos turned slowly and took deliberately unhurried steps back to his desk. He counted out his testing instruments and took his time putting them in a carisack before exiting the lab.

Anna fumed over his actions. She'd get rid of him if only he weren't so damn smart. He was the best biotechnician she had here, which wasn't saying much.

It seemed that some of the best minds had deserted Eternity over the past year or so. Rumor had it that most of them had either joined the Church of Dreams or simply dropped out of society. Eternity's security got down right irritable when key scientists could no longer be tracked. Sometimes Anna wondered if she'd missed an opportunity somewhere. Perhaps she should have developed her relationship with Rohin Chawla, rather than severing it.

No, she told herself emphatically. He doesn't have any real power. Only romantic, idealistic suckers would fall for his entertainment show and the Church of Dreams. No educated, technically trained individual would follow his farfetched dreamer notions for long. Shaking such thoughts from her mind Anna returned to the data on her terminal.

Two hours later Anna caught up with Janos on his way back from the pig's holding area. "So? What are the prelims?"

Janos slowed reluctantly. "Well, I'm not sure yet; but from examining them I'd say they probably have the Ager virus. The vet has identified at least two of the diseases that were introduced in the experimental group, and she feels that three more of the test infections are in their beginning phases. I'm going to run the new test for the Ager virus as soon as I get back to the lab."

"I'll come with you," Anna stepped ahead of him and walked toward the lab, expecting him to follow.

"I'd work faster without you," Janos said, refusing to follow her lead.

"I don't care what your problem is," Anna said. "Now move it!"

Janos moved in the direction of the lab, but again he was frustratingly slow. Finally, Anna could stand it no longer. She grabbed the sealed case of blood samples from him. "Dammit, Janos, why do you have to make everything so difficult? I'll do the damn test myself. Now get out of my sight. I don't want to see your ugly face for the rest of the day."

Smiling, Janos turned away from her, throwing his final words over his shoulder. "Thanks all powerful one. I could use a day off." Then he jauntily took his leave.

When she got back to her lab, Anna noticed it was deserted. She marched directly to the bench and began the preparation for the analysis. I'd rather do it myself anyway. That's the only way to make sure it's done right. Damn technicians.

After the better part of an hour the results displayed on the MC screen, verifying her suspicions. Five of the six control group pigs did indeed have the Ager virus.

Tired, Anna rose from the chair and began walking a course within arms reach of the walls of the lab. Every few paces, she stopped and stared toward the blood vials on the far desk; then she'd pace again. On her third circle around the lab she went back to the desk and called up both initial and recent data from other animal groups. All night long she ran comparisons: cross matches, disease incubation times, immune system responses, analysis of specific cells in infected animals vs. control animals. She also ran historical record searches for disease transmission types and incubation periods; then she ran comparisons against her current experiments.

By 0600 she was firmly convinced that the Ager virus was transmitted much more easily than the Eternity virus. Whereas the Eternity virus had a short lifespan outside the body and was transmitted only within the target blood stream—hence the required injection from Eternity—the Ager virus had a lifespan outside the body of three hours and could be transmitted by casual contact. The incubation time, transmission type, and antibody acquisition matched most closely with that of Influenza C. She double checked the matches before continuing her historical comparisons.

Influenza C, unlike the A and B types, was the only one that acquired antibodies that provided immunity against the type C virus for life. Though anyone infected with a certain strain of the type A or B viruses also acquired immunity to that strain, both the A and B type viruses occasionally altered to produce new strains that could dodge the immunity built up from a previous attack, thus leading to a new infection.

Anna wondered why the MC had related the Ager virus to Influenza C, rather than A or B. The amount of data from the cross matching could take her months to go through. If the match was as close as she suspected, it might also mean that some people could actually have a genetic immunity to the Ager virus. That possibility prompted the next important question. Could that immunity be transferred to another person at will?

Anna laughed aloud. Wouldn't it be just perfect, she thought, if the majority of the population turned out to be immune? She would love to see the look on Miki's face then.

She decided to keep her immunity theory to herself. It might come in really handy if Kant ever decided not to trust her. She set up a new security encoding for the data. Checked it twice. Stored it on her personal mind chip, then destroyed her encoding notes everywhere else.

The first order of business would be to prove the contagion. Then she needed to somehow make sure she was the first one protected from the Ager virus—either by immunity or vaccine. If she was lucky, the Ager virus would do the work of infecting most of Eternity's elite, maybe even Kant himself. Her final step would be to ensure that Kant, and other equally frightened members of The Ten, knew how contagious this was. She was sure their fear could only work to her advantage. She smiled. It wouldn't be long until she was number one.

Anna moved to her viewscreen and punched in Kant's code.

"Do you have that Ager test perfected yet, Hollinrake?" Kant asked when his image filled the screen. Anna grimaced at his return to using her last name. They'd been working pretty much as equals until this Ebola thing with John backfired on her. Since then, Kant's paranoia included everyone, especially her.

"Yes, I do," Anna responded.

"And it's tested fully?"

"As fully as it can be under the circumstances."

"Good. Let's start with The Ten first then work our way down the personnel hierarchy."

"Absolutely," she said, smiling. "In fact, I think you would want to start at the very top level first. Yourself for instance."

"What? Are you crazy, Hollinrake? I don't want any of your needles or infectious personnel near me."

"Then at least your closest allies," she continued. "I'll even take it myself to prove to you I'm not infected."

"What aren't you telling me?" He leaned closer to the screen.

She lowered her voice and leaned toward her viewer. "There's something I've discovered in the past twenty-four hours, and I haven't told anyone yet."

"So? "

"The Ager virus is significantly more contagious and much more easily transmitted than we thought."

After several moments he quietly asked, "How contagious?"

"Like the flu. Do you remember the massive influenza outbreaks of the twentieth century and the early part of the twenty-first? The infection could be spread if someone sneezed on you, touched you with unclean hands, or it could even be passed through a poor air filtering system. That is how contagious the Ager virus is. It's not transmitted at all like the Eternity virus. You don't have to be injected. No wonder it went through the population like wildfire in Helios' novel."

"And the diseases we've been seeing?"

"They are the same ones we've been using to infect the animals. Of course, with our current medical capabilities we can stop most of them. Don't worry, you probably won't die quickly...like John."

She noticed a grimace on Kant's face at the mention of his previous security chief. She decided this was not the time to mention the pre-Eternity Virus diseases for which doctors had never found vaccines—like many of the cancers. She would bring those up in her next conversation, when she wanted to increase his fear.

"You will, of course, die of old age," she continued. "And medical doctors will have to bone up on all these aggravating diseases, like the common cold, that we haven't had to deal with in the last two hundred years. They'll have to revitalize the entire field of diagnostic medicine in order to identify and combat them."

She could see Kant growing more and more worried as she described the possibilities to him. When his right eye began to twitch involuntarily she figured she'd said enough.

After what seemed like several minutes Kant finally spoke. "Run the test on every member of The Ten first."

"Then what?" she asked, willing herself not to grin like a Cheshire cat.

"Then," he hesitated a moment before continuing. "Then inform me of the results. Only me, do you understand? If anyone close to me has the virus I will take the necessary steps to ensure they no longer pose a threat to me...or to you." Again he paused before speaking. "I'll schedule The Ten for the test tomorrow. Then we will create a follow on schedule for every Eternity employee. If any one of The Ten fails to show up for the test, inform me immediately. Is that understood?"

"Yes sir." She smiled and tilted her head to one side. "I'm so glad I told you."

"And I want the results on you too, Hollinrake."

"Of course."

"Janos will do the test on you."

She laughed. "Don't trust me?"

"I trust no one," Kant said. "You may think you have total control in that lab, but I still have those who are loyal only to me."

So, that explained Janos' arrogance in the lab, she thought.

"Janos has no reason to protect you."

Smiling, Anna said, "And I have nothing to hide."

"Let's hope not, Hollinrake. Let's hope not." Then he signed off.

Anna leaned leaned back in her chair, contemplating the blank screen in front of her. "Let's hope you have nothing to hide, either, Kant," she said to the empty room. "I'd so hate to see you catch the Ager virus."

22

———————

Miki sat in the courtyard, anxiously glancing about for Rohin as she tried to converse with the woman across the table from her. She wondered if Rohin would look as different as she did. Miki had shaved her head and bleached her eyebrows a light blond in order to match the agent she was replacing. Additionally, she had used extensive body makeup to considerably lighten her skin, making her appear almost translucent. But at the moment most of her disguise was covered by the floppy hat, sunglasses, and oversized tunic she wore.

She wondered if their exchange of clothes would be enough to complete her disguise and get her past the video security and into the assembly hall. Studying the woman across from her, she decided it would work. They were close to the same size, and the normal Eternity uniform was bland enough to provide a very homogenous look for all employees. She took some comfort that so far everything had gone exactly as planned.

By eight that morning the group of six had already begun the first stage of their plan. The initial steps went smoothly. Jasmine reported the arrival of Volney, and Scully called only minutes later about Penn. Evidently each one had been issued a two day temporary employee card, then escorted into the facility to separate areas. It was 1145 when Rohin and Miki arrived separately at the front gate. They waited, as did the other visitors who came to enjoy lunch with a friend or family member inside the Eternity complex. Once more Miki cast an anxious glance in the direction Rohin and his contact had gone. She had seen neither of them since she began eating.

"Now, do you have the directions to get to the assembly hall?" her companion interrupted her thoughts. "You only have ten minutes after the tone to get there."

"Yes, I'm fine, "Miki answered. "Is the uh . . . entertainment ready?"

"It should be." The woman stood and motioned to her right. "If you're ready, let's get changed." Miki followed her toward the bathroom.

Five minutes later Miki escorted the woman with sunglasses and a floppy hat to the front gate, made a point of hugging her and thanked her for coming. Then the guard escorted the woman outside the security area, and Miki hurried back toward the assembly hall.

Once she entered the correct corridor she had no trouble finding her destination. She simply followed several hundred people who were all heading in the same direction. A moment after she entered the door, a man stepped to her side and took her elbow guiding her toward the back of the auditorium.

"Hello Angel," he whispered.

She stifled a gasp when she realized it was Rohin, who had also exchanged clothing with his contact. In addition to his sunglasses, he must have put some type of quick fade cream on as his face and hands as they were almost white, distinctly different from his usual near-black skintone. And the stray hairs escaping under his hat were blond instead of black.

Soon they were seated and apprehensively awaited the fireworks to come. The two of them only half listened to the presentation on acceptable filtration techniques for amino acid separation and identification. About twenty minutes into the presentation, the lights dimmed and the speaker pointed to video examples of the technique.

Suddenly there was a low reverberating boom, the first of several small explosions which filled the hall with an acrid smell.

Miki and Rohin silently dropped to the floor and covered their noses with a small filter from an inner pocket in their uniform. They waited until a swell of people began screaming and running toward the doors. Joining the stampede, Miki and Rohin exited the auditorium and headed straight toward security and the identigraph inside the secure area.

At first the guards screamed for everyone to halt, beamers targeted; but as the panicked crowd continued to push forward, shouting in fear and raising ID discs, the guards lowered their weapons. They stepped aside, frantically disabling the conveyor system and computerized destination codes as they commed the emergency to some control point. The panicked crowd continued to press forward and passed through security without violence.

Miki and Rohin remained with the main bulk of the group until everyone seemed to calm. As a feeling of safety returned, practiced judgement ensued and people dispersed to their various workstations. Miki checked Rohin's forward motion, pulling him aside and into a large, crowded vertical transport. After keying level ninety-seven as their destination, she worked her way toward the back, carefully noting how each person or small group exited at succeeding floors. She knew the most difficult aspect of the plan was yet to be executed.

Jasmine had previously verified that the lab where Anna was most likely to be found was on level ninety-seven. Though none of Rohin's spies had actually seen Anna, a couple of lab employees had spoken out about the new "bitch" they had for a boss. That managerial style and description fit Anna perfectly. When pressed further, they did describe her enough to verify her presence to the spies; however, these same employees had shut up quickly when asked about what work the lab was undertaking, stating that a class-one security assignment was in effect and they couldn't talk about their research.

By the time the vertical transport passed level ninety-two Rohin and Miki were the only ones remaining in the lift. At level ninety-seven the transport doors opened and Miki stepped out first. Rohin kept the doors ajar, waiting for Miki's signal that it was safe to join her. Taking a deep breath, he randomly pushed buttons for three more floors above them and quickly stepped out of the transport. Together they cautiously moved down the hall toward the doors they were seeking.

Rounding a corner, they suddenly stopped short. Within twenty meters of their destination stood a line of five people waiting to enter the lab.

"Here for the Ager test?" A short, squat man in line waved at them.

"Uh, yeah," Rohin answered quickly for both of them. "We haven't been on this level before. We weren't sure if this was the right place. The Hollinrake lab, right?"

"Yup, this is it," the man answered, remaining friendly. "Well, join the line," the man gestured behind him. "It seems to take about ten minutes a person. They take only two to three people at a time."

"Thanks," Rohin continued in a friendly manner. "Do you know any more about this than I do?"

"Uh," the man hesitated.

"I mean," Rohin picked up to reassure him, "is it true if you got this virus you could get sick and all?"

The man let out a pent up breath with relief, then eagerly spoke in a conspiratorial whisper. "Yeah. Evidently Eternity had to steal it from that fanatical group that wants to kill everybody off." Now the man was talking effusively. "Can you imagine? Who would want to do a crazy thing like that? I'm just thankful Eternity looks out for our interest. Without them we could be dead already."

"Yeah," Miki said sarcastically, "they really look out for our interest all right." Rohin pointedly nudged her in the side to quell her sarcasm.

Then the door opened and three people came out. A woman dressed in the Eternity uniform and a lab jacket motioned to the next two in line to enter. Then the door closed again.

"Have they been taking two, or three people at a time?" Miki asked, concerned that on the next turn she and Rohin would be separated.

"Usually two," the man said. "That last one was Fraimin. He'll probably be in there awhile. He's sweet on the tech and usually hangs around talking."

"That would do it," Rohin said, continuing to engage the man. "Is she worth a look?"

As the man rambled on about the general benefits and hazards of women, Rohin half turned toward Miki, arching an eyebrow questioningly. She shrugged, not sure what they should do now.

"Oh damn!" she said, as an idea formed in her mind. Pulling a piece of paper out of her pocket, she glanced at it quickly then put it back.

"Something wrong?" the man asked.

"Well, yes," she said sweetly. "I was supposed to remind someone from my section to come up with us. I forgot. And my section chief will have my ass." She looked down, trying to play on the man's sympathies.

"Gee, I know what you mean. I work for a pretty tough boss too. Hey, maybe I can help you."

"Yeah?" Miki looked up hopefully, opening her eyes wide in an innocent pose. "How?"

"Well, I have an internal comm on my timer," he answered, showing her his wrist. "Go ahead, punch in whoever you want to talk to." Miki looked at him apprehensively. "Really, it's OK," the man assured her. "I work in communications, and they usually don't monitor above level ninety during lunch shifts. There's just too much going on and too few people on hand."

"Well, if you're sure," she hesitated coyly, knowing he would press her further. When he took the timer off and handed it to her, she said, "Gee, thanks." Then quickly punched in Volney's code. She hoped he was there.

Within moments a feminine voice was heard over the comm channel. "Is Loder Volney there?" Miki asked anxiously. She didn't have to feign her fear at contacting him. She heard the beep of a hold signal, then another pickup.

"Volney," the familiar voice answered, and Miki let out a sigh of relief.

"I forgot to remind you about your test on level ninety-seven," Miki spoke slowly, emphasizing the level number. "You know, the Ager virus test we're all supposed to get?" There was a long pause before he finally answered.

"Oh yeah," he said. "Thanks for the reminder. I'll be right there."

"Hurry," Miki added. "You were scheduled ahead of me, and the next group will be called in about five minutes."

Volney acknowledged and signed off. Miki thanked the man, handed back his timer and then stepped back against the wall, leaning into its solid support. If Volney didn't get here in time, and Anna was in that room, this plan would be over before it had a chance to begin.

Rohin moved in front of her, squeezing her elbow as he passed. He took it upon himself to continue talking with the man in front of them, keeping her from trying to make any more light conversation. Four minutes later, Volney came running up to them. Miki raised her hands in warning, flicking her eyes sideways to indicate the man ahead of her.

"Thanks for the reminder," Volney said, stepping in line in front of Miki and Rohin. While he was introducing himself, the door opened, two people exited and the tech requested the next two people to enter. Volney entered with the man in front who had loaned her the timer, leaving Miki and Rohin alone in the corridor. They waited silently, wondering what Volney was facing.

After seven minutes, Rohin looked at his timer. "It's past the five minutes. We should consider forcing our way in if something doesn't happen soon. You know they don't have Volney scheduled for that test. Who knows what's going on in there?"

"Give him a chance," Miki answered. "He may be able to convince them it's their mistake. Besides, if he gets into trouble he can take care of himself. I've seen him hold off five strong men on his own. I can't believe lab workers would be that much of a challenge for him."

"I'll go along with you, for now," Rohin said tightly. "But if he doesn't come out within the fifteen minute timeframe we're going in after him."

"Easier said than done," Miki muttered. "The door is opened only by a recognizable palm print from the outside. I'm sure neither one of our palms will budge it."

"Damn!" Rohin glanced about nervously. "How long should we wait, then? If something went wrong it could well be that security has already been notified and we are sitting ducks!"

Just then the door slid to one side and a lab tech shakily pointed toward Miki and Rohin, indicating they were next.

Miki noted, however, that no one had come out this time. "What about the people already in there?" Miki asked cautiously. "I don't want it to get too crowded for you," she added, hoping her questions didn't tip her hand. The tech didn't respond, he only gestured again for them to enter. Then Miki heard Anna's laugh behind the worker.

"You might as well come in, Miki," Anna said. Miki still couldn't see her, though the voice was undoubtedly hers. "And bring Rohin with you. I've already called security. Would you rather be beamed in the hall or in here?"

That did it. Rohin pushed by Miki. "Run," he said, as he laid the lab worker out flat and stood ready to take on anyone else on the inside.

Miki followed right on his tail. She wasn't going to let him get hurt. Not for her sake when she'd been the one to talk him into this whole scheme.

The door closed resoundingly behind her and they both stood facing Anna. She was armed with a beamer and laughing gustily.

A quick glance verified their worst fears. Volney was stacked against the opposite wall, looking like a large stuffed doll that had lost half the stuffing. Evidently he had taken out three lab techs before being brought down. Their bodies were scattered like bowling pins near the desk at the front of the room.

"Did you really think you could come in and steal the virus back?" she asked. "Do you think we're fools?" Miki took a cautionary step forward, but Anna immediately waved the beamer at her. "I wouldn't try to be a hero, Miki. Though I prefer not to be the one to pull the trigger, I will if I have to." She motioned them away from the door, toward the center of the room.

"Why, Anna? That's all I want to know. Why?" Miki asked, glancing about the lab, evaluating what could be used for defense and what might be turned into an offensive weapon.

"You are so stupid, Miki," Anna answered with disgust. "You really thought that I could believe in your idealistic fight against Eternity. Actually I'm surprised you didn't know better. You, of all people, are most familiar with my cynicism. Though I must admit, for a little while I thought you might really be the one to come out on top. You did the first time. And if it were to happen again, of course I wanted to be there to share in the glory."

"What makes you think we won't?" Miki said.

Anna laughed again before answering. "You're here, aren't you? Does it look to you like you're the one winning this game? You really are the fool if you can't see that Kant has the real power." She paused, licking her lips, tasting the power like a sweet forbidden fruit. "And soon it will all be mine."

Suddenly Miki lunged at her, but Anna deftly kicked her in the stomach and shot the beamer within a few centimeters of her position, scorching a hole in the floor.

"I wouldn't try that again, Miki," Anna said, backing toward the door. "As you can see, this beamer is set on maim. I'll leave the killing to someone else, but I'll disable you easily and it will hurt like hell. And let's face it, the wimp here can't help you much." She threw the last statement at Rohin with vicious glee. "Actually, maybe killing Rohin would keep you in line even better." Then she aimed the beamer at Rohin, blistering a small section of skin on his shoulder.

"Damn you, Anna!" Miki yelled, moving to his side to examine the wound. "Stop playing games! If you're going to kill us, get it over with."

"It's not bad," Rohin said through clenched teeth. "It's just a surface burn."

With determination Miki moved to the refrigerator to look for ice. She figured if Anna wanted them dead there wasn't much she could do right now. And if she didn't, she could at least ease Rohin's pain a little.

She opened the refrigerator door, noting several shelves of labeled slides. They looked very similar to the contents of the unit at Ager command. She paused a few moments to make a mental note of some of the labels.

"You won't find the reference sample here," Anna said, noticing Miki's pause at the refrigeration unit. "But I wouldn't worry about it, you can easily generate the virus from anyone who has it. As a matter of fact, chances are both of you have already contracted it."

"What do you mean?" Miki asked angrily. "What have you done?" Finding the ice she moved back to Rohin's side, applying the cooling agent to his skin.

"Whether you live or die, Miki, your virus will take over the world just as you wanted. You just didn't realize that the minute you introduced it back into the world you had already accomplished your goal." Anna laughed again with such animosity that it made Miki's skin crawl. "So now you can go to your death knowing that you have won your personal war."

"How is that possible?" Miki asked, unwilling to believe it had happened without all the careful planning she'd been implementing.

"Your wonderful Ager virus is transmitted more like a flu virus than like the Eternity virus," Anna responded, happy to dole out information Miki didn't have. "A simple sneeze, an unwashed handshake, a kiss, any of these can pass your Ager virus."

"Then you have it too?" Miki asked with vicious hope.

"No. At least not yet," Anna answered with a knowing gleam in her eye. "It also seems that some people can be immune, and so far it looks like I may be one of them." She paused to let the impact of her statement show itself fully in Miki's face. "Wouldn't it be funny if you, the thorn in Eternity's side, die from your own virus and I survive?"

Miki edged closer, threatening to launch an attack. But Anna willingly backed further toward the door. Anna opened the door. Miki sprang toward her. The door closed in her face and she heard the lock snick. Miki and Rohin tried unsuccessfully to open it again from the inside; but Anna had already ensured they would not escape.

As if she couldn't leave without one final jab, Anna's voice was heard over an intercom within the lab. "Nice try, Miki. I'm glad I wasn't forced to kill you myself. I'll leave that to security when they arrive. Now I've given you my final gift, your last chance for love, Miki. Isn't that romantic? Just think, you and Rohin will be dead before the evening is out; so make your declarations to each other now if you have any." Anna's characteristic, ringing laughter echoed through the intercom. "Or maybe you should just let your hormones go crazy. You're so good at that Miki. Should I give you enough time for a last fuck before I send in security?" Anna's laughter rolled around the room, then it went silent. Rohin moved to examine Volney. "He's dead," Rohin said. "Broken neck." Then he moved to check each of the other three lab techs Volney had evidently killed. "All dead," he finally confirmed.

"This one is unconscious, but still breathing," Miki said bending over the lab tech she had decked earlier. She decided to secure his hands and legs, tearing pieces of cloth from his lab coat to use for bindings. Then she used another piece to gag him. She was not a cold blooded murderer, but she wasn't going to let him call for help or work against them.

Then she and Rohin looked around the room to plan their defense.

The center of the room contained three stationary lab benches running parallel to each other, approximately two meters apart. In the front of the room was a large desk. Miki surmised this was probably the throne from which Anna ruled the lab and her technicians; the desk would be a good barrier to the door right now. With significant grunting and groaning Miki and Rohin were able to move it in front of the door.

"At least that will cause the security detail to pause before entering," Rohin commented.

Next they quickly gathered all glass items. They broke several of them to be used as sharp weapons, then stacked select pieces in strategic locations around the room.

The most difficult task was disabling the lighting. Each lighting circuit was controlled through MC central processing and had to be individually disabled. Both Miki and Rohin stacked stools on top of benches, pulled wires and shorted circuits. With each foreign sound they braced for the onslaught of Anna's promised killing.

Tying off the last circuit, Rohin climbed down from the bench. "I get the feeling they're waiting on the other side of the door. Just waiting for us to give up," he said, nervously shifting from standing to leaning against the lab bench then standing again.

"Why don't they call out or something?" Miki asked angrily.

"Too cautious, I suppose."

Though they were in a tight and dangerous situation, Miki grinned at the irony of it all. What a way to finish her life, she thought.

"Rohin, I'm sorry," she said.

"For what, Miki?" He paused. "For winning? You got what you wanted."

"But I had plans," she said. "Plans to get people used to the idea, so it wouldn't be such a shock. I would never have just let it go wild like this."

Rohin laughed. "Power. Here Anna thought she had the power when you had it all along."

"I don't feel all that powerful right now," she said.

"Come here." He pulled her to him. "We will get out of this, Angel...together. I'm planning on a lot of years to fight with you over right and wrong."

Miki looked at him and smiled. He somehow had faith they could pull through this. She didn't want to tell him otherwise. At the moment she was not too successful in actually believing they would make it out of here alive. But she knew she wasn't going to give up easily.

He looked at her in a way she barely remembered—that look that said you are my life—my everything.

Uncomfortable, she said, "I guess all we can do is wait them out. They'll have to report soon. Someone will want to know what the situation is."

"You're really serious about still trying to make a run for it, aren't you, Angel?"

"No, I'd rather fly, actually. You know how we could do that?"

"Don't be a smart-ass."

"Smart or not, I'm trying to save our butts."

Rohin became serious, taking Miki's hands in his. "Miki, I want you to know ... "

"Listen, Rohin," she interrupted. "There is a natural time for death for each of us. I believe my time has come—but not yours."

"What are you saying? We might still get out of here, only a minute ago you said ..."

"No," she denied. "*We* won't. But maybe *you* can." Rohin began to interrupt again, but she stopped him. She withdrew her hands from his lingering hold, but continued to look directly into his eyes. She wanted him to understand why death was right for her now. "The search for death has been the focus of my life now for 70 years. I'm tired. My work is done. It's my time to go—the perfect time."

Rohin held her gaze, unable to say anything.

"But you," she continued, "you are committed to life. And it is especially important now for you to continue your dreams. As death becomes a natural part of life again, humanity will need you and your vision more than ever. So at all costs, you must be the one to survive, Rohin."

"But, I ... "

She took his face in her hands and crushed his mouth to hers, making promises with her lips, her tongue, her hands raking over him—wishing they could both live, wishing they could run and hide from the world.

Maybe even take off on one of those planned spaceships the Church of Dreams kept talking about. She'd never had a chance to really be with him, to live life together as husband and wife, and now she never would.

His lips responded in kind. When they'd wrung out the kisses as much as they could, they both clung to each other trying to catch a breath.

They were interrupted by the sound of the doors sliding open, then a masculine voice swearing as someone ran into the upended desk.

"Well, it's show time," Miki whispered, pulling Rohin down behind the bench.

Clearly visible in the bright light from the hall, two security personnel were standing before the door. Miki could see them framed by the desk and open door leaving only a crack for their entrance. They were both of medium height, and appeared well-muscled. Both were wearing the lose tunic type uniform of Eternity security, with folds of material for hiding a variety of weapons. Beneath the tunic, she could only assume were the skin tight pants worn by all personnel. One was dark and had a broad and high-cheekboned face, with black hair hanging in an even cut just above earlobes. She guessed the gender to be female. The other, probably male, had a prominent nose and large ears easily seen because of his bald pate. She heard the desk being forced aside, then the female guard squeezed past it, stepping into the darkened room. Silhouetted against the background lighting in the hall, the bald one reached into a fold of his tunic and pulled out a beamer. "If you come peacefully, you will not be harmed," he said in a monotone.

"Don't move," Miki whispered to Rohin.

After continuing to talk and offer assurances for several minutes in a feminine voice, Miki noticed a reflection of light. She assumed the second security guard had also pulled out her beamer. And, for the first time, Miki noticed the shadow of possibly a third person.

"They're going to start shooting!" Miki said, pulling Rohin even closer to the floor.

Miki pointed to the bottles at their side and mimed throwing them, whispering "when one attacks." Then she spun, and ran back to get behind the next bench, grabbing several additional broken pieces of glass to use in the attack.

Miki did not see the bright spot of the beamer until it was past her. It missed her by only a few centimeters. Though the guards could not see her, she was sure they were listening carefully for movement.

She knew there would not be time for her to return with the broken glass, so she found a large stool, got behind it and hefted it to the side, drawing the female guard away from the desk enough for Rohin to take aim.

"Got her," Rohin said loudly, as the guard fell from the well-aimed blow to her head. This caused the bald one to come barreling in, beamer shooting wildly. Rohin turned in the opposite direction and ran toward Miki, taking cover behind the next lab bench. Just as he arrived, she saw the woman he'd hit with glass getting up from the floor and crouching at the ready. The bald partner was still closer to the door.

Miki handed him a long thin piece of glass, and then helped him get more bottles stuffed in pockets.

The soft illumination from the hallway was suddenly cut off. She surmised the remaining security man must have realized that it silhouetted him and made it difficult to see into the lab. Fortunately, she and Rohin had long ago adjusted their eyes to the darkness. She hoped the security man could not adapt so quickly.

She peeked over the bench to get a position on the attackers. The entrance was still mostly blocked by the desk, leaving only a narrow area for someone to get into or out of the lab. It would be very difficult to get through there and out the door without getting hit, she thought.

She mimed to Rohin to move forward. They both got down on all fours and crawled silently ahead to be shielded by the bench closest to the door. Miki peeked over the counter once more.

One of the men called, "Yokoyama! Chawla! Surrender and you won't be hurt."

Miki clasped her hand over Rohin's mouth before he could be tempted to reply.

"Come on, Yokoyama! We just want to talk to you."

The silence was as thick as the darkness.

"Chawla, come on out. We won't hurt you. We wouldn't hurt a member of the Church of Dreams." Finally giving up the soft sell, the same man called, "Give it up now, you sons of bitches, or we come in after you. We'll shoot if we have to."

Miki wondered if they knew what this lab contained, and how important it was to Eternity. Would that data, if they knew it, keep them from entering, beamers blazing and destroying half the lab?

She got down on her hands and knees again, and worked forward inch by inch, moving a few feet in the opposite direction of Rohin. It would not do for them to make an accurate guess about just where her voice was coming from. Especially not if they meant to shoot her.

"Do you know where you are?" she asked. "Do you know you're in a lab containing a number of lethal viruses, including the Ager virus which negates your long lifespans?"

One of the men cursed softly. Then there was another mutter, two voices this time, verifying the shadow she noticed earlier was indeed a third person.

"We don't have time for that crap!" the second man said harshly. "There is nothing here that negates the Eternity virus. Eternity would have informed us of that before sending us in here. This lab was used only to check if people had already contracted the Ager virus. "

Miki laughed harshly, then shut up just as quickly, moving to another position before they located her.

"Are you willing to take that chance?" she asked again. "You may kill me, but not before I make sure these viruses are free to infect all of Eternity first."

The first man cursed quietly again.

"Besides," Rohin piped up from several meters away, "we have a beamer too! Anna missed one hidden on our guy, Volney. We don't want to use it, but we will! You charge on in and I'll kill you while Miki empties the viruses into the ventilating system."

Then Rohin rolled away to his right, half-rose, and moved his hand to indicate that Miki should back away. She was too far to make out the movement in the darkness. On her own she moved toward the wall a few feet.

Rohin motioned that she should lie down. Instead, she crouched close to the wall, ready to spring if necessary.

"Sure you got beamers!" the first man said sarcastically. "Anna checked everyone before she let you in. And why didn't you just blast us when we came through the door?"

"Can you be sure?" Miki questioned the guards assumptions again. "Anna had to leave quickly. We tell you she missed this one. She didn't know how Volney hides his weapons."

"And the Church of Dreams preaches non-violence," Rohin added, hoping his status in the Church would convince them of that statement. "But we will defend ourselves, and the world, from the misuse of these viruses if need be."

"No more time," the first man said. "We got orders! I give both of you 60 seconds to come out! Keep your hands high! We can see your outlines!"

"Toss your beamers in first so we'll know you can't shoot us!" Miki said.

"Sure, we'll do just that!" the second man said, and both laughed.

Miki crawled back over to Rohin. Her mouth close to his ear, she whispered, "When I give the signal, like this . . ." she raised her hand, and mimed rapping twice on the floor, "you say something loudly, then roll to hell fast toward the other end of the room. That way." She pointed to her left. "If they fire, scream as if you'd been hit."

He nodded.

"Wait. I have to get back to the other side."

Having resumed her former location and position, she rapped twice on the floor.

Rohin threw one of the glass bottles then yelled, "I hope you all die, you bastards!"

As Miki had expected, the two men guessed his location from the direction of his voice, though they could not know his exact position.

The air crackled and two holes appeared in the wall very close to where Rohin had been.

Screaming like a wounded animal, Rohin had spun away as soon as he finished speaking, but the closest beam still nicked his shoe, burning away the sole. His scream stopped as if blood had choked in his throat. Then the blinding white light came again, this time spaced wider and higher. But Rohin had rolled clear.

"Rohin!" Miki called softly, but not so softly, she hoped, that the two men would not hear her. "You all right?" Then, shrilly, "You damned murderers, I'll kill you!"

There was more muttering from the hallway. The first man called out then, "Cut the crap, Yokoyama! We're not some thick-headed fools!"

"You killed him!" Miki shouted again, and she rolled toward the wall until she was against it. Face close to the floor, she inched along to the center of the doorway behind the desk. She turned over and reached for the largest sharp piece of glass from the pile she had left there. Her groping fingers found it, and she carefully placed it on the floor by her right hand. She did not intend to speak any more. The two would make a rush very soon. They could not afford any more time.

A beam of white energy shot over Miki, causing her to jump inside her skin. Then she heard the desk being pushed further to one side, followed by one set of footsteps carefully entering around the far side. As the man cleared the desk she sprang toward him, but he easily rolled away shooting his beamer wildly. She shrank back behind the desk and regrouped.

Hearing the scuffle, another man cautiously placed first his beamer and then his arm around the desk. Pushing the desk as hard as possible, she startled him, grabbed his arm, forcing him to drop the beamer, then jerked him into the room. As his voice cried out in protest the glass she carried bit into his neck, silencing him immediately.

Hoping Rohin could take care of the guard still in the room, Miki cautiously moved toward the hall. She inched around the side of the desk, now holding the beamer she had recovered from her victim.

Rohin carefully watched the guard inside the lab. Slowly the man got up and followed Miki back into the hall. Rohin took that opportunity to jump him, keeping him inside the room. With his advantage of surprise the struggle didn't last long. Once he made the decisive blow, Rohin quickly turned to go after Miki.

Just before he reached her he heard the whine of a beamer and a heavy thud against the wall. Without thinking of the consequences he propelled himself through the opening and grabbed the first person he saw. It was the final guard.

Struggling from behind, Rohin used his sharp glass to make a quick slash across his throat. The guard collapsed, dropping his beamer to the floor. Rohin grabbed the beamer, and turned quickly, ready to face another attacker. But none appeared.

Looking back toward the floor, against the wall, he finally saw Miki. She was bleeding profusely from the abdomen. A gaping hole revealed her singed intestines. Her eyes were wide with surprise, though unseeing. He felt for a pulse. There was barely any life left.

With his heart hammering and tears threatening, he pulled out drawers in the lab until he found a first-aid bag. He used all of the newskin bottle to make a type of compress on her stomach and wrapped her tight with skintape. He took off his shirt and covered her, then grabbed her up in his arms and held her fast against him as he ran for the vertical transport. Talking himself into remaining calm, he struggled to review their preplanned exit strategy.

"Don't you dare die on me, Miki. You owe me that fight. I want to hear you arguing with me for the rest of my life."

He reached the floor above the main lobby and shouldered through a door to an emergency exit staircase. He saw Patrick's hover waiting at the bottom. As he approached, the door opened and he slid inside.

"Hospital." He said and reached for the medical kit they'd kept for emergencies.

Patrick set the codes and the hover streaked into the horizon along the path he had programmed.

Rohin injected Miki with starter. He'd seen this combination of drugs bring others back from the brink of death after being beamed. It worked with their enhanced immune system to speed up repairs.

But there was no longer a pulse. No longer a breath..

With the hover on autopilot, Patrick moved back where Rohin held Miki tight to him. Patrick felt for a pulse, listened for a breath. "Let's try juice," he said. He filled the hypospray with another drug. He injected Miki and then waited again.

Rohin looked into her open eyes. He no longer saw life. "No," he whispered.

Patrick reached over and closed Miki's eyes. "She's gone, Rohin."

"No!" Rohin held even tighter as if he could transfer his own life-force into her. "Her immune system is enhanced. I've seen medicos bring people back as long as ten minutes after their system shuts down."

Patrick shook his head. "Not this time. The injuries are too much."

Rohin gritted his teeth together and looked Patrick in the eye. "You just get us there. I'll make sure she lives, even if they have to cut out my own organs and give them to her. Go!" He rocked with her tight against him.

Patrick moved back to the pilot seat, his shoulders slumped in resignation.

Rohin refused to let her go.

"Dammit, Miki," he whispered to her. "Why did you have to play the hero. It was my turn, Angel. It was my turn to save you."

He rocked her against him and tightened his grip. "You can't leave. You won. The Agers won. Fight, Dammit! Fight."

He buried his face in her hair and wept.

23

Helios waited anxiously by his vidcomm at Ager command, Muru next to him holding his hand. He had just completed his fifth call of the evening, and still there was no news of Miki. Surely, if she couldn't contact him, Penn or Volney would, he thought. Was it possible that the mission was a dismal failure and the entire Eternity infiltration team was captured—or worse, killed? He shuddered at the thought and Muru put his arm around him, hugging him close without a need for words.

"What if she's gone?" Helios finally voiced his concern choking back tears. "How could we go on?" He realized now how fond of her he had become—maybe even loved her like a sister. Though it was difficult to love someone who always held everyone at arms length.

They often had harsh words about her unrelenting drive and absolute dedication to the Ager goal. Yet, just as often he likened her dogged belief to that of a saint. She was unwavering in placing her faith in the Ager plan, and with almost religious fervor she pursued it above everything else."Let's not jump to conclusions," Muru soothed. "Someone will call and let us know. Let's just try to keep positive."

Muru was worried too, but he wanted to be strong for Helios first. The original plan had been to confront Anna, get the reference sample of the virus back, then return to Ager headquarters by 1900 local. Now it was nearing midnight and they hadn't heard a word.

Bzzz.

Both of them jumped when the vidcomm's message alarm finally went off. Helios fumbled with the acknowledge switch. Finally succeeding, they both saw a scarred, puffy-eyed visage of Patrick McLean fill the screen.

"My God!" Helios and Muru both choked in surprise. "Patrick, what's wrong?" Helios asked. "Are you all right? You look like you've seen hell itself."

"She's dead," Patrick said, without preliminaries. "She tried to be the hero one last time and she's dead."

In shock, Helios heard but refused to comprehend Patrick's words. From the hollowness of his stare, Helios could only guess the emotional turmoil he had already been through.

"And Chawla? Is he dead too?"

"He might as well be," Patrick answered. "He's still at the hospital refusing to believe Miki's gone. He won't let them take her to the morgue. He's waiting. Dreaming, I suppose. I couldn't take it anymore. I couldn't watch him."

"What happened?" Muru asked numbly, as he grasped Helios' hand even harder.

Patrick relayed the events of the evening in fits and starts, as best he could based on what Chawla had told him while Miki was in surgery. Finally, he ended with Miki's daring attempt to disable two security men and Chawla's horror at finding her beamed, most of her stomach leaking onto the floor as she lay against the wall just outside the door.

Helios and Muru simply sat staring at the screen, unable to believe that she was gone.

"So, she died for nothing," Helios finally broke the silence, the words catching in his throat as he fought back angry tears. "We don't have the reference sample, and the Ager plan will never be executed."

"No, Helios," Patrick corrected him. "Her plan is already working.

In spite of everything that went wrong, she won. That's the irony of all this."

"What? We don't understand." Muru wiped his eyes with a large fist. He wasn't able to be as strong as he thought.

"It turns out the virus is transmitted like the flu," Patrick continued. "Probably half of Eternity already has it, and Chawla figured that most of the Ager organizations have it too. And, because Dreamers have been involved with the Agers, as well as inside Eternity, for quite some time, he expected the Church will soon be riddled with carriers, if we aren't already."

Patrick allowed a tired smile to relax his emotions a moment. Then he continued. "Yes, nothing could keep Miki from winning, even death. Not Chawla and the Church of Dreams, and certainly not Anna."

"Go to bed, Patrick," Muru said. "Thanks for the report.

Patrick nodded in silent assent, then his features disappeared from the screen as he signed off.

Helios slowly turned away and looked out the window. The moonlit silhouette of a tall pine tree wavered in the breeze. He watched with mixed feelings, until a drifting cloud temporarily blotted the moon. Relieved, he looked away from the window and closed his eyes. Helios knew he would never see a pine tree again without thinking of Miki Yokoyama.

Before coming to Ager command he had known only the harshness of the desert. Though the desert had its own beauty, it was won by surviving years of brutal wind and rain, flood and drought. One had to learn to look past the pain to appreciate its glory.

Whereas here, the abundance of water and greenery surrounding the command center had accurately reflected the fullness and undaunted energy of its leader. That fullness seemed inappropriate now, with the organization's destiny fulfilled and its leader gone. Helios looked once more toward the window, but the cloud still covered the moon. Though he knew the outside had not changed, he felt the inside had become barren.

He turned to Muru. "It's time to return home. It's time for us to renew our vows. Let's return to our desert once again and heal."

Muru held him again, his fingers playing through his hair as he drew his head closer. With an odd combination of sorrow and hope, they deliberately moved toward the bedroom to begin packing.

ROHIN HELD Miki's hand tight. He'd been talking to her, watching her for three days. The Eternity doctor's had written her off and advised him to turn off life support. He'd refused and had her moved to a facility under Dreamer control. Then he'd contacted his top researcher and Miki's personal physician.

His researcher verified that Miki was not a carrier of the Ager virus. She was one of those who were immune. It appeared so far that about 10% of the Dreamers were immune. Miki's physician concurred. She also assured him that Miki's system would eventually repair itself. It was just a matter of time.

Rohin wept at the news.

Then he had the facility leak the news that Miki had died.

Soon after the Agers and Dreamers signed a permanent treaty to work together—even though their ends may still be different. Having won the fight for shortened lives, the Agers agreed to help in the transition—help those who were infected to see their shortened lives as a gift. The Dreamers agreed to learn how the immunity worked and to determine if there was a way to share that immunity with others. Over the next decades both groups would determine next steps.

ANNA WATCHED Kant step from the vertical transport tube into his office. She sat at his desk, feet crossed on top of it, watching his angry approach with a lethal grin.

"How in the hell did you get in here, Hollinrake?" Kant walked briskly to the desk and pushed her feet aside.

"I have my loyal friends too, Wojin," she answered, drawing out the use of his first name. Confident and relaxed, she replaced her feet on his desk and leaned back in the chair.

"Do you realize what your little escapade just cost me?" He scowled, but didn't move toward her again.

"Your loss was insignificant compared to what the next few minutes will cost you," she said smugly, noting he did not try again to remove her feet.

"I have three dead security guards," Kant continued, pacing in front of the desk as if he were the one reporting to Anna. "Your lab assistant is alive, but just barely, and Chawla escaped with an injured Yokoyama."

Anna twirled a piece of hair in her fingers. "Yokoyama's dead. The Ager contact at the hospital just announced it to all the inner circle."

Kant stopped pacing. "That's the only thing that went right, then," he said. "But there's more trouble. A rumor is running rampant that we have the Ager virus and are testing it on employees. What can you possibly tell me that's worse?"

Anna slowly removed her feet, rose and solicitously guided Kant back to his chair. He glanced at her warily, but refused to sit.

"You better sit down, Wojin. It gets much worse."

Reluctantly, Kant descended behind his desk.

Anna perched on the desktop and crossed her legs as if she was delivering a social invitation. "You see, Wojin, what's running rampant through Eternity is much worse than rumor. It's the Ager virus. And you are one of the carriers." She exerted extra control to hold back a victorious laugh when she told him the news.

"What in hell are you talking about? There's no way I can have it. Don't you try your cheap tricks on me, Hollinrake. I know better."

Anna stood and leaned toward him, one hand on the desk. "You have the Ager virus. There is absolutely no doubt about it. Do you want to call Janos yourself?"

Without giving her an answer he immediately keyed in the comm number to Janos. Anna watched with barely concealed glee as he asked the question, then stoically heard the answer. He asked several more questions to confirm the testing procedure. Then his eyes closed and his chin noticeably dropped as he carefully disconnected.

"Damn." Kant mumbled, slumping in his chair. "You're right." He pounded a fist onto the desk. "But I feel fine, dammit."

Anna looked toward one of the wall screens. Her chest puffed out and she filled with anticipation of her new power. With some restraint, she allowed time to permit Kant to absorb the full impact of his drastically shortened lifespan.

"But," she paused dramatically, "*I* might be able to stop it."

"I don't need you. I'll take the Eternity virus again. It won't be as effective as taking it at puberty. But it will still work."

Anna strode to his desk and punched up her research. "Look," she pointed at the screen. "Have you forgotten that once the Ager virus takes hold the Eternity virus can no longer be introduced?"

Kant looked at her with disbelief in his eyes, but he said nothing.

"The only one's safe from the Ager virus are those who are immune."

"So find me someone who's immune and we'll put all our researchers on creating a vaccine," he said.

She held her head high and looked him in the eye. "I'm immune."

His mouth opened and he shook his head.

She laughed softly. "Can you imagine the look on Miki's face when I told her I might be immune? It was priceless! Me, the one she considered the nemesis of all humanity, destined to be one of the few to still be around another four or five hundred years."

"What makes you think you're immune?" Kant asked.

"I've tested myself continuously since we developed the Ager virus indicator. Then, two days ago, I did a marrow transplant from our lone control pig—the one that has shown the same immunity. I transplanted that marrow into one of the infected pigs. And whammo! Within twenty-four hours I could see a marked improvement in the infected pig's immune system response."

"That isn't conclusive evidence, and you know it," Kant said. "You may have just provided the pig with some specific disease immunity, not Ager immunity. What's your proof?"

"The proof is in the making, so they say. But if you want to throw away the only chance you have right now, be my guest." She noticed Kant wince slightly at the thought of the immunity not working. Then she continued, "If it doesn't work, you're no worse off. However, if my analysis is right, I believe we have room to negotiate."

"I figured you would want to negotiate something," Kant said. "But before we discuss anything, I want incontrovertible proof." Then he rose from his desk. He was no longer the same imposing figure, but Anna could tell he hadn't given up either. "As far as I'm concerned, you're on my black list, Hollinrake."

Anna stood also, ready to leave.

Kant continued, "I have a public relations nightmare because of *your* two friends, and the loose ends *you* didn't cover. Furthermore, I have three good security guards that are dead and have to be replaced. Right now I see no reason to listen to you or your theories. If you want to talk negotiations you have to give me something better than your maybes."

"Oh, you'll get it, Kant," she answered. Then she marched to the vertical transport and closed the door, keeping her back to him until the tube darkened.

Anna paced in her office waiting for the meeting of The Ten to begin. It had taken her three weeks to get the definitive proof she needed, but it was worth the work. She was indeed immune and had proven it through exhaustive testing. Even Janos verified her findings. This time, rather than going directly to Kant, she'd called an executive meeting of The Ten. Since Kant had made her number six, she had the right to demand a meeting for cause. Only with the full support of The Ten could she hope to overrule Kant. This time she was certain no one would stop her from reaching the pinnacle of power she had so long sought.

The meeting convened with all ten present, seated around a specially made decagonal shaped table. Nine of the places were exactly equal in width and angle. The tenth surface, where Kant sat, was twice the size of the others. The representation of the seat of the power was always evident, even within The Ten.

Anna assumed her place at the table. She eyed his position with envy. Today that seat will be mine, she thought. I will insist on it, and no one will dare deny me. But for now she waited impatiently for Kant to begin the meeting.

Kant took his time calling the meeting to order. He made a point of speaking with every member in the room, except Anna, often exchanging jokes and generally engaging in pleasantries. Anna sat quietly in her chair, putting on her best smile. She was willing to accept a few moments of procrastination on his part. Her moment of glory was only minutes away now. Finally, the group settled down and Kant called them to order.

"It appears that Hollinrake here," he began, indicating Anna derisively, "has demanded this meeting. Though I can't imagine why she wants to take up our time when we have so many other important problems to resolve." He paused and looked at her directly, not bothering to hide his irritation. "But, as a member of The Ten, she has the right. So I will turn it over to her and hope that we all receive some enlightenment soon."

Anna took a moment to look about the room, judging each member's mood before beginning. She felt they were neither antagonistic nor supportive toward her. Fine, she thought. They'll support me when I'm done.

"I've called you together to report on new evidence regarding the Ager virus. The virus will soon become one of the worst plagues in the history of humanity. Already people are getting sick. Nothing that will kill them yet, just irritations they'd never thought about before— allergies, colds. Within two years they will notice the aging process. Each year they will feel significantly older. More importantly, I have conclusive evidence that each of you will become infected and die within the next hundred years. If not from one of the many diseases that will ravage this planet, then from the ravages of old age itself." She paused to let the murmurs and denials die down before continuing. "Unless," she interrupted the whispers. "Unless, *I* choose to make you immune."

"You bitch!" Kant whispered ferociously in her direction. "You wouldn't deny us."

"Just try me," Anna answered back *sotto voce*, then continued being sure everyone could hear. "I shall determine which of you will continue to live long lives and which of you will die shortly." She paused for dramatic emphasis. "Kant already knows he has the virus," she pronounced. "He has already willingly passed this plague to you!"

"That's a lie!" Kant stood and roared at the top of his lungs.

Aghast, The Ten all began talking at once. Interrupting them, Anna continued loudly, "And furthermore, I have personally confirmed the results of the Ager test performed on each of you. There is only one person in this room who does not have the virus!"

Then complete silence filled the room, each member, certain that he or she was the one spared. Then they consciously tried to distance themselves from each other, shifting uneasily in chairs, moving a little further from the table, pulling their hands closer to themselves as if even a breath from their neighbor would contaminate them.

Anna began to laugh harshly at their antics. "You fools! Don't you see that it was your very presence in this room that exposed you to it. Every time you met with Kant, every time you touched him, shook his hand, he was transmitting the virus. And, of course, he never told you."

Several voices rang out at once, calling Kant a bastard and even more unsavory names. Without thought of repercussion, many voices questioned his very right to be there now.

"Shut up, all of you!" Kant roared, pounding the table with his fist. "Can't you see she wants to turn us against each other? Next she'll be suggesting immediate euthanasia for each one who is infected." All eyes turned to Anna questioning the truth of his accusation.

"Hmmm." Anna smiled. "That's certainly one option." When the upswell of negative comments went beyond her little joke she spoke again. "If you will all be quiet I'll show you a better option. For only I have a way to stop the Ager plague in all of you."

Once again the room became silent. Anna could read the hope in each of them. Then slowly and deliberately she began speaking.

"My extensive testing has revealed that some people may be immune to this virus. I am one of those people."

"Where's your proof?" Kant interrupted. "Don't believe anything she says until she has proof." No one paid him any attention.

With an air of certainty Anna reached down to lift the case next to her chair. Placing it on the table she extracted a single keydisc. "I direct your attention to the table viewers," she began. "This keydisc will unlock my secure test files with all the biological data you need, and their verification by Janos." She placed the disc into a small slot embedded in the table surface. Immediately, the data was simultaneously available on the recessed viewers in front of each of The Ten.

For the next two hours Anna patiently reviewed her experiments. She answered every question with confidence and a promise of even further proof. She emphasized the experiments on her own blood and bone marrow, pointing out the positive effects it created during transplant to unsuspecting lower-level infected employees. By the end of her exhaustive presentation she knew The Ten would grant any demand she had.

"I will share my immunity with each of you over the next ten years only if you meet my conditions." All eyes focused intently on her. Two or three of the members were already nodding their heads in agreement, before even hearing her requirements. "One," she continued, "is that the ten of us go into hiding until the plague has passed."

"But why?" a member from across the table asked. "If we have immunity we don't need to hide."

"Do you think the general population will let anyone live who is immune?" she asked, as if posing a question to a recalcitrant child. "They'll be so enraged, they will form mobs to hunt you down and kill anyone who is revealed as a member of The Ten. The mobs will believe that Eternity has a way to cure them and won't release the information. The media will begin a campaign of aggression, reminding the populace of Eternity's past record. You remember, when you tried to keep the Eternity virus to yourselves, or when you committed mass genocide by denying it to certain countries or ethnic groups."

"But we don't have to worry about the Yokoyama woman anymore," another member interrupted. "She was always the troublemaker before. We've been told that she' dead."

"She is dead," Anna agreed. "But her organization remains. And what about Rohin Chawla, the charismatic leader of the Church of Dreams? Do you honestly believe that he and his organization will sit idly by and let this go unchecked? Our only option is to go into hiding until this has passed."

"We can easily hide and still run Eternity," Kant finally spoke up, his voice cracking slightly. "What is your second condition?"

Anna looked directly at him, unwavering as she spoke. "That I become the leader of Eternity."

Kant didn't flinch. He held her gaze for a moment then looked to each of the others in the room. It was as if each one was holding their breath, waiting for his response. He knew no one would dare to speak against him; but he also knew the game was over, and Anna had won.

"Obviously, you've made it so we have no choice," he began, and as if a refreshing breeze circled the room, the others let out their breaths. "I will resign my presidency after . . ." he paused for emphasis, "after each of us has received your marrow transplant."

"That is not acceptable," Anna responded. "I have no assurance you will keep your word after it's done."

"And we have no assurance you will keep yours," Kant countered angrily.

"No you don't." Anna's lips curled in a triumphant smile. "But, if I don't keep my word you can still remove me. If you don't keep your word I have no recourse."

"Kant," the woman to his left reached over and covered his hand, almost motherly. "As you said, we have no choice. We have to meet her demands. If we don't we will lose our lives, and in the process lose

Eternity and its power in the world. At least this way we have a hope of keeping both." Her eyes beseeched his understanding. "Please Kant, don't make it more difficult than it is already."

Kant removed her hand and stood. "You will have my resignation by the end of this week—providing, " he paused for emphasis, "you meet my conditions. One, we will all be installed *jointly* in hiding. I want to make sure our lovely Anna doesn't pit us against each other. Two, I must be assured that we can continue to run Eternity effectively while we are in hiding. And three, I am the first one to receive the marrow transplant." He paused and looked each member in the eye. He ended with Anna and stared, unflinching.

"These are my demands. If they are met I will resign." Then he turned and left the room before any discussion could occur.

Each of the others slowly stood, staring at the spot he had vacated. No one seemed to have anything more to say. One-by-one they left the room.

When no one was left, Anna went to Kant's chair. First she stroked the back, running her fingers along the seamless construction. Next she stood behind it and viewed the other nine spots at the table, carefully noting the increased size and power of this position.

Finally, she sat in the chair, pulling it into position at the table. She leisurely surveyed the realm before her, imagining the others seated and looking to her for leadership. She nodded her head slightly at each place, like a Queen to her lowly subjects. The thrill of victory worked it's way up from her toes under the desk, to her chest as it expanded with anticipation and pride. By the time the thrill reached her face, her satisfied smile stretched from ear to ear and her eyes sparkled with victory.

It had all been worth it. All the years of being second to Miki. All the years of playing the double agent for Kant. Finally, power was hers. At least for the next six hundred years.

24

Rohin walked into the private room at the Dreamer hospital. Miki looked exactly the same as she had for the past two months. He watched the monitor connected to her. Everything was still steady. She no longer had machines helping her breathe or keeping her heart pumping. But she still hadn't come out of the coma.

Several Dreamer experts had examined her. They confirmed Miki didn't have the Ager virus. It was her immunity that had saved her and would rebuild her system again. It was just a matter of time. No one knew how much time. All their tests showed everything was working, all her organs had regenerated. It was her mind now that needed to catch up. When she woke, would she be angry she was immune? Would she want to be one with the people who did contract the virus?

He shook his head. He couldn't worry about that. He would cross that bridge later, when he had to. Right now his only objective was getting her well and taking her home—in whatever manner she could live, he would be happy.

Rohin sat on the edge of the bed and brushed a kiss across her lips, just as he did every morning when he came to spend the day with her.

"Good morning, Angel." He rubbed his thumb along her jaw.

Each day he'd shared the events around them. Over the past month, he'd told her how the Ager virus was spreading and how doctors were relearning how to treat disease. He told her how the Dreamers and Agers had come together to help in the transition. He told her about the ten percent who were immune and how somehow she and he had that immunity. He brought her news of the ongoing research work that both teams were doing and how much it would help humanity in the future. He didn't' know if she heard any of it, or if she understood his words. But he told her anyway.

He removed her hairbrush from the bedside stand and began brushing it from the crown to the ends. It was still pretty short, only shoulder length. It was one more thing he could do for her—one more thing to keep her close.

"I've come to give you you're back rub," he said after sharing the days events again and returning the hair brush to the drawer.

He carefully turned her onto her stomach, making sure the monitors remained attached. He made sure her head was turned to one side, so she could breathe easily. He knew the nurses could do this to help prevent bedsores, but he wanted to do this small thing for her. She had given her life for him. He didn't have the chance to stand in front of the beam. She didn't give him that choice.

He opened the back of her hospital gown and his breath caught as he looked at her still body. How long would it be until he saw her move again? He didn't even care if they could never make love again, as long as she would wake up...as long as she could speak...as long as she could hear him say once more "I love you."

Squeezing the massage oil on his hands, he rubbed them together to heat the oil. He started at her neck and worked down to her shoulders. Then to her back, carefully moving across it and on both sides.

The beeps on the heart monitor increased and his own heart stuttered. No, he reminded himself. This had happened before. The doctors said it was a reaction to the massage, nothing more. A sign she might wake, but not yet.

He moved lower, gently working the small of her back and her buttocks where most bedsores would appear. Fortunately, her skin was still perfect and supple. It was warm to the touch which renewed his hope that she would come back to him soon. Between himself and the nurses she was massaged three times a day to make sure the blood was flowing.

His hands moved down her thighs and he took extra time with her calves. He wanted to keep her muscles as limber as possible. When she woke, he wanted her to know she could walk. He didn't want her to worry about not being whole.

He turned her on her back once more. Her eyes fluttered open and his breath caught. Then they closed again. He let out the breath. That had happened before too. Some kind of automatic response the doctors said. It didn't mean anything yet.

He sighed and finished massaging her arms and her legs. No other responses today.

He changed her from the open gown to a pajama bottom and a top. It was time for her exercises. He lifted each arm and tried to add resistance to get her muscles to work. He did the same with her legs, making sure that at least they were lifted several times. He knew that when she woke, she wouldn't be able to walk immediately. But he would do everything in his power to help her.

He counted the repetitions aloud. "One." He bent her leg at the knee then straightened it and laid it down. "Two." He repeated the same procedure. Ten on the right leg. Then he moved to the left. "One."

"Errggg."

He laid her leg down. She'd never made a sound before.

"Miki?" He leaned over her, his finger tracing her cheekbone. "Miki, I'm here."

Nothing.

Should he signal the doctor? He didn't want to be told once more that it was nothing. After waiting several minutes he went back to the exercises for her right leg. "Two." He lifted her leg, pushed it back bent at the knee.

"Errgggg."

This time a nurse came running in. "She's waking!" She punched something into a mobile. "I saw the blip on the screen. The first one I wasn't sure, but the second one left no doubt."

Dr. Fander ran into the room. He checked all the monitors. He asked the nurse questions. He examined Miki.

"She may be coming around," he said. "It may be minutes or hours. Talk to her, Rohin. Let her know you're here."

He twined his fingers in one of her hands and held them close to her heart. He felt a slight squeeze from her.

"Yes! Come back to, Miki. Come back to me, Angel."

She squeezed again.

"That's right. I see you. I know you can hear me. Fight, Miki. Fight your way back."

Her eyes fluttered open, then closed, then open again.

He smiled, holding back the tears in his eyes. "Hello, Angel."

"Rohin?"

The tears streamed down. "Oh God, you're back. You're back."

Her eyes fluttered close, and he held his breath.

Then they opened again. "I heard you," she said. "I heard everything."

He didn't know what to do. Should he lift her into his arms? Should he barely touch her? He looked at the doctor, and raised a brow in question.

"She won't break," he said with a smile. "I'll leave you two alone."

Rohin gathered her to him.

She lifted a hand to his face and wiped away his tears. "I love you, Rohin Chawla."

He gazed into her deep brown eyes and saw everything he wanted. His past was gone. She was his future.

"Whoa," she said with a smile. "I just had an amazing flashback."

"Really? What did you see?"

"You and me having incredible sex together."

He laughed. "Really? I don't think we've ever had sex."

"Hmmm...it was a great dream then. Maybe I'll have to re-enact it with you?"

He looked at her seriously. "We have the rest of our lives for that. Right now you just need to take your time getting well."

"You don't even want to know about the dream," she asked, her lips forming a teasing pout.

He brought her hand to his lips and kissed each finger. "Are you trying to kill me, woman?"

"The first time," she said, "We were in a bed." She looked around the room. "This one would do."

"Really?" he moved to brush her lips.

"The second time we were in the shower."

Now he knew that was a dream, because they hadn't ever made love in the shower. "That's interesting. Any more?"

"Oh yes," she responded. "On your desk, against the glass wall in your office, in the..."

"The glass wall?" he interrupted. "Now you're getting kinky."

"Oh, the desk and the wall were in the same night."

He ran his fingers through her hair. "I see we have some catching up to do. What else did you dream, Miki?"

"I dreamt of children, our children."

He stopped. Maybe she was still a little delusional. Surely she remembered she was unable to have children. He was unable to make her children. That was part of the Eternity virus when you took it well after puberty.

"Miki..." he started. How would he tell her?

She looked up at him, all the trust in her eyes made him swallow.

"I know," she said. "Not children of our bodies. Hive children that we adopt. We can help them. We can get others to help them. We can stop the desperation in their lives."

He caught her up again in his arms, and this time he kissed her passionately and she returned his kisses. He should have known she'd figured it all out. She must have planned for the next fifty years while she was in that coma.

He looked at her again, and tucked a stray hair behind her ear. "We can adopt as many children as you want. My life is in your hands."

She laughed and moved her hand down to his pants. She trailed her finger along its front, "And what else will you put in my hand?"

Surprised, heat rushed downward and he gave her an immediate reaction. He cleared his throat. "Let's take one thing at a time," he said. "I want you more than you can imagine, but I want you only when you're completely recovered."

"Take me home, Rohin," she said. "I'm done with this place. Take me home so I can share the same bed with you, so I can always feel you at my side."

"Do you think you could stand me for the next six hundred years?"

"Only six hundred?" she asked. "I was hoping for Eternity." The smile she flashed made his heart flutter.

"God, I love you, Miki. Eternity sounds wonderful to me." He couldn't say anymore as his throat closed with the knowledge he had come so close to losing her. He'd felt her with every beat of his heart and hers. She was in the air that he breathed. She was in his head. She was everywhere he wanted to be.

Her eyes glistened and her smile was so wide he thought he would burst with gratitude. "I love you, too." She rained kisses along his chin. She pulled him down and kissed the tops of his eyelids. "I love the way you stood by me, even when we were in opposition." She kissed down his throat. "I love the way you challenged me to live." She laid her head on his chest and he enveloped her once more. "I love the way you never lied to me. You never walked away. I love the way you kept the dream alive...for both of us."

His heart had never felt so full. Nor had he ever been so scared. He wanted to live up to all her expectations. He wanted to make her happy for the rest of her life. He hoped he could do that. He hoped that as the Ager virus took hold and more people ran scared, he'd find the strength to be everything she thought he could be

"All of my dreams involve you," he said. "I will love you forever, no matter what comes." He pressed his lips to hers, sealing his promise.

25

———————

Six Months Later

"Miki, come back to me," Rohin said in his sleep, tossing and turning. "Fight, Miki. Fight to come back. I need you. Fight!"

Miki struggled to wake him from his nightmare, the same one which had tormented him over the past three months. When she'd come back from the brink in the hospital, Rohin had been there. His hands intertwined in hers. Everyone else had given up, but he had believed. He had kept the medicos ministering to her, artificially pumping her heart, filling her lungs, giving all the drugs a chance to work. It was ironic, that after the Ager virus had been unleashed she was one of the few who were immune.

She soothed him as he came awake, trying vainly to make him focus on a different dream, the one he had started with the Church. He still had nightmares of their last day in Eternity. Fortunately, she had no recollection of anything after she'd been shot with the beamer. Her last memory was the regret she'd felt for never telling Rohin she still loved him.

Rohin roused slightly and rolled toward her, pulling her against him. "You came back," he said.

"As always," she answered and snuggled into him. "I will never leave you again."

"Promise?"

She kissed him, at first softly but then more deeply as he came more awake. "Promise," she said. "What worries bring on these dreams, Rohin?"

"The 'casts are growing more frightening each day. The growing knowledge of the spread of the Ager virus can't be contained by Eternity much longer."

"Have any of The Ten come forward yet?" Miki asked.

"No. No one seems to know where they've gone. Some say they're dead. Some say internal spies killed them."

"But you don't believe it." Miki echoed the thoughts he had shared several times this past week. She wanted to believe what the 'casts said. But the fact that Eternity still controlled a lot of money and a lot of people made her wonder.

Rohin turned to his back and gazed at the ceiling. "I'm sure Anna had a plan. In her last moments with us she was so cocky. . . so sure of her eminent power." He paused. "She had a definite plan, which means that they all must be hiding. If she really is immune, then I'm sure she found some way to make that immunity work for her."

"And *you* will make the dream work for all of us," Miki insisted.

He leaned over and kissed her for a very long time.

When he released her, she asked, "What was that for?"

"For loving me." He brushed his lips along the curve of her neck. "For believing in me." He moved down to the vee between her breasts. "For understanding the dreams."

She stared at him for a long time in silence. For the past six months both of them had taken refuge in each other as the world around them descended into panic and chaos, and others led the Dreamers and the Agers. But she knew they couldn't continue to hide. She knew it was time for the groups to be together as one, to lose their separate identities. It was time for her to take her place beside Rohin and lead again.

Perfunctorily she bounded from the bed and began dressing. Rohin looked at her in utter surprise.

"Where are you going? What are you doing?" he asked.

"I'm getting dressed," she said. She walked to the closet and removed the white cassock she'd asked Shandra to make for her.

"Oh no you don't." Rohin came up behind her and put his arms around her, pulling her back to the bed. "Come back to bed. I have something much more fun for you."

She put all her weight into resisting him. "You know I would like nothing more than to while away another day in your arms. But it's time we both return to leadership."

He stared hard at her. She watched the emotions flit across his face. She could see the fear. She sighed and traced his strong jaw.

"Don't you see? The Dreamers and the Agers have only got a shred of faith in themselves left. We have to bolster that faith by keeping to our original plan of innovation and progress. Now, more than ever, people are looking to escape the wave of despair that is sweeping the earth. Now, more than ever, we must press forward with your vision for moving into space."

He sighed, resigned. "And all I've been doing is running away."

"You were dreaming," Miki said. "But now its time to make the dreams a reality." She held his eyes with hers, allowing him to see all the love inside her, the truth that they could do this together.

When he finally nodded she pulled him to her. "One for the road?" She winked at him and he carried her back to the bed.

"A quickie?" he asked.

"When were you ever quick?" she taunted.

For the first time since her recovery, they made love with the same vigor and enthusiasm they had enjoyed two hundred years ago—before they took on the Eternity mission.

THE MORNING ARRIVED cool and clear on the New Mexico high plateau, and Rohin Chawla stood meditatively in the suite at the pinnacle of the Church of Dreams, enjoying its beauty. He lowered his gaze from the horizon to take in the long line of people inching around the building. Taking a careful breath he finally smiled with only a little pain in his heart for sharing Miki with the world once more.

During the last six months the Dreamers and Agers had worked at a feverish pace to reach more people and to offer hope for an eventual cure. Unfortunately, they were still unable to produce a serum to fight the Ager virus. However, they were making good progress in fighting the multitudes of diseases that had come in its wake.

The sweet welcoming melody of Dreamer services sounded throughout the building, and the entry doors on the first floor opened automatically to admit the line of people.

Miki stepped into the room and took his hand.

"All the Agers in the area are at the service," she said. She smiled. "I think my entrance will be a bit of a shock."

She pulled him toward the transit tube. As they stepped inside he kissed her, long and deep.

"Are you ready for this?" he asked

"It's the perfect time to be reborn, don't you think?" she said. "We'll have to come up with a new name, you know, for our joint organization."

"I don't know," he said. "I think after this performance, the church will be no more. We'll all work together as the human race—without names to divide us.

Miki giggled. "It's pretty big, isn't it? My return from the dead?" She paused. "Do you think Anna and The Ten will be watching?"

Rohin smiled. "Their spies are among the invited. They will know immediately."

"We will live the dream!" Miki responded with the Dreamer motto.

"No, Miki," Rohin said. "We *are* living the dream."

The transit tube began to move and he wrapped his arms around her.

In the large auditorium the ceiling lights dimmed to black and the conversations silenced. Only the diffused light of the stage floor remained, focusing all eyes to the center as the music swelled. A fog curled over the edge as a spotlight directed the congregations' eyes upward.

Descending from a darkness near the roof, without apparent support, were two white cloaked figures with arms wrapped around each other. The figures were bathed in the palest rose colored light. They stepped out onto the floor together and their images were enlarged on every screen.

The audience gasped and Rohin and Miki smiled.

The music slowly quieted and Rohin and Miki said their parts in tandem with Rohin beginning the first line.

"We come for all humanity"

"We come to work together."

"We come with love." He squeezed her hand.

"We come with trust." She turned and smiled as she looked into his eyes.

"We come with hope," they both said together and then turned toward the audience and raised their hands, inviting them forward. "Join us."

ABOUT THE AUTHOR

Maggie Lynch is the author of 20+ published books, as well as numerous short stories and non-fiction articles. Her fiction tells stories of men and women making heroic choices one messy moment at a time. Her nonfiction focuses on helping indie authors be successful in their careers.

After careers in counseling, the software industry, academia, and worldwide educational consulting, Maggie chose to devote her time to her career as a full time author. Her fiction spans romance, suspense, fantasy and science fiction titles. Her non-fiction focuses on guiding authors to success in planning, distributing, and marketing their work.